"Maybe my coming here was a mistake."

Arden was surprised by the plea for reassurance in Rachel's statement.

"*Neh.* It wasn't a mistake." Upon seeing the fragile vulnerability in Rachel's eyes, Arden's heart ballooned with compassion. "Trust me, the community will *kumme* to help Ivan."

"In that case, I'd better keep dessert and tea on hand," Rachel said, smiling once again.

"Does that mean we can't have a slice of that pie over there?"

"Of course it doesn't. And since Ivan has no appetite, you and I might as well have large pieces."

Supping with Rachel after a hard day's work, encouraging her and discussing Ivan's care as if he were, well, not a child, but *like* a child, felt… It felt like how Arden always imagined it would feel if he had a family of his own. Which was probably why, half an hour later as he directed his horse toward home, Arden's stomach was full but he couldn't shake the aching emptiness he felt inside.

She is going back, so I'd better not get too accustomed to her company, as pleasant as it's turning out to be.

Carrie Lighte lives in Massachusetts next door to a Mennonite farming family, and she frequently spots deer, foxes, fisher cats, coyotes and turkeys in her backyard. Having enjoyed traveling to several Amish communities in the eastern United States, she looks forward to visiting settlements in the western states and in Canada. When she's not reading, writing or researching, Carrie likes to hike, kayak, bake and play word games.

Patricia Johns writes from Alberta, Canada. She has her Hon. BA in English literature and currently writes for Harlequin's Love Inspired and Heartwarming lines. You can find her at patriciajohnsromance.com.

CARRIE LIGHTE

The Amish Nurse's Suitor

&

PATRICIA JOHNS

The Nanny's Amish Family

LOVE INSPIRED
INSPIRATIONAL ROMANCE

Recycling programs for this product may not exist in your area.

ISBN-13: 978-1-335-50996-3

The Amish Nurse's Suitor and The Nanny's Amish Family

Copyright © 2021 by Harlequin Books S.A.

The Amish Nurse's Suitor
First published in 2020. This edition published in 2021.
Copyright © 2020 by Carrie Lighte

The Nanny's Amish Family
First published in 2020. This edition published in 2021.
Copyright © 2020 by Patricia Johns

This edition published by arrangement with Harlequin Books S.A.

For questions and comments about the quality of this book, please contact us at CustomerService@Harlequin.com.

Harlequin Enterprises ULC
22 Adelaide St. West, 40th Floor
Toronto, Ontario M5H 4E3, Canada
www.Harlequin.com

Printed in U.S.A.

CONTENTS

THE AMISH NURSE'S SUITOR

Carrie Lighte

For the kind *Englischers* and Amish people of Unity, Maine, who enthusiastically helped me with my research, and with thanks to my brother for "talking shop" about lumber.

But the wisdom that is from above is first pure, then peaceable, gentle, and easy to be intreated, full of mercy and good fruits, without partiality, and without hypocrisy.

—*James* 3:17

Chapter One

"Toby probably didn't think I was ambitious or smart enough for him," Rachel Blank told her roommate, Meg.

It had been nearly two weeks since her boyfriend had broken up with her—the same amount of time Meg had been away on vacation—and by this point Rachel was more angry than sad.

"Not ambitious or smart enough?" Meg's voice rose with incredulity. "What else would he call someone who started out with an eighth-grade education but later earned her GED, her BSN, and is going to school to become a nurse practitioner?"

"He doesn't know I applied to the MSN program, and I haven't actually been accepted into it yet, either," Rachel protested feebly. Meg didn't seem to hear. She was pacing in front of the sofa, counting on her fingers as she reeled off Rachel's accomplishments.

"You've learned to drive, you've learned to swim and you've mastered more technology than many people who've grown up surrounded by it. Not to mention you're fluent in three languages—English, German and *Deitsch*. If the tables were turned, Dr. Toby Grand wouldn't last a week living like an Amish person."

Rachel appreciated her roommate's impassioned defense of her, but she was uncomfortable with her praise. When she left her Amish community and family ten years ago, they'd accused Rachel of *hochmut*. Highmindedness. Pride. They said her pursuit of higher education was, among other things, an attempt to draw attention to herself. The implication stung so deeply that even now at twenty-eight she resisted it when anyone pointed out her accomplishments. Which, fortunately for her, Toby had rarely done. Instead, he'd pushed her to reach more difficult goals, which was one of the reasons Rachel hadn't told him she'd applied to an MSN program; she didn't want to disappoint him if she was rejected.

"Well, those weren't his exact words. But even if they were, I suppose I understand why he wants to date Brianna. She's a doctor, too. I'm only a nurse."

"*Only* a nurse?" Meg stopped pacing and thrust her hands on her hips. Meg was also a nurse, although she worked in a hospital, whereas Rachel worked at a clinic in the suburbs.

"*Neh, neh, neh*, I'm not saying *I* think nurses are inferior." Rachel sometimes accidentally reverted to *Deitsch* when she was flustered. "That's what *Toby* thinks. He says Brianna has more in common with him than I do."

"Yeah. They're both sneaks."

Toby had only broken up with Rachel *after* he'd been on several dates with Brianna, the practice's newly hired doctor. That's what vexed Rachel most—the betrayal.

"They probably thought it would be easy to pull one over on the naive Amish girl. And they were right. I had no idea Toby and Brianna had been seeing each other."

"That's not because of your Amish background. It's because you're an honest person who extended trust to someone you loved."

Did I love *Toby?* Rachel asked herself. During the ten months of their relationship, she'd definitely developed stronger feelings for him than for any man she'd dated, and she'd thought those feelings were reciprocated. In fact, when Toby came over to break up with her, his expression had been so somber she'd suspected he was about to propose. The ironic thing was, she wasn't sure how she would have answered. Afterward, as devastated as she was by the circumstances of their breakup, a small part of her felt relieved he hadn't asked her to marry him.

Meg shook a finger at Rachel. "You'd better not ever take him back."

"I doubt he'd ever want to *come* back, but no, I absolutely wouldn't go out with him again. He crossed a line that can't be uncrossed," Rachel assured her friend. "With God's grace I'll forgive him eventually, but right now, it's hard enough to even *look* at him at work."

Regardless, each day she held her head high and made a point to greet him and Brianna with a big smile, knowing the kind of office rumors that would erupt if she gave any indication of how deceived or miffed she really felt. She wouldn't give her coworkers the satisfaction. *Maybe I have more* hochmut *than I care to admit*, she mused.

"You should take a vacation. Maybe go to Maine for a few days…"

Rachel recognized Meg was hinting she should visit her family. Her roommate was one of the few people Rachel had confided in about how much she missed them sometimes. But missing them and visiting them were two different matters. Rachel hadn't been baptized into the Amish church before she left for the *Englisch* world, so she wasn't in the *Bann*, but in some ways, she felt like she might as well have been.

Both of her parents had passed away before she left her Amish community in Serenity Ridge, Maine. Rachel had two older married brothers, Colin and Albert, and one younger brother, Ivan, a bachelor. Initially her family members had been understandably hurt, disappointed and angry when Rachel told them she was moving to Massachusetts to pursue an education in nursing. Colin's wife, Hadassah, claimed she spoke for the entire family when she told Rachel unless and until she returned to Serenity Ridge and the Amish for good, she shouldn't bother to return at all.

Rachel thought in time they'd come to accept her decision even if they disagreed with it. Yet her monthly letters went unanswered, except by her youngest brother, Ivan, who wrote twice a year—at Christmas and Easter. But Easter had passed a week ago without a note from him, either. She was beginning to accept that although she'd never stop praying for or loving her family, the same might not be true for them.

"I've had enough rejection for the time being."

"Then you should go somewhere fun." Meg snapped her fingers. "A Christian singles' cruise! Wouldn't Toby and the people at work faint if you came back from the Bahamas with a new boyfriend? That would shatter their assumptions about you."

As well as Rachel had adapted to the *Englisch* life-style, she couldn't picture herself going on a singles' cruise, even if she were desperate to meet a man, which she most definitely was not. If she'd made it through the heartache of leaving her family behind at eighteen, she'd make it through life without a boyfriend at twenty-eight. Her faith, career and friendships were all she needed to be fulfilled. In fact, the breakup couldn't have come at a better time, since she'd soon have to devote herself to furthering her education. "No, I'm saving every cent I have for tuition. If I get in to the MSN program, I'll be too busy studying to have time for a relationship."

"First of all, it's not *if* you get in to the MSN pro-gram, it's *when*. Secondly, you'll be too busy for a re-lationship? Wow. You sound more *Englisch* than I do!"

Rachel chuckled again, but the truth was, she didn't feel particularly *Englisch*. Nor did she feel Amish. She felt…alone. No—she felt *independent*. And that suited her just fine.

Arden Esh had stacked so much mail on the little desk in the workshop the pile slid like an avalanche onto the floor. He stooped to pick up the envelopes. Sooner or later he was going to have to open them. He hoped they were bills and not customer orders; he and his business partner, Ivan Blank, needed all the sales they could get. They'd sunk every spare cent into ad-vertising their shed-building business, and after three years of barely profiting, this spring they hoped to see an increase in revenue.

Arden couldn't imagine how, exactly, that was going to happen with him manning the shop alone. Not that money was the most important matter at the moment—Ivan's recovery was. He'd been sick for almost two weeks, and two days ago he wound up in the hospital.

Last evening when Arden visited him there, Ivan had barely opened his eyes. Arden had chatted about the shed he'd just finished. He didn't even know if Ivan was awake until Ivan pulled aside his oxygen mask and rasped, "Would you write to Rachel? Ask her to *kumme* as soon as she can. She'll help you in the shop. Don't..." He was having difficulty breathing. "Don't tell anyone, though."

Initially, Arden had been taken aback by the request. Ivan often spoke fondly of his sister, who'd left the Amish a decade ago to become a nurse. They'd kept in touch, but Ivan had confided that his sister-in-law Hadassah made it clear Rachel wasn't welcome to visit. Arden felt a pang of guilt, aware that Ivan wouldn't have subjected his family to the tension of a reunion if he believed Arden could manage the shop—specifically, the paperwork—by himself. Long ago the two men had come to an unspoken understanding about the division of their responsibilities. For lack of a better expression, in many ways Ivan was the brains of the operation and Arden was the brawn.

Considering Ivan's family hadn't supported his business venture from the beginning, Arden understood why Ivan was reluctant to ask one of his brothers for help with administrative tasks during his illness. Ivan said Rachel was a very intelligent, capable woman who'd often expressed her desire to see him again. But her presence would undoubtedly create controversy. Regardless, Ivan was the one who had founded the business, so even though Arden had eventually become an equal partner in it, he deferred to Ivan's judgment in the matter.

Now, as Arden searched the desk for Ivan's address book, a disturbing possibility occurred to him: Ivan wanted Rachel to visit because he believed he was dying and wanted to say goodbye. The very thought stopped Arden cold. He immediately dropped to his knees. *Dear Gott, if it's Your will, please heal Ivan. Give those caring for him wisdom and fill him with a sense of Your loving presence. Amen.* Then, knowing no request was too small or too big for the Lord, he added, *And please help me find that address book.*

He stood, brushed the knees of his trousers and lifted a stack of catalogs. Beneath them was a blank piece of paper with the salutation *Dear Rachel* scrawled at the top, and beneath the stationery was an addressed, stamped envelope. Ivan must have begun writing his annual Easter letter to his sister—he was nothing if not conscientious—but he had been too sick to finish it. Silently thanking the Lord for the unexpected way He'd answered his prayer, Arden cleared a space at the desk, sat down and picked up a pen.

As he stared at the blank page, his hairline beaded with perspiration and his tongue tasted sour. This was why Ivan handled virtually all of the paperwork while Arden compensated by doing whatever heavy lifting Ivan's slighter frame couldn't handle. It wasn't that

Arden *couldn't* read or write—it was that it took him so painfully long because the letters often seemed to jump around and didn't make any sense. It had been that way for as long as he could remember, and although his schoolteacher had thought he'd outgrow it if he practiced more or tried harder, he never did. The only thing more daunting to Arden than a page filled with text was a completely blank sheet of paper. He threw down the pen and strode to the other side of the workshop to pick up a hammer. Now *this* was a tool he could use as deftly as if it were an extension of his own arm.

How could Ivan ask me to write to his sister, of all people? When Ivan spoke of Rachel, there was nothing except admiration and affection in his voice. But there were others in Serenity Ridge whose opinions of Rachel weren't as high; they indicated she thought herself a tad superior to those in her family and community. If their assessment of her character was correct, Arden expected she'd have a good laugh about the "ignorant" Amish man's spelling.

No, Arden couldn't write to her. As he drove a nail into a floor joist, he thought, *If I can find that address book, I'll look up her phone number and call her instead.* But by the end of the day, he'd turned the desk upside down and inside out and come up empty-handed. He was going to have to face the page. Maybe his mother or his younger sister, Grace, would proofread the letter. *No, I can't show it to them. Ivan said not to tell anyone else he wants Rachel to* kumme.

He took a deep breath and stared at the stationery. What should he say? "Your brother is in the hospital with pneumonia"? He doubted he could get the spelling right for the word *hospital*, much less *pneumonia*. One thing he'd learned over the years—when it came to writing, reading and speaking, shorter was better. With his hand shaking as much as if he'd just downed four cups of coffee, Arden positioned his pen under the words *Dear Rachel* and inscribed:

> Your brother is very ill. Please come soon if you can.
> Signed,
> Arden Esh

Arden chewed the end of the pen. Had he spelled *signed* correctly? Words that were spelled differently than they sounded gave him the most trouble. But if he crossed it out, it would look too messy and he'd have to start over with a new sheet. The prospect made him shudder. He folded the paper in quarters, slid it into the envelope and carried it to the mailbox at the end of the long driveway.

Even though he was doing exactly what Ivan had asked him to do, Arden couldn't escape the feeling he was letting him down. If only Arden didn't have such difficulty with words, he could take care of the paperwork himself. Of course, if Arden didn't have such trouble with words, he never would have moved to Maine, because he would have been able to get through an interview and secure a factory job in Indiana. *I'd probably be married with two or three* kinner *by now, too.*

Arden was glad Serenity Ridge's Amish community was small with very few single women; it gave him a plausible excuse for not courting anyone. The couple of times he'd walked out with anyone in Indiana had been utterly discouraging. His verbal difficulties had made him more nervous than usual, rendering him speechless. The women must have construed his silence as disinterest or else thought he was stupid, because none of them walked out with him for long.

It's just as well, he consoled himself, remembering. *Courting is intended to lead to marriage, and marriage leads to* bobblin. Arden's father had suffered the same problem as Arden, but to a lesser degree. Assuming the issue was hereditary, Arden couldn't knowingly subject his offspring to a lifetime of the kind of shame, frustration and struggles he'd faced. He'd decided years ago not to torment himself—or disappoint a woman—by engaging in courtship when he knew it wouldn't progress to marriage.

Just because I can't be a husband or a daed *doesn't mean I'm not responsible for making the most of the opportunities* Gott *has given me, including supporting my* schweschder *and* mamm, he thought. *So I've got to do whatever it takes to keep the business afloat during Ivan's illness.* Even if that meant working side by side with Ivan's condescending *Englisch* sister.

"You got in so late last night I didn't get to ask how Ivan is," his sister said to Arden later over a supper of *bottboi*, an Amish version of pot pie made with chicken and noodles.

"He was resting well." Arden didn't want to worry Grace. She had her hands full taking care of their mother, Oneita, who was experiencing a severe flare of lupus symptoms.

As supportive as their community in Maine was, Arden frequently regretted he'd had to relocate his mother and sister so far from their beloved district in Indiana. Since he couldn't get a factory job and there was a surplus of carpenters in the area, Arden had moved to Maine some three years ago when he heard about the shed-building opportunity with Ivan. Shortly afterward, Arden's father had died, so Arden had brought his mother and sister out to live in Serenity Ridge, as well.

"I wish I could visit him," Grace said. "So he knows how much I—*we*—care about him."

Arden appreciated his sister's sentiment, but she couldn't leave their mother alone in her current condition. Even if Grace wanted to go to the hospital after Arden returned home for the evening, cab fare was an expense they could scarcely afford. "I told him you were praying."

"*Jah*, but I want to do something tangible, the way other people do for *Mamm* when she's ill. Maybe I could make meals to put in his freezer for when he comes home."

"He'd probably *wilkom* that," Arden agreed. He forced himself to dismiss his niggling fear about Ivan's health declining even further.

"I can clean the *haus* for him, too. Make sure he has fresh sheets and do the dusting and window washing. I'll do it when Jaala comes over to visit *Mamm* tomorrow."

"That's a *wunderbaar* idea." Arden figured even if Ivan didn't get out of the hospital for a while, at least Ivan's sister would appreciate arriving to a clean house.

On Thursday evening Rachel described to Meg how mortified she'd been when she walked in on Brianna and Toby kissing in the break room that day. She'd quickly grabbed her lunch from the fridge and eaten it in her car, which would have been enjoyable because the weather was so warm, but her allergies caused her eyes and nose to run. When she returned to the office, her coworkers assumed she'd been crying over Toby and Brianna's break-room canoodling.

"Unbelievable," Meg empathized. "But it might brighten your day to know you have mail on the hall table."

Was it news from the university? Even though she knew it was immature, Rachel couldn't wait until Toby found out she'd been accepted into the program. Countless times since he'd broken up with her she'd imagined his stunned expression when she oh-so-casually told her coworkers she was resigning to get her MSN… Unless she *didn't* get into the program. At the possibility, Rachel's stomach twisted into a knot. Then she remembered she would receive the decision via email, not regular post. When she retrieved the letter, she noticed the address was written in her brother's familiar cursive.

"It's from Ivan!" she announced, chagrined that she'd doubted he wanted to keep in touch. But when she scanned the letter, her knees wobbled and she dropped into a chair. "Oh *neh*."

"What is it? What's wrong?"

Rachel extended the paper to her roommate. "My *bruder* is sick."

It only took a second for Meg to read the message. "This is upsetting, but I'm sure everything's going to be okay," she said, giving Rachel a hug. "C'mon, I'll help you pack so you'll be ready to go first thing in the morning."

Following her, Rachel fretted, "Ivan's so ill he couldn't even write to me himself. I can't believe my other brothers didn't contact me sooner. What if he's dying? What if I'm too late?"

Meg twirled around and placed her hands firmly on Rachel's shoulders. "You won't know how sick Ivan is until you get there. It's not helpful to imagine the worst-case scenario."

"That's true," Rachel hesitantly concurred.

Meg pulled a suitcase from the closet and opened it across the bed. "Do you think you'll be calm enough to drive? If you need me to take you, I will."

Meg was the closest person Rachel had to a sister and she loved her for her generosity and support, but Rachel knew she'd used the last of her PTO to go on vacation. "Thanks, but I'll be fine. And you're right—I can't let my imagination get the best of me."

But as she lay awake in bed an hour later, Rachel's apprehension about Ivan's health returned. *Very ill*, the note had said, but what did that mean? Ivan always described his business partner in glowing terms, but Arden must have been quite dense not to have provided more details. Or maybe he was deliberately terse; it was possible he only wrote the note because Ivan pressed him to write it since no one else would. Either way, Rachel hoped their paths wouldn't cross too often while she was in Serenity Ridge. After Toby broke up with her, Rachel had made up her mind to stay as far away from thoughtless, insensitive men like him as she could.

Leaving early the next morning, Rachel prayed during most of the three-and-a-half-hour drive from Boston to Maine, but the closer she got to Serenity Ridge, the queasier she became. Not only was she anxious about Ivan's health, but she was uneasy about the reception she'd get from her family. As she crested the long hill leading to her old home—the house Ivan, the youngest boy in their family, had inherited according to their Amish tradition—her hands were clammy on the steering wheel. Would she find her brothers in the yard? Maybe her sisters-in-law would be in the kitchen, making soup for Ivan.

On first glance she didn't spot any buggies when she pulled up in the driveway, nor did she see anyone as she crossed the lawn and climbed the porch stairs. It seemed strange to knock on the door of the place she'd once called home, but Rachel rapped twice and waited, stealing a look around the front yard. When no one came, she knocked again, louder. No response. Like most of the Amish in Serenity Ridge, the Blanks didn't lock their doors, so Rachel pushed it open.

"Ivan? Hello?" She timidly crossed the threshold. "Anyone home?"

She passed through the kitchen and stuck her head into the living room—no one was there, either. Then she went upstairs, announcing her presence. If her brother was sleeping, she didn't want to startle him by bursting into his room. "Ivan, it's me, Rachel."

His room was empty, the bed made. *This was where Ivan slept as a boy—now that he has his choice of rooms, he probably moved into the bigger one at the end of the hall.* But he wasn't there, either. As she darted to check the other two bedrooms, Rachel noticed the unmistakable scent of vinegar—someone had recently washed the windows. In fact, the entire house had been scrubbed clean. It was immaculate, as if no one had ever lived there. That could only mean one thing—the women from church had cleaned Ivan's house, as was their practice when someone died. It was a way of caring for the family of the bereaved, who were expected to host the community after a funeral. Rachel collapsed onto the bed in her old room and sobbed, her worst fear realized: she was too late.

Arden stopped hammering. He thought he'd heard a vehicle pull up the lane, so he waited for the customer to enter the workshop. When no one did, he resumed pounding until a couple of moments later, when he realized maybe it was Ivan's sister who had arrived. He set his hammer down and blew a curly lock of hair from his forehead. Meeting new people, especially *Englischers*, wasn't something he relished or excelled at doing.

Outside he noticed the little green sedan had Massachusetts plates, so Arden ambled slowly toward the house and pushed open the door. Taking a deep breath, he mentally prepared to say hello, but Rachel wasn't in the kitchen. Figuring she was in the bathroom, he waited for her to come out, but after a few minutes he concluded she wasn't in there, either.

"Hello?" he called as he entered the living room. "Hello?"

There were footsteps on the staircase, and then a young, slender *Englisch* woman dressed in a long green skirt and black top appeared in the doorway of the living room. Her auburn hair hung to her shoulders in soft layers. She must have either had a cold or else she'd been crying, because she dabbed her red-rimmed nostrils with a tissue.

"Hello," she murmured, glancing up at him. She had the same broad forehead and narrow jaw as her brother, although her almond-shaped eyes were hazel instead of brown, and now that he looked into them, Arden was convinced he had indeed caught her weeping. As if an introduction were necessary, she said, "I'm Ivan's sister, Rachel Blank."

"I'm Arden Esh, the one who wrote to you. I'm your brother's business partner."

Rachel nodded solemnly. "Ivan told me about you. He was very…" There was a catch in her voice. "He was very appreciative of your skills."

"Denki," Arden muttered. He wasn't used to receiving compliments from a woman, nor was he accustomed to chatting with someone who was clearly fighting back tears. Generally speaking, the Amish were less demonstrative about their emotions than the *Englisch*.

Rachel broke eye contact and took a seat on the sofa. She smoothed her skirt as she spoke. *"Denki* for writing to me. When did Ivan…how did he…"

As her chin dropped to her chest, her hair made a curtain obscuring her face, but from the way her shoulders were quivering, Arden could tell she was crying. Whenever he'd interacted with medical professionals, they came across as calm and collected, no matter how severe an injury or bleak a diagnosis, so Rachel's behavior caught him off guard.

"I'd, uh, I'd say it was about ten or twelve days ago when he came down with a bad case of bronchitis. But it turned out it wasn't really bronchitis—or maybe it started out that way, but then it developed into—" Arden paused, afraid he'd stumble over the word *pneumonia*. It was easier to describe the symptoms instead. "Each day it became more and more difficult for him to breathe. But then yesterday his condition, uh, took a turn…"

Rachel lifted her head to look at him, and Arden knew his cheeks were flushed. "It's okay. You don't have to tell me anything else right now," she said tearfully.

He thought learning that her brother was improving would have made her happier. "Do you want tea?" he suggested, hoping she didn't so he could go. "Or to lie down upstairs?"

"No, thanks. I'd rather not. Too many memories. I'll book myself into a hotel."

Arden expressed his surprise. "Oh. I think Ivan hoped you'd stay here. You know, to care for the animals and keep an eye on the *haus*. But I can continue doing that if you'd rather not."

She slowly shook her head. "No. If that's what Ivan wanted, I'll honor his request. It's only for a few days. I imagine the livestock will go to Colin or Albert after the funeral, right?"

"The funeral? Whose funeral?"

Rachel's mouth gnarled into a frown. "Whose do you think? *Ivan's* funeral," she sobbed.

The room tilted as it usually did when he panicked, and Arden couldn't find the words fast enough to explain. He couldn't find them at *all*, not with Rachel bawling into her hands like that, her shoulders convulsing, and Arden knowing he was somehow the cause of her distress.

"Your—your—your *bruder* isn't ha-having a funeral," he stuttered. Then he clarified bluntly, "Ivan's not dead."

Rachel's shoulders lifted and dropped a few more times before she turned her head toward him, still bent forward, her arms crossed against her chest, her face red. "What did you say?"

"Ivan's not dead. He's in the hospital. He has pneu-pneu-pneum…" The word wouldn't come out, but it didn't matter anyway. Rachel shot from the room and within seconds Arden heard her retching in the bathroom. He pushed his hand through his hair and circled the braided rug, wondering whether he should check on her.

Before he could decide, she flew back into the room, her eyes blazing. "What is *wrong* with you?"

Humiliation scalded Arden's face and reduced him to being a schoolchild at the chalkboard again, struggling to solve what should have been a simple word problem. *What is wrong with me* was a question he'd asked himself countless times since then, and he still didn't know the answer.

"How could you send me a note like that? How could you stand there and tell me about my *bruder* fighting to breathe and his condition taking a turn, especially since I came here to find the house empty and immaculate? You had to have known I thought Ivan died!" She gasped and then pressed a hand against her lips and the other against her heart, as if to quiet them both.

She was right; the misunderstanding *was* his fault. He should have expressed himself better. He had no defense; all he could do was apologize. "I'm sorry. It was a miscom-commun-communication."

"*That's* putting it mildly," Rachel uttered, but the fight had gone out of her voice, and her shoulders drooped, too. She wiped beneath her eyes and stated more than asked, "Ivan's still alive?"

"*Jah.* He's in the hospital, but he's getting better."

Rachel sniffed, nodding. Then she said, "I think I need a glass of water."

"I'll get it." Arden was relieved to have an excuse to leave the room. When he returned, Rachel was perched in a straight-backed chair on the opposite side of the coffee table. He handed her the glass and reluctantly lowered himself onto the sofa. After apologizing again, he told her he'd be too busy filling orders to manage the administrative side of their business, which was why Ivan had requested Rachel come to Serenity Ridge.

"I'm surprised he didn't ask Colin or Albert or their wives. Or someone else from the district."

"Our community is still relatively small, and spring is planting season. Your brother Albert and his wife went to Ontario because her mother is sick. As for Colin, his roofing business picks up at this time of year, too. Ivan didn't ask Hadassah because she's, uh…"

"Too bossy?"

Arden suppressed a chuckle. Ivan *had* mentioned Hadassah's habit of giving him unsolicited advice, but that wasn't the only reason he hesitated to involve her in their business. "She's, uh, with child. Twins, apparently. She tires easily."

"Oh, so Ivan didn't have any choice other than to ask me."

"*Neh, neh.* That's not why. I'm sure it's because of how *schmaert* and competent you are." His response brought a sliver of a smile to Rachel's lips.

"I'm glad to help for as long as I'm needed," she replied.

"Ivan will be relieved to hear that," Arden said. *But not half as relieved as I'll be when it's time for you to go.*

Sitting across from Rachel with his large hands resting on his knees as he squeezed his legs into the space between the sofa and the coffee table, Arden appeared as tentative as a young boy who'd just been scolded and was afraid to move for fear of further punishment. Pale blue eyes and a mass of curly, dirty-blond hair contributed to his youthful appearance, but given his manly physique and the faint crinkle of skin at the corners of his eyes, Rachel figured he was about thirty-one or thirty-two years old. His thick, level brows emphasized the rectangular shape of his forehead, but it was his mouth that captured her attention—she wondered what it would take to put a smile on those broad lips.

I suppose it's my fault he looks so grim. It's possible I overreacted. Before Rachel could think of a way to lighten the mood, an approaching vehicle interrupted the silence.

Rising, Arden said, "That might be a delivery. I should get back to the workshop."

Rachel stood, too, subconsciously estimating Arden's height at six-one or six-two as she walked him to the door. She watched as he hurried down the stairs and across the driveway. She knew men in the *Englisch* world who spent hours at the gym trying to develop a similar physique: small waist, broad shoulders and biceps so muscular she could see their outline beneath his cobalt-blue cotton shirt. That must have been what Ivan meant when he jokingly wrote one of Arden's strengths was his strength, which was a good thing, because one of Ivan's weaknesses was his weakness.

My poor bruder *is probably weaker than ever right now.* Keenly aware that pneumonia severe enough to be hospitalized sometimes could be a touch-and-go condition, Rachel thanked the Lord that Ivan was still alive and after ten years, she was finally about to see him again.

Chapter Two

After bringing her suitcase in from the car, Rachel washed her face and took her cell phone out of her purse. The low-battery warning flashed, so she quickly texted Meg—Rachel had promised to let her know when she arrived—and made a mental note to pick up a phone charger she could use in her car, since there was no electricity in the house. She was about to get back in her car when she realized she hadn't asked which hospital Ivan was in, nor had Arden volunteered the information. *I wonder if there's much information that he* ever *volunteers,* she mused as she walked toward the back-yard. *He might not be as thoughtless as I suspected he was, but he's definitely a man of few words.*

Remembering how Ivan had written he'd converted the barn into a workshop and the smaller workshop into a stable, Rachel thought back to when her family moved to Maine from Ohio some twenty years ago. Her father had built a barn big enough for their milk cows, horses, buggy and equipment. He'd also constructed a small workshop for personal use. He and his cousin started a metal roofing supply and installation business, but because the cousin's land was more centrally located to the *Englisch* community, their main workshop was housed on his property, which Colin now owned. Rachel's brother Albert was a partner in the business, too.

Ivan was the only one who hadn't taken up the family trade. He had a deeply rooted fear of heights, a fear Colin and Albert had reportedly accommodated by assigning Ivan administrative responsibilities in the shop. Although he was adept at accounting and customer service, Ivan soon grew restless. Rachel understood perfectly why building sheds was a better fit for his blend of carpentry skills and temperament, but Colin and Albert undoubtedly believed Ivan should have derived satisfaction from participating in the family business. Although he'd never written about any conflict directly, Rachel could imagine Ivan's professional choice was met with nearly as much family opposition as Rachel's decision to leave the Amish.

Entering the barn through a new side door labeled Customer Entrance, Rachel surveyed the workshop, impressed by how bright and tidy the spacious interior was. Four small buildings in various stages of construction were situated in separate quarters of the work area. Metal shelving held an assortment of equipment, tools and other supplies along the periphery of the room on one side. A substantial quantity of lumber was stacked in racks near the wall on the other two sides, and what appeared to be recently installed overhead doors ran the length of the fourth wall. Rachel paused and inhaled the piney scent.

Because Arden wasn't in sight and the hum of the

nearby generator was so loud, she shouted his name. Hunched over, he emerged from a little wooden structure that looked more like an oversize dollhouse than a shed. When he straightened to his full height beside it, he reminded her of an illustration of a giant in a children's book, and she giggled.

"If that's the size of the house, I can only imagine how tiny its shed is."

Arden glowered. "It's a playhouse for an *Englischer*'s eight-year-old *dochder*. It might seem frivolous to you, but it's what the customer ordered and we need the business."

Rachel instantly regretted her joke. She wasn't mocking his work—with its scalloped eaves and miniature window boxes, the tiny house was beautifully designed. It took her by surprise to see him come out of it, that's all. "I forgot to ask which hospital Ivan is at, the one in Waterville or in Pittsfield?"

"Neither. It's the one in Belridge."

"Belridge? That must be new since I lived here. Can you tell me how to get there?"

Arden squinted and rubbed his neck as if it was giving him a headache. "You take 202 through Unity."

"And then?" she prompted.

"Don't you have PSG?"

Finding it ironic an Amish person would suggest she use technology, Rachel chuckled. "You mean GPS?"

"*Jah*. You should use that. It's more accurate, and I'm busy."

"Oh, okay," Rachel replied, but Arden had already ducked back into the playhouse. His abrupt departure made her feel foolish. It could have been he was stressed out about his workload, but she got the feeling he was annoyed with her for joking around.

At the end of the driveway, Rachel let the car's engine run idle. If she turned right, the same way she came in, she'd head toward the highway. If she turned left, she'd travel directly past Colin's property. Colin or Hadassah surely would be able to tell Rachel how to get to the hospital, assuming they were home and willing to talk to her. *But if they give me the cold shoulder, I might end up blubbering again, and I need to stay as upbeat as I can before visiting Ivan.* Without further hesitation, Rachel turned right. If her Amish family and Ivan's coworker couldn't be counted on to give her directions, she'd just have to stop at the nearest gas station, where she'd ask an *Englisch* stranger to help her find her way.

Arden waited until he was certain Rachel had driven away before coming out of the playhouse again. He felt like such a *dummkopf* in her presence. The rumors he'd heard were proving to be more accurate than not; Rachel *was* rather smug, giggling at the way he'd botched up that acronym. As for directions to the hospital, he saw the trip in his mind's eye so clearly he could have led her there blindfolded, but *telling* her how to get there was another story. Arden might as well have tried to talk her through the Sahara Desert and back again.

What really irked him, though, was the way she'd looked down her nose at his work on the playhouse. It was one thing for her to be amused by his verbal inadequacies, but Arden took great care to produce high-quality products. Even if it seemed impractical by Amish standards, the playhouse was meaningful to the customer, Mrs. McGregor, and Arden was committed to surpassing her expectations for craftsmanship and service. Not to mention, he was dedicated to doing whatever he could, in good conscience, for the business to prosper.

And as Arden had just discovered, sometimes that meant completing customers' orders sooner than originally promised. Mrs. McGregor had come to inquire if he could finish the project the following Friday, a week ahead of schedule. Since it was the end of April and several customers wanted their sheds ready before summer, Arden was juggling other projects simultaneously. But because painting the playhouse was virtually all he needed to do before the project was completed, Arden agreed. Mrs. McGregor subsequently produced two gallons of her daughter's favorite shade of paint for Arden to use. Lovely Lavender, she'd called it. Or was it Lively Lilac? Either way, it looked purple to him.

I'll have to ask Rachel to schedule the earlier delivery, he reminded himself. Sometimes Arden kept so many details in his head he was surprised his skull didn't tilt to the side, but recording information in his brain was far easier for him than jotting it down on paper.

As he took a swig of water from his thermal cup, he heard another vehicle in the driveway—too loud to be Rachel's—and went outside. Two men jumped down from the cab of a large flatbed truck and headed his way.

The stockier one, who had the name *Bob* emblazoned on his shirt pocket, said, "The shake shingles will arrive from our Montville site on Tuesday, but as you can see, we've brought your two-by-sixes."

"That can't all be mine," Arden objected, surveying the load.

The taller, wiry guy snorted. "Funny."

Arden wasn't joking. "I didn't order that much. Our customers have been choosing pine, so we only need half as much cedar as usual. That looks like twice the amount."

"Hang on a sec." Bob retrieved a clipboard from the cab and brought it to Arden. Tapping it with his knuckle he said, "Yup. Someone named Allen put in the order. Signature's right here."

"Arden," Arden corrected the man. "That's me, but that's not the quantity I ordered."

For as much difficulty as he had with reading and writing, Arden didn't have any problem with math. Knight's was a new lumberyard; maybe they'd made a mistake. Arden and Ivan had only been contracted with them for a couple of months, so perhaps the employees were confusing theirs with an *Englisch* business.

"Your paperwork shows you did. Check for yourself—it's a photocopy of the order you placed. The note says you mailed it in." Bob handed the clipboard to Arden.

Arden distinctly recalled the afternoon he'd tried to phone in the order—the *Ordnung* allowed cell phones and solar chargers for business use—as he'd done with the previous lumberyard he and Ivan patronized. The clerk insisted he'd have to place the order online, by fax or in person, because they required a customer signature. Arden explained he didn't have a computer or fax machine and the lumberyard was too far away for his horse to get there in one day, which caused the woman to crack up. When she realized Arden was indeed Amish, she'd apologized profusely.

"You can make up an order sheet yourself. Just use the product codes from the catalog and indicate the amounts. You don't even have to write the sizes down, because we can tell exactly what you want by the codes, but don't forget to sign your name at the bottom."

Studying the sheet now, Arden's mouth went dry. It looked right to him, but then again, he misread things more often than not.

After a minute, Bob took the clipboard back. He pointed to the left of the page, "See here? This is the product code for cedar two-by-sixes. This is the amount you ordered. Here's the product code for the shake shingles, and again, you wrote the amount right beside it."

That explained it: Arden had been so concerned about accidentally transposing letters when he copied the product codes from the catalog that he'd proofread them three or four times. Unfortunately, he didn't pay as careful attention to the quantities. He must have matched the quantity of two-by-sixes with the product code for the shake shingles and vice versa. Red-faced, he admitted his error to Bob.

"We only need half as much cedar, and we'll need double the amount of shake shingles."

"Doubling the shake shingles won't be a problem since they haven't shipped yet," Bob said. "But if we return half of this load, you're going to have to pay a handling fee plus the standard mileage rate for us to return it to the yard. Those are the terms of your contract."

Arden didn't know what to do. He and Ivan had budgeted down to the penny for inventory. They couldn't afford to pay for a surplus like this right now. But it would be a complete waste of money to pay for the drivers to return the wood to the lumberyard.

"All right. We'll keep it."

When they finished unloading and stacking as much of the lumber as they could on the racks that weren't already filled with pine, they piled the rest of it on the floor.

"Per your contract, there's a 10 percent discount if you pay us now," Bob told him.

Arden wished he would have read the contract or that Bob had reminded him of the discount while they were unloading—it would have given him more time to write the check. Arden wrote especially slowly if he felt as if someone was breathing down his neck. His pen hovered over the payee line.

"How do you spell *Knight's* again?" he asked, and the taller guy snickered while Bob dictated the spelling.

As they sauntered away, Arden heard the wiry man remark to Bob, "I guess someone who graduated from a one-room schoolhouse isn't going to win any spelling bees, huh?"

"Maybe not, but he sure does nice work," Bob replied, gesturing toward the playhouse. "Wish I could afford something like that for my kid. It's nicer than my *own* home."

Arden's face was still hot when his sister walked through the door some ten minutes later. "What's wrong, Grace? Is *Mamm* okay?"

"*Jah*, she's fine. Rebecca Miller is visiting her, so I came over with cheeseburger *supp* to put in Ivan's freezer, along with *kuche* for his pantry. I know other

women in the district will be bringing him meals when
he's discharged from the hospital, but I want him to have
plenty to choose from while he's recovering."

"Oh. I, um, don't know if that's a *gut* idea."

"Why not? Doesn't he like cheeseburger *supp*?"

"*Neh*, that's not it." Arden knew Ivan hadn't wanted
anyone to find out about Rachel coming, lest Colin in-
terfered and stopped her. Now that Rachel had arrived,
Arden figured it was only a matter of time until Colin
and his family learned of her presence—and even when
they did, there was little they could do about it. Still,
he was reluctant to be the one to spill the beans. "His,
uh, *schweschder* is visiting. She's staying in his *haus*."

"His sister? The *schmaert* one who became an *Englisch* nurse?"

Arden bristled at the mention of Rachel's intelli-
gence. "Ivan only has *one* sister. And *jah*, Rachel's a
nurse."

"She's *kumme* to take care of him?"

While Arden would have preferred it if other people
believed Rachel had come specifically to take care of
Ivan rather than to help Arden with business matters,
that wouldn't explain why she'd arrived when Ivan was
still in the hospital. "*Jah*, and to, uh, help with some of
the administrative tasks at the shop—since I'll be too
busy making sheds to do the paperwork."

"That's *wunderbaar*. Since she's a nurse, maybe
she'll take a look at the skin on *Mamm*'s fingers. Is
Rachel at the *haus* now? I could go introduce—"

"*Neh!*" It was going to be challenging enough to
work with Rachel every day; Arden didn't want her
flaunting her smarts in his home, too. Nor did he want

his mother trying to pair them up; she'd been nagging him for nearly two years to go to a matchmaker in a neighboring district in Unity. She claimed she couldn't go home to heaven in good conscience until both of her children found spouses. Arden invariably replied if that was the case, he had a responsibility to remain single indefinitely. It had become a running joke between them, but Arden sensed his mother was more serious than she let on. Knowing her, it wouldn't matter that Rachel was no longer Amish—she'd insist Rachel could be wooed back into the fold. Arden, however, was not in a wooing state of mind.

"Rachel's not home. If *Mamm* needs medical care, we'll take her to the *dokder*. I don't want you to ask Rachel for help. For all intents and purposes, she's an *Englischer*. We can work with her, and of course we'll be kind to her, but that doesn't mean she's invited to our *haus* to socialize. Besides, she probably prefers her privacy. In any case, Ivan asked me to keep the news of her arrival to myself, so I trust you'll do the same."

His sister narrowed her eyes, but she didn't argue. "Okay, but I'm going to go put the *supp* in Ivan's fridge so Rachel can enjoy something *gut* to eat when she comes home, just like you do every evening, Arden. Except *she'll* have to eat hers alone."

Her point made, Grace tugged the door shut behind her. The force caused the mail to slide from Ivan's desk for the umpteenth time, as if to emphasize just how much Arden needed Rachel's help.

Rachel spoke with a nurse before entering Ivan's room, confirming what she already imagined; for a few days, Ivan's health had been hanging in the balance. He'd had a severe case of bacterial pneumonia and then suffered a reaction to the antibiotics, rendering it difficult for the doctors to determine the most effective course of treatment. He was still on oxygen and needed to remain in the hospital for several more days, but yesterday there had been indications his condition was finally improving.

After not seeing him for ten years, the sight of her brother would have moved Rachel deeply even if he hadn't been lying in a hospital bed, but his pale, manly face and thin, limp body overwhelmed her, despite her professional training. She spent the better part of the afternoon sitting beside him, stroking his dark wispy hair or resting her hand on his arm, praying. Whenever a nurse entered, she'd inquire about Ivan's medication and symptoms. Although plenty of patients in various stages of pneumonia visited the clinic, she'd never actively cared for them in an ongoing capacity, and she wanted to know what to watch for once Ivan returned home.

Some time around five o'clock, she must have dozed off, because she was awoken by a slight fluttering beneath her hand. Ivan was reaching to remove his oxygen mask.

"Neh," she said, slipping into *Deitsch*. "Don't try to talk, Ivan. Just let me look at you."

Now that he'd opened his big brown eyes, Rachel spotted a trace of the fourteen-year-old boy—her little brother—he'd been the last time she saw him, and she smiled as she bent forward to give him a hug. "I'm sorry you've been so sick. I came as soon as I heard."

She felt him nodding against her cheek, and she held him a moment longer before letting go. She pulled her chair closer and peered into his eyes. "I don't want you to worry about anything at the shop. I'll stay as long as you need. You just focus on resting and getting better."

He nodded and reached for the mask once more. Pulling it up, he asked in a whisper, "Have you seen…" That was all he could manage, so she had to guess what he meant.

"The workshop? It looks great. So large and professional. You've clearly done well." .

But he shook his head so she guessed again.

"I've met Arden, *jah*." But Ivan closed his eyes to indicate that wasn't his question, either. "Have I seen Colin and his family?"

Ivan nodded, wincing. It occurred to Rachel he was worried. But was he worried for her or for Colin and his family? Probably both. Ivan had been put in a difficult position when she left Serenity Ridge; he was so fond of Rachel and yet he was still under Colin and Hadassah's thumbs. By the time he was an adult and Colin and Hadassah had moved into their own house, Ivan had probably had enough of a challenge convincing his brothers he could start a business without creating more trouble by inviting Rachel home or traveling to visit her.

"I haven't seen them yet, *neh*. But don't worry, I'll do my best not to say anything to upset them. I won't let anything they say upset me, either." *It's not as if they can upset me more than they have by refusing to have any contact with me for the past ten years.* "We all just want you to get better."

Ivan nodded, his eyelids drooping. Now that she'd

seen him, Rachel was reluctant to let her brother out of her sight again, but he'd rest more soundly without her there. She gave him another hug. "I'm going to go, but I'll visit again tomorrow afternoon. I'll call the nursing station and check in on you in the morning, and they can call me any time you want them to, as well."

She thought he'd already fallen asleep, but as Rachel turned to leave, Ivan's fingertips brushed her sleeve. She paused as he lifted his mask a third time. "*Denki*, Ray-Ray," he said. It was what he'd called her when he was learning to talk, and the nickname made Rachel smile and tear up at the same time.

I haven't cried so much in one day since...since the day I left Serenity Ridge, she thought.

On the way home, she stopped at a superstore to purchase a cell phone charger and some groceries. She was so weary she grabbed a couple of microwave entrees and didn't realize her mistake until she was driving out of the parking lot, but she was too tired to turn around. Maybe she could pry the frozen food out of its plastic containers and heat it in the gas oven.

Arden's been caring for the animals. I wonder what he's done with the eggs he's collected... Rachel didn't realize how fortunate she'd been to grow up with an endless supply of fresh eggs until she moved to Boston. On Saturdays she'd drive fifteen miles to the farmer's market to buy them, although they were outrageously expensive. As far as she was concerned, she'd be happy to eat fresh eggs morning, noon and night for the duration of her stay in Serenity Ridge.

Then she wondered if Arden would still be working. No, it was close to seven o'clock, and he would have gone home for supper by now. Ivan never wrote about Arden's family, but since Arden didn't have a beard, Rachel deduced he wasn't married, which didn't exactly surprise her. While Arden was undeniably handsome, the Amish valued good character over good looks, and Rachel didn't know quite what to make of his personality. Not only was he uncommunicative, but he seemed humorless, too. Still, he'd appeared sincerely apologetic about having given her such a scare, and Ivan thought highly of him, so he had to have redeeming qualities, even if Rachel didn't know what they were yet.

There was no buggy or horse in the yard when she arrived home, although she hadn't remembered seeing one the first time she'd arrived, either. Maybe Arden lived close enough to walk? Suddenly Rachel felt uneasy staying alone in the big house, without any neighbors within shouting distance. She had to remind herself she wasn't in the city anymore. She was safer here, but she intended to lock the door anyway.

When she set down the groceries, she discovered a note on the kitchen table.

Welcome, Rachel—
I thought you'd enjoy soup—it's in the fridge, and I've filled the cookie jar with snickerdoodles.
    I hope to meet you soon.
Grace Esh (Arden's sister)

Why such a sweet note and an even sweeter act of kindness should reduce Rachel to tears—*again*—she didn't know, but they did. And few things made Rachel as ravenous as crying, so after a day of bawling her eyes out, she tossed the frozen dinners into the freezer of the gas-powered refrigerator and heated the soup instead. When she finished eating a large bowl of it, she still felt hungry, so she had a second bowl, followed by two cookies.

Finally, too full and exhausted to think another thought, Rachel collapsed into bed.

On Saturday morning, Arden was relieved to find the cow had been milked and the eggs collected at Ivan's place. He'd been caring for the animals and bringing the surplus dairy products home so the deacon's wife could share them with those in need. Ivan was glad to relinquish the responsibility, but it surprised him a city girl had gotten up so early on a Saturday.

When he came out of the barn, he was further surprised to see Rachel crossing the lawn carrying two cups of coffee. Tinted red by the morning sun, her hair was an eye-catching contrast with her creamy complexion. For an *Englischer*, she didn't seem to wear much makeup. *Not that she needs any, but I wonder if she's going without it so she'll fit in with the Amish women in Serenity Ridge?* Arden quickly dismissed the curious thought. *"Guder mariye."*

"Guder mariye."

It wasn't until Rachel replied in kind that Arden realized he'd greeted her in *Deitsch*. She didn't seem to bat an eye, but he wondered if he ought to address her solely in *Englisch* instead. She extended a mug to him. He'd already had coffee before leaving his house, but he never refused another cup. He accepted it and held the workshop door open for her.

"Ivan must have told you we usually work from seven or eight o'clock until noon on Saturday. But I didn't think you'd be up and at 'em at this hour."

Rachel's response was peppered with even more *Deitsch* words. "I get up earlier than this to commute to work. Besides, I couldn't wait to have fresh *oier* for breakfast. They were *appenditlich*. So were the *kuche* and *supp* your *schweschder* made."

"My *schweschder*?" Ivan wondered how Rachel knew it was his sister who'd left the goodies in her kitchen.

"*Jah.* That's how she identified herself in her note. Grace Esh. She *is* your *schweschder*, isn't she?" Rachel tittered, and Arden gritted his teeth. By saying such stupid things in front of her, he kept opening himself up to her teasing. Or was it mockery?

He motioned toward the desk, ignoring her question. "You might want to get started on the paperwork by going through that stack of mail. Our calendar is somewhere beneath all those papers, and it'll show you what we've got scheduled when. The checkbook's in the bottom drawer. We had a delivery from Knight's yesterday and got a 10 percent discount. I wrote out a check, but I didn't record the amount in the ledger yet. Also, Mrs. McGregor wants the playhouse completed a week early, so please call our delivery guy and arrange for that."

"Whoa! Wait a second," Rachel protested, setting her mug on a large manila envelope. "How do you expect me to remember all of that? Let me grab a pen… Where *is* a pen?"

Before Arden could answer, the door swung open, and Colin Blank walked in. Rachel was crouched behind the desk, searching the drawer for a writing utensil, and she didn't immediately see him, so Arden announced loudly, "*Guder mariye*, Colin," which caused Rachel to jump up.

"*Guder mariye*, Arden." Then, catching sight of his sister, he said stiffly in *Englisch*, "Hello, Rachel."

"*Guder mariye*, Colin. It's—it's *gut* to see you," Rachel replied. Arden noticed her hands were trembling as she lifted her arms, presumably to embrace her brother, who remained motionless. Rachel quickly dropped her arms, knocking her hand against the desk and jostling her cup, which sloshed coffee onto the mail.

As Rachel used a blank sheet of paper to blot the spill, Arden took advantage of the pause to edge away, saying, "I'll, uh, let the two of you talk in private."

"*Neh*, don't leave. What I've *kumme* to say concerns you both." Colin announced, "Last evening Hadassah and I visited Ivan in the hospital. Imagine our surprise when the nurse told us Rachel had been there to see him, too. And that she'll be helping care for him after he's discharged."

Uh-oh. Arden had known this moment of familial reckoning would come, but he hadn't expected to be in the middle of it. Neither he nor Rachel spoke—Colin had a commanding presence.

"Even more perplexing was that Ivan indicated Rachel will be helping with the paperwork here," Colin said. Arden noticed he avoided addressing his sister directly; instead, he referred to her in the third person, as if she weren't standing a few feet away. "Since he couldn't elaborate, we figured we must have misunderstood him. Would you care to explain?"

Arden swallowed, unsure if Colin was speaking to him or to Rachel. "I-I-I'll be too b-busy constructing the sheds to take care of our orders and accounting."

"I understand what it's like to be short-staffed," Colin said. "What I'm confused about is why you didn't ask me or Hadassah or someone from our district for assistance."

Arden tried to think of a diplomatic yet truthful explanation. He couldn't well say, *You're so reproachful Ivan was worried you'd find fault with our business and try to convince us to close shop.* Nor could Arden admit he didn't want others in their district to discover the extent of his reading and writing difficulty. Fortunately, Rachel piped up.

"From what I understand, many in the community are preparing for planting season, and spring is an extremely busy time for you at work, too, especially with Albert being in Canada. And Hadassah's pregnancy is wearing her out, so Ivan didn't want to burden the two of you."

Colin's face visibly reddened, and Arden didn't know if it was because the Amish in their district avoided using the word *pregnancy*, especially in mixed company, or if he was angry because Rachel had answered instead of Arden, but there was no mistaking his insinuation when he said, "Ivan, Hadassah and I are *familye*, and *familye* help carry each other's burdens."

Rachel lifted her chin, clearly unfazed. "*Jah*, which is exactly why *I'm* here—to help my *bruder* Ivan, as well as my *bruder* in Christ, Arden."

Upon being reminded of their shared Christian faith, Colin appeared to momentarily back down. His posture softened. "It was kind of you to *kumme*, Rachel, but I'll help Arden with the accounting and orders, and Hadassah and the other women in our district will care for Ivan when he comes home from the hospital. I'm sorry for the inconvenience of traveling all this way, but there's no need for you to stay any longer."

"*Denki* for your concern about me, Colin." Rachel's response was equally tempered. "But it's a privilege, not an inconvenience, for me to be here. I gave Ivan my word I'd stay and help, and I intend to honor my promise."

Colin acted as if she hadn't spoken. Directing his gaze toward Arden, he said, "Ivan is ill, so I understand his lapse in judgment, but I would have thought you'd know better. You should have asked me for help."

Arden resented Colin scolding him as if he were a child, but not as much as he resented it when Rachel called attention to Colin scolding him as if he were a child. "Arden's not a *bu* and you're not his *daed*. You wouldn't appreciate it if someone came into *your* shop and took over *your* business," she pointed out.

Now the brother and sister were speaking as if *Arden* weren't there, and it riled him to no end, but even if he had known what to say, they didn't give him an opportunity to say it.

"Your opinion is not *wilkom*, so I'd thank you not to interfere," Colin authoritatively declared. "This matter is between Arden and me."

"*Neh*, this matter is between Ivan and Arden. *You're* the one who's interfering."

Colin must have been surprised by the fire in Rachel's voice, or else he recognized he was overstepping, because he faltered. "All—all right, then. Arden, do you want Rachel or me to help you with the administration of the shop?"

Some decisions were easier than others. "Rachel," Arden stated definitely.

Both Rachel's and Colin's mouths dropped open. Colin recovered first, saying, "If that is your decision, I'll respect it." He clapped Arden on the back. "But if you change your mind or if there's anything else I can do to support you, let me know."

Once the door closed behind Colin, Rachel clasped her hands beneath her chin and gushed, "*Denki* for standing up for me like that. It means a lot to me."

Considering how poorly Colin had treated Rachel, Arden could understand why she'd feel like Arden had stood up for her, but he didn't want her getting the wrong idea. "I wasn't standing up for you. I was abiding by an agreement I made with my business partner," he told her. "If Ivan had suggested we ask Colin for help, I would have agreed to honor that request, too."

"*Jah*, I know. I just meant…never mind." Pressing her lips together, Rachel turned her back toward him and began tearing open an envelope.

If her presence is going to cause me this much stress every day, I might need to convince Ivan to take Colin up on his offer to help, Arden thought to himself as he strode to the opposite end of the workshop, where he could labor in peace.

Chapter Three

On Sunday morning as Rachel drove into town to attend a local church, she passed the little building the Amish used for worship. Although most Amish throughout the country took turns hosting biweekly services in their homes, the Serenity Ridge and Unity districts were two of a few exceptions that worshipped in church buildings. However, they did keep the custom of only gathering every other week as a congregation; on alternating Sundays, families met in their own homes. Rachel was surprised to see the number of buggies neatly lined along the perimeter of the property; could the community have grown that much since she'd been away, or did a lot of folks have relatives visiting?

She sighed. The Amish practice of visiting each other on Sunday afternoons had been one of her favorite customs when she was young. As a girl outnumbered by three brothers, Rachel relished any opportunity that allowed her to socialize with female friends. Once she became a teenager, she better appreciated having older brothers whose male friends dropped in at their house.

Although Colin and Albert's friends were too old to have any romantic interest in Rachel, that didn't stop her from developing crushes on them. By the time she was mature enough to have a suitor, she'd already made up her mind to leave the Amish, which was probably just as well, considering there weren't any eligible bachelors her age in their tiny district anyway.

Maybe there are more courting opportunities now that the community has grown, she thought. Ivan hadn't ever written about walking out with anyone, but she wouldn't have expected him to, since the Amish were more discreet about their romantic relationships than the *Englisch* were. Still, she couldn't help but wonder if he was courting anyone. Then she found herself wondering whether Arden was courting anyone, and if so, whether they'd be walking out tonight, the way Amish couples often did on Sunday evenings. *Why would I care?* she asked herself. *It's certainly not as if I want him to pay* me *a visit instead.*

But as she headed home after church, Rachel had to admit she wished *someone* would drop by; the house seemed too large and lonely. *Maybe I should make the first move and visit Colin, Hadassah and the children,* she thought. *I could offer to take them to see Ivan.* Ultimately, she wasn't that brave, however, so she journeyed to the hospital alone, where her brother slept through most of her visit.

A downpour broke out as Rachel drove home, and when she trekked across the lawn, her shoes left a trail of indented footprints behind her. "Mud season" was what Mainers called the period in between late March and early May when the ground was oversaturated with

melted winter snow and fresh spring rain. Rachel recalled how she and Hadassah sometimes had to mop
the floors three times a day to keep up with the muck
her brothers tracked in.

Being back in Serenity Ridge was stirring all kinds
of memories, some happier than others. Rachel remembered sledding with her brothers in the winter and the
long afternoons her mother had spent teaching her to
bake and sew. She even recalled how excited she'd been
to help plan for Colin's wedding to Hadassah—and how
that excitement turned to disappointment when Hadassah moved into their house and Rachel found out how
controlling she was. Then there were her parents' fu-
nerals, as well as her own leaving…

Aware her mood would darken if she thought too
much about the past, Rachel took out the ingredients
she'd purchased on Saturday and set about making a
batch of sticky buns the way her mother had taught her.
Because the recipe made far more buns than she could
eat by herself, she decided to bring a half dozen of them
to the workshop the next morning, along with coffee for
Arden and her. They'd gotten off on the wrong foot, but
as her mother always told her, there was nothing like
fresh confections and friendly conversation to draw
people together. Granted, Arden had made a point of
letting her know it made no difference to him whether
he worked with her or with Colin, as long as Ivan's
preference was honored, but Rachel figured since she
was the one working there, she'd try to foster a cordial
environment. She was tickled when her efforts seemed
to pay off.

"These are really *gut*," Arden said, his mouth half-full.

"*Denki.* I was worried I may have lost my touch. It's been ages since I've made them."

"Why? Don't you like them?"

"I *love* them." Rachel pulled a bun off the loaf for herself. "I got out of practice because, well, my ex-boyfriend, Toby, used to lecture me about the detrimental effects of sugar."

"Is he diabetic?"

"No. He's a *dokder.* And he's right—an excess of sugar *can* be bad for you."

"An excess of *anything* can be bad for you." Arden took a swallow of coffee before adding, "I'm surprised you'd let his opinion stop you from doing something you wanted to do."

Despite her intentions to establish a congenial relationship, Rachel was immediately defensive. "Just because I left the Amish against my family's wishes doesn't mean—"

"I wasn't referring to your leaving the Amish," Arden interrupted. "I was referring to your refusal to back down to Colin's demands the other day. *I* even had a difficult time saying no to him, but you held your own. So it surprises me you'd give in to your boyfriend's opinion about sticky buns. Seems to me, if he didn't want to eat them, he didn't have to, but why should that stop you from making them if that's what you enjoy doing?"

Rachel shrugged, dumbfounded. For all the times people had implied she was strong-willed, it had never come across as a compliment until now, and she treasured Arden's words. At the same time, she felt criticized by his remark about her deference to Toby... Was that because Arden was right? "I guess I sort of figured he…well, he's a *dokder* and he knows a lot more about health than I do."

Brushing the crumbs from his lips with the back of his hand, Arden remarked, "*Jah*, he knows a lot more about health than I do, too, but that doesn't mean I'm not going to have a second sticky bun after lunch today."

As she watched him effortlessly pick up a drill and ladder and carry them across the workshop, Rachel's heart skipped two beats in a row. *It's probably from all the sugar I just ate*, she tried to convince herself.

Arden leaned the ladder against the double wood storage shed and climbed a few steps to inspect the roof a final time before it was picked up for delivery the following day. Made from rough-cut lumber, the structure required no painting, which was a relief, since painting was the task Arden favored the least. As it was, he was dreading painting the inside of the playhouse. Although the cost of any building they constructed included a painted exterior, Ivan and Arden agreed it wasn't worth it to them in terms of time to paint the interiors, so they left that chore to the customers. Mrs. McGregor, however, had insisted she'd pay extra if they'd accommodate her request this one time. It was important to her that the playhouse be delivered in "move-in–ready condition," as she put it, which was also why she'd supplied her daughter's favorite hue of paint.

It's strange, the things Englischers *will indulge in*, he thought. *And even stranger what they won't.* He could understand why too many sweets could be bad for a person—it didn't take a medical degree to realize how important a healthy diet was—but he took Rachel's ex-boyfriend's opinion about sticky buns as a criticism of the Amish lifestyle. *It's probable some of us eat more sweets than Englischers, but our desserts aren't loaded with preservatives. Not to mention, we get a lot more exercise than the average Englischer, and we've been eating farm-to-table food since long before they came up with the term.*

Arden hopped down from the ladder and glanced across the room at Rachel, who was holding a paper in one hand and running her finger down another paper that lay flat on the desk. She appeared to be cross-referencing documents. Arden hoped she could figure out her brother's abbreviations, notes and figures, because Arden sure wouldn't be able to offer any input—a fact he didn't want her to discover. *Someone who dates a doctor would find it hard to fathom how a grown man can't comprehend simple record-keeping.*

Rachel happened to look up and caught him watching her. Giving a little smile, she asked, "Is there something you need from me?"

"I—I wanted to be sure the pickup is scheduled for this shed for tomorrow."

She set down the paper she was holding and opened the planner; like Ivan, she was very organized and had already decluttered the desk. After surveying it, she rose and brought the planner to him. Pointing at a line halfway down the page, she said, "I think this *PU* means pickup, right? But what's *RCWS*? The customer's initials?"

Arden chewed the inside of his cheek. He would have been hard-pressed to answer even if Rachel hadn't been standing so close to him, but he was especially distracted by the little scar above her right cheekbone. It reminded him of a tiny chip in a delicate teacup. "I, uh, I think the cu-customer's last name is Johnston. There should be a customer folder in the filing cabinet."

"I'll check on the name and address, but that still won't tell me if the pickup has been scheduled. To be safe, I'd better call the trucking company," she decided. Motioning to the shed, she remarked, "It's beautiful. I love the look of natural wood. What do you call wood like that?"

"The wood is cedar, but the way it is sawn is called rough cut. I like rough-cut sheds best myself, too."

"That's it!" Rachel grabbed his forearm. "*RCWS* means rough-cut wood shed."

It was either her hand on his arm or sheer embarrassment about his ignorance that was making Arden feel overly warm. He pulled away and reached to retract the ladder so she couldn't see his face. "*Jah*, that makes sense. Sorry, I must have forgotten."

"Don't apologize—it's a crazy recording system. I'm just *hallich* we cracked the code."

Relieved Rachel didn't think he was a dolt for not knowing the acronym, Arden confessed, "To be honest, Ivan takes care of most of the paperwork around here, so your guess is as *gut* as mine when it comes to figuring it out—actually, your guess is *better* than mine."

"If that's true, it's because I'm related to him. Our minds must be wired the same way." Rachel's eyes twinkled with more green than brown today. "Which probably explains why we were so close as *kinner*."

"Seems like you're still pretty close, otherwise he wouldn't have asked for your help," Arden acknowledged, which seemed to brighten Rachel's expression even more.

"Do you have other *brieder* or *schweschdere*?"

"*Neh*, just Grace," he answered. "She lives with me, along with my *mamm*. I moved here from Indiana when I heard about the opportunity to work with Ivan. Then I brought my *mamm* and Grace out after my *daed* died a few years ago."

"Do you miss your community in Indiana?"

"*Jah*, but this is my community now. It's where my *familye* and my *kurrich familye* live, so it's home to me."

A shadow crossed Rachel's face, and Arden realized he might have sounded as if he were judging her for leaving the Amish, which he wasn't. That's what happened when he volunteered too much information—he said the wrong things even if he managed to use the right words.

"That reminds me, I'm going to visit Hadassah during my lunch break today," Rachel said. "I'll take the business phone with me, in case a customer calls."

"Are you sure you want to do that?" Arden asked. He meant was she sure she wanted to take the business phone, but she must have thought he was asking if she was sure she wanted to visit Hadassah.

"*Jah.* I'm going to offer her and Colin a ride to the hospital whenever they want to visit Ivan," she answered. "And that offer is open to anyone in the community, including you."

Given how quickly rumors spread in Serenity Ridge, Arden couldn't imagine traveling alone with *any* woman, much less with a woman who'd "gone *Englisch*." Still, he thanked her for her thoughtful offer, and they resumed working until their one o'clock lunch break.

"I left your sugar fix wrapped up in the bottom drawer," Rachel said with a sassy grin before she exited the workshop.

"My sugar fix?"

"*Jah*, the sticky buns, remember? I'm not going to eat any more of those since I have plenty at the *haus*, so help yourself. There's four left."

"Only four?" he joked back. "The Amish require six servings of fresh goodies a day."

"*Ach*, I forgot," she said, pretending to smack her forehead. "I'll bring more tomorrow."

It made Arden inexplicably happy that he could still hear her laughing even after she'd closed the door behind her.

Rachel hesitated in the driveway, wondering whether she should drive or take the buggy. She didn't want to offend Hadassah by showing up in a car, but she didn't have a lot of time to spare, so she went inside to fetch her keys. Passing a mirror, she realized she should do something to her hair, which hung loosely about her face and shoulders. It would have been hypocritical to pull it back in a bun the way the Amish women did, but out of respect to her sister-in-law, she brushed it into a ponytail. She was already wearing a long navy blue skirt, and while her cotton top was short-sleeved—most Amish women in Serenity Ridge wore sleeves that covered their elbows—it was plain white and had a modest neckline.

Although she'd felt encouraged her attempt to break

the ice with Arden had been so successful, when Rachel pulled into the driveway leading to Colin and Hadassah's home, she lost her confidence. She didn't expect to be *welcomed*, but what if her sister-in-law wouldn't even *acknowledge* her? There was only one way to find out. As she followed the path to the house, Rachel carefully avoided the puddles leftover from yesterday's rain. Muddy shoes would give Hadassah an extra reason not to invite her in, and Rachel really wanted to meet her nieces and nephews who hadn't yet been born by the time she left.

Colin and Hadassah had gotten married when Rachel was fifteen, and by the time she left home, they had one daughter, with a baby boy on the way. Two years later, Ivan wrote that Rachel's sister-in-law had had another girl, and three years after that, another boy. Sadly, she'd lost a baby, too—Rachel had sent a letter of condolence, which, like the other letters, went unanswered. Although it would be considered too bold to inquire, she hoped Hadassah's current pregnancy was progressing smoothly and the unborn twins were healthy.

Rachel's legs felt weak as she reached the front porch, where a boy about five years old was sitting on the steps. "Hello," she greeted him. "I'm your *ant*. You must be Thomas."

The boy furrowed his brows. "My *ant* went to Canada with *Onkel* Albert."

"*Jah*, that's your *ant* Joyce. I'm your *ant* Rachel."

"I don't have an *ant* Rachel," the boy contradicted. He wasn't being rude—Rachel doubted Colin or Hadassah had told him about her. It stung, but she couldn't blame his parents. They would have feared they'd negatively influence their children by merely presenting the possibility someone could leave the Amish.

"Would you please tell your *mamm* that Rachel is here to see her?"

Hadassah appeared at the screen door. "Thomas, your lunch is on the table. Take your boots off by the entrance and go join your *bruder* and *schweschdere*." She held open the door and turned to the side so he could pass.

Squinting up at her from the bottom step, Rachel noticed Hadassah's belly was so large she appeared to be nearing the end of her pregnancy, although with twins, it was sometimes difficult to tell. "Hello, Hadassah." Her voice quavered as she fought to control her emotions. Her sister-in-law had always had a way of making Rachel feel she was intruding, even when Hadassah came to live in *Rachel's* house.

She remained on the other side of the door. "What can I do for you, Rachel?"

Her manner told Rachel what she'd already suspected; she was going to be treated like an outsider, or at best, like a customer. *You could invite me in and introduce me to my nieces and nephews.* "I wanted to say hello and ask if you need a ride to the hospital. I'm *hallich* to—"

"*Neh*, we don't want to ride in an *automobile*. We'll get there on our own."

"But it's too far away to take the horse," Rachel began to say. Then she realized it wasn't that Hadassah didn't want to ride in a car—it was that she didn't want to ride in *Rachel's* car. She swallowed, trying not to feel slighted. "Okay, well, if you change your mind, let me know. And once Ivan is discharged, please feel free to stop by the house any time."

"*Denki*—I mean thank you," Hadassah said as if Rachel no longer understood *Deitsch*. "It's good to know you're allowing Ivan's relatives to visit him. His brothers will be so pleased."

There, that did it; Rachel's eyes welled with tears. "I didn't mean I was *allowing* you. I meant I'd *wilkom* your company." *Even though you're being terrible to me.*

The silence that followed was punctuated by birdsong and the muffled conversation of the children inside. If Rachel heard correctly, her name was mentioned. She waited another moment before saying, "I'd better get back now. I've been helping Arden with the bookkeeping, and I'm having a hard time making heads or tails of Ivan's notes," she nervously admitted.

"Colin could take over if you're struggling," Hadassah suggested.

Rachel's cheeks burned. Hadassah was just *looking* for a reason to get rid of her. "*Denki*, but I'll figure it out. Besides, it keeps me busy until Ivan is discharged."

"If you're bored, you should consider returning to your job in the city. Joyce will be back from Ontario soon. Between the two of us and the deacon's wife, Jaala, we can care for Ivan. We might not have nursing degrees, but we'll see to it he recovers."

Rachel refused to respond in kind to Hadassah's barbed insinuations. As genuinely as she could, she replied, "*Denki*, but I'd rather stay here until Ivan is better. I'd *wilkom* your help caring for him, though. And if you change your mind about a ride, let me know…"

Rachel forgot she'd been standing on the first stair

and she stumbled as she backed away, narrowly missing a puddle, but she didn't stop moving until she reached the end of the road, where she pulled over and put the car in Park. Resting her head upon her arms on the steering wheel, she tried to gather her swirling thoughts. *Why does Hadassah tear me down like that?* I'm *not the one who acts as if I'm better than she is—she's got so much* hochmut *she'd rather pay exorbitant cab fare than accept a ride from me! And I never implied she couldn't effectively help Ivan recover—even if I do* know *more about health care than she does.*

The abrupt honking of a loud horn caused Rachel to lift her head and peek in the rearview mirror. She rolled down her window and motioned for the driver to go around her; there was plenty of room. *You might as well pass me,* she thought belligerently, *because I'm not leaving until I'm good and ready to leave.* And that warning went double for her sister-in-law.

Arden sighed as he put away his insulated lunch bag. Having completed the shed for pickup, he could move on to the next one. He also had a doghouse to build. Arden and Ivan frequently joked the business should be named Blank's Little Buildings instead of Blank's Sheds, because they accepted orders for everything from sheds to ice shanties to doghouses. They'd even built an outhouse once. As long as a building's dimensions fell within the state's regulations for transportation, they could make it, but Arden was looking forward to the day when they could focus solely on sheds, because they could be more efficient that way. But until their business grew, they couldn't turn away any projects, including playhouses. Which meant this afternoon Arden had to tackle the task he least enjoyed: painting.

He'd just finished rolling paint over the first wall when someone entered the workshop. Unable to tell whether it was Rachel or a customer, he squeezed through the playhouse door. It was Rachel. Her face was blotchy and her eyes pink-rimmed, like on the day he met her. Uh-oh. Her visit with her sister-in-law must not have gone well.

Arden could sympathize; Colin's behavior toward her the other day had been downright spiteful. You'd think under the circumstances, he'd extend Rachel a little grace. After all, Ivan had been gravely ill and Rachel was volunteering in the shop. Arden supposed it was none of his business how the Blanks interacted, but it wouldn't hurt if he showed a little more appreciation of Rachel himself.

"Hi," he said casually, strolling in her direction to grab a rag from the bin.

"Hi." She barely glanced up from the planner she had already opened in front of her. "If I'm reading this right, it looks like there's another shed that's due on Monday."

"*Jah.* I'll get right on that as soon as I finish painting the inside of the playhouse."

This time she paused to look up. One side of her mouth lifted in a wry smile. "Lavender?"

"How did you know?"

Rachel pointed to her own hair, which he noticed she'd pulled into a ponytail, to indicate he had something on *his* head. "The flecks gave you away."

Arden scowled, pulling a curl straight and checking his fingers for paint. "It's *lecherich*, the things the *Englisch* want."

Now Rachel scowled, too. "*Jah*, we're a *lecherich* group, aren't we?"

"*Neh*, I wasn't referring to *you*."

"I'm *Englisch* now."

Arden was trying to cheer her up, not offend her. He would have been better off if he'd remained inside the purple playhouse. "*Jah*, but—but—"

She waved her hand. "It's okay, I agree. Some *Englischers* buy their *kinner* too much stuff they don't need. I mean, considering the homelessness problem in our country, it seems extravagant for someone to buy a *kind* a playhouse she'll outgrow in a year or two. But at least if they're going to buy something like that, it's *schmaert* they're investing in a playhouse as nice as the one you made."

"*Denki*," Arden said as warmth traveled from his ears all the way down his spine. "I hope the customer still thinks it's nice when it's delivered on Friday and she sees my paint job. I'm not the best painter, and it's close quarters in there."

Rachel snapped her fingers. "Oh no, I forgot to reschedule the pickup for that. Listen, how about if I make the call and then I'll do the painting so you can start on the next shed?"

Arden was taken aback. "That's very kind, but you don't have to do that. It's enough that you're managing the paperwork—"

"Really," she insisted, looking directly at him. Maybe it was because her hair was drawn up or because she'd been crying, but she appeared pallid, almost gaunt.

"There's not enough paperwork for me to do while I'm waiting for a customer to call. Besides, I find the monotony of painting soothing. Especially when I'm using a soft color, like lavender."

"Lavender paint has the opposite effect on me," Arden said with a laugh. "But even with its windows open, the playhouse doesn't have a lot of ventilation. I don't want you to get dizzy."

"I carry surgical masks wherever I go. I'll grab one from my car."

So, while Arden went to work on the next shed, Rachel painted the playhouse interior. Every once in a while he'd call out, asking how she was doing in there, and she'd indicate in a muffled voice she was fine.

Toward the end of the afternoon, she stuck her head out and pulled off the mask. "*Kumme* take a look. Tell me if you see any spots I've missed."

Arden gingerly ducked into the playhouse—Mrs. McGregor had insisted he shouldn't add an adult-size door to the back of the structure because she wanted the house to be "child-centric"—and straightened his posture to three-quarters of his height. Rachel was as meticulous with her painting as Ivan was about his work. "I hate to admit it, but it looks really *gut*."

"Hate to admit it? Why? Because *Englischers* can't paint as well as the Amish?"

"*Neh*, because it's purple."

Rachel blushed. "Sorry, I guess I'm a little defensive."

"A little?"

She chuckled. "I think it could use another coat, don't you?"

"It's hard to say until this coat dries."

"*Jah*, you're right. So what color do they want the trim painted?"

"I think she called it cloud white or cotton white—it was something fluffy." Arden instantly wished he hadn't admitted that was how he remembered the name of the paint—he sounded so juvenile.

"Poodle white, maybe?" Rachel joked, and from the way she rolled her eyes, he recognized she was poking fun at the names of the paint colors, not at him.

Suddenly, aware of how close they were to one another—not that there was any other way to position themselves in such a tight space—he felt heady and needed air. "I think the fumes are getting to me," he said. As he backed toward the door, he inadvertently stepped on the rim of the paint tray, upending it.

"Oh *neh*!" Rachel tried to scoop the spilled paint from the floor with her hands.

"Here, let me help," Arden offered, snatching the nearby rag. As he bent to swab the floor, she stood up, catching him beneath his chin, and he staggered backward. She reached for his arms to keep him from knocking into the wall, but it was too late; he could feel his shirt dampen with paint along his shoulders as well as on his arms where Rachel had clutched them.

"I am such a kl-l-lutz. I am so sorry. I ruined your wall."

"*I'm* sorry. I ruined your shirt. Look—your sleeves have handprints on them."

"Purple, my favorite color," Arden quipped as he gave Rachel the rag so she could wipe off her fingers. He twisted his torso to inspect his lower pant leg. A thick glob of paint dribbled down his calf to his ankle. "At least my shirt is color coordinated with my trousers."

That sent them into peals of laughter. Every time they tried to stop laughing, they'd start again, harder than before, until they were nearly breathless. Suddenly, Rachel went quiet. She held a lavender fingertip in the air in front of her lips. Arden listened. Someone had entered the workshop.

"Arden?" a man called.

Arden scrunched his shoulders forward so he wouldn't rub against the door frame as he exited the playhouse and Rachel followed. Colin was standing a few yards away, shaking his head. "What is going on here?"

"W-we—we," Arden stuttered, both embarrassed and angry. He could imagine how ridiculous he and Rachel looked, but who was Colin to demand to know what was going on in *his* workshop?

"We spilled paint," Rachel said, an edge in her voice.

"That much is clear," Colin retorted. "Spilling paint is a waste of money—and time. It hardly seems like a laughing matter."

"I guess that depends on how good your sense of humor is," Rachel shot back. Sometimes it was difficult to say whether Colin was goading her or she was the one goading Colin, but Arden wished they'd both knock it off.

"Is—is Ivan okay?" he asked, concerned about the reason for Colin's visit.

"*Jah.* I spoke with the *dokder* this morning, and he said Ivan should be discharged by the end of the week. It would be a shame if he came back to find the workshop like this." He pointed at the hem of Arden's pants, which were dripping paint onto the floor.

So that Rachel wouldn't have a chance to interject a snippy reply, Arden quickly said, "Praise *Gott. Denki* for coming all this way to share the *gut* news with us, Colin."

"*Jah*, well…" Colin seemed thwarted by Arden's expression of gratitude. "I also brought you this estimate of Ivan's hospital bill. It's based on the premise he'll be in the hospital another four or five days. They won't tally the final amount until he's discharged, but I understand you and Ivan use your business earnings to cover medical bills. This will give you an idea of whether you can pay it or not."

The Amish oftentimes negotiated a steep discount with health-care providers by paying their bills in full at the time services were rendered. Ivan had always been more than generous in using their business profits to help cover Arden's mother's medical expenses, even forgoing his own salary on occasion. Now Ivan was the one who needed financial help. Arden had no doubt the community would cover whatever portion of Ivan's bill they could. But the collective funds were stretched to the limit, and he didn't want to strain them further. Arden knew roughly how much money he and Ivan had in their business account, and he could give up his salary for a couple of weeks, but with his mother sick, he couldn't be sure she wouldn't need to see a doctor again soon, too. Then what would happen? He didn't want Colin to find out they were financially strapped, lest he argue their situation was more evidence of why they should close their shop.

"Denki." Arden held out his hand for the estimate; his palm and fingertips were purple.

Colin shook his head. "I'll leave it on the desk so you can read it once you and Rachel are finished… spilling paint."

"What a grump," Rachel muttered as the door shut behind her brother. "So listen, I think the best thing is for you to take off your boots right there. Otherwise, you're going to leave purple prints everywhere you walk." She giggled, but Arden was no longer in a joking mood. She must have caught on, because she strode to the rag bin and returned with several more rags.

Blotting paint from his boots and pants, Arden realized Colin was right; he *had* wasted both money and time this afternoon, and he hoped Colin wouldn't tell Ivan about the paint incident. It wasn't so much that Arden cared about Colin's opinion as it was that Arden wanted Ivan to be confident Arden was doing everything that needed to be done in order to cover the hospital bill and meet their financial goals for the spring. And because the sooner Arden completed a project, the sooner he got paid, he was going to have to increase his productivity and decrease his distractions. *Which means keeping my conversations with Rachel to a minimum*, Arden decided. *Starting now.*

"I'm going to work late tonight, but after you've cleaned up the paint mess, you should leave for the evening," he told her when he finished wiping off his clothes.

"Are you sure? I could help—"

But Arden cut her off. *"Jah*, I'm sure," he said. *I'm absolutely positive.*

Chapter Four

Although Rachel visited Ivan on Monday and Tuesday, he'd been so groggy she'd barely begun to converse with him when he drifted off, so Wednesday evening she was thrilled to find him sitting up in bed, eating dinner—both good signs. Also, his oxygen face mask had been replaced with a nasal cannula, which made it easier for him to talk. "So, how are you and Arden getting along?" he asked in between spoonfuls of soup.

"He's kind of quiet, but we get along fine." In reality, except to thank Rachel for her help each day, Arden had hardly spoken two words to her since Colin's visit on Monday afternoon. The sudden switch in his attitude both offended Rachel and hurt her feelings, especially since they'd just broken the ice with each other, but there was no need to tell her brother that.

Ivan chuckled before responding, "*Neh*, I didn't mean how are you getting along with each other. I meant how are you getting along with the workload?"

"Oh!" Flustered, Rachel quickly recounted how, in between reconciling the business's accounts, fielding customer inquiries, stocking inventory and scheduling deliveries, she'd spent the past two days painting both the interior and exterior of the playhouse.

"You're really going above and beyond what we hoped you'd do for us. I appreciate it and I know Arden does, too, even though he's not much of a talker. It takes a while for him to open up, but once you get to know him, I think you'll find he's a *wunderbaar paerson*."

A wunderbaar paerson *wouldn't be influenced by such an* unfreindlich paerson *as our* bruder *Colin*, Rachel thought. Aloud, she paid Arden as much of an honest compliment as she could, admitting, "He does beautiful work on the sheds."

"*Jah*, I've learned a lot from watching him. I'm blessed to have him as my business partner and my *freind*," Ivan said, and it struck Rachel that as quick as Colin was to find fault with someone, Ivan was equally quick to compliment a person. She loved that quality in her younger brother, whether or not Arden deserved his praise. "Has he said anything about how his *mamm* has been feeling lately?"

"*Neh*. Why, what's wrong with his *mamm*?"

"She has lupus."

Rachel was surprised. Knowing Arden's mother had a chronic illness instantly made her feel less annoyed at him. As a nurse, Rachel frequently witnessed the toll a chronic illness could take on a patient's family members, as well as on the patient with the disease. "If she's having a flare, he didn't mention it."

"That figures. Arden tends to keep his struggles to himself. Have you met his *schweschder*, Grace?"

"*Neh*, although she left an *appenditlich* meal and

dessert for me at the *haus*. I haven't met anyone from the community yet. I haven't seen anyone I used to know, either—except Colin and Hadassah." Until she said it aloud, Rachel didn't fully realize how much it bothered her that no one at all had dropped by Ivan's house to say hello.

"People from the community probably don't know you're here. I haven't been able to tell anyone because whenever I've gotten visitors, I've either been too sleepy or the oxygen mask has made it difficult for me to say much."

They know I'm here—everyone in Serenity Ridge always knows everything that's happening with everyone else, Rachel thought. *No one is stopping by because Colin and Hadassah have poisoned the well against me.* "It's all right, I don't mind being alone. Besides, pretty soon you'll be coming home, and you're the one I came to Serenity Ridge to see."

But for as independent as she thought she was, Rachel felt especially lonely that evening when she returned to the empty house. She called Meg, who launched into a story about how their upstairs neighbor had flooded the basement by cramming too much clothing into the washing machine. Meg didn't care about the puddles in the basement as much as she cared that the washer's agitator broke, so the machine was out of order and she had a mountain of laundry piling up. "What am I supposed to do now, wash everything by hand?"

"You mean like the Amish do?"

"The Amish wash their clothes by hand?"

"Sure. They beat them on rocks down at the river."

"They do?"

"No! Of course not, silly." Rachel giggled; some of the illusions *Englischers* held about the Amish amused her. Even though she'd educated her roommate on many Amish practices, apparently she hadn't mentioned how the Amish in Serenity Ridge did their laundry. "They use old-fashioned wringer washers, which are powered by diesel generators. But they never use dryers—clothes are always hung on a line. I kind of miss doing that, because it makes everything smell fresh."

"I know exactly what you mean—my mother always hung out our laundry, too. It's funny, because these days people act so smug about buying energy-efficient dryers, but those same people wouldn't be caught dead hanging their clothes outside on a line."

Rachel laughed again. "Well, the Amish would consider using a dryer—even an energy-efficient one—to be as taboo as…as talking to *me*." She meant the comparison to be tongue-in-cheek, but Meg picked up on how alienated she really felt and clucked her tongue sympathetically.

"Do you want me to visit you this weekend? I work Friday and Sunday, but I could come for the day on Saturday."

"Oh, that's really sweet, but it's too far to drive for one day. I'll be fine. I think I'm feeling sorry for myself because I was just getting over Toby dumping me the way he did and then I came here only to face more rejection. If it wasn't that Ivan's going to need extended care when he comes home, I'd be tempted to leave sooner rather than later."

"Yeah, he's going to have a long recovery," Meg acknowledged. "Have you told them at work you won't be coming back for a while?"

"I'll let them know at the end of the week. I dread making that call, though."

"Why? You can legitimately take family medical leave."

"Yeah, but only the people in human resources will know *why* I'm taking a leave of absence. Everyone else is going to assume I'm heartbroken because of Toby and Brianna." Rachel recognized she shouldn't care what they thought, but it still bugged her to imagine anyone pitying her, especially Toby. *Wait until I get accepted into the MSN program and quit my position at the clinic—then they'll see I'm not as naive or needy as they think I am.* "Anyway, if you run out of clothes, feel free to borrow some from my closet. It's not as if I'll be using them any time soon."

After she said goodbye to Meg, Rachel realized she should do a load of laundry herself, especially since she had a thick smudge of lavender paint down the front of her navy blue skirt, and in addition to her green skirt, she'd only brought one other dress. *It's either I wash my clothes in the wringer tomorrow morning or I sew new ones.*

Thinking about sewing reminded Rachel of the time Toby and his younger brother, also a doctor, had held a contest to determine whose suturing technique was better. They each cut the skin of a grape and then sutured it closed again to present to their father, an orthopedic surgeon, for him to judge. Watching them, Rachel decided to give it a try, too. When Dr. Grand Sr. saw the results of her attempt, he declared *her* the winner. She credited all the time she spent quilting, as well as sewing capes, aprons and dresses, for her coordination and steady hand.

Suddenly it occurred to Rachel that she'd be expected to suture patients' wounds once she became a nurse practitioner, and she decided to stop by the local fabric store at her next opportunity. Not only would sewing a skirt or two give her more wardrobe choices, but it would allow her the chance to improve her manual dexterity for the future. *Who needs visitors anyway?* she asked herself. *In a little while, Ivan will be coming home, and I'll have his company. Meanwhile, I'll keep myself busy by focusing on what's really important— preparing for my career as a nurse practitioner.*

"*Mamm*'s fingers seem to be getting worse," Grace said as she set a box of cereal in front of Arden on Thursday morning. Usually, she made a big breakfast, but she'd woken up late; she'd probably been up most of the night, trying to keep their mother hydrated and her fever down. "I really think we should ask Rachel if she'll take a look at them."

"*Neh*, I've already told you that's not a *gut* idea," Arden objected. He shook the box above his bowl, and only a half cup of grain poured out. It didn't matter; his sister always sent him off with a hearty lunch, and he could take his break earlier than usual.

"Why not? You just told me you're so busy at the shop you have to work until seven thirty again tonight and tomorrow evening. If Rachel takes a peek at *Mamm*'s hands and says it's nothing serious, it would spare you from taking time off to bring her to the *dokder*."

Arden's sister had her own horse and buggy to use for running errands nearby, but she was nervous about driving to the hillier, western section of town where the medical clinic their mother went to was located. The *Englischers* in Serenity Ridge, while respectful, weren't as cautious as the *Englisch* drivers in Indiana, who were accustomed to slowing their vehicles as they crested hills, never knowing if a buggy was just out of sight and traveling at a much slower pace on the descending side. More than once since she moved to Maine, Grace had experienced a car approaching her too quickly from behind, which not only spooked the horse but frightened Grace to the point she was unwilling to travel to the clinic unless absolutely necessary. So it was up to Arden to either transport his mother to her medical appointments or arrange for a cab or someone in the district to take her.

He silently dithered over what to do. Grace was right; he could ill afford to take time away from the workshop, especially since yesterday he'd accepted a rush order— something he virtually never did, but it was only for a chicken coop, and the customer was willing to pay handsomely for the inconvenience of the short notice. However, his sister had also told him their mother was experiencing a strange discoloration of the skin on her fingers. Although her lupus flares primarily included a classic butterfly rash on her face, extreme fatigue and a chronic fever, their mother been advised to seek medical attention for any new symptoms. She'd said the discoloration didn't last long and wasn't painful, but Arden didn't want to take any chances.

"I understand you don't want Rachel coming to the

house for a social visit, but this would be for medical purposes only," Grace said. "We could compensate her for her trouble, if that's what you're worried about."

"*Neh*, that's not it. It's that… It's that Rachel is only a nurse, not a *dokder*. I want *Mamm* to get the best care. I'll use the work phone to schedule an appointment for her at the clinic. We'll figure out the transportation logistics once we know what time she has to be there."

"I'm not sick enough to go to the clinic. Grace worries too much," Oneita said as she shuffled into the kitchen with a water glass in her hand. "Next time I go to the rheumatologist, I'll tell him about my fingers. Who's Rachel?"

Pleased that Grace had honored Ivan's request not to tell anyone about Rachel, Arden ignored his mother's question. "Are you sure you're okay?"

"Jah," she answered and then was overtaken by a coughing fit. Grace hovered over her, wringing her hands. When Oneita stopped wheezing, she took a sip of water and then said, "I'm fine, but I need to lie down again. Would you make some white willow bark tea with a drop of honey, Grace? I think my fever is back."

Grace placed her hand over her mother's forehead. "*Jah*, you're *waarem*. I'll walk you to your room."

When she returned, Grace scowled at Arden and picked up their conversation right where they'd left off. "I don't understand you sometimes. If Rachel is anything like Ivan, she'll be *hallich* to help. Or is it that you're afraid *Mamm* and I won't be polite to her because she went *Englisch*? I promise we'll *wilkom* her into our home as warmly as we'd *wilkom* any Amish woman."

That was exactly what Arden was worried about.

Once Grace and his mother got to chatting, there was no telling what they'd say to Rachel. *I've got enough on my mind without worrying whether they're going to try to convince an* Englischer *to take pity on a* dumm *Amish bachelor and* kumme *back to Serenity Ridge for* gut *so I can marry her.* "If *Mamm*'s fingers get worse, call me on the business phone," he instructed his sister and bolted from the house.

It wasn't until ten thirty when he caught a glimpse of Rachel dipping a piece of a sticky bun into her coffee that Arden realized he'd forgotten the lunch his sister packed for him. His mouth watered. Rachel glanced up, and he hastily averted his eyes. For the past couple days, he'd been careful not to even comment about the weather in her presence, lest she take it as an invitation to strike up a longer conversation. She must have noticed him looking at her now and interpreted that as a sign he wanted to chat, because she dipped the last piece of the bun into her cup, popped the dripping morsel into her mouth and then sauntered in his direction as she licked a dab of icing from her upper lip. Arden's stomach growled. It was going to be a long day without any sustenance to tide him over.

"You're making *gut* progress," she said about the coop.

"*Jah*, but the customer wants to pick it up on Saturday, which means I need to finish building it by tomorrow morning or else the paint won't dry," he replied. He stammered when he added, "W-would you, uh, b-be willing to help?"

"*Me?*" Rachel's voice squeaked with disbelief. Arden knew he shouldn't have asked; when she'd volunteered to paint the playhouse, it was probably a onetime offer only.

"Nev-never mind. Y-you don't have to. I thought because you s-s-said there wasn't enough for you to do you wouldn't mind. And you did such a *g-gut* job painting the playhouse," he stuttered.

"Oh—you want me to *paint* it!" The tiny scar on Rachel's cheekbone leaped higher with her smile. "When you asked for my help, I thought you meant you wanted me to help you *build* the coop. I'm *hallich* to paint it—I'll do any work around here that doesn't involve swinging a hammer, using a saw or wielding a drill. What color does the customer want it painted?"

Delighted by Rachel's response, Arden grinned. "You'll never guess."

"Please don't say lavender."

"*Neh.* Guess again." Despite being pressed for time, Arden was in no hurry to have their conversation end.

She guessed turquoise, yellow and pink before giving up.

"Eggshell white." He kept a straight face as he waited for her reaction.

"Oh. White's no so bad—" she started to say before she got the joke. "*Eggshell white for a chicken coop. Voll schpass!*" When she tipped her head back in laughter, her hair spilled over her shoulders and down her back. Amish women sometimes wore their long hair loose at home in the evening, so Arden had seen locks of all different textures and colors, but never had he so closely beheld hair as lustrous as Rachel's. As she moved, he caught a whiff of coconut mingled with…almond? Hunger clawed at his stomach.

"Actually, the family wants red, like a barn. They wanted the inside painted, too. They claimed a dark color is more conducive for the hens to lay than natural wood, but that's where I drew the line. I don't have the time, and I'm concerned the chickens will end up pecking the paint off anyway. They were awfully disappointed when I said *neh*."

"Who, the family or the poultry?" Rachel was tipping her head coyly to one side, clearly teasing him.

"Probably both." Arden was so at ease he didn't have to think about what to say or how to say it—his words and jokes were flowing readily.

"*Jah*, everyone knows what high expectations those *Englisch* chickens can have. You're just fortunate they didn't ask you to *wallpaper* the inside of their coop," she replied. When Arden stopped laughing, Rachel added, "I'm actually being serious. I know some *Englischers* who wallpapered the inside of their coops. They used vinyl wallpaper, like the kind people use to line their drawers, because they say it makes cleaning the coop a lot easier."

Arden shrugged. "That wouldn't be my choice, but if it's what they want to do, who am I to convince them otherwise?"

He picked up his hammer and got back to work, but inwardly he was savoring their exchange. It occurred to him Rachel not only had a terrific sense of humor, but her work ethic was as diligent as any Amish woman's he'd ever known. And most of those women would have chewed him out something fierce for ruining their paint job the way he'd ruined hers the other day, but she found it comical. *Colin is too hard on her*, Arden realized once again. *Rachel might not be Amish anymore, but she's a gut woman.*

* * *

Who knew taciturn Arden could be so humorous? Rachel swallowed the rest of her lukewarm coffee and set the cup back on her desk. She was glad to have another painting project to complete, and now that Arden was warming up to her again, she hoped things around the workshop wouldn't continue to be so dreadfully dull.

After taking a quick peek at her phone to confirm she hadn't received an email from the MSN program yet, Rachel spent the rest of the morning rechecking the figures in the ledger. One of the few comments Arden had made to her on Tuesday was that he was concerned there might not be enough funds in the business account to cover Ivan's hospital bill. But after reviewing the ledger twice, Rachel was confident they could withdraw the amount in full and still have a few thousand dollars left over.

She was about to break for lunch when a tall, redheaded *Englischer* entered the shop and introduced himself as Chris Jones, the hardware and tool supplier for the business. There was something familiar about him, but he didn't show any sign of recognition when Rachel told him her name, so she concluded she must have seen him in passing at the grocery store or maybe in church on Sunday.

"I was on my way to Unity, so I thought I'd deliver these since they were special order so we couldn't pack them with the supplies they received last week. Seemed kind of silly for Ivan or Arden to hitch up the buggy and come all the way to the store for a single box of nails."

"That was thoughtful. If you give me a moment, I'll

pay you for the entire order. I just saw that invoice," Rachel suggested. When she located the paperwork and finished writing out the check, she lifted her head to find Chris studying her intently.

He immediately apologized. "I don't mean to stare, but I feel like we've met before."

"So do I but I don't know whe—wait, Chris Jones. You're Paige Jones's brother!" His surname hadn't registered with her right away, because it was so common.

"Ah, you're one of Paige's friends." The crease across his forehead indicated Chris still couldn't place Rachel.

"Sort of. She tutored me ten years ago when I was studying to get my GED. We met at your house, and your parents often invited me to stay for supper. I think I only met you once or twice when you were home from college for the holidays," Rachel explained.

Chris palmed his forehead. "How could I forget? Paige talked about you all the time. She said you were a really quick learner and you caught on to everything right away."

Rachel briskly shook her head. "If that's true, it's because Paige was such an effective teacher. I lost touch with her years ago. What's she doing now?"

"Teaching, of course. On a reservation in New Mexico."

"I'm not surprised. She had a keen interest in connecting with people whose cultures are different from her own. So did your parents. They were intrigued by my Amish background." Rachel stole a glance in Arden's direction. His back was turned as he searched the shelves along the wall, but she felt self-conscious, worrying whether he was within earshot. She could understand why it might be considered disrespectful for her to stand in the presence of an Amish person and casually chat with an *Englischer* about her decision to leave the community. She didn't want to offend Arden, but neither did Rachel want to cut her conversation with Chris short, considering his sister had been instrumental in helping her.

"So, did you, er, decide to stay after all?"

Rachel giggled softly; she could imagine how confusing it was for Chris to see her working in an Amish shop dressed as an *Englischer*, especially considering the last he knew, she was planning to leave the Amish. "No, after I got my GED, I moved to Boston, went to college and became an RN. And right now, I'm waiting to hear if I've been accepted to an MSN program to become a nurse practitioner." Then, to further clarify, she added, "Ivan's my brother and he's been in the hospital with pneumonia, so I'm only in Serenity Ridge temporarily to help out."

Chris congratulated her on her academic and career successes before saying, "I had no idea you were related to Ivan. That's too bad he's been so sick. Your family is fortunate to have you here."

I wish they *felt that way.* "Please give Paige my fond regards when you speak to her. And greet your parents for me, as well."

Once Chris was gone, Rachel sat down again and mindlessly filed away the invoice, but her thoughts harkened back to the evenings she'd spent conversing with Paige and her parents. They'd been nonjudgmental as they listened to Rachel ponder aloud the pros and cons of leaving her Amish family and community, neither

encouraging her to go nor persuading her to stay, even
when she was so conflicted she begged Mrs. Jones to
tell her what she should do.

"I think you should keep praying for wisdom," Mrs.
Jones had responded. Rachel had been hoping for a
more definitive answer, but when she pushed for one,
Mrs. Jones merely added, "It might help to remember
whether you choose to leave or stay you can always
change your mind later if you believe God is leading
you in a different direction."

I can't imagine ever living here permanently again,
Rachel mused. Then she spied Arden's broad shoulders
as he stood in front of the supply shelf, and as she reflected on their playful morning banter, she smiled and
thought, *But I suppose visiting isn't so bad after all.*

Arden slid the box of hinges—they weren't what
he was looking for—back into its slot among the other
boxes of nails, screws, nuts and bolts. He hadn't been
able to keep from overhearing Rachel and Chris talking,
and their conversation had distracted him and damp-
ened his sunny mood. While he was disconcerted to discover their trusty hardware supplier's family had helped
Rachel leave the Amish a decade ago, he was even more
dismayed to learn about Rachel's career plans. *Why
should I be surprised she has ambitions to become a
nurse practitioner?* he asked himself.

No, Rachel wasn't as haughty as she was rumored
to be—nor was she even as snooty as Arden's initial
impression of her. In fact, when Chris complimented
her for being a quick learner, Arden noticed Rachel
had deflected his praise; she'd demonstrated *demut*,

or humility, the opposite of *hochmut*. But as Rachel's goals for the future demonstrated, she had an insatiable appetite for knowledge. *She may be Ivan's sister, she may be a hard worker and she may be* schpass*, but I'd do well to remember she's still an* Englischer. *A very* schmaert *one at that.*

"I'm going to go eat now." Rachel's voice cut into Arden's thoughts. Although they routinely took their lunch break at the same time, she went to the house to eat while he ate in the workshop or outside on the bench beneath a peach tree. "How about you? It's nearly one thirty."

"I'm working through lunch today," he answered, although the very word *lunch* made his stomach raw.

"You can't go without eating. You'll get a *kop-pweh*," she warned. "Trust me, I know these things. I'm a nurse."

As if I could forget. "A nurse, soon to be a nurse practitioner," he muttered.

"You heard me tell Chris that?" Rachel cocked her head.

Intending to clarify that he hadn't been eavesdropping, Arden said, "It would have been hard not to. This is an open space with high ceilings. If it was a secret, you should have lowered your voice."

"I have nothing to hide." Rachel sounded insulted, and Arden realized he'd been too gruff. Maybe she was right; he was getting peckish.

"Not even the 5/32-inch wood screws?" he ribbed, trying too late to make her smile. "I thought we had half a box left."

"They're right in front of you." She was already turning on her heel.

"Where? I don't see them."

She pivoted around again and pointed. "If the box gets any closer, it's going to bite you in the nose—532WS. Read the product code."

Arden lifted his hand midway to the shelf, but he still didn't see which box she meant. What was the code again? He and Ivan never paid attention to codes—they'd arranged the hardware according to what they used most often, and Arden had memorized where every last item was located on the shelves. He touched the box he thought the screws were in and Rachel tugged his sleeve to move his hand away.

"Are you putting me on or do you seriously need glasses? Those ending in *DWS* are the drywall screws, not wood screws." She reached in front of him to remove a box from the shelf near his opposite shoulder.

"Aha, when you said nose level, you meant *your* nose level, not mine." He tried to cover his mistake with humor, but it was lost on her as she hurried toward the door. His hand must have been shaky from hunger, because the box slipped from his fingers, spraying screws across the floor. He was squatting to pick them up when the door opened and in walked Grace. Arden's heart raced, but before he could ask her, she assured him their mother was fine.

"Anke Beiler came by to *qwilde* with her. *Mamm*'s not ready for that yet, but the white willow bark tea she drank must have helped a lot, because her fever is gone. Anyway, Anke said she'd stay there and visit so I could run a few errands, including bringing you your lunch."

"*Denki.* You didn't have to do that, but I'm glad you did." Arden realized sometimes he was so stressed out about what was happening at the workshop he didn't thank his sister often enough for all she did to care for their mother and keep the household running smoothly.

"It's okay. It was on my way to the fabric shop." Looking around, Grace casually inquired, "So, where's Rachel today?"

"She's up at the *haus* eating lunch."

The words had barely left his mouth when Rachel burst through the door. "I forgot my phone," she announced breathlessly as she swiped it off the desk. It must have taken a moment for her to register Grace's presence, because Rachel came to an abrupt halt. Single-handedly gathering her hair and holding it against the nape of her neck, she stuttered, "H-hello."

"Hello. You must be Rachel. I'm Arden's sister, Grace."

Rachel immediately dropped her hand, and her hair swung free as a smile illuminated her features, from forehead to chin. She squeezed Grace's arm. "It's so nice to meet you, Grace! *Denki* for the meal you brought the other day. It was *appenditlich.*"

"I'm glad you enjoyed it. I'm actually delivering Arden a meal today, too." Grace impishly put her hand to the opposite side of her mouth, pretending to whisper behind it, "He forgot his lunch, and he gets cranky when he doesn't eat."

"Oh, that explains a lot," Rachel joked. Or maybe she wasn't joking—Arden couldn't tell, but hearing how quickly Grace and Rachel teamed up to tease him made him uneasy.

"Grace is on her way to the fabric shop," he told Rachel, cupping his sister's elbow. "I'll walk you back to the buggy."

"I'm in no hurry." Grace planted her feet where she stood. "How is Ivan, Rachel?"

"He's getting a little stronger every day. He'll probably *kumme* home this weekend," Rachel said. "But if you'd like to go visit him in the hos—"

Arden cut her off. "Grace, you're keeping Rachel from her lunch. She has to go now."

Grace raised an eyebrow at him before addressing Rachel, whose cheeks were flushed. "You'll have to forgive my *bruder* for interrupting you. Not only does he become irritable when he's *hungerich*, but he forgets his manners, too."

"It's okay, I understand. That's what happens when someone's blood sugar drops too low. You really ought to eat now, Arden," Rachel advised. She sounded so genuinely concerned Arden felt bad for having interrupted her like he did—until she turned to Grace and said, "You know, I was planning to go to the fabric store, too. How about if we go together?"

"Perfect! It will give us a chance to get better acquainted."

Now Arden was really desperate. "Y-y-you're going to be gone that long, Rachel? What if a cu-customer calls?"

"I'll take the business phone with me," Rachel told him. To Grace she added, "But he's right, it might take more time than I can spare if we travel by buggy. Are you comfortable going in my car?"

"Sure, as long as I don't have to drive," Grace said, giggling.

Arden must have appeared as apprehensive as he felt, because when Rachel looked at him she said, "Are you sure you're going to be okay? You look peaked."

"*Jah*, once I have lunch, I'll be fine," he resigned himself to saying, even though he was no longer the least bit hungry.

Chapter Five

"You sound a lot happier tonight," Meg said a few minutes after Rachel called Thursday night on her speakerphone as she drove home from visiting Ivan. "Did you find out you got into the MSN program?"

Rachel groaned. "I'm sorry I've been so moody lately, but you're right, I do feel a lot happier tonight, and no, it's not because I found out anything about my application. It's because I had a *gut* afternoon at the fabric store with Arden's *schweschder*, Grace."

Meg cracked up, and when Rachel asked what was so funny, she imitated, "A *gut* afternoon with Arden's *schweschder*. You're sounding more and more Amish every day."

Rachel laughed, too. "If you think I *sound* Amish, wait till you see how Amish I look in the dress I'm making."

"What?" Meg's tone suddenly changed. "Why are you making Amish clothes? You're going to stay there permanently, aren't you?"

"Don't be *lecher*—ridiculous. I'm making a dress because I brought so few skirts, and it gives me some- thing to do in the evenings until Ivan is discharged."

"Sewing doesn't sound like a fun way to spend an evening. Haven't you met any handsome, eligible bachelors who could take you out?"

"Only Arden." Rachel's answer slipped out of her mouth before she realized how it sounded. "I mean, he's the only bachelor I've met, and his sister told me he's not courting anyone. Which obviously is neither here nor there, because he's Amish. My point is, no, I haven't met any eligible bachelors I'd consider going out with." She was grateful Meg couldn't see her face, because her cheeks felt aflame.

"For as much as you've told me about Arden, you've never told me what he looks like. Is he handsome?"

"Not that it matters, but yeah, I suppose he's good-looking. He's tall and has blond—blond*ish*—curls and light blue eyes. And a nice smile, when he smiles, which is rare."

"He's still being Mr. Morose?"

"Well…sometimes. It's hard to say. He sort of turns on a dime. Like this morning, he was cracking jokes right and left, and then all of a sudden, he became surly again because I was talking too loudly to a customer or he couldn't find where I put the inventory. And when his sister came by, he all but tried to drag her out of the workshop rather than let her talk to me. Who knows, maybe he's afraid I'll be a bad influence on her and she'll go *Englisch*, too."

"But she's friendly to you?"

"Very. Although I suspect part of that is because she's interested in my brother."

"But you're not interested in *her* brother?"

"Not at all," Rachel insisted. "He's Amish, remember?"

"*I* remember. Do *you* remember?"

Rachel gave an exaggerated huff. "Just for that, I'm saying goodbye now, Meg."

"*Gut nacht,*" Meg chirped, and they both laughed before hanging up.

I don't know why she'd suggest I'm romantically interested in Arden, Rachel thought. *I think she's just being* lappich *on purpose, to amuse me. The idea is as* narrish *as the thought of me lingering in Serenity Ridge. The moment Ivan is well again, I'm out of here.*

Meanwhile, she was glad she'd gone to the fabric store with Grace, who'd filled her in on the news in Serenity Ridge. Ivan rarely mentioned people other than their family members when he wrote to Rachel, so she was surprised to discover how the population had grown and changed since she'd lived there. The fledgling community was only a little over twenty years old, and already it had nearly tripled in size, despite the fact several of the people who originally settled there had either returned to their home states, married and moved away, or passed on.

Maybe I'm being too sensitive to think people are avoiding me—they might not even live here any longer, Rachel realized. *I suppose I could try to introduce myself to the Amish. But how?* Showing up at church after having been gone for ten years would likely be awkward for everyone, as would dropping in on someone she used to know. And she wasn't about to attend a singing. Ah well—for tonight she literally had her work cut out for her; she'd purchased fabric in a bright spring color Grace said would look pretty with her hair and eyes. It wasn't until she'd already cut into it that she realized she'd chosen almost the exact shade of lavender Arden had spilled inside the playhouse, and the recollection made her laugh all over again.

"Arden, *kumme* look at this," Grace called from the living room when he walked through the door on Thursday evening. It was after eight o'clock and he was beat, but hearing the urgency in his sister's voice, he raced through the kitchen without removing his muddy boots.

She was standing over their mother, who was reclining on the sofa in a housecoat. "Stop fussing," Oneita said to Grace. "Let your *bruder* eat his supper."

Grace wouldn't listen. "Look at *Mamm*'s fingers, Arden. *That's* what I've been telling you keeps happening. Please show him, *Mamm*."

Oneita sighed, but she held up her hands. Although her thumbs were spared, the top halves of all eight of her fingers were so white they nearly glowed.

"Do they hurt?"

"They tingle a little, like when your foot falls asleep, but they don't hurt."

"Were you leaning on them?"

"*Neh*. I just got out of the tub."

Arden tugged at his ear. "Did you use a new soap or something?"

"What is this, twenty questions?" Grace snapped. "She didn't *do* anything. It just happens. See—now they're turning blue. This is the sequence it follows. It's not going to do us any *gut* to guess what's happening. We need a medical professional's help."

"But if it doesn't really hurt…" Oneita said, even as she winced and wiggled her fingers.

"*Mamm*, there might be an underlying reason this is happening. If that's the case, it needs to be addressed now, before it progresses. I don't want you to end up suffering needlessly." Grace's tone indicated she was struggling to remain patient. She shot a look at Arden and added, "The longer we wait, the more expensive the treatment might be."

Although money might have been a prohibitive issue a few days ago, it was no longer Arden's primary consideration. Thank the Lord, his concern over Ivan's hospital bill had finally been put to rest this afternoon when Rachel confirmed she'd combed through the ledger, checking and rechecking the figures, and she'd assured him they had money to spare, even if Ivan wasn't discharged on Saturday or Sunday as expected. Arden didn't quite know how to explain their extra funds, but who was he to doubt Rachel? She'd carefully tracked every bill paid, supply bought and delivery scheduled and insisted they were in the black.

What he was more concerned about now was meeting the deadlines for the projects he'd taken on in an attempt to bring in as much money as possible during Ivan's hospitalization. He was already working from six thirty in the morning until seven thirty or eight o'clock each evening. He hadn't even begun the shed that was scheduled for pickup on Monday and he couldn't work on the Sabbath, so how could he take time off to bring his mother to the clinic? Granted, he or Grace could ask someone else to take her, but there was no guarantee anyone would be available. Oneita taking a cab was even less likely than Grace taking the buggy to that side of town; cabs made her nervous, and she'd only ride in one if absolutely necessary.

"Has it gotten worse or happened more frequently?" Arden asked his mother.

"*Neh.* Definitely not."

Grace threw her hands in the air. "Arden! Are you going to wait until her fingers fall off to do anything about this?" She stormed from the room, and Arden rubbed his eyes, stupefied by her comment.

His mother merely chuckled. "Don't listen to her, Arden. If my fingers fall off, we'll sew them back on again."

Arden didn't find the thought amusing. He sank into a cushion at the opposite end of the sofa. "Grace is right, *Mamm*. We need to get this checked out sooner rather than later. I'm sorry I hesitated. It wasn't that I don't want to take the time or spend the money. You're more than worth it. It's…" He stopped speaking, realizing if his mother's health truly was his priority, he wouldn't offer the flimsy excuse of needing to meet his work commitments.

"I know, *suh*." His mother leaned forward to pat his knee. "You're shouldering a lot of responsibility at the workshop—more than usual. That's important not just for the customers, but for you and your *familye*, and especially for Ivan. Unless my hands get worse, this can wait."

"*Neh*—"

His mother pointed a finger at him; it had almost returned to its normal hue. "You and your *schweschder* take excellent care of me and I appreciate it, but I am still your *mamm* and this is still my body, so I'm making this decision, not you. I'll tell my rheumatologist about my fingers at my next appointment."

Arden shook his head. "Can we compromise? Since I have a shed due on Monday, I'll schedule an appointment for you for Tuesday. If your hands get better before then, we'll cancel it. But if they get worse, we'll go to the *dokder* immediately."

"All right, all right. But the only reason I'm agreeing to this is because otherwise Grace is going to be upset with you."

"*Jah*. Remember the time I procrastinated installing a heater in her buggy and she served meat loaf every night until I got around to doing it?" Meat loaf was Arden's least favorite food.

"Do I ever! Even *I* didn't like meat loaf anymore after that," his mother joked. "And if we don't want it for supper tomorrow night, you'd better wipe up the floor. Look at that mud."

Arden gamely went into the kitchen to take off his boots and wipe up the footprints before returning to the living room to mop the floor there, too. As he worked, his mother said, "I'm surprised Grace flew off the handle tonight. She came back from the fabric store in such a *gut* mood."

"Oh?" Arden didn't look up from wringing the cloth into the bucket. Rachel had seemed almost giddy after the trip to the fabric store, too. All afternoon he'd had to fight the temptation to worry about whether Grace told Rachel something he wouldn't have wanted her to disclose, such as that he had trouble reading or that their *mamm* wished he'd meet someone to court.

"*Jah*, she said Ivan's *schweschder* took her in her car—don't fret, she made me promise I wouldn't tell anyone Rachel is here, although I can't imagine it will stay a secret for very long. Anyway, afterward they drove around so Grace could show Rachel some of the new farms and Amish *heiser* in Serenity Ridge."

That would explain why they were gone so long. "Hmm."

"Grace said Rachel is in her late twenties. There aren't too many people that age to socialize with here. You ought to invite her to our *haus* for supper after work one evening."

I knew that was coming, Arden thought. *I wish the weather were as predictable as my* mamm *and* schweschder. "She goes to visit Ivan in the evenings after work."

"Ah, that's right. She offered Grace a ride. I'm surprised she didn't offer to take you, too, considering your relationship with Ivan."

"She did offer, *Mamm.*" Arden shifted himself upright and picked up the bucket.

"But you didn't accept? Don't the two of you get along? Or are you uncomfortable about how it would appear to be alone with her? If that's it, Grace could go with you, too."

Arden felt trapped; no matter what he said, his mother would likely draw the wrong conclusion. "W-we wo-work w-well together." The repetition of *W*s made his stutter even more pronounced. He edged toward the door, adding, "I-I've b-been working late and I wa-wanted to give her time alone with her *br-bruder* since it's been so long since she's seen him. She went *Englisch* ten years ago, you know. She hasn't been b-back since then."

"*Jah,* Grace mentioned that." A frown pulled at his mother's mouth. Satisfied she'd gotten the message, Arden moved toward the kitchen on his way to dump the dirty water outside. Just as he turned the door handle, his mother called, "When Ivan comes home from the hospital, we'll have to invite both him and Rachel to have supper with us. Won't that be *schpass*?"

Rachel kicked her sheet aside. Between the rainy weather and the warming temperatures, there was already a hint of summer humidity in the air. It was a good thing she could sew quickly, because if the heat kept up, she couldn't continue to wear the clothing she'd brought with her, with the exception of the short-sleeved cotton top she planned to put on again today.

The clamminess in the air not only made her cranky, it caused her hair to wilt, too, so she swept it into a high ponytail. It felt good to have it off her neck, but Rachel realized if she leaned forward while she was painting the chicken coop, her ponytail might brush against it and she'd wind up with even redder highlights than her natural ones. She released her hair and gathered it in a bun at the nape of her neck instead. *I can imagine what Meg would say if she saw me now...*

The rain was coming down in sheets as she sprinted across the lawn to the workshop a few minutes later. The instant she reached the door, she realized she'd left her cell phone at the house and had to race back. The battery was running low—she didn't drive often enough to keep it charged—but it had enough power for her to check her email for news from the university. The second time she got to the workshop, she was so soaked she felt as if she'd been swimming.

"Guder mariye," Arden greeted her from behind the

wall of a shed that hadn't been there when she'd left the previous evening. He was *fast*.

"Guder mariye," she echoed. Noticing she was dripping on the catalogs on the desk, she asked, "Do we have any towels in here?"

"Neh," Arden replied as he came around the shed into view. He did a double take when he spotted her. "The rags in the bin are clean, though. Let me get you a couple."

"Denki," she said when he handed her several cloths in assorted sizes a moment later. She patted one along the length of her sleeves before using the second one to blot her hair and then her face. Lowering the cloth, she spied Arden watching her. "I know, I look like a drowned rat."

His ears turned pink. "D-do you wa-want me to run to the *haus* and get a r-real towel?"

"If you do, it'll be wet before you make it halfway back to the fence," she replied. "Just listen to it coming down." They both paused and looked toward the roof of the barn, which was being pelted with raindrops. "Even *you* don't make that much noise when you're hammering, and you've got a really quick, powerful swing," Rachel said.

When Arden's cheeks and neck ignited with color, Rachel realized her comment may have sounded flirtatious, but she didn't know how to indicate that wasn't her intention. Changing the subject, she said, "I guess if there's one *gut* thing about wearing my hair like this, it's that it doesn't look any different when it's wet than when it's dry."

Terrific, now it sounded as if she was insulting

Amish women's hairstyles. Rachel didn't know what was wrong with her brain and mouth today, but they weren't doing her any favors. "Ivan really should keep an umbrella in the *haus*," she added feebly.

"I suppose he figures since he wears a hat, he doesn't need an umbrella," Arden remarked with a shrug, and Rachel was glad he walked away before she could embarrass either of them again.

As Arden pulled out his tape measure and measured the length of a joist, he fought to keep his hands steady. Ordinarily, he might have felt complimented if a young woman noticed his strength, but coming from Rachel, it unnerved him.

But why? Because she's Englisch? he asked himself. She sure didn't look *Englisch* today; with her hair combed into a bun like that, for the first time Arden could envision the young Amish girl she'd been before she left Serenity Ridge. The severe hairstyle was an unsettling contrast with her *Englisch* clothing, and he wished she'd worn her tresses loose, the way she usually did, but that was beside the point. It wasn't her hair or clothing or the fact she'd gone *Englisch* that made him feel upset by her flattery. Arden was upset because he realized a comment about his strength was going to be the best compliment he'd ever get from Rachel. *It's not as if someone that bright would ever think of me as clever or wise.*

His tape measure snapped his thumb as he retracted it into its casing; he had the reflexes of an amateur this morning. Last night he'd lain awake in bed for hours, worrying about his mother and Grace eventually inviting Ivan and Rachel to supper. Board games would inevitably follow their meal, and if any of those games involved reading aloud… Arden yawned. He was tired. Tired from having spent the night tossing and turning, tired from trying to stay one step ahead of their customers, and tired from trying to hide his shortcomings. How ironic that the one thing people noticed about him was his strength, when at the moment, he felt as weary as could be. He closed his eyes and prayed. *Lord, please empower me to do Your will today and to meet the commitments I've made to others.*

"Arden? Are you okay?"

His eyes flew open; Rachel stood in front of him. "*Jah.* Do you need something?"

She extended him the phone. "Grace wants to talk to you. She sounds upset."

He pressed the phone to his ear. "What's wrong, Grace?"

"It's *Mamm*'s…this time it's not just…and her…" Whether it was because of the rain, the phone shanty or the cell phone's reception, Grace's voice kept cutting in and out.

"I can't hear you, Grace. But I'm coming home right away. I'm bringing Rachel. We'll be right there." He turned toward the desk to ask Rachel for her help, but as he'd mentioned the day before, sound carried well in the workshop and she'd heard everything he'd said.

"I'll run to the *haus* to get my keys. You lock up here and meet me at the car."

Reaching the car before Rachel did, Arden prayed, *Please,* Gott, *keep* Mamm *well.*

A moment later Rachel slid into the seat behind the

steering wheel. "Which road do I take?" she asked as they neared the end of the driveway.

Arden's mind clouded, and his tongue felt thick. Two of the three streets he usually traveled to access the road he lived on were washed out, so he'd taken a roundabout way to the workshop that morning. He couldn't have told Rachel the names of those streets if his life depended on it—not even if his *mother's* life depended on it.

"Arden." Her voice was firm but calm. "Which way?"

"R-r-right," he said, and she turned in the opposite direction of where he wanted her to go.

He hadn't mixed up right and left for years—it only happened when he was stressed or tired. As a child, it had taken him much longer than the other students to learn the concept of right and left. He was finally able to memorize the two directions when the teacher told him, "Think of it this way. *Right* is on the same side as the hand I *write* with. The other hand is left." Except Arden always completed the mnemonic as, "The other hand is wrong."

"Neh!" he barked now. "Wrong! Go wrong!"

Rachel tapped the brake, and his upper torso swung toward the dashboard before the seat belt jerked his momentum to a stop. "Which way do you want me to go? Right or left?"

Arden pointed. "That way."

"Okay." She reached over and tapped his hand, repeating, "Okay. It's going to be okay."

For the rest of their trip, each time they came to a stop sign or the end of a street, he'd squint into the rain and point in the direction he wanted her to continue. The downpour pelted the rooftop so hard it made it difficult for them to hear each other, and twice they temporarily lost all visibility when passing vehicles shrouded them in water.

"Ivan told me about your *Mamm*'s lupus. Has she had a flare of symptoms recently?" Rachel asked as they approached another four-way stop.

"*Jah*, a fe-fever." Arden pointed. "Up the hill. Then t-turn by the *Grischtdaag* tree farm."

Rachel did as he said. "Anything else?"

Arden was confused; couldn't she see the tree farm? "There's a small b-barn."

"No, I meant any other symptoms?"

"She's tired. And her ha-hands are—" He rapidly tapped the dashboard. "Here, turn here. Down this road at the end is wh-where I live."

"Hold on, I haven't stopped the car yet," Rachel said when she pulled up to the house, but Arden already had one leg out the door. How many times had she treated patients who'd wound up injured because they'd panicked while trying to help a family member during an emergency?

She turned off the ignition, nabbed her first aid kit from beneath the seat and hurried behind him into the house, through the kitchen and into the living room. There a thin, older woman whose head of dark hair didn't contain a strand of gray was placidly resting in an armchair while Grace stood beside her holding a glass of water.

"Why, hello. You must be Rachel Blank. I'm Oneita Esh," the woman greeted her as if she'd been expecting Rachel to stop by for a sister day.

Before Rachel could respond, Arden began firing off questions. "Are you okay, *Mamm*? Is it your hands? Grace, what happened?"

"Her nose changed color, just like her fingers. It was the oddest thing."

Oneita looked at Rachel and raised her hands as she shrugged. "They're better now, as you can see. I only wanted Grace to tell Arden we might need to schedule an appointment after all, but I guess they didn't have a *gut* phone connection. I'm sorry you came all the way out here in the rain. Grace—please make Rachel a cup of tea. She's dripping wet."

"*Mamm*, as long as we're here, you should let Rachel look at your hands. And your nose," Arden suggested.

Oneita rolled her eyes. "My *kinner* fret so much you'd think *they're* the *eldre* and *I'm* the *kind*."

Rachel laughed. Then, sensing Arden and Grace's frustration with their mother, as well as Oneita's resistance, she suggested, "A cup of tea would be *wunderbaar*, Grace. Perhaps while you're making it and I'm chatting with your *mamm*, Arden will go remove his shoes and get a towel for me. I'm afraid we've made a mess of your floor."

Arden looked at her askance, but Grace sighed and nudged him out of the room, saying, "Okay, we'll give you privacy to chat."

"You're going to want to look me over, aren't you?" Oneita asked.

"It might help keep those two from breathing down your neck," Rachel whispered, causing Oneita to chuckle.

She proceeded to take Oneita's temperature and discuss her symptoms. Rachel was almost certain she could identify the phenomenon, as she'd read about it and seen several lupus patients treated for it in the clinic over the years. She didn't think Oneita's case was urgent, but since Rachel wasn't qualified to offer a diagnosis, she encouraged her to see a doctor soon.

As Arden and Grace reentered the room, Oneita argued, "I understand that, but I'd still like to hear what you think it is and what I can do about it until I get in for an appointment."

"*Mamm*, if she doesn't know for sure—" Arden started to say.

"She *does* know. And she knows what I can do to treat it or prevent it." Oneita pointed her finger at Rachel in a way that reminded her of her own mother. "*Kumme* now, you've studied and learned a lot about *Englisch* medicine. I understand some people might think that's a matter of *hochmut*. But it's false *hochmut* to act as if you don't know something when you clearly do."

Flustered, Rachel was at a momentary loss. Somehow Oneita's words sounded less like a scolding and more like...like *encouragement*. She felt the same way now that she'd felt when Arden pointed out how she'd held her ground with Colin—it was as if Oneita and Arden appreciated the very attributes in Rachel that the people in her family condemned as character flaws.

"Okay," she agreed. "I'll tell you what I know, but first I have to admit there's something that's confusing me. If this is what I think it is, usually it's triggered by cold temperatures, but the weather's been so warm lately. It seems odd you'd be experiencing it now—especially after bathing."

Grace clasped her hands together. "*Mamm*'s been

taking tepid baths, not hot baths. It's what she does for her fever."

"But she didn't have a bath this morning, did she?" Arden countered. "And even if she did, it's not as if she put her nose under water."

"Maybe today was an exception," Oneita said.

"Did you do anything else with cold water today, *Mamm*?" Arden pressed. "Rinse vegetables? Make lemonade?"

"*Neh*. Grace has been doing all the food preparation. She thinks I'm so weak she barely allowed me to get my compress from the freezer before she was chasing me out again."

"*Mamm*, that's it! You opened the freezer, which is right at nose level, and you've been handling the compress. Could being exposed to the cold for such a short time trigger it, Rachel?"

"*Jah*. I think you've solved the mystery, Arden," Rachel said, silently admonishing herself for making assumptions about Oneita taking hot baths and for not asking additional questions, as Arden had done. But now that she was more confident about the diagnosis, she told the Eshes everything she knew about the disease, including how to prevent it, what to do when it happened, what tests the doctor might want to run and what alternative medicine options she might consider. She concluded by again urging Oneita to schedule a doctor's appointment.

"Arden will do that for me, but I doubt the *dokder* will tell me anything you haven't already said." Oneita brought her teacup to her lips. "Oh, this is cold. Would you put another kettle on for us, Grace?"

"Actually, Rachel and I ought to get back to the workshop now." Arden was shifting from foot to foot, but Rachel noticed the color had returned to his cheeks and he wasn't stuttering anymore. He was probably nervous about meeting his deadlines, and she didn't want to add to his anxiety.

"*Jah*, we should go," she agreed, hoping she didn't appear rude for dashing off.

"Then you must *kumme* for tea another day, shouldn't she, Grace?"

"Absolutely." Grace smiled at her brother. "Arden and I have been talking about Rachel visiting since she got here, haven't we, Arden?"

"*Denki*, I'd like that," Rachel agreed, and in that moment she realized just how much she'd longed to be welcomed into an Amish family's home again.

On the return trip, Arden could hardly speak, except to indicate in which direction Rachel should turn. Now that he wasn't so distraught over his mother's condition, he had the wherewithal to verbalize left or right instead of just pointing, but beyond that, speech eluded him. He needed to process the gamut of emotions he'd just experienced, from his fear about his mother's health to his admiration of how skillfully Rachel managed the situation, to his apprehension about her coming to their house socially. Fortunately, either Rachel understood his need for silence or she was deep in thought, too, because she was as quiet as he was.

Although the rain had let up and Rachel only used her intermittent wipers to clear a fine mist from the windshield, the unpaved back roads were soft with puddles. More than once she navigated onto the shoulder in order to bypass the standing water, but when they came to a particularly large pool that extended across the road's width, she stopped the car and bit her lip.

"Uh-oh. That looks deep. I better not cross it. I don't want the engine to seize." She glanced into the rearview mirror and at both sides of the road. "It's too narrow to turn here. I'm going to have to back up a little first, and then I can maneuver a three-point turn."

Rachel put the car into Reverse and Arden could hear the engine revving, but they went nowhere. "Are we stuck?"

"I think so. I'll look." Rachel shifted into Park and reached for the door handle, but Arden pressed her shoulder to stop her from getting out.

"No need for both of us to get dirty," he said. As soon as he placed his weight down, he sank far enough into the soggy ground that the muddy water nearly covered the top of his boots. The muck created noticeable suction as he trudged to the front of the car, where he confirmed the driver's side wheel was stuck indeed. "Put it in Reverse," he instructed Rachel, who was sticking her head out the window.

"It is," she confirmed.

"I'm going to rock it a couple times first. On the count of three, apply the gas." Arden bent to place his hands against the front bumper, shoulder width apart, thinking, *This is never an issue with a horse and buggy.* "One… Two…" He could feel the car begin to budge, and he heaved with all his might. "Three!"

Rachel must have pushed the pedal to the floor, because the driver's side wheel gyrated in place, wildly throwing blobs of mud at him before both tires gripped the ground and the car shot backward with such force Arden lost his balance and thumped onto his bottom in the ooze. Fortunately, he was able to halt his backward momentum by bracing his torso with his arms, so he remained in an upright sitting position instead of lying flat in the sludge.

As he wiped dirt from his eyelid with a clear patch of his sleeve, he saw Rachel charging toward him on foot, waving something white in the air. "Arden, are you okay? I'm so sor—" One of her feet was submerged in mire, and as she extended the other leg forward, it lost traction and slid beneath her. Her knee hit the soft ground first, followed by her elbow on one side and then her palm on the other. By the time she stopped moving, she was lying flat on her belly with her chin in the mud.

Arden scrambled to his feet to help her up, too. "Are you okay?"

"Jah," she said once she was upright. Blinking at the damp, dirty wad she still gripped in her fist, she added, "But I'm afraid these were my only napkins."

The notion that a couple of flimsy paper napkins could have made a difference to them caused Arden to howl with laughter, and Rachel clutched her stomach and joined him. Noticing that the grime on her face made her bright teeth appear even brighter as she laughed, he couldn't think of any woman he knew who would be as good-natured as Rachel was being right now. If her attitude in the face of being drenched with rain and gunk wasn't a demonstration of *demut*, he didn't know what was.

Chapter Six

Once she maneuvered the car into a turn, Rachel offered to take Arden home so he could change his clothes and wash up, but he insisted on continuing to the workshop.

"After the, uh, paint incident, I brought a change of clothing to work. Didn't think I'd need to use them so soon, but..."

Rachel giggled. "But you've never been around me before. I seem to foster all kinds of messy mishaps."

"*Neh*, the paint spill was definitely my fault. But here's a little hint for the next time someone is pushing you out of the mud. You want to apply *light* pressure to the gas pedal."

"How was I supposed to know? I've never been stalled in a swamp before," Rachel countered genially. "Besides, what makes you the expert? You don't drive."

"*Neh*, not anymore. But my running-around period lasted three years, and let's just say there's a lot of snow in Indiana in the winter and flooding in the spring..."

Rachel's mouth fell open. She couldn't imagine staid

Arden going through a three-year *rumspringa.* "Wow. My running-around period only lasted four weeks when I was sixteen. I tried out the *Englisch* lifestyle with my friends, but I honestly wasn't drawn to it."

"But you—" Arden didn't complete his thought.

"I left two years later, *jah.* Despite what people think about me seeking attention or rebelling against my Amish upbringing, that's not why I left. I left because I—" Rachel swallowed the rest of her sentence. She'd said too much.

"You left because...?" Arden twisted toward her in his seat, as if he was truly interested in hearing her answer.

"I left because when my *mamm* was sick, I wished I could do something besides rub her temples and feet with apple cider vinegar or bring her ginger tea." Remembering, Rachel sighed before she clarified, "That doesn't mean I don't value natural remedies, because I do in many instances. But as a young *maedel* watching my *mamm*'s *dokder* and nurses, I developed a curiosity about *Englisch* medicine, and I secretly dreamed of becoming a nurse. But that would have meant leaving the Amish, and after *rumspringa,* I had no desire to go *Englisch,* so I put the idea out of my mind. Then when my *daed* became ill, my fascination with medicine returned and, well, as you know, I eventually became a nurse."

To Rachel's astonishment, instead of Arden pointing out how prideful it was to pursue an *Englisch* education instead of being satisfied with her Amish schooling, he said, "And you became a very *gut* one. *Denki* for helping my *mamm* today."

* * *

If Arden didn't know better, he might have suspected it was a tear instead of a trickle of mud dripping down Rachel's cheek as they pulled into Ivan's driveway. She pushed it aside with the back of her hand and flashed him a smile.

"I'm glad to help your *mamm* any time."

Arden was about to say he hoped his mother wouldn't need help again when he spied movement out of the corner of his eye. An Amish wagon was parked in front of the workshop in the area designated for loading sheds and unloading supplies. Unlike the buggies the Amish in Serenity Ridge used for travel, this type of wagon was pulled by a draft horse instead of a standardbred and had an open seat. Although Arden couldn't see the face of the man who owned the wagon, the steel roof panels piled on the flatbed indicated it belonged to Colin.

"Uh-oh. Look who got caught in the cloudburst."

"I suppose since he's wearing a hat, he figured he didn't need to bring an umbrella," Rachel said, quoting Arden's earlier remark as Colin turned toward them, glaring. On the surface her gibe might have seemed facetious, but beneath it Arden heard a note of fear.

"Hi, Colin. That was quite some del-deluge, eh? Sorry to keep you w-waiting. I see you brought the panels I ordered for the sh-shed roofs." Arden hoped in vain his friendliness would allay Colin's ire.

"I've been sitting here for over an hour. I'm sopping wet and so is my horse. You'd better have a *gut* reason for closing the shop in the middle of the day." As Colin strode in their direction, droplets flew from the brim of his hat. When he removed it to shake it dry, he must have gotten his first full gander at Arden and Rachel, because he abruptly halted and hollered, "Exactly what kind of nonsense have you two been up to this time?"

In the face of confrontation, Arden was usually tongue-tied, but today he struggled to *hold* his tongue. He stood tall with his fingers balled into fists at his sides. "I told you I'd pick up the panels from your shop myself. It was your choice to deliver them and your choice to set out in bad weather. You also chose to *waste time* sitting in the driveway when you could have piled the roofing by the door and left. But then you would have missed the opportunity to scrutinize the business. You can see we're bedraggled and the car is filthy, yet your first inclination isn't to ask about our welfare. It's to cast judgment on me—and on Rachel."

Colin faltered backward two steps before regaining his balance. "If you don't want to tell me where you've been, maybe you'll have to tell Ivan."

Without acknowledging Colin's threat, Arden walked around him to unlock the workshop door and then ambled back to the wagon and began pulling the steel panels from its bed. "Rachel, would you please write a check for Colin for this order?"

"Of course. How much do we owe you?" Rachel sweetly asked her brother.

While she and Colin went inside, Arden finished stacking the metal sheets against the side of the workshop wall. Passing Colin on the way in, he thanked him for the delivery, but Colin didn't reply.

Once inside, Arden headed straight to the rag bin and toweled the grime from his face and hands. Rachel was quiet except to suggest Arden go to the house to change and clean up first, while she minded the shop, and then she took her turn. She came back with two mugs of piping-hot coffee, which Arden found surprisingly refreshing on such a warm day. By then he'd calmed down, but he didn't want to discuss what had happened between Colin and him. He was relieved that once again, Rachel seemed to have an implicit understanding of his need to ruminate in silence. The only thing she told him before they began their separate tasks was that she must have dropped her phone at some point, because she'd discovered it submerged in a puddle on the way to the house.

"Does it still work?"

"*Neh.* I'll stick it in a bowl of dry rice. That sometimes helps."

"You can use the business phone if you need to make any personal calls."

"*Denki*, Arden," she said and when she placed her hand on his arm and held his gaze, he had the feeling she wasn't just talking about the phone.

As she dabbed white paint on the trim of the coop, Rachel tried to sort out her feelings about everything that had happened so far that day. She wished she could talk to Meg, but she didn't want to tie up the business phone. Besides, her roommate might tease her about the jumble of feelings she was experiencing concerning Arden, and Rachel didn't want to joke about it, even in good fun.

She was surprised at herself for confiding in Arden about why she went *Englisch*. Most of the Amish people she'd discussed the subject with had a tendency to *tell* her why she wanted to leave—that was, because of *ho-chmut* or some other sin—but Arden had truly listened to her explanation, and he didn't seem to judge her for it. *He even said I was a gut nurse.* Toby never would have said that—Toby would have criticized her for being confounded by what was triggering Oneita's condition.

As much as she appreciated Arden's kind words, what Rachel found most commendable was how he'd responded to Colin upbraiding him. Without rudeness or rancor, he'd firmly called out Colin's hypocrisy. She was especially touched Arden had made a point to defend Rachel as well as himself against Colin's unfair condemnation.

Colin had appeared so appalled Rachel might have pitied him, had he not threatened to tell Ivan on Arden, as if Arden were a child. How Arden managed to keep his temper Rachel didn't know, but his response inspired her to be civil, too. *How insulting of Colin to insinuate Arden was irresponsible for closing the shop*, she thought. Rachel had witnessed firsthand how much Arden was doing for the business, and this morning she'd seen the burden he was carrying for his mother's health, too. *He's got so much weight on his shoulders.*

Thinking of Arden's shoulders made her pulse skitter, and she set down her paintbrush.

"You dizzy?" Arden called. Had he been watching her?

"A little. I'm going to take my lunch break now, okay?"

"*Jah.* Me, too."

After what they'd been through that morning, it seemed fitting to suggest they eat together, but Rachel resisted the impulse. Her emotions were running high;

it was better to put a little distance between Arden and herself until she'd had a good night's sleep. Besides, she intended to spend her break scrubbing the floors. *Ivan's coming home soon. If Colin tells him I've done nothing but made messes, a spotless* haus *will help prove him wrong.*

Arden didn't make it home until nine o'clock on Friday, and after checking with Grace to be sure his sleeping mother hadn't had any more issues with her skin, he took a shower and went to bed. Lying there, he reflected on how Rachel reminded him of Ivan; not only was she finicky about the quality of her painting, but she was discreet like he was, too. She'd promised Arden she wouldn't bring up their altercation with Colin when she visited Ivan that evening.

"We have nothing to hide," she'd said. "But I'd prefer Ivan didn't know about the tension between Colin and me."

"Between Colin and me, too. I shouldn't have responded to him in anger."

"Are you *narrish*? You may have *felt* angry—and justifiably so—but your response wasn't angry. It was truthful and direct. It was very well said, Arden. And you gave him every opportunity to reciprocate with grace."

It was very well said. Arden had never received that compliment before, and he played it over and over in his mind before his thoughts turned to why Rachel had said she'd left the Amish. Despite the rumors, it didn't seem her intention in leaving was to gain knowledge so she could promote herself; she'd left because the *Englisch* gave her an opportunity to serve others in a way she couldn't serve them if she remained in Serenity Ridge. Her decision seemed neither rash nor rebellious—she'd waffled about it for years, primarily because she preferred the Amish lifestyle.

Yet ultimately she did *choose to go* Englisch, Arden reminded himself. *And she* is *going back, so I'd better not get too accustomed to her company, as pleasant as it's turning out to be.*

Although Arden was putting in a full day's work on Saturday, Rachel left the workshop at twelve to pick up Ivan from the hospital, since the staff had confirmed the previous evening he'd be discharged sometime in the afternoon. Arden suggested she take the business phone with her in the event an emergency arose.

"Don't worry," she razzed him. "I learned my lesson yesterday. I'm sticking to the main roads."

"Even the main roads might be flooded. You'll have Ivan with you, and...well, it seems wise to take the phone if case you need it."

Rachel was puzzled by his suggestion, since the Amish relied on the Lord, not on technology, in times of emergency. *I suppose he thinks since I'm not Amish, it's not incongruent for me to carry a phone.* It wasn't, but somehow she didn't want her status as an *Englischer* emphasized.

"Okay, but only because I'm expecting a call from my roommate." Because the business phone didn't have internet access, on Friday Rachel had used it to call Meg to ask her to periodically check her email account for a message from the university. Meg hadn't answered so Rachel left a confidential message along with her email password.

When she arrived at the hospital, an aide was assisting Ivan with his clothing, so Rachel wandered outside and perched on a bench in the sunshine. As a balmy breeze played with the ends of her hair, Rachel watched doctors and nurses entering and exiting the building, their expressions mostly intense. She wondered if that's how she appeared when she arrived for work. There were so many sick people in the world and so many loving family members and friends who worried about them. It often felt overwhelming, and today Rachel was grateful for the slower pace of caring for just one patient, her brother.

When she went back inside, she met one delay after the next in the processing of Ivan's discharge paperwork, even though she'd arrived with his checkbook ready for him to pay the bill. Eventually everything was sorted out, and she brought the car around to pick Ivan up at the entrance. As she and an unfamiliar patient-care assistant helped him into the passenger seat, Ivan tottered, breathless from the brief exertion of standing.

"You sure you're ready to leave? You can stay another night," the assistant jested.

"*Jah*, I'm in *gut* hands. My *schweschder* is a nurse."

Rachel might have been mistaken, but she thought she heard a trace of pride in his voice.

At four o'clock, the customer who ordered the coop came by with several buddies and a truck to transport it home. Afterward, Arden continued working on the shed that was due Monday. Although he'd made enough progress to be confident he'd finish it well before the scheduled pickup time, Arden puttered around the workshop, hoping to greet Ivan. If her brother was as weak as Rachel indicated, he might need help getting into the house.

By six o'clock when they hadn't shown up, Arden began to worry. *What if there is damage to Rachel's car from yesterday and it's acting up now?* His stomach constricted with cramps, and he didn't know if they were from nerves or hunger, but he was determined to stay until Rachel and Ivan arrived.

Unable to focus on work, he took a seat on the bench beneath the peach tree. It had bloomed early this year, and as he leaned against the trunk, inhaling its fragrance and listening to the bees buzzing within the pink blossoms overhead, he quietly prayed until calmness settled over him. Within minutes, Rachel's car wound its way up the driveway. Another soaking rain on Friday afternoon had washed off most of the mud, and her car glinted in the late-day sun.

Arden lifted his hand. He strode to them and opened the front passenger door as Rachel got out on the other side. He was surprised by how loosely Ivan's clothes fit and how much paler he'd become since Arden had seen him last, but his humor was still robust. Grinning at him, Ivan asked, "You didn't think I was coming back, did you?"

"I never doubted it for a second," Arden said, a catch in his voice, because he *had* doubted it. He bent forward so Ivan could sling an arm around his shoulder for support as he rose into a standing position. Arden bolstered Ivan across the lawn at a snail's pace. By the time they got to the porch, Ivan's stamina was depleted.

"Let me rest here in the fresh air," he requested, so Arden lowered him onto the porch swing and took a seat on the bench nearby.

"I made *supp* last night. You'll stay for supper, won't you, Arden?" Rachel asked.

"Supper? I thought Ivan and I would get back to work. There's a shed we need to finish by Monday."

"Oh, sure, now that my *bruder* is back you're going to kick me out of the shop, aren't you?"

"Of course not," Arden objected. "After all, Ivan never brings me *kaffi* and sticky buns in the morning the way you do."

"*Jah*, and I doubt he'd be as forbearing as I was if you ruined *his* paint job."

"*Neh*, probably not, but *he's* never propelled me into a mud puddle like *you* have." Arden recognized they were teasing exaggeratedly for Ivan's benefit, and Ivan seemed to enjoy the entertainment. It felt like a celebration to have him home. That his hospital bill was paid and Arden had nearly met all of their work deadlines added to the festivity.

"It sounds like you two have quite a few stories to tell me," Ivan said. "I can't say *denki* enough to both of you—" He coughed weakly.

"Then don't try," Rachel told him before disappearing into the house for a glass of water.

"She's right. Or I'll have to try to figure out a way to say *denki* for all the times you've helped me. And we both know how *gut* I am with words." Usually Arden didn't acknowledge his speaking difficulties, even in jest, but this evening he felt less self-conscious than ever before. Rachel reappeared with the water for Ivan and then went back into the house, telling them supper would be ready in a few minutes.

"How is your *mamm*?" Ivan questioned.

"She was struggling for a while. She experienced some new symptoms, which are already improving, thanks to your *schweschder*."

"That's *gut*." Ivan closed his eyes and smiled as a breeze passed over the lawn, carrying the scent of peach blossoms and new grass.

They sat in comfortable silence until Rachel announced supper was ready. She stepped outside to steady the swing so Arden could assist her brother out of it. He used his shoulder to truss Ivan beneath one arm while Rachel did the same on the opposite side. The three of them were about to angle toward the door when Ivan said softly, "Well, look at that. I think my first visitor has arrived."

Perplexed that someone could have come up the driveway without her hearing them and nervous it might have been Colin, Rachel followed the direction of Ivan's eyes. In the gloaming she could just make out a form on the far periphery of the front lawn. A bear? An enormous deer?

"A moose!" Arden uttered in a hushed tone, and the great animal swung its head in their direction. For nearly a full minute, it kept utterly still before it turned and lumbered into the woods bordering the property.

"That was amazing. I've never seen a moose the whole time I've lived here," Ivan said.

"Me, neither," Rachel said. "I mean, when I lived here before. I wish my phone worked. I would have liked to take a photo to show to Meg. Maybe it'll come back."

"If he does, it's *schmaert* to steer clear of him," Arden said. "He might look docile, but moose are unpredictable. His antlers haven't fully *kumme* in this year, but if he charged, he could kick or trample a person to death."

After the trio squeezed through the door, Ivan said, "It must have been all the excitement, but I'm too bushed to eat. Arden, could you help me out? I'd like to go to bed, but I feel as unwieldy as that moose."

While Arden was assisting her brother in the bedroom down the hall, Rachel filled two bowls with soup and placed a loaf of bread on the table and then poured the milk. When Arden reentered the room and seated himself opposite her, she felt strangely shy to be eating alone with him, even though they worked together side by side every day.

"I'll say grace," she offered, bowing her head. "Lord, *denki* for healing Ivan and bringing him home. And *denki* for bringing me home at this time, too." Her voice quavered, so she paused a moment. "Please continue to heal Arden's *mamm* and help her to get the care she needs. Soften my heart toward Colin and soften his heart to me and both of our hearts to You. Please strengthen us with this food, especially Arden, who needs endurance as he continues to labor so diligently in the workshop during Ivan's recovery. Amen." Rachel furtively dabbed a tear away before lifting her head.

Arden's celestial-blue eyes searched hers. "Are you

okay?" he asked. She was embarrassed he'd caught her tearing up until he added, "Your hand is bleeding."

"Bleeding? Where?" She turned her hands palm up and then over again.

He leaned across the table and gently twisted her hand to indicate the space between her ring and middle fingers. "There."

Rachel's breath hitched. Instead of taking her hand from his to get a better look, she leaned forward to see the red stain. Although she instantly recognized what it was, she didn't want to say. Not yet, not if saying it meant he withdrew his touch.

"See it?" Arden asked.

"It's paint, from the coop," she replied, embarrassed that she'd washed her hands countless times but clearly hadn't done a good enough job. To her surprise, he allowed her fingers to linger in his.

"Oh. I guess it's a *gut* thing *I'm* not the one taking care of Ivan, since I can't even tell the difference between blood and paint," Arden joked, giving her hand a little squeeze. Only then did he release it, sliding his arm back across the table and picking up his spoon.

The soup scalded Arden's tongue and gave him something to distract him from the topsy-turvy way he was feeling. As he chugged down half a glass of milk, Rachel remarked how tired Ivan still seemed.

"*Jah*, he practically dozed off midsentence in his room."

"I'll have to wake him soon for his medication. And to check for a fever. They said to watch for that. A relapse of pneumonia can be even worse than the initial bout."

"You're going to need endurance, too."

"What?"

"You prayed I'd have endurance. You're going to need it, too," Arden explained. "There were a lot of nurses in the hospital, but here you're on your own."

"Don't you think I'm qualified to take care of him by myself?"

That wasn't what he'd meant at all. Arden was surprised by the plea for reassurance in Rachel's question; usually she seemed so confident. "I can't think of anyone better qualified to take care of him. But he's got a long road to recovery ahead, and you're going to need help so you don't wear yourself out."

"I told Hadassah I'd *wilkom* her help, but I don't think I can count on her. Joyce and Albert won't return from Canada for a couple more weeks, according to Ivan."

"In addition to Grace, there are others in the community who will be *hallich* to help."

"I don't know about that. I'm worried they'll stay away because of my presence. Maybe Ivan would have been better off without me here. Maybe my coming here was a mistake."

"*Neh.* It wasn't a mistake." Upon seeing the fragile vulnerability in Rachel's eyes, Arden's heart ballooned with compassion. "Trust me, the community will *kumme* to help."

"In that case, I'd better keep dessert and tea on hand," Rachel said, smiling once again.

"Does that mean we can't have a slice of that pie over there?"

"Of course it doesn't. And since Ivan has no appetite, you and I might as well have large pieces."

Supping with Rachel after a hard day's work, encouraging her and discussing Ivan's care as if he were…not a child, but *like* a child, felt…well, it felt like how Arden always imagined it would feel if he had a family of his own. Which was probably why, half an hour later as he directed his horse toward home, Arden's stomach was full, but he couldn't shake the aching emptiness he felt inside.

Having checked on Ivan throughout the night, Rachel was wearier in the morning than she'd been when she went to bed. Since it was an off Sunday, she suggested she and Ivan hold their own worship services together. She was delighted when he told her he'd kept their father's old Bible in a drawer upstairs. Rachel read aloud from it in German. Although she hadn't practiced the language in years, the words returned to her as readily as the vistas of Serenity Ridge, so familiar and beautiful she wondered how she'd gone so long without them.

When she finished reading, she prepared a light lunch and then Ivan needed to sleep again, so Rachel helped him into the bedroom and then tiptoed away, leaving the door slightly ajar so she could hear if he summoned her. She was drying their dishes when a buggy approached; it was Arden's.

"Grace wanted me to deliver these whoopie pies. She thinks they'll whet Ivan's appetite for home-cooked food again." He handed her a square plastic container with a note taped on top of it, reading:

Rachel,
Mamm and I are expecting visitors this afternoon
or I would have *kumme* to see you and Ivan myself. We are praying for you both.
Grace

"Oh, that's so thoughtful. These *are* Ivan's favorite, but it feels like there are plenty in here. Would you
like one?" After experiencing such an enjoyable time
with Arden at supper the previous night, Rachel didn't
hesitate to invite him to share dessert this afternoon.

"*Jah*, please. When I asked if I could have one at
home, Grace refused. Apparently, whoopie pies are
only for people with pneu-pneumon-pneumonia," Arden
complained as he lowered himself onto the bench. "Or
for p-people taking care of p-people with pneumonia."

"*Neh*, they're also for people visiting people taking care of people with pneumonia," Rachel said with
a giggle.

A few minutes later as they were indulging in the
treats and tea, another buggy pulled into the driveway.
Upon seeing it was Hadassah, Rachel nearly fell off
the porch swing. *Maybe she's had a change of heart!*

Smiling, Rachel waved as Arden hurried to help
her sister-in-law from the buggy. Two of the children
scrambled down in front of her. Hadassah's pregnant
belly seemed to have grown impossibly larger in the
past few days.

Aware questions about her sister-in-law's health
would be unwelcome, Rachel greeted her by saying,
"Hello, Hadassah. It's so nice to see you." Then she
bent to speak to the children. "Hello again, Thomas.

And you must be Sarah. Your *onkel* Ivan wrote to me about you. I'm your *ant* Rachel."

Without responding, Thomas took off to chase a squirrel across the yard, but to Rachel's amazement, Sarah said, "Hello, *Ant* Rachel," and then joined her brother. Rachel couldn't help but notice the girl looked more like Rachel than like Hadassah—with one unfortunate difference; Sarah's nose was running. In fact, Thomas had a runny nose, too. The nurse in Rachel wondered how long they'd been ill.

Without acknowledging Rachel's greeting, Hadassah said, "The *kinner* want to see their *onkel*. Is he inside?"

"*Jah*, but he's sleeping."

"That's okay. We've *kumme* all this way. Thomas and Sarah can play in the yard until he wakes. I'll sit beneath the peach tree." She began plodding across the sodden ground.

"You're *wilkom* to join us on the porch, Hadassah," Rachel called after her. "But I'm afraid today isn't a *gut* day for you and the *kinner* to visit Ivan. It seems Sarah and Thomas have colds, and we don't want to jeopardize Ivan's recovery."

Hadassah slowly pivoted toward the house, her features contorted into a scowl. Breathing heavily, she approached the porch and shook her pointer finger at Rachel. "It's one thing for you to believe you're superior to the Amish. But how can you can be so puffed up as to think you know more about health care than the *Englisch*? Not one of those nurses in the hospital ever prohibited me from seeing Ivan, and I'm not going to let you stop me, either!"

As peeved as Hadassah's remarks made her, Rachel

had enough experience dealing with patients' families to respond calmly. "If the nurses in the hospital saw Sarah and Thomas today, they wouldn't allow them to visit Ivan, either. He simply can't be exposed to any infections right now. Even a common cold could wreak havoc on his immune system, because it's already severely compromised."

"My *kinner* do *not* have colds. They have allergies."

"*Neh*, they have colds. Their mucus is not running clear—"

"*Absatz!* I don't want to hear you describe such a thing to me. Even if you're right—which you are *not*—I do not have a cold and *I'm* going to see Ivan." Her face and neck were crimson as she set one foot on the bottom stair.

"You may not have a cold yet, but you've been in close contact with least two *kinner* who do." Rachel planted herself in front of the doorway. "We must guard Ivan's health. And I hope you'll guard your own health, too, because you don't want to *kumme* down with something this late in your pregnancy. I appreciate what an effort it was for you to *kumme* here, and I'd *wilkom* your company here on the porch. How about if I bring you and the *kinner* some refreshments?"

Without answering her, Hadassah questioned Arden, "Do you hear how she's speaking to me?"

"I think Rachel's right, Hadassah," Arden replied. "Please don't get so worked up about it, though. As soon as the *kinner* are over their colds, you can visit."

"Pah!" Hadassah puffed. She leaned on her knee with one hand and used the other to point at Arden this time. "Colin warned me about you two. I believed what he said about Rachel, but I didn't want to believe him about you, Arden. You'd better be careful cozying up to an *Englischer*. It wouldn't sit right with the bishop."

As she trudged away, Arden scurried down the porch steps, offering, "Let me help you into the buggy, Hadassah," but she batted at his hand. Instead she leaned on the shoulders of her children, who teetered beneath her weight.

So much for the community helping me, Rachel lamented to herself. *I'll be fortunate if I'm not ousted from Serenity Ridge altogether once Hadassah and Colin are done wagging their chins about me.*

Chapter Seven

After Hadassah's buggy rolled down the driveway, Arden went to bid Rachel goodbye, but she'd gone into the house, undoubtedly to tend to Ivan.

On his way home, he wondered, *Why wouldn't Colin accompany his wife to his* bruder*'s* haus *when she obviously has a difficult time with mobility? What could possibly be more important than seeing to Hadassah's comfort and safety?* Deep down, Arden suspected Colin was deliberately slighting Rachel—at his wife's expense—as a demonstration of his anger. He could only imagine how much angrier Colin would be once Hadassah told him Rachel had turned her away and Arden had defended Rachel's decision.

Their behavior is unfair. I'm *the one who should go to the bishop about* them, Arden thought. *I'd be perfectly justified.* But he wouldn't do that, because while the Bible said God required His people to "do justly," it also instructed them to love mercy. Besides, Arden was confident he'd done nothing wrong, so he wasn't overly concerned about what Colin or Hadassah might say if they actually did report him to the bishop. Still, Arden decided, for Ivan's sake, he ought to tread carefully. For Rachel's sake, too. There was already enough tension between the Blank family members; he didn't want to add to it by appearing to side with Rachel. Hadassah and Colin could make her time in Serenity Ridge very unpleasant, and Arden didn't want her being squeezed out before Ivan was better. The very fact that Hadassah had brought sick children to visit their uncle showed just how much Ivan needed someone like Rachel there, advocating for his health. *The less time I spend with her outside the workshop, the better it will be for everyone*, Arden concluded.

When he arrived home, Arden was dismayed to find Ike and Eva Renno, whose buggy he'd passed on the road as he set out to deliver the whoopie pies, were seated in the double wooden glider on the porch. Although Arden liked Ike and Eva was a nice enough person, she was as chatty as Arden was reserved, and his head throbbed whenever he spent more than fifteen minutes in her presence.

"*Mamm* went inside to nap. She said she couldn't think of a better way for any *mamm* to celebrate Mother's Day," Grace informed him when he hopped up the steps. Because Mother's Day fell on the Sabbath, the Amish in Serenity Ridge didn't make a fuss over it, although Arden and Grace had gifted their mother with a subscription to her favorite publication, *The Connection*, which was published out of Indiana and included articles written by Amish people throughout the country. "I made iced tea. *Kumme* join our discussion."

"I've, uh, already had tea," Arden hedged.

"Oh, were you out visiting someone special?" Eva questioned.

Arden could have kicked himself for letting that slip. "On second thought, I'm kind of hot. I would like a glass, please."

"Were you visiting someone special?" Eva repeated.

"I, uh, stopped by Ivan's *haus*."

"Ivan's *haus*? I heard his *Englisch schweschder* is staying there."

I guess the cat's out of the bag now. Holding out his hand to take the glass from his sister, Arden replied noncommittally, "*Jah*, that's correct."

"Sit down," Grace insisted and waited for Arden to take a seat before giving him the iced tea. "How was Ivan?"

"He was asleep again, so I didn't get to speak to him. Rachel said he had a restless night—he was coughing a lot."

"Oh, the poor dear. I have a tried-and-true honey-cider cough remedy I could bring him, don't I, Ike? Remember when I gave it to you last October when you were sick with bronchitis?" Eva didn't wait for her husband to reply before resuming her earlier train of thought. "Maybe I shouldn't bother bringing it to Ivan, though. Hadassah said the *Englisch schweschder* has taken control of his health—in addition to his *haus* and his business, but I don't have to tell *you* that, do I, Arden?—so I don't know if my gesture would be *wilkom*."

Arden felt the hair on the back of his neck stand on end, and he reminded himself it was better to say nothing; that way, his comments couldn't be misinterpreted.

Grace, however, piped up, "I'm sure Rachel would appreciate an act of kindness from someone in our community. She might be pleased to receive visitors, too, provided they don't overstay their *wilkom*."

There was no mistaking the implication in Grace's remark, but it seemed lost on Eva. "To be frank, I don't know if I want to visit Ivan while the *schweschder* is there. Hadassah said she's been flaunting her *Englisch* ways in front of her *familye*. Showing up at Hadassah's *haus* uninvited in her car, or wearing inappropriate hairstyles and clothing in front of her *dochdere*, that kind of thing. I don't want her pushing her lifestyle on *me* like that."

Arden could no longer censor himself. "I've been w-working with Rachel at the shop, and she never w-wears or does anything in-in-inappropriate. *Jah*, she's *Englisch*, but she's also very m-modest."

Eva raised an eyebrow. "You find her becoming, don't you?"

How could she twist my words like that? No matter how he replied, Arden figured he'd incriminate himself, so he refused to say another word. Grace, on the other hand, let loose.

"*Jah*, Rachel is very fetching, and she's very *schmaert*, too. More importantly, she's extremely helpful," she said. "She helped *Mamm* when she was experiencing new lupus symptoms, and she told us about as many alternative forms of treatment as *Englisch* ones. So if that's your concern about sharing your remedy, you have nothing to worry about. She demonstrates every bit as much respect toward the Amish as the Amish demonstrate toward her."

Although Arden wholeheartedly agreed with Grace's characterization of Rachel, he was concerned if her comments got back to Hadassah, they'd make things worse. Fortunately, once again his sister's words seemed to go right over Eva's head; she'd turned her attention to swatting at a bee.

"Ike! It's going to sting me," she whined, flapping her hands about her ears. Her husband jumped to his feet and fanned his hat through the air.

Arden took advantage of their alarm to change the subject. "Guess what I saw yesterday? A moose!"

Eva immediately stopped flailing to inform everyone moose had been spotted in the deacon's yard, on the Christmas tree farm and at the lake, as well. Arden asked enough questions to keep her talking on the subject for half an hour until another bee chased her from her chair and her husband suggested they'd better be on their way.

As she lay in bed on Sunday evening, Rachel reflected on Hadassah's earlier remarks. She vacillated between feeling utterly incensed and being racked with guilt. On one hand, her sister-in-law had been completely out of line to speak to her as she did. Couldn't Hadassah see Rachel's refusal to allow her to visit Ivan wasn't personal? She was only looking out for her brother's best interests.

Yet, having witnessed how labored Hadassah's breathing was and having watched her struggling to walk even a short distance, Rachel was worried about her sister-in-law's health, too. It wasn't good for her to get so upset. As necessary as it was to keep Hadassah from seeing Ivan, Rachel regretted having caused her distress, especially when she belatedly realized today was Mother's Day. Knowing Colin, Rachel doubted he'd given Hadassah a card or even verbally acknowledged her devotion to their children, so she was probably in need of encouragement.

Even so, why should I be the one lying here feeling sorry for upsetting her? I doubt she feels guilty for hurting my feelings by announcing my own bruder *warned her about me.* Actually, Hadassah had said Colin had warned her about *them*—meaning both Rachel *and* Arden. Rachel didn't know exactly what that meant, but she had an inkling. And if Colin and Hadassah really did go to the bishop with their grievances, who would the bishop be more likely to believe—an *Englischer* who abandoned her community or an Amish couple who'd lived in Serenity Ridge since they were *kinner*? Rachel didn't want to find out. Nor did she want to put Arden in the position of having to defend himself.

My main objective is to help Ivan with his business and his recovery. I'm only here temporarily, she reminded herself. Long after she returned to Boston, the others would still be working and living in Serenity Ridge. It was important to Rachel that their long-term relationships with each other didn't suffer because of her short-term presence among them now. For that reason, she decided she'd try to do whatever she could to prevent and ease any discord between them. *I should distance myself from Arden whenever possible, too, so no one else can accuse him of "cozying up to an* Englischer."

Yet the idea of giving up her budding friendship with

Arden made her so resentful Rachel rolled out of bed and knelt beside it in prayer. *Dear* Gott, *I want You to use me to reflect Your love, but I don't feel very loving at the moment. Please change my heart and give me strength.* Upon hearing Ivan's coughing downstairs, she added, *And please give Ivan strength, too.*

But the next morning, Rachel's brother seemed even weaker than he'd been on Sunday, and despite his objections, she refused to go to the shop to work. Instead, she decided she'd gather whatever paperwork she needed and bring it back to the house, where she'd also field customer calls while keeping an eye on Ivan. When she scurried to the workshop to tell Arden her plan, he barely glanced up from the tiny structure he was building.

"What's that, a dollhouse to go inside Mrs. McGregor's playhouse?" she joshed.

"It's a doghouse," he replied flatly and then resumed hammering.

Rachel squinted at him, wondering if he'd simply gotten up on the wrong side of the bed or if something else had gone awry. Was it possible Colin and Hadassah had already filled the bishop's ear with their tales about him and her? "Is everything all right?"

"*Jah*, just busy," he mumbled and drove another nail into a joist. Rachel waited for him to stop hammering.

"Then you won't like what I have to tell you. I have to work up at the *haus* today because I don't want to leave Ivan alone. I'm afraid of what might happen if he gets out of bed by himself. His legs are still a bit rickety. One *gut* spring breeze and he'd collapse like a *haus* of cards." Rachel tittered nervously.

"There's no need for you to be here today anyway, so that's fine."

Keeping my distance from him isn't going to be such a loss after all, Rachel thought as she collected what she needed from the desk and returned to the house.

But by the end of the day, she almost would have preferred Arden's grouchy company to no company at all, since Ivan slept most of the day. Although she was aware his recovery would be slow, Rachel fretted over her brother's condition, second-guessing whether he'd been released from the hospital too soon. On Tuesday morning, however, he awoke looking bright-eyed and declaring how hungry he was. She settled him into a chair at the kitchen table and poured them each a cup of coffee.

"I'll make *oier* and *pannekuche*," she offered, retrieving eggs from the fridge and a mixing bowl from the cupboard.

Ivan said something that sounded like, "Don brfr," and she twirled around to catch him with a mouthful of the whoopie pie he must have taken from the container on the table. He swallowed before repeating, "Don't bother. I'll just have one of these." When he smiled at her, his teeth were comically blackened from the dark cake, and she laughed so hard she dropped into a chair opposite him.

"What's so funny?" he asked, so she took a whoopie pie for herself, bit into it and then grinned back at him. They both cracked up until she begged him to stop because she was afraid he'd lose his breath and wind up back in the hospital.

"Nonsense," he said. "I haven't felt this *gut* in weeks."

Circling the table, Rachel wrapped her arms around

his scrawny shoulders and kissed the top of his head. "Neither have I."

"You ought to go back to the workshop," he told her when she released him.

"*Neh.* Maybe tomorrow, if you keep improving."

"Arden probably needs your help today more than I do."

Rachel hesitated. Arden had likely finished the dog-house by now, and it would need to be painted. "Let's compromise. At lunchtime, I'll send Arden here to visit you during his break, and I'll go get a few things done in the shop."

When she trekked to the workshop shortly before one o'clock, Rachel spotted Arden in the driveway talking to an *Englischer* she assumed was a customer, so she went inside and set the folders she'd been carrying on the desk. The business phone buzzed, and as she reached for it, she accidentally knocked a file to the floor, scattering invoices everywhere.

"Hi, Rach. It's me, Meg. I know this is your business phone, but—"

Her heart leaped to her throat. "Did I get into the MSN program?"

"No," Meg said. "I mean, that's not why I'm calling. I checked your email, but there wasn't any notice yet. I'm sorry to get your hopes up. It was just that your message was so cryptic the other day I wanted to be sure you're okay."

"Oh." Rachel sighed. "Yeah, I, well… Friday was a long day, but everything is fine now. Ivan's home now."

"Hey, that's great! That means *you'll* be home soon, too. Unless you decide to stay."

"How many times do I have to tell you, I am *not* staying here," Rachel contended. *And I might be returning sooner rather than later if Hadassah has her way.*

"Uh-oh. Does that mean Mr. Morose hasn't gotten any nicer to you since you've been in Serenity Ridge?"

"What? Do you mean Toby?" Distracted by picking up the invoices, Rachel didn't have the foggiest notion why her roommate would have thought she'd been in touch with Toby.

"No, not Dr. Deceiver. I was referring to Amish Arden. You know, Mr. Morose. The kind of thoughtless, insensitive man you're supposedly trying to avoid."

"Oh, him. Well, like I've said, he isn't always *that* dull. I definitely wouldn't put him in the same category as Toby," Rachel said. She knew Meg's nicknames were her impish way of sticking up for Rachel, but she was relieved she hadn't shared her ambivalence about Arden with her roommate. It wasn't something she wanted to make light of. "So, anything new happening with you?"

"Aside from the landlord finally fixing the washing machine? Nope, not a thing."

"I am so envious," Rachel joked. "Nothing that exciting has happened here, although we did see a moose last evening…"

After a few minutes of chitchat, Meg promised to let Rachel know as soon as she got an email from the university and then hung up. As Rachel stood to stack the mess of papers she'd gathered on the desk, she noticed Arden in the doorway.

"Hi, Arden. I've *kumme* to switch places with you. How about if I stay here and paint the doghouse while you take your lunch break at the *haus*, where you can keep an eye on Ivan? He's been guarding the whoopie pies, but if you arm wrestle him for one, I'm sure you'd win," she jested.

"*Neh.* I got waylaid by another project, so I haven't completed the doghouse yet. I'm not taking a lunch break. So there's no sense in you hanging around here this afternoon."

His reply was so curt and his tone so dismissive that Rachel stalked off thinking, *As if I'd want to be around you anyway,* Mr. Morose!

Arden sawed through a two-by-six, letting the end segment clatter to the floor before stopping to take a swig of cold water. It quenched his thirst but not his fuming. He'd been mad ever since he overheard Rachel talking on the phone. It wasn't as if he'd intended to listen in on her conversation, but now that he'd overheard it, her words echoed ruthlessly in his mind.

"He isn't always *that* dumb," she'd said. Or had she used the word *dull*? It hardly mattered; they meant the same thing—she'd been calling someone stupid. Maybe it was self-centered of Arden to suspect *he* was the one she'd been referring to, but who else could she have meant? Her brothers were the only other men she'd crossed paths with in Serenity Ridge, and she regarded Ivan too highly to speak about him that way. As for Colin, he was cantankerous, maybe even cruel, but Arden doubted Rachel considered him dumb—not even compared to Toby, who apparently was so intelligent he was in a class all by himself. That left Arden.

He felt humiliated. He felt infuriated. And, ironically, he felt extraordinarily stupid—not because of his speaking and reading difficulties, but because he'd sincerely believed Rachel respected him. Come to find out she was looking down her nose at him, maybe even at the entire Amish community. *I guess Colin and Hadassah were right about her after all.* Her phone conversation had made it clear not only how she felt about Arden but about being in Serenity Ridge, where apparently nothing exciting happened. *Sorry we don't live up to your standards for entertainment*, he imagined saying to her. *If you're so bored, why don't you hire a visiting nurse to take care of Ivan so you can go back to the* Englisch *lifestyle you claimed you were never drawn to in the first place?*

Arden's foul mood followed him throughout the afternoon, but at least he channeled his orneriness into constructing the small, simple garden shed that was due the following morning. It was a quick project that required no painting, but without Rachel on-site to remind him of the deadline, he'd forgotten about it. Unfortunately, that meant he'd have to stay late to complete the doghouse that was due on Thursday, which would have to be painted tomorrow. He was so engrossed in his work he didn't notice anyone had entered the workshop until Grace appeared at his side.

"What's wrong—"

"Don't worry, *Mamm*'s fine. She insisted I bring supper to Rachel and Ivan. And to you, too. She thought we'd enjoy sharing a meal together."

I'm sure she did. "That's a nice gesture, but I'm too busy to stop for supper."

"But you've got to eat."

"Eating can wait. My deadline can't."

"You don't have to stay long, but surely you can spare

the time to gobble down a plate of *yumsetta*," Grace argued. "C'mon, Arden. If you don't join us, it will look like...you know."

"Like you're here specifically to see Ivan because you like him?" Although he had never mentioned it before, Arden had his suspicions about how his sister felt about Ivan. The color rising in her cheeks now indicated he'd been right.

"*Neh*, it will look like you're being rude. Which you *are*, in more ways than one!" Grace retorted. Arden hadn't meant to insult her; he'd just wanted her to back off about eating supper at the house.

"Ivan knows how much work I have to do. He'll understand why I can't stop."

"*Jah*, but what about Rachel? Have you considered how she might feel if you don't join us for a meal? She might think it's because she's *Englisch*."

"Rachel *is Englisch*, and I have no obligation to socialize with her. My only obligation is to *work* with her."

"Eh-hem." From the doorway, Rachel cleared her throat. "I, um, was coming to ask whether you prefer water or *millich* with your meal."

"*Millich*, please," Grace answered. "Arden can't eat with us tonight—he's got to keep working."

"I understand." Rachel looked squarely at him. Arden couldn't read her expression, but after she and Grace left, he wondered, *Did she hear what I said about not being obligated to socialize with her?* Then he shrugged it off, reasoning, *Now she knows what it's like to overhear someone express how they* really *feel about you.*

But the truth was, Arden *didn't* really feel about Rachel the way his comment might have made it sound, even if *she* thought *he* was dumb. Which he had to admit was kind of presumptuous—maybe even egotistical—of him to believe, since he couldn't be certain she'd been talking about him on the phone. The more time that passed, the hungrier he became, and the more he wished he had joined the others for supper. *Maybe if I hurry I can finish this up and get to the* haus *before Grace leaves. If I'm fortunate, I can at least get a piece of dessert.*

By the time he'd completed his work on the dog-house, it was after seven, so he didn't bother to put his tools away before locking up for the night. As he crossed the driveway, he spotted Ivan and Grace rocking on the porch swing, and he wondered if they'd already had dessert or if Rachel would serve it to them there. But from this vantage point, he could see the backyard, too, and he noticed Rachel was taking in the laundry—an indication her hosting duties had ended.

The clothesline was a bit too high; she had to stand on tiptoes to grasp it and then tug it down while she unclipped the pins. As Arden quickened his pace so he could give her a hand, he spied something looming near the back perimeter of the property. At first he thought it was a shadow or the dusk was playing tricks on his eyes, but then the creature slogged several steps in Rachel's direction. *The moose!* Arden's heart battered his ribs. Although the animal's eyesight likely wasn't good enough for it to see Rachel behind the linens, its hearing and sense of smell were excellent, and it seemed to home in on her. By contrast, Rachel was completely oblivious to the danger lurking on the other side of the sheet hanging in front of her.

Aware a loud noise could frighten the moose, Arden

crept closer and said, "Rachel, *absatz*," just loud enough
for her to hear. She swiveled her head sideways to look
at him, an annoyed expression on her face as she continued unpinning the sheet. "Do. Not. Move," he com-
manded gruffly, terrified she'd flounce off rather than
speak to him. "There's a moose coming toward you."

His tone must have convinced her he was gravely
serious, because Rachel froze with her arms stretched
above her head, her spine straight. She locked her gaze
on him, and her face went whiter than the sheet she'd was
unfastening. "Arden, help me," she whimpered. Then,
"Please help me, Lord. Please, *Gott*, make it go away."

Arden tried to reassure her from where he'd sought
protection beside a maple tree some ten yards away. The
tree wasn't especially wide, but he knew it was vital to
keep something sturdy in between him and the moose
at all times. "It stopped walking, but it's looking your
way. You must do exactly what I tell you to do. If I say
run, you need to sprint over here to me, behind this tree
as fast as you can."

"Now?"

"Neh!" Arden exclaimed, and the moose lowered its
head and flattened its ears, both signs of aggression.
"Don't run unless I tell you to."

"Please, Arden, please," she pleaded, as if he held
any authority over the large bull. "It's getting closer. I
can hear it making a clicking sound."

"Rachel, listen to me. I want you to back away very,
very slowly." She immediately let go of the clothesline
and sheet and inched away as the moose flattened its
ears—not a good sign. Arden's back and leg muscles
were so tense they burned. Little by little Rachel was

putting distance between herself and the moose, but she was still out in the open. She couldn't outrun the animal if it charged; she'd never make it around the house or even to the maple tree.

Arden considered his options. If he waved and yelled, there was a chance the moose might scram, but it seemed more likely he'd incite the beast to charge. So he did the only thing he could count on to be effective: *Please, Gott, get that animal out of here*, he prayed.

"Arden, what are you looking for over there?" Grace questioned loudly as she came traipsing around the house toward the backyard.

"Shh." Arden gestured for Grace to stop just as the dangling sheet billowed in the breeze. At that the moose thundered forward. "Run!" Arden shouted, but instead Rachel collapsed right where she stood. Arden started to race toward her when he noticed the moose had come to an abrupt standstill a few yards in front of the clothesline, so he halted, too. The bull's first charge was a bluff. Would it leave or would it charge a second time for real?

"Don't move," he growled at Grace, who'd also stopped dead in her tracks. He waited as the moose stared at the sheet. Was that what it was after all along? One, maybe two agonizing minutes passed before the animal slowly raised its head again and galumphed from the yard.

Grace and Arden both sprinted toward Rachel. He reached her first, and she was already rousing, or trying to. He rolled her from her side onto her back and directed Grace to elevate Rachel's feet twelve inches above her heart. Then he bent to put his ear by her mouth so he could hear her raspy voice.

"Did the moose knock me down?"

"*Neh.* He didn't have to. You fell down on your own."

"Where did everyone go?" Ivan asked, stumbling toward them in the twilight.

"Wait right there!" Grace ordered. "We don't need a second Blank passing out tonight." She gently set Rachel's feet down and ran to Ivan's side, saying, "I'll take him inside."

When Rachel lifted her head and propped herself up on her elbows, Arden warned, "You shouldn't get up too quickly. You might get dizzy."

"Who's the nurse here, you or me?" she asked, sitting all the way up.

"I might not be as *schmaert* as you are, but I'm definitely stronger," Arden replied. He slid an arm beneath her knees and wrapped his other one around her torso. In one swift motion, he stood upright and pulled her closer to his trembling heart.

Arden's gesture was so unexpected and his embrace so gentle Rachel felt as if she might faint a second time. As he carried her toward the house, she exhaled, allowing herself to go limp against his chest. She was so accustomed to being a nurse—to caring for others—she didn't realize how soothing it was to have someone coddle *her*, and she closed her eyes to bask in the feeling.

"You okay?" Arden's breath warmed Rachel's face.

"*Jah.*" She peered up at him. "*Denki* for rescuing me. If you hadn't warned me the moose was there or talked me through the situation, who knows what might have happened."

"I hardly *rescued* you. That was *Gott*'s doing."

"True, but *Gott* allowed you to be in the right place at the right time, so He could use you for my *gut*."

They reached the house, and Arden climbed the porch stairs and opened the screen door one-handed, not setting her down until they'd reached the living room, where Grace was coaxing Ivan to take another sip of water.

"Rachel!" Ivan exclaimed. "Grace told me what happened. Praise the Lord you're all right."

"Praise the Lord you're all right, too," Rachel echoed. Arden still had his arm looped around her waist, and he assisted her to the sofa so she could sit next to her brother. Once seated, she patted Ivan's hand. "You hardly have enough strength to walk from the bedroom to the living room, much less hike through the yard. What would you have done if the moose had charged *you*?"

"That would depend."

"On what?"

"On how much money I had," Ivan deadpanned.

"Voll schpass." Everyone laughed until Rachel clapped her hand over her mouth, realizing she needed to pick up a prescription. The pharmacy at the superstore was open until ten, and the druggist had said they'd have the medication ready, since Ivan needed to take it that night before bed.

"I don't think you should drive," Arden protested. "Not so soon after fainting."

"I'll be fi—"

"Neh, she definitely shouldn't drive." Grace agreed with her brother for once. "You ought to take her in the buggy, Arden. I'll stay with Ivan."

"Neh. It will take too long. Your *mamm* will be worried."

"Our *mamm* will be asleep," Grace countered. "She told me she was going to bed early and we shouldn't hurry home if we're having *schpass*, especially Arden. She's always pestering him to be more social."

Rachel got the feeling *Grace* was the one who was in no hurry to return home; clearly she desired to spend more time talking with Ivan alone on the porch. While Rachel empathized, she could tell by Arden's lack of response how hesitant he was to bring her to the pharmacy. All of a sudden, she remembered his words from earlier that day: "Rachel *is Englisch* and I have no obligation to socialize with her." In her hysteria over the moose, she'd forgotten about that and how hurt and disappointed she'd felt. Granted, it was a small offense compared to the enormity of saving her life, so she couldn't hold a grudge. Neither could she impose on Arden to spend more time with her than he wanted to—especially since she'd already committed to distancing herself from *him*.

"*Neh*, that's okay. I'll be fine driving," Rachel said. Then to show she held no expectation of him, she added, "Arden's not obligated to take me."

"I know I'm not obligated," Arden said, his tone as assertive as when he'd instructed Rachel not to move as the moose was eyeing her. "But I'd *like* to take you, if you'll let me."

Concerned he may have felt put on the spot, Rachel questioned, "Are you sure you don't mind?"

Arden didn't reply—he was already on his way outside to hitch up his horse and buggy.

Chapter Eight

Arden's ears were scorching; Rachel had *definitely* heard what he'd said to Grace in the workshop. As he adjusted the leather straps on the horse's harness, he wondered how he was going to explain why he felt it was necessary to avoid her outside the workshop. The horse whinnied, and Arden glanced around the driveway to make sure the moose hadn't returned. A shiver prickled his spine. *Rachel could have died tonight*, he thought. Suddenly, he felt resentful of Colin and Hadassah's pettiness. If they didn't value the opportunity to have a relationship with Rachel, that was their choice, but he wasn't going to let their opinion—their self-righteousness and spite—ruin *his* friendship with her.

So, after he assisted Rachel into the buggy but before he directed the horse to walk on, he turned to her and said, "I kn-know you overheard what I told Grace in the w-work-sh-shop about not being o-obligated to s-socialize with you. I only said that because I—I—I felt bad Colin and Hadassah were so upset, and I thought by not sp-spending time with you except at work, maybe it would help e-e-ease the ten-tension." It had been a while since Arden's speech had been that choppy in Rachel's presence, and a bead of sweat dribbled down his neck.

She nodded thoughtfully. "I understand. I actually decided something similar about limiting the time I spend with you. Not just for Ivan's sake, either—I don't want you to get a bad reputation if you hang out with me socially. You know, guilt by association."

Arden shrugged. "Neither of us is guilty of any wrongdoing, so if people are going to judge us unfairly, I guess there's not much we can do to stop 'em."

"So then…" Rachel dipped her head shyly. Arden had the urge to tuck her hair behind her ear so he could look into her eyes. "Does that mean you still want to take me to the pharmacy?"

"*Jah*, of course! And anywhere else you want to go."

As the horse clip-clopped along the country roads toward the *Englisch* superstore, Rachel chatted away about how she couldn't believe it had been ten years since she'd been in a buggy. She said she'd missed the rhythm, the pace, the sounds and even the smells of traveling that way. Arden sneaked a glance at her animated silhouette and grinned; her exuberance was charming.

Catching him looking at her, she said, "I'm babbling, aren't I? I assure you, it's not a post-concussion syndrome symptom."

"A what?"

"Oh, sorry. I was referring to symptoms that can be red flags after someone suffers a blow to the head. Like confusion or sensitivity to sound. Or like feeling a pressure to talk too much, the way I was just doing."

Arden's mouth went dry. "You think you have a c-con-concussion? It d-didn't seem like you h-hit your h-head when you fell, and th-the ground is so soft."

Rachel must have known she'd alarmed him, because she touched his shoulder. "*Neh!* I didn't hit my head, and I definitely don't have a concussion. It was intended as a joke because I'm jabbering so much. Nurse humor, that's all." She rested her hand on her lap again.

"Then what *do* you have that's making you gab so much?" Arden cracked.

"Well, it could be one of two things. It's possible I've *kumme* down with a bad case of homesickness—or I'm recovering from one. A person doesn't really know how much she's missed something until she has it again. Then she can't seem to get enough of it," she said, her voice quavering. Was that from the vibration of the carriage or something deeper?

"What's the other diagnosis?" he asked to lighten her mood.

"Too-much-sugar-itis." She grinned at him and confessed, "We had whoopie pies again for dessert."

He smacked his lips. "Now that's one illness I wouldn't mind catching."

Rachel lay in bed with her eyes closed, imagining herself in Arden's arms as he carried her from the backyard into the house. As terrified as she'd been by the moose attack—or pseudo-attack—she was equally enraptured by Arden's protective embrace. And his watchfulness hadn't stopped there; he'd persuaded her to give him the business phone that night because he wanted her to get a good night of rest and to sleep in as late as she needed the next morning. Even Arden's willingness to distance himself from her had been a demonstration of caring for Rachel, a way of looking out for her best interests, as well as those of her family. It was no wonder she was falling for him.

Rachel, you only think *you're falling for him*, she could hear Meg warning. *That's natural after someone saves your life. You know full well it's just a rush of hormones—dopamine, oxytocin, serotonin and endorphins. It will pass.* But that was exactly the problem; Rachel didn't *want* the feelings to pass. She wanted them to linger. She wanted them to *grow*.

Sighing, she rolled to her side. She couldn't wait to see Arden the next day. They had agreed if Ivan was well enough, she'd change places with Arden at lunchtime so she could paint the doghouse. As the rain thrummed on the rooftop, Rachel realized she'd never finished taking in the laundry. Now what would she do? Both of her skirts were on the line. She hadn't noticed until she was getting ready for bed that the back of the dress she'd worn tonight was dirty from when she'd fallen. She didn't want to knowingly go to work looking unkempt—especially in front of Arden.

That's when she remembered the lavender dress she'd begun sewing. She got up and padded downstairs to the living room. After checking on Ivan, she brought her fabric and sewing supplies back to her room. Stitching the dress again reminded her of the grape-suturing competition Toby had held against his brother. Maybe it was because she really *had* eaten too much sugar that evening, but the idea of suturing a patient repulsed Rachel to the point of nausea. Certainly she'd experienced queasiness before in her role as a nurse, but tonight she felt overwhelmed by it. *It's only nerves—a post-traumatic reaction to the moose scaring me*, she told herself.

Nevertheless, she tied a knot in the thread and clipped it from the spool. Holding up the garment by its shoulder seams, she realized how closely it resembled the dresses she'd made as a girl. She hadn't intended to replicate the pattern—she hadn't even *used* a pattern—but with its long skirt, boxy top and clean, simple lines, it looked more like an Amish dress than an *Englisch* one. Amish women didn't use buttons or zippers on their garments, relying instead on straight pins or hooks. Rachel hadn't meant to imitate this practice, either, but sheer exhaustion caused her to abandon the idea of sewing a zipper into the dress, and she'd forgotten to buy buttons anyway. *This will have to do until I can rewash and dry my other clothes.* It was past two when she finally turned in and after seven when she woke the next day.

It was no longer raining, but the air was heavy with humidity and Rachel was glad she'd stayed up making the lightweight cotton dress. Since she'd be painting that day, she pulled her hair into a soft bun and then made her bed and went downstairs. To her relief, Ivan was still asleep—he'd stayed up until Rachel and Arden returned home the previous evening, which was much later than usual for him. Although she sensed he relished visiting with Grace as much as Grace did with him, Rachel hoped he wasn't overdoing it. She didn't want him to suffer a setback.

I might as well bring the laundry in, she thought, but she made coffee and swept the kitchen floor first.

Then she swept the living room floor. After wiping out the fridge and reorganizing the pantry shelves, she recognized she was deliberately procrastinating going into the backyard. *That's silly. I'd be far more likely to encounter the moose again at dusk or dawn than at this time of day...*

She gathered her courage and stepped outside, nearly upending the laundry basket that was sitting in front of the door. Who knew she'd ever be so delighted to find a load of dirty linens and clothes! Arden must have collected them this morning. She brought the basket into the basement, and as the washer tub was filling, she examined the clothes. They weren't dirty, just wet from the night's rain—there was no need to rewash them after all. However, the sheet she'd been taking off the line when the moose disrupted her task was grimy along its edges where it had hung to the ground. Rachel filled the basin, added soap, put the sheet in the tub and turned on the agitator, allowing the machine to churn while she swept the basement floor. Afterward, she fed the sheet through the wringer and then carried it and the other items upstairs to hang on the line a second time.

But first she ducked into the bathroom to wash her hands, since they'd gotten dirty handling the sheet. Glancing at the mirror, she caught sight of her reflection and didn't immediately recognize it as her own. Upon taking a longer look at her lavender dress and Amish hairstyle, she gasped and promptly burst into tears as the past came rushing back. She didn't just re-call how she'd *looked* before she left Serenity Ridge, but how she'd *felt*, how consumed she was with her dream of becoming a nurse. But she *had* become a nurse, so why was she crying now?

"Why are you crying?" Ivan's question from the hallway echoed hers.

She moved toward him, tears streaming down her cheeks. "I d-don't know—don't know who I am anymore." She hiccuped, her shoulders heaving.

"I do. You're my lovely *schweschder*," Ivan replied, which made her sob harder. He took her by her hand and led her to the couch in the living room, where he waited for her to stop crying before he brought her a glass of water.

She pushed a tear from her cheek with her wrist. "I'm the one who's supposed to be helping *you* feel better. You need your rest."

"*You* need *your* rest. Why don't you go back to sleep for a couple more hours?"

"I can't. I have to hang the laundry."

"It will still be there when you get up, because even if I had the energy, you wouldn't want me hanging it. It would end up more wrinkled than it is now."

Suddenly it occurred to Rachel to ask, "Who was doing your laundry before I got here?"

"Hadassah," he admitted sheepishly.

"But it's been years since they moved into their own *haus*."

"*Jah.* I told her she didn't have to do it, but I guess she didn't like the way I looked when I washed and hung out my clothes myself. Like I said, they somehow end up looking worse."

Rachel chuckled; say what she would about her sister-in-law, Hadassah had been looking out for Ivan for years, and in some ways, Hadassah probably thought of him as *her* little brother, too. "I'll hang the clothes first and then I'll go back to bed for a while. Just don't let me sleep past noon. I have a doghouse to paint."

As he worked alone for the third day straight, Arden tried to convince himself it wasn't Rachel in particular he missed—it was the silence that was getting to him. But he knew that wasn't true; he'd been working alone for weeks when Ivan first came down with bronchitis, and the hours had never dragged on like this before. How was it that two weeks ago he'd never even met Rachel Blank and now, after only two and a half days without her in the workshop, Arden was keenly aware of her absence?

He kept scanning the area by the desk to catch sight of her chewing the end of a pen the way she sometimes did when she was reconciling the invoices, but of course she wasn't there. *I'd better get used to it*, he reminded himself. *In another few weeks, she'll be back in Boston.* And if Ivan didn't start regaining his strength, Arden wouldn't see Rachel very often until she left, either, because she'd continue to do the paperwork up at the house.

Even though they'd agreed she would paint the doghouse that day, Arden wouldn't be there at the same time—he'd be at the house with Ivan, since Rachel was concerned about him being too weak or becoming lightheaded and falling. *It's too bad her phone is broken, otherwise Ivan could use it to call the business phone if he needed help. That way, Rachel would be free to work here with me.*

Just then the phone's ringer cut through Arden's thoughts. He jogged across the workshop to pick it up as an Amish woman he didn't recognize breezed through the door. He held up one finger to indicate he'd be right with her, but as he pressed the phone between his shoulder and ear, Arden's attention was focused on jotting down the details for a change in the customer's order. Capturing the information on paper was a challenge, and it didn't help his concentration to have the Amish stranger hovering nearby. Arden had to ask the man on the phone to repeat the spelling of his last name twice, but even then he transposed the letters when he read them back to the customer. When Arden finally had it right, he said goodbye and snapped the phone shut, scratching out his errors while simultaneously asking the woman, "How may I help you?"

"I'm here to inquire if you construct fences, or only sheds."

"Only sheds and small buildings," Arden said, frowning at the square of paper. It was a mess; he hoped Rachel could read it.

"Oh, that's too bad. I've had a problem with a thirteen-hundred-pound trespasser in my backyard, and I heard your sheds are so durable I hoped you could build me an equally strong fence."

"A thirteen-hundred-pound tres—Rachel!" Arden dropped his pen. Her appearance had completely thrown him off. "I didn't recognize you."

She smiled. "*Jah*, I didn't recognize myself in the mirror, either. As you know, all of my other clothes had to be rehung. *Denki* for bringing them to the doorstep for me, by the way."

Arden couldn't concentrate on what she was saying. Although he'd seen her with her hair in a bun before and the dress she was wearing now wasn't all that different from the long *Englisch* skirts or modest dresses she normally wore, there was something about the simplicity of the ensemble that emphasized the uniqueness of her eyes. Previously he might have described them as almond shaped, but now he saw they were actually upturned and fringed with lashes that were thicker and longer at the outer corners. Even the little nick above her right cheekbone stood out against the plain backdrop of her outfit, enhancing the originality of her countenance.

She smoothed her skirt. "I know lavender is your least favorite color, but I won't be around much today, so you won't have to look at me in it for very long."

Arden hadn't realized he'd been staring. "I don't mind looking at you in it. I mean, I m-mean, the color is becoming on you. Or you are b-becoming in it."

The skin around her eyes crinkled with her smile—something else he hadn't noticed when she'd worn her hair down. "I might be wearing a polka-dotted dress by the time I'm done painting the doghouse, especially since I'll to have to hurry. I hope I can finish it quicker than you and Ivan can eat your lunch."

Arden couldn't stop himself from asking, "I, uh, I wa-was wondering if your cell phone works yet?" He presented his idea of giving it to Ivan so he could call her on the business phone if he needed help, which would allow her to spend more time in the workshop.

"Oh, that's a *gut* idea, but my cell phone has officially expired." She momentarily looked almost as disappointed as he felt, but then she brightened. "Hey!

Instead of painting during your lunch break, I could go buy a disposable phone. I've wanted to get one while I'm here anyway. It doesn't feel right to use the business phone for my personal calls."

"That's a *wunderbaar* idea—"

Just then Grace entered the shop. "Oh, Rachel, your dress is lovely! Didn't I tell you? Arden, don't her eyes look pretty in that color?"

"Her eyes look pretty in any color." The words rolled off his tongue, and Arden couldn't tell who was most stunned by them—him, Rachel or his sister. Of the three, Grace recovered the quickest. She asked if they'd celebrate Ivan's birthday with her on Friday evening.

Rachel clapped her hand to her cheek. "I forgot his birthday is on the thirteenth!"

"I don't think he remembers, either—he said he's lost all sense of time. Which will make it more festive, kind of like a surprise party." After Rachel and Arden agreed a quiet celebration was in order, Grace said, "Today I've brought Ivan *hinkel supp* from *Mamm*. This morning I told her about the moose incident, so she also sent me off with a jug of chamomile sun tea to calm your nerves, Rachel."

"*Denki.* Ivan would probably like to have *supp* for lunch instead of the sandwich I fixed for him. You came at the perfect time if you'd like to join him and Arden at the *haus*. I have an errand to run."

"Actually, I need to get a smaller level—my three-foot one is too big for the shelves I need to hang in our next shed," Arden said. "So, I, uh, I'd like to go with you, Rachel. If Grace doesn't mind staying with Ivan, that is."

"That's fine," Grace agreed.

Arden didn't know if his sister's smirk was because it was obvious he wanted to spend time with Rachel or because Grace was pleased to visit Ivan alone again. *Probably both*, he decided, feeling a bit smug himself.

Rachel was glad she was wearing a long dress, because her knees were wobblier today from Arden's compliment about her eyes than they had been last night when the moose was coming her way. Fortunately, she was able to steady her hands against the steering wheel, and as she drove, she questioned Arden about Oneita's health.

"Her skin is so much better she doesn't want to go to the rheumatologist next week for her regularly scheduled appointment. Which reminds me, I was supposed to cancel it for her."

"Oh?" Rachel was concerned. "I'm not sure that you should do that. Her situation with her skin discoloration wasn't urgent, but it is something the *dokder* should be aware of so he can track it. He might want to make adjustments to her treatment plan, too."

"That's what I tried to tell her, but she thinks you gave her all the help she needs. And my *mamm* is as stubborn as...as a moose!"

Rachel giggled. "My *mamm* was like that, too. No one knew better than she did, because she was the *mamm*."

"*Jah*, that's why I was so surprised when my *mamm* listened to you." Arden added, "You must be very *gut* at talking to your patients because you're so considerate and easygoing, but you're very knowledgeable, too."

Rachel felt her cheeks flush. Two compliments from Arden in one day. That was more than she'd sometimes received from Toby in a month. "How about if I go talk to her before you cancel the appointment?"

Arden groaned. "She's going to think I put you up to it."

"*Neh*, she won't. Tomorrow when Ivan's asleep, I'll drop in casually to return her pitcher."

"*Denki*. I'd appreciate that."

"It'll be my pleasure." Building relationships with patients was one of Rachel's favorite parts of nursing, and she hummed the rest of the way to the superstore.

As they pulled into the parking lot, Rachel scanned the opposite corner. Since the Amish community was still small, there wasn't a covered area for horses and buggies the way there sometimes was in larger Amish communities. But in Serenity Ridge, the *Englisch* residents respected that the horses needed a quiet place where they wouldn't be disturbed, and someone had built a simple hitching post on the southernmost edge of the lot. Even though Arden had insisted the night before that he didn't mind if anyone saw them together, Rachel was relieved to find the area devoid of other Amish people. But in case any showed up, she suggested she and Arden separate inside the store and meet again outside at her car.

He wrinkled his forehead, his blue eyes dimming. "Don't you want to be seen with me? Are you afraid the *Englischers* will see you in that dress and assume we're courting?"

Flustered by the mere suggestion of Arden as her suitor, she stammered, "*Neh*, I just, I—it—it might take me a while because I've never bought a disposable phone before, so I have a few questions. I don't want you to stand around being bored."

"You mean because you'll be discussing technology and I won't understand it?"

"*Neh!* It's not that. I—"

Arden gave a satisfied grin; she hadn't realized he'd been jesting. "I'll go get what I need to purchase and then I'll meet you by the phones," he said.

Rachel's first order of business was to buy Ivan a birthday present, and she knew exactly what to get him: waders so next spring when he went fishing in Serenity Lake he wouldn't get so cold—which she suspected had played a role in his pneumonia *this* spring. After selecting a pair, she made her way to the electronics and technology section but couldn't find a staff person to help her, so she perused the back of the boxes of several different phones, comparing them. She'd narrowed her selection down to four possibilities by the time Arden arrived.

"Oh, wait—that one might be better," she said, indicating a phone on the shelf level with her chin. "Could you read me what that says about talk time and apps?"

Instead, Arden offered to hold on to the other four boxes so she could examine the fifth option herself. She was reading its list of features aloud when someone in the aisle interrupted.

"Is that you, Arden?" It was an Amish woman and a man who appeared to be her husband—or somebody's husband, because he wore a beard, as was customary for married Amish men. He also wore a neatly trimmed mustache, which was another anomaly practiced by the Amish in this part of Maine, as well as in a few other communities in the country. Unlike beards, mustaches weren't required for married Amish men living in Serenity Ridge—Colin and Albert had never grown them—but they weren't forbidden, either.

"Are you buying a phone?" the man asked, and Arden scrambled to set the boxes back on the shelf so quickly he dropped one of them on his toe. When he bent to retrieve it, he dropped it a second time.

For someone who supposedly isn't concerned about being seen with me, Arden sure is nervous, Rachel thought.

Of all the Amish people we'd run in to, it had to be the Rennos. Arden almost would have preferred to cross paths with Hadassah and Colin, because they would have ignored him and Rachel; Eva was going to ask a hundred and one questions.

"*Neh.* I'm not buying a phone. Rachel is." Arden felt like a schoolchild tattling on his classmate. "It's for her *bruder*, Ivan."

"Why does Ivan need a cell phone? Is it for work?" Eva asked him, as if Rachel weren't standing right there.

"He's going to use it while he's in the *haus* to call me at the shop if he needs me," Rachel said. She was making things worse by explaining. Even though Ivan was sick, most Amish people considered it unthinkable to use a phone at home, much less to use one to call a family member on their own property. "I'm Rachel Blank, by the way."

Whoops. Arden had been so surprised to see the Rennos he'd forgotten to introduce her, and after a pause he realized Eva and Ike weren't going to introduce themselves. "This is Eva and Ike Renno."

"*You're* the *Englisch schweschder*?" Eva questioned.

"That's not my *title*, but my *name* is Rachel, *jah*." Arden didn't blame Rachel for being annoyed to be referred to as the English sister, but her uppity tone wasn't going to win anyone over.

"Hadassah told us you were visiting. I guess she must have spoken to you about dressing appropriately in her *dochdere*'s presence."

"What?" Rachel's cheeks were going red, so Arden tried to steer the conversation in another direction.

"Eva's husband works with Colin and Albert," he said. "How *is* work, Ike?"

Eva wasn't to be deterred from her line of questioning, and she spoke over her husband. "I didn't see your buggy when I came in, Arden. Where did you hitch your horse?"

"I—I—I—"

"He rode with me in my car. It doesn't need a hitching post," Rachel quipped. Arden's one consolation was that Eva wouldn't catch on to her sarcasm.

"You left your workshop in the middle of the day to buy a phone?"

"And t-t-to get this," Arden said, displaying the level. It didn't occur to him to ask why Renno wasn't at work. "We're on our lunch break."

Eva looked at Rachel. "I was considering calling on Ivan. Arden told us he's had a terrible cough. I can make a honey-and-cider cough remedy that will stop him from hacking, although I'll have to drop by the organic market for honey on the way home."

"Oh, don't trouble yourself to do that," Rachel said.

Eva narrowed her eyes. "*Neh?* You only allow him to take *Englisch* medicine, is that it?"

"Not at all. Your remedy probably works as well— maybe even better—than an *Englisch* cough suppressant, but Ivan can't use one of those, either. You see, after having pneumonia, it's important he gets the *rotz* out of his lungs. It's *gut* for him to cough it up."

She wrinkled her nose. "I wasn't aware of that."

"You're *wilkom* to visit him any time, provided you haven't been sick. He's very susceptible to infection right now."

Eva huffed. "I'm *never* sick."

"*Gut*, then I hope to see you soon. For now, I need to find a sales clerk. As you mentioned, it's the middle of the day, and we need to get back to work." Rachel exchanged the box in her hand for one on the shelf, and after they both bid the Rennos goodbye, Arden followed her toward the customer service center.

Rachel couldn't believe the interaction they'd just had with Ike and Eva. What did she mean about dressing appropriately of front of Hadassah's daughters? Rachel had only seen little Sarah very briefly. "Wow, they really gave us the third degree," she muttered.

"What does that mean?"

Realizing the idiom in *Englisch* was foreign to Arden since the Amish rarely interacted with the courts or the police, Rachel chuckled. But before she could explain what she meant, Arden snapped, "There's no need to laugh just because I don't know that term."

"*Neh*, of course you don't," she acknowledged, surprised by how defensive he sounded. "It means they gave us a hard time. Interrogated us. Asked a lot of questions."

Arden didn't say anything most of the way home. Although he'd told Rachel he didn't care who saw the two of them together or what they thought if they did, she wondered if he minded more than he first let on. Not that she could blame him; Eva apparently was friends with Hadassah, and Rachel had a feeling Eva would repeat their conversation verbatim to her sister-in-law as soon as she could.

"You seemed a little nervous in the store," she finally remarked.

"What makes you say that?"

"Well, for one thing, you were stuttering a lot."

"That doesn't mean I was nervous," he barked.

Rachel was puzzled by his increasingly sour mood. Was he angry she'd implied a gossipmonger like Eva could make him nervous? If he wasn't irked because of the Rennos, it had to be because of something Rachel had said or done, but she didn't know what that might have been. "Have I upset you somehow?"

"I'm not upset," he said, scowling as they waited for the light to change. "If you're taking North Main instead of returning the same way we came, you'll have to turn right here. One of the drivers told me there's a detour because Fourth Street is washed out."

When Rachel put on her blinker and eased into the intersection, he frantically tapped the dashboard, saying, "*Neh*—other way!"

Waiting until she could safely change course, Rachel laughed nervously. "Someone who isn't upset doesn't mix up a simple thing like left and right. Do you want to tell me what's going on? Are you afraid Ike will tell Colin you were away from the workshop again? Or that you were buying a disposable cell phone?"

"I'm not *afraid* of anything. This trip was a necessity, not a social outing, and I'm on my lunch break. As for the phone, even if I was buying one, Colin would assume it's for my business. He knows I'd never flirt with buying technology for my own use. It's not as if I'm in danger of going *Englisch*."

That's exactly *what Colin would think and you know it, so why are you defending him all of a sudden?* Rachel was crushed. She couldn't comprehend why Arden was shutting her out like this, but maybe his behavior was the reality check she needed so she wouldn't continue to entertain the kind of ludicrous romantic notions she'd been having about the two of them.

"Jah," she said, crossing her arms against her chest. "I can't picture you going *Englisch* any more than I can imagine myself staying among the Amish."

Chapter Nine

Never in his life had Arden felt so humiliated. He stared out the passenger side window, stupefied by how Rachel had pointed out his stuttering, mocked him for mixing up left and right, and ridiculed him because he wasn't familiar with an apparently common *Englisch* phrase. And then, after insulting him, she had the good nerve to ask if anything was wrong!

But mostly, Arden was disgusted with himself for ever giving her the benefit of the doubt, especially after he'd overheard her talking on the phone. *Whether or not she was referring to me, she was calling someone dumb, and that should have shown me enough about her character to recognize how truly arrogant she is, no matter how unpretentious she appears on the surface.*

Not only had Rachel made fun of Arden, but she'd indirectly scorned the Rennos by rejecting Eva's offer to bring Ivan a homemade cold remedy. Eva might have been a blabbermouth, but her intention toward Ivan was kind. It wasn't as if Rachel actually had to administer the remedy to her brother, but why couldn't she have accepted it graciously instead of acting like a big show-off and delivering a lecture on phlegm? *If anyone should feel embarrassed, it should be* her, *not me!*

"I'm going to go show Ivan how to use this cell phone before I begin painting," she announced when finally they pulled to a stop in the driveway. Arden was already halfway out of the car.

"That's fine. I've got an errand to run. I've set the paint by the doghouse. The customer wants black trim, the rest in blue. I'll be back by three thirty or so." Then, as more of a demand than a statement, he added, "You should be finished painting by then."

"An errand? Why didn't you tell me?" Rachel questioned, her voice tremulous. "I could have taken you when we were out."

"I wanted to go by myself." Arden slid the rest of the way out of the car and shoved the door shut without a backward glance.

After getting his lunch bag from the workshop, he hitched his buggy and guided his horse toward Serenity Lake. It didn't matter to him how long he was gone; if necessary, he'd work from the time he returned until midnight rather than be in the same room with Rachel. Cutting across town toward the valley, Arden journeyed down a dirt road only the Amish were allowed to use, per the private landowner, to gain access to the water. After stopping at the edge of the woods to secure his horse, he followed the foot path to where the trees opened to a small clearing. There, jutting into the lake water loomed a boulder the Amish called Relaxation Rock, because its flat top was an ideal location for reclining. But Arden was far too wound up to relax. Pacing the narrow stretch of sand along the water's edge, he picked up a few stray stones and hurled them as far as he could into the sparkling clear lake.

As he chucked them, he snickered bitterly, thinking, *Too bad Colin and Hadassah or Eva and Ike aren't around to catch me playing hooky now.* He knew he should feel guilty, but he only felt tired out and fed up. His energy waning, he gripped the lunch bag between his teeth and scrambled to the top of the boulder. He ate his lunch slowly, reveling in the view until his eyelids grew so heavy he set his hat beside him, leaned back, folded his arms behind his head and fell fast asleep.

The last thing Rachel wanted was to be in the workshop when Arden returned, so she completed painting the doghouse as quickly as she could and cleaned the brushes and tray and put away the rest of the supplies. Then she gathered the ledger, a folder of invoices, two supply catalogs and the scheduling calendar, along with the business phone. From now on, she was going to stay far away from Arden for as long as possible. If he wanted her help, he was going to have to ask for it, because she was sick of volunteering and even sicker of his moodiness. *He wants to be by himself? Fine, he can be by himself. I'd rather run into the moose again than to cross* his *path!*

Thinking of the moose reminded Rachel she still had to take in the laundry. No sooner did she bring it inside than she changed out of the lavender dress and into her navy blue *Englisch* skirt and white blouse. As she put the dress she'd made on a hanger, Arden's compliment—"Her eyes look pretty in any color"—flitted through her mind, quickly followed by what he'd said about her being effective with patients. How could he go from saying such lovely things to behaving like such an oaf? The more she brooded about it, the more addled she became until she finally gave up trying to figure it out. *Why am I wasting my time speculating about Arden? Whatever happened to me being an independent and career-focused woman?* she chastised herself.

If only she could go to the bookstore to purchase the medical book on assessments and management protocols she'd been wanting to read, perhaps she could get her mind back on her future. But going to the bookstore would have meant leaving Ivan alone, and even though they both had phones now, Rachel was reluctant to be away from the house for that long. She'd noticed her brother's coloring looked off and she was convinced he was overly tired, especially later, when he turned in for the night at seven thirty.

As helpful as Grace had been by bringing meals and staying with Ivan in Rachel's absence, Rachel worried Ivan was sacrificing his sleep in order to visit with her. But how could Rachel broach the subject? The young couple were clearly in love. Besides, Grace was the only person who had come to see Ivan since he'd been discharged. Although he never mentioned this conspicuous lack of visitors, Rachel was disappointed by it. "That goes to show how wrong Arden was when he said the community would be *hallich* to help during Ivan's recovery," she said aloud to herself as she turned off the lights and went to sleep early, too.

Both she and Ivan were up at the crack of dawn the next morning, and he looked even livelier than Rachel did.

"You really don't have to stay at the *haus* with me today. You can go down to the workshop," he said when Rachel returned from collecting eggs and milking the cow. "I'll be fine on my own."

"Something tells me you won't be on your own for long," Rachel absently replied as she counted the eggs. She was craving angel food cake but was one egg short.

Ivan chuckled. "You're right. Grace is stopping by with more *supp*. You and Arden should join us for lunch. I don't know how I'll ever eat it by myself."

"*Denki*, but since you'll have company, I'd like to go to town." It would be the perfect opportunity for Rachel to get the book she wanted. Maybe she'd even treat herself to an iced espresso and a muffin at the popular coffeehouse in town. Or buy eggs from the grocery store. She might even wear lipstick—no more plain dresses fastened with straight pins for her; Ivan was getting better, and Rachel needed to start acting like an *Englischer* again.

But her afternoon plans were thwarted when Ivan was taking a shower and Grace arrived with a large pot of soup in hand but wouldn't enter the house. Teary-eyed, she explained her mother had a mild fever again. "I don't know if it's a recurrence of her lupus symptoms or if she's coming down with something, but if it is an illness, it's possible I'll get it, or that I'm already carrying it. Which means I might have exposed Ivan to it!" she wailed.

Rachel took the pot and set it aside before calmly leading Grace to the porch swing. After asking about her mother's symptoms, as well as about her own health and hand-washing practices, she ventured Ivan didn't have much to worry about; Rachel's bigger concern was Oneita's lupus. Remembering she'd promised Arden she'd speak to his mother about keeping her upcoming doctor's appointment, Rachel provided Grace a face mask and asked her to stay with Ivan until she returned from checking on Oneita. By the time Rachel retrieved her keys and purse, Ivan had joined Grace in the kitchen, where she was setting bowls on the table.

"I'll be back soon. Remember, no kissing, you two—it spreads germs!" Rachel cautioned on her way out the door to make Grace and Ivan blush. Teasing her brother was something she'd never outgrow. Besides, she wanted to take advantage of the opportunity to prompt Ivan to ask to be Grace's suitor, if he wasn't already courting her. *Grace's* bruder *may be a grouch, but Grace is a* wunderbaar *woman.*

As she was getting into her car, Rachel spotted Arden helping an elderly couple load the doghouse into the back of a pickup. His curls were springs of light in the noon sun, and a damp spot bloomed across his bright blue shirt between his shoulder blades. As she watched him dexterously hoist the structure, Rachel remembered how he'd swept her into his arms after she fainted. She pinched her eyes closed to block the memory and exhaled heavily. When she opened them again, Arden was gone.

Arden stood by the desk, chugging down a cup of water. It was seeing Rachel as much as it was the humidity that had made his temperature rise. As steamed as he still was at her, he needed her help. In the past day alone, he'd received a dozen phone calls about orders, delivery dates and supplies, as well as a voice-mail message from the bank requesting a return call. Even if Rachel had left the relevant paperwork behind, Arden still would have been hard-pressed to field the inquiries and process the information he was receiving. He just couldn't read and write fast enough, and he was tripping over his tongue more often than usual today, on account of having had insomnia the night before.

But apparently Rachel had somewhere to go—probably to an *Englisch* store, guessing by her appearance. She was back to wearing her usual clothes, and instead of pulling her hair into a neat bun, she'd piled it in a sloppy knot atop of her head. *She looks like she's been in a windstorm.* Arden instantly regretted the thought; by criticizing something as superficial as Rachel's wardrobe or hair, he was behaving no differently than Hadassah, and he liked to think he had far better reasons for finding fault with Rachel than that.

Then it occurred to him since Rachel had left the house, it was the perfect time to say hello to Ivan and drop off the notepad containing what little bit of information he managed to capture from the phone calls. To his surprise—he hadn't noticed his sister's buggy by the stable—Grace greeted him at the door wearing a blue mask. His pulse drummed in his ears; was Ivan okay?

"The mask is only a precaution," Grace said. "*Mamm* had a fever this morning, and since I've been in close contact with her, I was concerned I might accidentally transfer an illness to Ivan. Rachel said she doubts it, but she went to check on *Mamm* anyway. I guess she's going to try to convince her to keep her rheumatologist appointment, although I can't imagine *Mamm* will agree."

"I wouldn't be too sure about that—Rachel has a *gut* rapport with *Mamm*," Arden replied, automatically giving credit where it was due. Despite being miffed at Rachel, he was grateful she was going to try to persuade their mother to follow up with her doctor.

Because Rachel hadn't left an extra mask for Arden, when he entered the kitchen, he stayed across the room from Ivan. They chatted briefly before Arden handed off the information he'd brought with him.

"I ought to have Rachel bring me up-to-date on the paperwork," Ivan said. "But I'm afraid I sleep so much sometimes I don't know what actually happens and what I dreamed happened. I'm eager for things to be back to normal at the workshop again, though."

Not half as eager as I am, Arden thought. "No hurry. It's better not to push yourself. I wouldn't want you to relapse." *Especially if it means your* schweschder *would have to stay longer.*

Although Grace invited him to join them for lunch, Arden was too hot to eat soup and he didn't want to be there when Rachel returned, so he plodded back to the workshop. He had just crossed the threshold when the phone rang. *Not again*, he thought. This time the caller asked to speak with Rachel.

"She's not here at the moment, but how can I help you?"

The man chuckled. "You can't, except to give Rachel a message. Let her know Toby phoned and I'd like her to return my call as soon as possible. She's got my number. Thanks, guy," Toby said and disconnected before Arden could reply.

Thanks, guy? No wonder Rachel had dated Toby; he was just as condescending as she was.

"Hello, Rachel." Oneita patted the empty spot beside her on the double glider on the porch. "*Kumme*, sit. You look a little wan, dear."

Rachel tucked a strand of hair behind her ear. The humidity was wilting her updo. "I may look as if I'm drooping, but I feel fine. How are *you* feeling?"

Oneita harrumphed. "Better than my *dochder* would have you believe. I assume she sent you here?"

Rachel laughed. "I was going to use the pretext of returning your pitcher, but I forgot to bring it. I would genuinely like to borrow an *oier*, though. But you're right, I came because Grace is worried about your fever."

"I honestly don't feel like I have one. I keep telling Grace she worries too much."

"I must say, you don't *look* sick. May I take your temperature?" Oneita agreed, so Rachel took a thermometer from her first aid kit and slid it beneath Oneita's tongue. When it beeped, she removed it and read aloud, "Ninety-eight point one. Nope, no fever."

"I knew that thermometer Grace was using was a piece of junk! I misplaced ours, so she picked up one on sale at the supermarket. I told her she was sacrificing quality for price, and this proves me right."

"I'm inclined to agree with you, but I can understand why Grace was worried," Rachel said diplomatically.

Even though no one else was anywhere around, Oneita lowered her voice. "I suspect she was even more worried about your *bruder* than about me. She's quite fond of him."

"I think Ivan's fond of Grace, too," Rachel confided.

"I reckon it's too early to plant celery for their *hochzich*, but I'd love to have Ivan as a son-in-law. He's been a blessing to our *familye*. Especially to my *suh*."

At the mention of Arden, Rachel shifted uncomfortably in her seat, but she acknowledged, "Ivan's very grateful to have Arden as his partner, too. I remember him writing to me that he was about to give up the idea of owning a business when Arden answered his ad. He was amazed a craftsman like Arden would relocate halfway across the country for an uncertain business endeavor."

"It must have been part of *Gott*'s divine plan for both of them, because your *bruder* gave Arden an opportunity he never would have had back home."

Despite being upset with him, Rachel's curiosity was piqued. "Really? Arden's so skilled—why wouldn't he start his own business in Indiana?"

"There are a lot of carpenters in that part of the country. They far exceed the demand. And of course, working in an *Englisch* job simply wasn't an option for Arden."

"*Neh*, of course not," Rachel murmured. Although she could understand why an Amish person might not want to work for an *Englisch* employer, hearing it still felt like an affront, especially since it was clear Arden would have preferred an Amish person to work with him during Ivan's illness, too.

Oneita continued, "He was crushed he couldn't work in the factory with his *daed*. But with Arden's reading and writing difficulties, well, he struggled through the application process, which included timed tests. And because his speaking problem is worse when he's tired or nervous, he didn't do well during the interviews, either."

His reading and writing difficulties? His speaking problem? It took a moment for it to dawn on Rachel. "Oh, you mean because he stutters sometimes? That doesn't seem fair for an employer to eliminate him for a job on that basis."

"His stuttering, *jah*, but it's more that he sometimes has trouble getting his thoughts out. You've probably noticed it takes him twice as long to read and write as anyone else, too. That's why working with Ivan is such a *gut* fit for him. Your *bruder* handles all the calls and paperwork—and now you do, too. Although Arden is too self-conscious to talk about it, I know it was a huge relief when you arrived."

Rachel's stomach dropped, and if her skin hadn't already been clammy from the heat, she would have broken into a sweat upon remembering she'd asked Arden to read aloud from the phone packaging yesterday. She'd also pointed out he'd been stuttering. And laughed when he mixed up right and left. *No wonder he was so terse with me! He must think I'm a total jerk!* Her eyes stung, and she scrambled to her feet, causing Oneita to ask whether she was okay.

"*Jah*, but it occurred to me there's something I need take care of at the workshop." Rachel zipped to the car without another thought about borrowing an egg or even encouraging Oneita to keep her medical appointment—all that mattered to her now was making things right with Arden.

* * *

When Rachel barreled through the door, Arden was sitting at the desk finishing the last of his lunch while he puzzled over an order that had arrived in the mail. Ordinarily, he wouldn't have opened the envelope, but the customer had just called asking to change the specifications from those he'd written on his original request, which, unfortunately, included a variety of acronyms. Because Arden was too confused to make heads or tails of the order, he was forced to tell the customer he'd call him back later.

"I assume you've *kumme* for this." Arden pushed the rest of the mail across the desk toward Rachel. He stood and put his utensils into his lunch bag, which he dropped into the bottom desk drawer, and then he strode across the work area toward the sawhorses.

Rachel scampered in front of him. Peering up into his eyes, she clasped her hands beneath her chin and said, "*Neh*, I'm here to apologize, Arden. I'm so sorry for saying you seemed nervous the other day. And for calling attention to your stutter and the fact you mixed up the directions. I promise I wasn't making fun of you. I had no idea you have dyslexia."

Arden couldn't believe his ears. "Dyslexia? Who told you I have dyslexia?"

"Your *mamm*. She didn't use that word, but she told me about your challenges reading and writing. And about how you mix up letters—"

Arden didn't think it was possible to feel more embarrassed than he'd felt yesterday. But to discover his mother had discussed his...his so-called *challenges* with Rachel was too degrading for him to bear graciously. "So you diagnosed me with dyslexia? I thought a specialist had to do that. I thought there were tests involved. Or are you so uniquely qualified you can diagnose a person at a glance?"

Rachel's nostrils were turning pink, and her chin quivered. "*Neh*, you're right. I don't know for certain you have dyslexia. I just, I—I—I—"

"You're stuttering now. Is that because *you* have dyslexia?"

"Arden, I don't blame you for being angry at me, but I'm trying to make amends. I'm very sorry." Tears spilled from her eyes, but Arden was relentless. It was as if he was taking out all of the frustration and humiliation and fear of failure from the past nearly thirty years of his life on Rachel.

"What are *you* crying about? Does it t-take you t-ten minutes to read a simple passage from the Bible? How many t-times do you have to check your s-spelling for errors? Do you constantly w-worry you wr-wrote down a product code wr-wrong? Has anyone ever refused you a job or called y-you lazy when y-you were trying your hardest?" Arden was utterly exasperated that he couldn't even tell Rachel off without stammering. He ended by leaning forward and glaring at her as he asked, "Do *your* peers think *you're* stupid?"

She passed her arm across her face to wipe her tears away. "Sometimes, *jah.*"

"Ha!" Arden scoffed, picking up a saw. "You? I doubt it."

"*Jah*, me," Rachel said, tapping her chest. "Not to the degree you've experienced, not even close, but I do know what it's like to try to prove myself to my peers.

To know they think I'm not quite bright enough for them. To feel as if I don't measure up."

"That's a self-confidence issue. I have an *actual* problem with my abilities." He balanced a board across the two sawhorses.

"That might be true to a degree, Arden, but despite your struggles, you're one of the smartest, most creative people I've ever met. You'd have to be, to design such beautiful, unique sheds." Rachel gestured toward the side wall of the workshop. "You memorized where everything on every one of those shelves is. You retain more information in your head than I can capture in a logbook. And you knew exactly what questions to ask your *mamm* when I was trying to get to the bottom of what was triggering her skin discoloration. I didn't—and I'm trained in that kind of thing. It put me to shame."

As much as he wanted to believe Rachel meant what she said, Arden wasn't going to be fooled twice. "*Jah?* If that's what you really think, why did you tell someone on the phone how *dumm* I am, especially compared to Toby?"

"I never said such a thing! You must have misheard—oh." Rachel suddenly interrupted herself. She looked away, chewing her lip; Arden knew it. Despite what she'd just professed, she couldn't deny she'd called him stupid. "I didn't say you were *dumm*. I said you weren't *that* dull and—"

"So I should feel c-complimented because you said I'm not quite as stupid as you first thought?" Arden picked up the saw and began vigorously cutting into the board, his back to her.

"*Listen* to me, would you?" she shouted over the

noise. "My roommate asked if you were acting morose because that was my original impression of you. But later, on the phone, I told her you weren't as dull as all that—*dull*, not *dumb*—meaning, you weren't so dreary. So morose."

Arden stopped sawing. He wanted to trust Rachel was telling the truth so badly his chest ached. He turned to face her. "You did?"

"*Jah*, I did." She added ruefully, "Although you're being so nasty right now I might change my mind again."

"Don't," he said, setting down the saw. He took both of her hands in his. "Please don't change your mind. I'm sorry. I—I—I've been trying to keep m-my difficulty a secret for so long. When y-you n-noticed it, I felt so... I thought you were being condescending. That you were looking down your n-nose at me."

"I could never look down my nose at you, Arden! I have nothing but deep respect and admiration for you."

He gently tugged her fingers, pulling her closer until they were only inches apart. "That makes two of us. I mean, I think that highly of you, too." His mouth went dry, and he licked his lips as she tilted her chin upward.

Rachel's legs turned to butter, and she felt her face flush beneath Arden's unflinching gaze. His eyes were bluer than blue, like the first patch of clear sky after a storm. As much as she wanted him to kiss her, Rachel couldn't let that happen—for his sake, more than hers. She forced herself to take a step backward and then she slid her hands from his grasp. He nodded in silent agreement and rubbed the perspiration from his forehead with the back of his hand.

Not two seconds later, the door creaked open. Arden jerked his head to the side, and Rachel spun around to see Jaala Flaud, the deacon's wife. *Wow, that was close!* Rachel thought, but her relief was short lived. *Uh-oh. She must be here to inform Arden the deacon and bishop want to speak to him about associating with me. Or worse, to suggest I leave Serenity Ridge.*

"So this is where you've been hiding!" Jaala exclaimed. "Rachel Blank, *kumme* give me a hug."

For an instant Rachel was too stunned to move, but then she nearly flew across the room into Jaala's open arms. As the deacon's wife enveloped her, Rachel inhaled the trace scent of nutmeg and cloves on her clothing. *The fragrance of my girlhood*, she thought, knowing Jaala must have made her renowned spice cake with cream cheese frosting that morning. Rachel whisked a tear from her cheek before letting her go.

Sizing Rachel up, Jaala remarked, "You look more like your *mamm* than ever. It is so *gut* to see you, but why did I have to hear about your arrival from Eva Renno? Nobody told me Ivan was out of the hospital, either."

"I'm sorry," Rachel replied. *And I'm sorry for assuming you wouldn't* wilkom *me back or visit my* bruder *while I was here, too.* "I assumed Colin or Hadassah would have told you."

"Ah, well, that doesn't matter now. We've got a lot of catching up to do. Will you join Abram and me for supper tonight? A few other young people will be there, too. There's plenty of cake for everyone. Arden, you're *wilkom* to *kumme*, too."

Rachel hesitated. "I'd love to, but I'm concerned about leaving Ivan—"

"I'll stay with him," Arden interjected.

"It's settled, then. We'll eat at six." Jaala linked arms with Rachel and started for the door. "*Kumme* with me while I visit Ivan. I figured since I'm one of the first to learn he's home, I'd better bring him a big vat of *supp*, and I need help carrying it in from the buggy."

Grateful but amused because Grace had already brought them so much soup they'd be eating it into next week, Rachel flashed a smile over her shoulder at Arden. When he winked and placed a finger to his lips, she wistfully thought, *That's not the only secret we'll have to keep to ourselves.*

Chapter Ten

"How is Ivan?" Rachel asked Arden when she returned from the gathering at Jaala's house. "Did he do his deep breathing exercises?"

"*Jah*. But he's tuckered out. He went to bed an hour ago."

"He needs as much rest as he can get. I meant to tell you I have to take him to a follow-up appointment tomorrow, so I'll only be in the workshop in the morning."

"That's fine. So, did you enjoy your visit?"

"It was *wunderbaar*. I met two couples—Maria and Otto Mast, and Sadie and Levi Swarey."

"Did you meet the Swareys' *kinner*, David and Elizabeth, too?"

"*Jah*." Rachel giggled. "I had to remove a tick from David's scalp. Sadie was concerned he'll get Lyme disease, but I could tell by the tick's color and size it was a male and males don't transmit—Oh, I'm doing it again. I keep forgetting other people aren't as fascinated by these things as I am."

It occurred to Arden that Rachel hadn't meant to

lecture Eva or to show off the other day—she was in the habit of sharing knowledge that was interesting to her and potentially helpful to others. "You're a natural teacher."

"*Denki.* Patient education is one of my favorite parts of nursing. They educate me by sharing what they've experienced, too." Rachel's voice lost its sparkle when she added, "Unfortunately, there's not much time to build relationships with patients in the clinic. We move 'em in and out. I spend more time entering data into their electronic health records than talking with the patients."

"Will that change when you become a nurse practitioner?"

"Ha! I'll probably have even *less* time."

"Yet becoming a nurse practitioner is what you want to do?"

"*Jah*, I suppose."

"Hmm."

"Hmm what?"

Somehow, now that Rachel knew about his trouble finding the right words, it was actually *easier* for Arden to express himself in front of her. "When you told me about becoming a nurse, you described it as a dream, almost an irrepressible one. You pursued that dream at great cost to yourself. That's a far cry from *supposing* you want to become a nurse practitioner."

Rachel chewed on the corner of her lip. There was a faraway look in her eyes but she simply shrugged and said, "*Jah*, well, maybe I won't get into the MSN program anyway."

"If you don't, you could always *kumme* back to Serenity Ridge for *gut*." Like most of his deepest-felt sentiments, this one sprang from Arden's lips, taking him by surprise.

Rachel seemed to think he was jesting. "*Jah*, I could ask Ivan to give me a job as painter in residence."

Arden attempted to cover the fact he'd been serious by kidding, "Or you could become Serenity Ridge's nurse in residence. We Amish need someone to lecture us about *rotz* and ticks and the dangers of cough suppressants."

"Lecture?" she asked. "You mean the other day? Was I really that bad? The only reason I told Eva not to bring the cough remedy was because she was going to buy honey from the expensive organic market just for that purpose, and I didn't want it going to waste."

I've really misjudged her, Arden realized again. "*Neh*, you're not *that* bad," he said, blithely imitating her tone when she said he wasn't *that* dull.

"Gee, thanks." She gently pushed on his bicep, frowning in mock consternation. How he wished he could kiss that fake pout from her lips… Her cell phone rang, and Arden wrenched backward. She pulled it from her purse and glanced at the display screen. "I'd better answer this. *Denki* for staying with Ivan. I'll see you in the morning?"

"See you in the morning," Arden echoed as she lifted the phone to her ear. Rachel had already shut the door behind him when he remembered he'd never told her that Toby had called that afternoon. *Maybe that's him on the phone with her now. Maybe he's wondering when she's coming home*, Arden conjectured. *What if he's calling because he wants to date her again?* He didn't know what had inspired that idea, but once he got it into his head, it was all he could think about.

"Guess who's going to be a nurse practitioner?" Meg taunted in a singsong voice.

"Who?" Rachel's mind was still on her conversation with Arden. *Was he serious about wanting me to stay in Serenity Ridge?*

"Do you really have to ask? *You* are, that's who. You got into the MSN program!"

"I did?" Rachel had been anticipating the university's decision for so long she thought she'd be exuberant when she finally heard, but instead she felt hollow.

"Yes, you did!"

"Oh." Her eyes filled with tears—and they weren't the happy kind, either.

"Oh? That's all you have to say? What's wrong? Aren't you glad you got in?"

"Yeah, I am," Rachel said, but Meg could tell she wasn't being completely honest.

"That answer lacks conviction, Rach. What's going on? Has Ivan had a relapse?"

"*Neh*, Ivan's definitely improving. It's just that, it's just…it's *everything*," Rachel cried, releasing a torrent of pent-up emotion. Meg listened to her recount a hodgepodge of anecdotes, from nearly being trampled by the moose to her argument and subsequent reconciliation with Arden to the lovely evening she'd just enjoyed at the deacon's house. She also lamented Colin and Hadassah's behavior, the fact her nieces and nephews hadn't known she existed, and the realization she'd wrongly made assumptions about the Amish community in Serenity Ridge. She ended by saying how conflicted she'd felt lately about becoming a nurse practitioner. "To be honest, I don't think I want to *be* a nurse practitioner as much as I wanted to prove I *could* be one. And I especially wanted to prove it to Toby. It was a matter of pride—what the Amish call *hochmut*."

"I'm not entirely surprised—you love nursing so much, I never really could imagine you changing roles. As grueling as the application process was, at least you figured out you don't want to go through with becoming an NP before you enrolled in the program or quit your job," Meg consoled her. "For a minute there, I was afraid you were going to tell me you weren't coming back to Boston…"

Rachel hesitated a spell before assuring her, "No, I'm coming back."

"Good, because I miss you. The only bad thing about returning is that you'll still have to work with—oh no!" Meg abruptly exclaimed. "I forgot to tell you. Toby called the other day. Please don't be mad, but I gave him your number. The one at the workshop, I mean."

"Meg!" Rachel groaned.

"I'm sorry, Rach, but he left me, like, five messages. When I finally picked up, he told me he and Brianna broke up and he seemed desperate to talk to you. I figured he was going to call and beg you to take him back and I, well, I kind of wanted you to have the satisfaction of telling him no way… And, hey, now that you've found out you got into the MSN program, you can rub his nose in that, too, even if you aren't going to enroll."

Rachel sighed. Two weeks ago she would have derived a certain satisfaction in spurning Toby or telling him she'd been accepted into a top-notch MSN program, but now she had no desire to do something so vengeful and vain. "I'll talk to him if he calls, but I'm not going to tell him about getting into the program."

"I know, I know," Meg muttered. "The Amish would consider that to be *hallich maage*."

"Hallich maage?" Rachel repeated.

"Yeah. Pride."

"You mean *hochmut*."

"What did I say?"

"It sounded like *hallich maage*, which loosely translated means *happy stomach*." Rachel giggled.

"Don't poke fun at me or I'll remind you of the time you called a phlebotomist a *lobotomist*."

The two roommates cracked up as they reminisced about other humorous things Rachel had said or done while she was acclimating to the *Englisch* lifestyle. Before they bade each other goodbye, Rachel told Meg to give Toby her temporary cell phone number if he called again—she didn't want him using the business phone.

She got ready for bed, but long after midnight, Rachel lay awake, mulling over Arden's suggestion that she might return to Serenity Ridge for good. It wasn't as if the idea hadn't occurred to her already, but as Meg had accurately pointed out, Rachel loved being a nurse. And as Arden had reminded her, she'd sacrificed so much to become one. *But if I love nursing so much, why do I feel so discontent when I imagine returning to my job in Boston?*

On Friday morning, Arden kept watching the door. Rachel hadn't been coming in as early as she did before Ivan was discharged, and he was eager to tell her about the phone call from Toby, which had been weighing heavily on his mind. Besides, he liked being in Rachel's company as often as he could.

She eventually ambled in at nine thirty, whistling. When Arden relayed the message, she didn't seem surprised. "Sorry about that. Meg gave him the business phone number," she said, which made Arden even surer Toby had been in touch with Rachel already. Was he also right in guessing what they'd spoken about?

It's none of my business, he reminded himself. "I've got two customers arriving shortly to discuss modifications to this shed," he informed Rachel, pointing at the structure. "If you'd listen to the rest of the voice-mail messages, I'd appreciate it. We had several I didn't attend to yesterday."

"Of course," she agreed and lifted the business phone from the desk. Her smile was especially winsome this morning, and Arden could no longer keep himself from fishing to find out why.

"Your eyes are gleaming. Have you got a secret?" he hinted.

She stopped tapping on the cell phone to squint at him, her head cocked. "As a matter of fact, I do."

"Do you want to share what it is?"

"Jah..." she stalled, looking at the phone again. "But not now. You'll find out at Ivan's birthday party."

Clearly she was being coy, and while Arden might ordinarily have enjoyed this kind of badinage, today it felt like torment. He shamelessly pleaded with her. "I'm really *gut* at keeping secrets if you want to tell me now."

"Well, I could but then—"

The couple Arden was expecting entered the workshop, enthusiastically greeting Arden before Rachel could complete her sentence. She gave him a one-shouldered shrug and a puckish smile, as if to say, *Oh, well.* Resigned to bearing the suspense until the couple left, Arden led them to the shed, where he listened to their proposed design modifications.

As they spoke, Arden glanced over at Rachel, who was frantically flipping through the ledger with one hand and holding the phone to her ear with the other. She must have slipped out the door a few minutes later, because the next time he looked up, she was gone. After the couple departed, he found a note on the desk reading, *Arden, I had to run an errand. I won't be back this afternoon since Ivan has his MD appointment. I took the phone in case a customer calls. I'll see you tonight at six.* She'd signed her name, and next to it she'd sketched a moose's head. The moose was winking, and beneath him she'd scrawled, *You* moose *not try to guess my secret—it will spoil the surprise!* And despite his impatience to find out her news, Arden had to laugh.

I've gone over the ledger so many times I was sure it was correct, Rachel thought as she drove to the bank. But obviously it wasn't, otherwise the bank manager wouldn't have left so many voice-mail messages the past couple days. The first were simply requests to return his calls, but in this morning's message he informed her there were insufficient funds in the business account to cover the check Ivan had written to the hospital. Because Blank's Sheds was a longtime customer in good standing, the manager was contacting Ivan as a courtesy, allowing him until noon today to reconcile the deficit in order to avoid bouncing the check and incurring a fee. Even more worrisome was the possibility the hospital might rescind the discount on Ivan's bill if it wasn't paid in full immediately, as agreed.

As she stopped at a traffic light, Rachel remembered Arden mixing up right and left, and it occurred to her *he* might have been the one who made an error in their records. *Everything was balanced perfectly when my brother relinquished the accounting responsibilities to Arden, so it couldn't have been Ivan's doing.* Aware that sometimes people with dyslexia also had dyscalculia, Rachel wondered if that was the case with Arden. She dreaded telling him about the error, anticipating how self-conscious he might feel.

And the timing was terrible—tonight she'd planned to confide in him, Ivan and Grace that she'd been accepted into the MSN program but wouldn't be enrolling. She had stayed up praying about it throughout the night, and she knew it was the right decision, but she was less certain about her other unshakable idea: *Maybe I should stay in Serenity Ridge permanently.* Tonight she wanted to test the waters, to hear if her brother and her new friends thought that was a plausible option.

For now, her sole objective was to prevent Ivan's check from bouncing. By speaking to the manager in person, she hoped to buy more time. Although he'd said the account was several thousand dollars short, Rachel prayed there might be a check from a customer in today's mail that would cover the deficit. Then, right before turning into the bank parking lot, she was struck by another solution: she could transfer the funds from her own account. Now that she wouldn't have to pay tuition fees, she couldn't think of a better use for her savings. She was thrilled when the manager accepted her proposal, not merely because it resolved Ivan's business problem, but also because it seemed like further affirmation that she'd made the right decision about the MSN program.

After contacting her bank and arranging for the transaction, she barely had enough time to get home and take Ivan to his appointment. The doctor said he'd made remarkable progress; his oxygen saturation level had come up, and his lung X-rays looked better, too. "You must be very committed to practicing your breathing exercises, aren't you?" the doctor asked.

"Not half as committed as my *schweschder* is to *making* me practice them." Ivan's comment made the doctor chuckle.

"I wish all my patients had someone like your sister to take care of them. You're very fortunate."

"That's true. I don't know what I would have done without Rachel," Ivan said, beaming at her.

It was such a relief to hear about Ivan's improved health and she was so eager to share her decision not to become a nurse practitioner that Rachel decided she'd wait until the following day to discuss the insufficient funds issue with Arden.

As it turned out, that evening Rachel discovered she'd have to wait to tell everyone about her career decision, too, because every time she tried to bring up the subject, she was delayed. First, Grace was upset because she overcooked the roast. It was so tough they ended up having soup—again. Rachel chose not to tell everyone immediately after supper because she wanted the focus on her brother as he opened his gifts. Then, as they were eating cake, Ivan suffered a coughing fit that was so extreme Rachel suggested he'd benefit from a steaming bath. Ivan reluctantly agreed, and Grace began stacking the dessert dishes, but it was Arden who dragged his feet about leaving. He had seemed so agitated all evening—squirming in his seat and picking at his food—Rachel was surprised he wanted to linger.

"I, uh, know Ivan needs his rest, but first don't you have news to share, Rachel?" he asked.

She smiled. "*Jah*, I'm glad you asked about that. I—" As she was speaking, the business cell phone vibrated on the coffee table where Rachel had left it so Arden would remember to take it home since he was expecting an early-morning call the next day. Rachel leaned forward to check the number. "I don't need to get that. What I was going to say is that I've decided to—"

Immediately after the business phone stopped vibrating, Rachel's phone began ringing from atop of the desk in the corner. Rachel crossed the room and picked it up. "It's Toby. He's going to keep calling until I answer, so give me one sec," she said before ducking into the kitchen.

"Ivan, you look miserable," Grace cooed. "I wanted our gathering to be special, but I'm afraid this party might have set your recovery back three weeks!"

"Don't be *lappich*. I'm sorry my coughing cut our celebration short. The party was so thoughtful—and I was genuinely surprised."

Arden shifted in the chair, feeling like a third wheel

as Ivan and Grace unabashedly exchanged sentiments of affection. From where he sat he could hear bits of Rachel's phone conversation with Toby. He caught phrases like "I've already forgiven you," and "what I want more than anything." *I* knew *it*, he thought, his suspicions confirmed. Rachel had reconciled with Toby.

"Can't you, Arden?" Grace questioned, jolting him back to their conversation.

"Sorry, what did you say?"

"I said, can you take Ivan to *kurrich* and back home on Sunday? He shouldn't be on his own, and I'll be going with *Mamm* to visit Aquilla King." Aquilla was a childless widow who had recently had hip surgery, and as was customary, the female members of the Amish community were either taking turns staying with her or bringing meals to her home.

"*Jah*, of course," Arden agreed, adding that since Rachel might be a while, he and Grace should leave so Ivan could take his bath. Since they were traveling in separate buggies, Arden said goodbye before Grace did. He retrieved the business phone from the coffee table and tried to creep past Rachel in the kitchen, but she excused herself from Toby and covered the phone with her hand.

"I'm sorry about this," she said, indicating the phone. "I'll tell you my news tomorrow."

"No hurry." Arden wasn't in a rush to hear her announce she was getting back together with Toby. *It doesn't make a whit of difference to me either way*, he thought bitterly, even though he'd been consumed by the possibility all day long...and even though the reality kept him rolling from one side to the other throughout the night, too.

In the morning he was surprised when his mother told Grace that Tuesday was their turn to spend a day and night with Aquilla.

"Tuesday? That's when you have your appointment with the rheumatologist," Arden reminded her.

"You were supposed to cancel that for me."

"I didn't because… Didn't Rachel talk to you about it?"

"*Neh.* Why would she? If the *dokder* doesn't receive forty-eight business hours' notice for cancellations, they charge a fee. Now I *have* to keep the appointment. I hope I can find someone to switch days with me at Aquilla's *haus*," his mother fretted. "I wish you would have kept your word, Arden."

"I'm sorry, *Mamm*," Arden apologized, begrudgingly wondering why Rachel hadn't kept *her* word to speak to his mother. Then he remembered: the two women had probably been too busy discussing his so-called dyslexia. *Oh well, that's water over the dam now*, he conceded. *At least* Mamm*'s still going to the doctor.*

When he got to the workshop, Arden received the call he'd been expecting. Before disconnecting, the customer informed him he'd tried to leave a message the evening before, but the voice-mail box was full. So Arden listened to the old messages to determine which ones he could safely delete. That's when he heard it: an urgent warning from the bank manager indicating they had until noon on Friday to avoid bouncing the check Ivan had written to the hospital. *How could we be short that much?* Arden was stumped, and his hairline and upper lip beaded with sweat. *Rachel assured me we were in the black.*

He opened the ledger and did his best to review the entries, but there were so many abbreviations and acronyms his vision blurred. Whatever had happened, it had to be his fault, since Rachel was fastidious about her calculations. But how could anything he'd done cause such a big discrepancy? Since Ivan had been sick, Arden had only written a handful of checks, and those were never for more than a couple hundred dollars—with the exception of the check he wrote to Knight's for the cedar two-by-sixes. But he'd told her about that and surely she'd recorded it, hadn't she?

His hands trembling, he thumbed through the ledger, scanning it first for the figure, which was easier for him to recognize than the product code. It wasn't there. He searched again and again one more time, unable to believe Rachel hadn't recorded it. *No wonder she thought we had more than enough funds to cover Ivan's bill.* At the time, Arden hadn't understood how that could possibly be the case, but since he was used to being the one to make errors and Rachel was so smart, he assumed she'd been right. Now he almost wished he *had* been the one who'd made the mistake. Rachel was so conscientious about protecting Ivan's health; she was going to be devastated to learn she'd caused harm to his business. Even worse than being charged an overdraft fee and blemishing their record at the bank was the possibility the hospital might not allow a discount now, since the check had bounced. Arden shut his eyes and prayed, *Please,* Gott, *if it's not too late, help me think of a solution to prevent that from happening.*

"Somebody must have stayed out too late last night," Rachel said, gently touching his shoulder. "Were you asleep or are you coming down with something?"

"Neh, I—I—I," he stuttered. "I'm afraid I have something upsetting to discuss with you." To Arden's surprise, after telling her about the bank, Rachel smiled.

"Phew. I thought you were going to tell me your *mamm* was sick. I've already covered the deficit. It's all set for now."

"Y-you covered it? C-covered it, how?"

Rachel picked at her thumbnail. "I transferred funds from my personal account. I, uh, I'd been saving up for tuition, but, well, my big news was that I decided I don't want to go back to school, so… I was in a position of being able to cover the deficit."

As relieved as he was the business wouldn't be fined and the hospital would be paid on time, Arden felt profoundly disappointed Rachel had tried to hide her mistake like that. Why hadn't she told him about it? Was she too proud to admit she made an error? "When were you going to *kumme* clean about this?"

"*Kumme* clean?" Rachel narrowed her eyes. "You make it sound as if I should be ashamed. I wasn't trying to deceive you, Arden. I was trying to *help* you. Sometimes when people struggle with language or reading and writing, they also have challenges with math and I didn't want you to feel bad. Especially because we were celebra—"

"Whoa!" Arden sputtered. "You are unbelievable! You assume because I have a problem with words, this accounting error has to be my fault, too?"

"*Neh*, I didn't assume this was your fault because of

anything other than the fact I've scrutinized the figures in the ledger a dozen times and everything adds up, so this had to have been an error that occurred before I got here. It couldn't have been Ivan, since he was ill, so it had to be you."

"Of all the condescending, self-satisfied, disparaging things you've ever said, *that* takes the cake!" Arden jumped up and stomped halfway across the workshop before he stopped, swiveled around and shouted, "Let me tell you something, lady! Even if I had made an error, I don't need you to protect me from the truth. I've been making errors and living up to the consequences most of my life! Trying to protect me from my own mistakes is not how you treat a man—it's how you treat a *kind*. Or someone you pity."

"I wasn't going to keep it from you, and I wasn't being condescending," Rachel cut in. "I covered the deficit because I care about you and Ivan and your business."

She tried to say more, but Arden wouldn't let her. "You want to know the great irony here, Rachel? I actually did think I was the one who made the error. That was my first thought—and apparently, it was your first thought, too. But here's the kicker—*you* were the one who made the mistake. It was *your* fault, not mine, so don't you dare act as if you were doing *me* any favors!"

Rachel pulled her chin back, her eyes wide with bewilderment. "*My* fault?"

"*Jah*, as hard as that might be for you to accept. You never recorded the payment I made to Knight's for a surplus shipment of two-by-sixes after I expressly asked you to."

She shook her head and furrowed her eyebrows. "I don't remember you asking me to do that—"

"*Neh*, and you didn't remember to talk to my *mamm* about keeping her appointment, either. But one thing I *can* do better than you, Rachel Blank, is remember. You were sitting right there at that desk and I told you we had a delivery from Knight's and we got a 10 percent discount. I said I wrote out a check but I didn't record the amount in the ledger yet. Then I said Mrs. McGregor wanted the playhouse completed a week early and I asked you to call our delivery guy and arrange for that. *Now* do you remember?"

Parts of what Arden said were vaguely coming back to Rachel, but his tirade was so venomous she could hardly think straight. "I suppose some of that sounds familiar," she said meekly.

Arden pounced on that, his voice booming through the workshop, "*That's* all you have to say for yourself? Not *I'm sorry*, not *I was really wrong*?"

"You aren't giving me a chance! And even if I did apologize right now, you wouldn't accept it. There's nothing about your demeanor that suggests you want to work this out—your entire intention is to tell me off. To put me in my place," she yelled back. "Well, let me tell *you* something, mister—for someone who's supposedly so humble, you're being thoroughly contemptuous!"

"And for someone who's supposed to be so *schmaert*, you're as dense as a brick!" Arden hurled the insult at her. "How did you ever manage to get into an MSN program when you can't even remember something as simple as telling a patient to go to the *dokder*?"

Her voice dripping with sarcasm, Rachel sniped, "Gee, Arden, I don't know. Maybe the *Englisch* are just more forgiving of my mistakes than the Amish are."

Arden's face was so red it was tinged with blue. "Then maybe you should just go back to the *Englisch* already, because as we've all seen, you don't fit in here!"

"I'd rather fit in with *Englischers* who are forgiving than Amish hypocrites like you and my *bruder* and sister-in-law," Rachel retorted before she spun on her heel and tromped out, slamming the door behind her so hard the building shook.

Chapter Eleven

Too angry to drive and too upset to let Ivan see her in this state, Rachel couldn't go back into the house, so she marched across the lawn toward the edge of the property. She and her brothers had blazed a trail through the woods leading from their house up a rocky incline to the southern end of the ridge that inspired Serenity Ridge's name. The path wasn't as well-worn as when Rachel left, so she found a large stick and hacked away at the spring underbrush, her vision blurred with tears.

How could I have ever imagined I was falling for Arden—or wanted to kiss him! He's even more critical than Toby, Rachel thought as she progressed deeper into the forest. Even if she'd made a mistake with the bookkeeping, she'd covered the deficit with her own money, so she would have thought he'd be grateful for her help, not pious about her error. She yelped as a black fly bit her upper shoulder; she'd forgotten how much pain those little critters could inflict. *That's one more thing I won't miss when I go back to Boston.*

Recalling Arden saying she didn't fit in and suggesting she leave now, Rachel shoved a thick tree limb off the path with her heel. *Nothing is going to get in the way of where I want to go or what I want to do,* she thought. But where and what *was* that? Just last night she'd imagined not only staying in Serenity Ridge indefinitely but rejoining the Amish and being baptized into the church. She'd even hinted at her plans to Toby over the phone.

He'd begun their conversation apologizing for dating Brianna behind Rachel's back and then asked if she'd consider seeing him again. Rachel said she'd already forgiven him, but that she wasn't interested in a relationship; that's when she let it slip she was contemplating staying in Maine among the Amish permanently.

He'd argued, "You can't live up to your potential there, Rachel."

"*Neh,* I can't live up to *your* expectations of me here," she countered. "But I *can* try to follow *Gott*'s plan for my life. And that's what I want more than anything."

"But you love being a nurse. You've said it hundreds of times."

"I think… I think I love being Amish more. Besides, I can still take care of people in my family and community in an unofficial capacity."

"You mean without getting paid for it?"

"There are more important things in life than money and prestige, Toby," Rachel scolded, only half-seriously. She knew Toby had deep faith in God, even if his recent behavior had been less than honest.

"Like what, sticky buns and *yumsetta* casserole?" he grumbled.

"Exactly!" Rachel laughed, glad they were ending

things on a better note the second time around, and saying her intention aloud made her gain confidence she was on the right track—returning to her Amish roots seemed to be what the Lord was leading her to do.

Her own words came back to her now: "I think I love being Amish more." The problem was, as Arden so cruelly pointed out, the Amish apparently didn't love her. Or at least, several of the Amish people she cared most about—which until today had included Arden—didn't want her around.

She slapped her neck, and a fly fell to the ground. A few feet ahead, a tree had fallen across her path, and she didn't know whether to climb over it or turn around and go back. *Where* am *I anyway?* She thought she knew, but now she wasn't so certain. Once, after she'd gotten lost in the woods as a girl, Colin had told her if it ever happened again, she should sit down and wait to be rescued. Too hot, itchy and tired to continue, Rachel leaned against the fallen tree. *Lord,* she prayed, *please guide my next steps*—all *of them.*

After a couple of hours, Arden's temper had cooled enough that he was able to devise a plan so he wouldn't have to work with Rachel any longer. First chance he got to speak to Ivan alone, he was going to tell him what Rachel had done. Her mistake could have cost their business and their reputation—with the hospital, as well as the bank—too much to allow her to continue managing the paperwork and bookkeeping. As an equal partner, Arden had decided it was time they either hired a temporary *Englisch* administrative assistant or recruited someone from the Amish community. *Who knows, Rachel's so arrogant this change might offend her so much she'll decide she's leaving Serenity Ridge before Ivan recovers. If so, Grace will be able to take care of him now that* Mamm *is well again...*

The more he thought about his plan, the more anxious he became to implement it. He would've gone to the house and told Ivan right then if it weren't that he couldn't stand the sight of Rachel. As it turned out, Ivan rambled into the workshop right before he left for the day at one o'clock. Arden figured Rachel had already given her brother her skewed version of what occurred.

"Feels *gut* to be in here again," Ivan said, inhaling. "Rachel's concerned about the sawdust irritating my lungs, but I've missed the smell. Where is she, anyway?"

Arden scrunched his forehead. "She left here a couple hours ago. I thought she went to the *haus*."

"*Neh*, and her car's still in the driveway."

"She must have gone for a walk. She, uh, was kind of upset. She made a pretty big error," Arden began. He delved into an account of what had transpired with the check for the hospital bill as impartially as he could, sticking to the details and refraining from suggesting they replace Rachel until Ivan had a chance to absorb the gravity of her mistake.

"You think my *schweschder* was upset she had to use her money to cover our deficit?"

Arden was surprised it didn't seem to be sinking in. "*Neh*, she said she had that money available because she decided not to enroll at the university. Besides, we'll pay her back. I think she was embarrassed she made such a potentially destructive mistake. And I have to confess, I expressed my displeasure she didn't tell me about it sooner."

"*Jah*, that was a big burden for her to bear on her own. I wish she would have told *me*, too. I suppose since we put her in charge of bookkeeping, she must have felt responsible for straightening it out with the bank manager."

Arden was dumbfounded; couldn't Ivan understand how careless Rachel had been? "I think it might be time to find someone else to manage our accounting."

"I agree. Someone who doesn't care about me— about *us*—so much wouldn't have given up their savings like Rachel did. I'd rather we hire an *Englisch* stranger than put her in that position. The only thing that puzzles me is how we got so far behind in the first place. You've been filling orders day and night, according to Rachel. Have customers been remiss in paying us?"

Arden felt as if he'd been whacked upside his head with a two-by-four. No—a two-by-*six*. And well he should have, for tearing into Rachel when the very reason she'd had to cover the debt was because of the mistake *he'd* made first. "I, uh, I'm afraid I, uh, ordered too much cedar. It set us back and I—I—I—I didn't want to have to pay the return fee, so I accepted the delivery."

Ivan nodded slowly. "Ah, I see. Well, we all make mistakes, and I'm sure we'll use the wood and profit from it soon. We'll work with Rachel to figure out a suitable repayment plan meanwhile."

"*Jah,*" Arden said, but in light of Ivan's grace, he felt so ashamed the word was barely audible.

"Anyway, I came to tell you your *schweschder* called

Rachel's cell phone from the phone shanty. She tried to call here but kept getting voice mail."

"I didn't hear it ring. Is my *mamm* okay?"

"*Jah*, but the two of them are making *supp* to take to Aquilla tomorrow, and they want you to pick up a set of freezable containers."

"Okay," Arden agreed. But his feet were leaden as he put away his tools and swept up the sawdust. His heart was heavy, too, with the awareness that every single insult he'd cast at Rachel—that she was condescending, self-satisfied and disparaging—was doubly true about *him*.

He dropped to his knees on the hard concrete floor. *Lord, I've been so proud and self-righteous. Please forgive me. Please help me to make amends with Rachel, and for her to forgive me, too. Wherever she is right now, please protect her heart from the rancor of my words.*

By the time Rachel returned home, she had a dozen fly bites on her neck and face, her dress was damp with sweat, and she was parched. She assumed Ivan would be taking his afternoon nap, but instead he threw open the screen door the moment her foot touched the first step.

"Rachel, I've been worried sick about you!" His sentiment caused her to break down in tears—at least *one* person in Serenity Ridge loved her. He insisted she sit on the porch swing while he brought her a glass of water and a cold compress. Sitting beside her, he wrapped his arm around her shoulders.

"I'm smelly," she apologized, but he drew her closer.

"Arden told me what you did for us. I'm grateful, Rachel—but also sorry you felt so responsible as to take on our debt. I promise we'll pay you back as quickly as we can."

While it didn't surprise her that Ivan had a different response to her actions than Arden did, she wondered what Arden had told him about their heated exchange. "I know you will, but as I said to Arden, I couldn't think of a better use of my savings than putting the money toward your hospital costs. I'd do it again in a heartbeat."

"But are you absolutely certain you don't want to become a nurse practitioner?"

"I've never been more certain about a decision in my life—except when Toby asked me to get back together last night and I said *neh*," she replied. *It's the decision about whether or not I should stay here I'm confused about.*

"He did?"

"*Jah*, but can we talk more about this later? I need to take a shower."

"You do that, and I'll warm some *supp*. We'll have an early supper."

Rachel groaned. "I don't know if I can swallow another spoonful of *supp*. Do you suppose you'd go with me to get pizza tonight?"

"In your car?"

"*Jah*. I'm too tired to hitch the horse and buggy."

"In that case, can we go to a fast food drive-through? I'm craving a burger and fries."

"Oh, and a nice, cold extra-large strawberry shake!"

Later, as they ate their takeout meals in the park, they didn't talk about anything more serious than old memories—bowling at the *Englisch* bowling alley, playing volleyball in the backyard, their father's rich singing voice and their mother's contagious laugh. Yet these lighthearted remembrances stirred a deep longing within Rachel's heart, and by the time they got home, she felt so emotionally and physically depleted she actually went to bed before Ivan did.

Long after he should have been asleep, Arden was mulling over how angry he'd gotten at Rachel. He'd suffered more than his fair share of derision before, but it had never provoked him the way it did when he thought Rachel was scorning him. To think, he'd gone so far as to devise a plan to force her out of her voluntary role in her brother's business! *What if Ivan* does *propose she relinquish her work in the business?* That might be just the impetus she needed to leave early. To go back to Toby. The thought made him shudder.

Whether she gets back together with him or not is beside the point. All I care about is reconciling with her. For as long or short of a time as Rachel had left in Serenity Ridge, Arden wanted their friendship to be like it was before... No, that wasn't the full truth. He wanted their relationship to be *better* than it was before: he wanted to admit to Rachel how he felt about her—which was unlike how he'd ever felt about any woman. But he could scarcely admit those feelings to himself, knowing he couldn't act on them. Not just because Rachel was *Englisch*, but because he could never get married, never have children. And since that was an impossibility, the best he could hope for was that the rest of his time with Rachel would be as good as their time together up until he'd acted like a genuine *dummkopf*.

Despite having a sleepless night, Arden woke early, milked the cow, ate and quickly got ready for church. He hoped to speak to Rachel before he and Ivan left, but her car wasn't in the driveway, and Ivan came out of the house alone.

"My *schweschder* made me wear it," he explained, sheepishly pointing to the blue paper mask covering his face. "She's concerned people might get too close."

She was right. During the after-church lunch, so many people gathered around Ivan that he and Arden were among the last to leave. By the time they got to Ivan's house, Colin and Hadassah's buggy was in the driveway, but Rachel's car was not. "Ah, there's Hadassah and the *kinner*. She said they'd visit. She felt bad about forgetting my birthday," Ivan explained.

Hadassah had brought all four children, and the two eldest were pushing the younger two across the lawn in a wheelbarrow. Hadassah was sitting on the bench beneath the peach tree. How in the world had she managed to get down from the buggy? She appeared to have gained an inordinate amount of weight—even her hands were swollen.

"*Kumme* out of the sun, Hadassah. I'll bring you lemonade," Ivan said, and Arden helped her up the porch stairs.

Arden knew he should allow Ivan and Hadassah to visit in private, but he wanted to stay until Rachel returned. Fortunately, she pulled into the driveway a few minutes later. She slowly strolled across the lawn, stopping to talk to the children at length, and Arden couldn't guess whether she was dawdling in order to avoid him or Hadassah.

"Hi, Rachel," he said at the same time Ivan greeted her.

"Hello," she replied to neither of them in particular. "Hello, Hadassah."

"Hello," Hadassah said with a sniff, angling her face away from the sun.

"How are you feeling?" Rachel scrutinized her sister-in-law.

"We don't have allergies anymore, if that's what you're worried about."

"*Neh*, I can see that." She paused. "That dress is a fetching color on you, but—and this is a concern, not a criticism—your…your face looks very swollen."

Hadassah turned and looked Rachel up and down. "*Jah*, and yours is covered in fly bites."

To Arden's surprise, Rachel laughed. "Isn't it awful? I feel like a pincushion, but I haven't got any witch hazel. I remember when you told me how soothing that is."

Hadassah's expression softened noticeably. "Especially if it's kept in the fridge." She squeezed her eyes shut.

"Do you have a *koppweh*?" Rachel was concerned; Arden could tell.

"*Jah*. It's been raining so much that my eyes aren't used to the sun anymore. I keep seeing flashing lights."

Ivan stopped rocking the porch swing, as if he was picking up on Rachel's uneasiness, too.

"I don't want to alarm you, but I think you ought to see a *dok*—a midwife."

"I *am* seeing my midwife on Tuesday."

"I mean now. I think we should call an ambulance—"

"Don't be *lecherich*." Hadassah shifted to her side and pushed off the chair, panting. It took her three tries to get into a standing position, and when she was upright, she wobbled forward. Arden reflexively jumped up and steadied her by her elbow. "I came here to wish my brother-in-law a *hallich* birthday, not to be lectured about my health."

Before Hadassah could take another step, Rachel grabbed each side of the railing, barring her from leaving. Her voice was low but firm as she said, "Hadassah, you're a *wunderbaar mamm*, and I know how much you love all of your *kinner* as well as the two *bobblin* you're carrying. For their sakes, you must go to the hospital now. You have all the signs of a life-threatening condition. Please, I am begging you, please don't reject this advice just because it's coming from me. I know what it's like to lose my *mamm*—please don't allow that to happen to your *kinner*. Please don't leave my *bruder* a widower."

Hadassah grimaced. "Okay," she agreed, causing Arden to marvel at Rachel's gift of persuasion once again.

Rachel began issuing orders. "Ivan, get my phone from my purse and call nine-one-one. Tell them Hadassah has signs of preeclampsia, and it's a multiple pregnancy—how far along are you, Hadassah?" Rachel questioned before instructing Ivan what else to say. "Arden and I will help you inside, Hadassah. You need to lie on your left side."

"Can't you take her in your car?" Arden asked. "I think I can carry her if I need to. It will be faster."

"*Neh.* The paramedic will start an IV if necessary, and they'll be able to administer medication quicker than I'd be able to drive to the hospital."

They couldn't all get through the door at the same time, so Arden entered sideways, supporting Hadassah by himself. Before they were across the threshold, the children had assembled on the porch, apparently sensing the crisis.

"Is *Mamm* okay?" the oldest asked.

"She has a bad *koppweh*," Rachel calmly explained over her shoulder. "An ambulance is coming to take her to the hospital, where they're going to help her feel better. I'll get your *daed* and bring him to the hospital, too. I'd like you to stay here with your *onkel* Ivan and make sure he takes it easy. If you play a quiet board game with him, you may all have a glass of lemonade and a piece of cake."

The children expressed their agreement as Ivan provided an address to the dispatcher. As soon as Hadassah was situated on the bed, Rachel directed Arden to bring her the first aid kit from her car so she could take her sister-in-law's blood pressure. Silently praying as she worked, she'd just begun to inflate the cuff when the ambulance siren blared outside. Rachel stayed with Hadassah until the paramedic and EMT rolled her on a stretcher into the ambulance. "I'm going to go get Colin now, Hadassah. We'll see you very soon."

When she arrived at Colin's home, she immediately spotted him on the front porch with Eva and Ike Renno. Wasting no time with pleasantries, Rachel beckoned to him, urging, "Colin, you must *kumme* with me. Hadassah's been taken to the hospital by ambulance."

"We'll go get the *kinner*," Eva volunteered. "I'll stay with them here at the *haus* as long as needed."

As they drove, Rachel explained she suspected Hadassah had moderate to severe preeclampsia. "It's a very serious condition. They may induce labor, but most likely she'll need an emergency C-section." Rachel stole a sideways glance at Colin. A single tear ran down his cheek, like a crack in a stone wall. She reached over and squeezed his fist.

"Please, *Gott*, watch over my wife and our *bobblin*," he began praying. "Please, *Gott*, please."

He continued to pray, and Rachel silently echoed his prayers all the way to the hospital, where she dropped him off at the entrance and then went to park. By the time she got inside, Colin had already been taken to be with Hadassah, who was, indeed, undergoing an emergency C-section. It seemed like forever before Colin came to find Rachel in the waiting room. The blue scrubs were a stark contrast with his traditional Amish clothing, and his skin was sallow and his eyes were bloodshot. Rachel's heart pummeled her ribs.

"They made it. All three of them," he said. "My wife and two *seh*."

Rachel gasped, erupting into tears of joy. "*Denki*, Lord!" she uttered as Colin enveloped her.

"I'm sorry, Rachel," he said when he let her go, and at first she thought he meant for squeezing her so tightly. "*Mamm* and *Daed* put me in charge of watching over our *familye*. When you left, I…"

He couldn't finish his sentence, nor did he need to. Rachel understood; his anger about her leaving had been masking his disappointment in himself and concern for her. Similarly, his criticism of Ivan's business wasn't because he wanted to be in control; it was because he wanted to protect Ivan from failure. Until now, Rachel had only seen the austerity of Colin's actions, not the sense of fraternal responsibility behind his intentions, just as he'd only seen pride, not her desire to help others, when she left to become a nurse. "I understand, Colin. I'm sorry, too."

After Eva and Ike came for the children and buggy, Arden arranged for a taxi to take him and Ivan to the hospital. They were deeply grateful to learn Hadassah and the babies were all right. Since there was a limit on the number of visitors who could enter the NICU room, Rachel came out so Ivan and Arden could see the babies once they'd washed their hands and put on sterile gowns and gloves. Although Colin's mouth was obscured by a paper mask, Arden could tell by the way his eyes twinkled he was grinning.

"There's Jacob, and this is Daniel," he said, pointing to where the babies slept in separate incubators.

"I know how that feels, *buwe*," Ivan joked about the skinny oxygen tubes strapped to their noses.

"They're so tiny," Arden said. "But praise the Lord they're okay."

"*Jah*. The *dokder* warned us about a host of conditions they might face in the coming years because of being born so early, but that's in the future. Just look at them. They are alive. They are *Gott*'s gift to us."

As he listened to Colin's expression of fatherly love, it occurred to Arden his own father must have felt the same way when he was born. Arden hadn't ever really thought about it before, but surely his dad knew his son and daughter might suffer the same difficulties he himself had suffered. Yet that foreknowledge hadn't prevented him from getting married, having children and cherishing them as gifts from the Lord. *Why should I let it stop me?* As Daniel waved his fist and began to cry, Arden wiped his own eyes, overcome by a rush of emotion.

A nurse entered the room and chased Ivan and Arden out to the hall, where Rachel was conferring with a midwife. Arden overheard her giving the woman her cell phone number, and then she drove Ivan and Arden back to Ivan's home. She was so eager to go tell her nieces and nephews about their new baby brothers she didn't even turn off the car when she dropped the men off, so Arden didn't get a chance to apologize to her in private.

"Uh, Grace can *kumme* early in the morning to stay with Ivan if you want to go to the hospital," he said before shutting the door.

"*Denki*, I'd appreciate that," she replied in a tone that was neither unfriendly nor warm.

Grace seemed pleased for an excuse to visit with Ivan again, and the next morning she collected the eggs and milked the cow before Arden awoke. "I'll make breakfast at Ivan's *haus*, so Rachel gets sustenance since she probably didn't eat much yesterday."

Within an hour the four of them sat down to a hearty breakfast casserole, toast and coffee. "What happened to your face?" Grace asked Rachel. The small red spots Hadassah had pointed out the previous afternoon had grown into welts overnight.

"I took a walk in the woods Saturday. I was swarmed by black flies."

So that's where she was. Arden cringed, knowing

he was the cause of both her emotional and physical irritation.

"We never got to hear your news the other night after Toby called. Was he part of what you were going to tell us?" Grace questioned.

"Toby? *Neh*. He was calling to…to reconcile." Rachel dabbed her mouth with a napkin.

"He's going to be your suitor again? I mean, to date you?" Grace pushed. "Was that your news?"

"*Neh*, he's not. My news was that I got accepted into the MSN program."

"That's *wunderbaar*!" Grace exclaimed. "Isn't that *wunderbaar*, Ivan and Arden?"

"*Jah*," they agreed, even though they both already knew. *But what's more* wunderbaar *is that Rachel's not getting back together with Toby*, Arden thought.

"*Denki*, but I've decided not to go," Rachel said.

"You're not going?" Grace sounded perplexed.

"*Neh*. I decided becoming a nurse practitioner wasn't…it wasn't really how the Lord was directing my steps. Anyway, I'd better get going. I'm sure Colin is itching to have me bring him a fresh change of clothing," Rachel said, pushing her chair away from the table. She hadn't taken more than three bites of her meal, but she felt too self-conscious in Arden's presence to eat. After experiencing an emergency like yesterday's, she was keenly aware of how petty it was to continue harboring ill will toward him.

The night before as she was reflecting on her conversation with Colin, it had occurred to Rachel that her brother might have meant to be helpful the day he suggested Rachel should go back to Boston and he could help Arden with the accounting. *I accused Colin of trying to take over Ivan's business, yet that's exactly what I did by covering the deficit. Even if my intentions were* gut *or I was pressed for time, I should have discussed it with Arden first.* She wanted to apologize, but she'd need privacy for that. Until then, she had a busy morning in front of her.

When she arrived at the hospital, Daniel and Jacob were asleep and Hadassah looked exhausted, too, so Rachel kept her visit short. Right before she left, Hadassah suggested Colin go change into the clean clothing Rachel had brought, so they could have a moment alone to chat.

No sooner did the door close behind him than Hadassah apologized. "I've been *baremlich* to you, Rachel, and I'm so sorry."

"It's okay. Some of that might have been from feeling ill or from hormones. During pregnancy, your estrogen and progesterone levels—" Rachel stopped. "Oops, sometimes I can't help myself."

"It's *gut* to share what you've learned. If you hadn't, I might not be alive now and neither would the *bobblin,*" Hadassah said. "But it wasn't illness or hormones—I've acted this way toward you for over ten years. I was so... so hurt when you left. I know how demanding I can be, but instead of blaming myself for your leaving, I blamed you. I said it was *hochmut.*"

Until now, it never dawned on Rachel that Hadassah thought she'd left because of *her.* "Hadassah, I didn't leave to get away from anything or anyone—I was going *toward* what I believed was *Gott's* will for me at that time. If anything, you were one of the very people who made me so reluctant to go—I consider you to be my older sister. And older sisters are supposed to be bossy."

"Well, younger sisters are supposed to be spoiled." They were both laughing when Colin reentered the room.

"Did you ask her yet?" he questioned Hadassah. When she shook her head, Colin said, "We, uh, we were wondering if you might be able to stay in Serenity Ridge a little longer than you planned? The staff here has suggested we line up a visiting nurse for the next couple of months to give us a hand…"

Rachel was stunned silent, so Hadassah interjected, "We promise not to pressure you to leave the *Englisch*."

Because she'd spoken about leaving the Amish so often, the notion of leaving the *Englisch* struck Rachel as funny, and she smiled. "I appreciate that, but I'd like a little time to think it over."

She didn't get any farther than the parking lot before she unequivocally knew what her decision would be. Leaning against her car, she dialed Meg's number to break the news to her. "You were right, Meg. I'm staying here," she blurted out without even saying hello first. "I'm returning to my Amish faith and lifestyle for *gut*."

"Oh, Rachel," her dear friend said with a sigh. "In your heart, you never really *left* the Amish for *gut*."

Although it was raining, as his sister prepared lunch, Arden waited outside on the porch in case a customer or delivery truck came by. Instead, it was Rachel's car that turned into the driveway. Arden shot across the lawn quicker than she could get out and close the door.

"Rachel, I owe you an apology," he began. As she looked up at him, wide-eyed, raindrops ran in tiny rivulets over the bright wheals on her face. "I—I—I am so ashamed of h-how I spoke to you yesterday. Everything I said was—was truer of me than of you. I was the one who m-made the m-mistake in the first place, but instead of being grateful for your help, I was rude and unkind. *Neh*—I was vicious."

She shook her head, and his hope for reconciliation crumbled until she said, "I forgive you, Arden, but I shouldn't have made that kind of decision without consulting you and Ivan. I can see now how patronizing my actions were. I'm very sorry."

"At least you were trying to be helpful. I was trying to be *hurt*ful, because…well, because *I* felt hurt." Although the rain was warm on his scalp and back, Arden shivered as he confessed, "I was also envious."

"Of what?"

"Of Toby."

"Why would you be envious of someone like *him*?"

Arden coughed, stalling. "He's so *schmaert* and—"

"And so are you! I meant it when I told you you're one of the smartest people I know."

"It isn't just that Toby's *schmaert*." A wet curl stuck to Arden's forehead, and he pushed it aside. "It's also th-that he symbolized something I thought I could never have."

"Such as?"

Arden couldn't face her. He looked over her shoulder, focusing on the trees in the distance. "M-marriage."

* * *

To whom? Rachel felt her insides melting like wax. Arden couldn't possibly mean *her*? "What's stopping you from getting married?"

"Nothing is now. But *I* w-was stopping myself before," Arden said. "I thought I should-shouldn't get married be-because my *kinner* w-would have the same problems I have."

"That's a possibility, but it's not an absolute. As you once said to me about my caring for Ivan, who would be better equipped to help that child than you?"

"I—I know that now. I figured it out when I saw how thrilled Colin was about his *bobblin*…"

Rachel giggled. "*Jah*, I didn't know he could still smile like that."

"Arden! Rachel! What are you doing out in the rain? Lunch is ready," Grace summoned them from the porch.

"We're coming." Rachel was disappointed their conversation had been interrupted, but she hoped they'd pick up where they left off once they had privacy again. When they got inside, they dried off and seated themselves at the table.

"I hope *rivel supp* is okay. *Mamm* and I were making it for Aquilla, so we figured we might as well make some for you, too," Grace said, and Ivan smiled politely.

After they'd thanked God for the meal, Rachel announced she had something for the other three to consider. "Grace, if your *mamm*'s health is stable and if Ivan and Arden agree to it, in a few days would you be willing to take over for me at the workshop on an ongoing basis—and check in on Ivan occasionally, too?"

Arden dropped the saltshaker right into his soup,

spraying chowder everywhere. "You w-w-won't be wo-working at the shop anymore?"

"I don't know." Rachel handed him a spare napkin, but he made no attempt to mop up the spill. "Hadassah and Colin have asked me to help them for a couple of months once she and the *bobblin* are discharged. I'd like to do it, but Ivan won't be able to return to work for a while, and I don't want to leave the two of you in the lurch, which is why I thought Grace might be—"

"I'd be *hallich* to step in," Grace said.

Ivan simultaneously remarked, "Hadassah needs you more than we do."

"Jah," Arden agreed as he fished the saltshaker from his chowder. "You definitely should help Hadassah and the *bobblin*. It's a better use of your skills."

Rachel wasn't expecting everyone to be quite so enthusiastic about her relinquishing her position at the workshop. She had intended to tell them about her decision to be baptized into the Amish church, too, but what if they weren't receptive to the idea? Suddenly she could hardly fight back the tears. *"Gut*, it's settled then. If you'll excuse me, these clothes are wetter than I thought and I'm uncomfortable in them. I'll go change."

Upstairs she kicked off her shoes and curled into a ball, quietly weeping into a pillow. She understood that even if Arden had the smallest romantic inclination toward her, he wouldn't have been likely to express it. Not while she was still *Englisch*. But did he have to seem so happy she wouldn't be working with him any longer? *And to think, I dared hope when he was talking about wanting to get married, he might have had me in mind—which just goes to show how much* hochmut *I really do have!*

She didn't remember falling asleep, but when she awoke, she changed into her lavender dress, went into the bathroom and splashed cold water over her face in an attempt to soothe her swollen eyelids and ease the sting of her bug bites. Downstairs she found the table had been cleared, Grace was gone and Ivan was taking a nap. Instead of soup, she opted to have a glass of lemonade. As she was putting the pitcher back in the fridge, she noticed a brown paper bag with her name on it. Inside was a bottle of witch hazel and a note.

Rachel,
Hadassah needs you so I can't be selfish, but I will miss you in the workshop. I wish you could stay in Serenity Ridge forever.
Arden

Rachel hugged the bottle to her chest as she reread the note three times. Then she put the witch hazel back in the fridge and, with every ounce of restraint she could muster, slowly picked her way around the puddles as she walked toward the workshop. The sun was breaking through the clouds, and once again, Arden's eyes mirrored the blue of the sky as he stepped outside. It was as if he'd been waiting for her.

Glancing at the note in her hand, he said, "As you know, I'm not very *gut* with words."

"This is the best *liebesbrief* I've ever received," Rachel gushed, and then she was immediately embarrassed she'd referred to it as a love letter. Was that how Arden had intended it?

"*Gut*, because it's the best—and the only—*liebes-brief* I've ever written," he replied, and for now, that was all he needed to say.

Epilogue

"Are you enjoying your work as a midwife's assistant?" Sadie Swarey asked Rachel.

"I can't think of anything else I'd rather do. It must have been *Gott*'s plan for me to be here when the twins were born—otherwise I might never have found out the *Englisch* midwives desperately needed an Amish person to work with them in Serenity Ridge."

"*Ach!* Speaking of twins, look—mine are getting in line for a third piece of *hochzich* cake." Sadie waved a finger at her two children, Elizabeth and David, across the church's gathering room. "*Gott segen*, Arden and Rachel."

After she walked away, Meg came over to where they were standing. "Rachel, you're glowing!" she remarked. "Oops, is that not allowed? Are compliments considered *hochmut*?"

Arden shrugged. "I hope not, because I keep telling Rachel the same thing."

"*Denki*," Rachel said to them both. "I'm so glad you took time off to be here, Meg."

"I wouldn't have missed it for anything. Although I feel a little out of place. Am I the only *Englischer* here?"

"*Neh.* The Jones *familye* is *Englisch.*"

"Did I hear you mentioning my name?" Chris Jones sauntered in their direction, grinning.

"*Jah.* Chris, meet Meg. She's my *gut* friend, and up until seven months ago, she was my roommate, too."

"Hello, Meg. If you'd like, I can stick close by. We'll be fish out of water together."

"That would be nice." A blush settled over Meg's face.

As the pair edged toward the dessert table, Arden teased Rachel. "I didn't realize matchmaking was one of your vices. You're worse than my *mamm.*"

"But wouldn't it be wonderful if Meg and Chris fell in love, got married and were as *hallich* together as Ivan and Grace, or as you and I are?"

"I doubt anyone else could ever be *this hallich.*" Arden discreetly nuzzled Rachel's ear as he whispered, "I didn't know I could be this *hallich*, myself."

"Just wait until we have *bobblin.* You'll be overjoyed."

"I can hardly wait. And I can't wait any longer for this, either," he said, before surreptitiously kissing his bride.

* * * * *

A father of the fatherless...
God setteth the solitary in families.
—*Psalm* 68:5–6

Chapter One

Thomas Wiebe pushed himself to his feet and headed toward the side door to look out at the warm August evening. Low, golden sunlight washed over the grass, and birds twittered their evening songs. His jittery nerves didn't match the peaceful scene. The social services agent who had come by the night before had said that they'd be here by seven, and it was a quarter past already.

"Stop fussing, Thomas," Mammi said, pulling a boiling kettle from the woodstove. Her crisp, white *kapp* was a shade brighter than her white hair. "She'll come."

Thomas glanced back at his family in the kitchen. They weren't all blood relatives, but this was as close to family as he had left in the community of Redemption, Pennsylvania. His older brother, Noah, sat with a glass of lemonade in front of him, his straw hat on the table. Thomas and Noah were both old enough to be married with families of their own by now, but not having found the right wife meant that they stayed here with Uncle Amos—an honorary uncle, not a biological one—and his elderly grandmother. It was a house filled with men, as Mammi described it.

And any minute now, Thomas's daughter would be joining them… *His daughter.* He'd known about her, but he'd never been given the option to be in her life. Thomas had made a mistake with an Englisher girl on his lengthy Rumspringa, and the breakup had been messy. Tina wanted nothing more to do with him. It wasn't that he forgot about his daughter, but he'd accepted that heartbreak as part of the consequences for his mistakes. Coming back home to Redemption four years ago was supposed to be his new start. But when a social services agent came to his house last night and told him of a fatal car accident that killed his daughter's mother, everything had changed.

His daughter, Rue, was now coming to live with him after never having met him even once in her young life. Would she hate him just a little? He wouldn't blame her. But at the age of four, he wasn't sure how much she'd even understand about her new situation.

Outside, a car rumbled up the drive, and Thomas pulled open the screen door and stepped out onto the raised patio next to the house. A clothesline full of men's pants and shirts flapped in a warm breeze.

Thomas waited while the car stopped, the door opened and the social services agent from yesterday got out. She shot Thomas a smile and waved. She was an older woman, plump and pleasant. Tanya Davis, she'd said.

"Good evening, Mr. Wiebe!" Tanya called.

Thomas would do just fine, but he didn't trust himself to speak just yet. He came down the steps toward the car and glanced back to see Noah and Amos in the door. Tanya opened the back door to the car and leaned in, undoing the buckles from a children's car seat. Then she backed out again, followed by a small, frail child.

The little girl stood there, a teddy bear clutched in front of her. She wore a pair of pink pants and a ruffled purple T-shirt. Her hair was stringy and blond, and she looked around herself with large, frightened blue eyes. She reminded him of a bedraggled bird.

Thomas came closer, unsure if he'd scare her or not.

"Hello," he said in English. He wasn't very eloquent in English... But then he wasn't very eloquent in German, either.

The little girl looked at him, silent.

"I'm your *daet*, it would seem," he said slowly. Then he realized she might not know the word. "I'm your... father."

"Hello, Mr. Wiebe." Tanya held out a hand and Thomas shook it. "Shall we go inside? Maybe you're hungry, Rue," Tanya said quietly, smiling down at the girl, then glancing up at Thomas.

"Yes, Mammi has made some sticky buns. She thought you might like that," Thomas said.

He turned around and led the way to the house, feeling that strange distance between himself and that little girl behind him. Rue had never met him, but he'd also never had a chance to even see her... He'd been a *daet*, but until this very moment, it had been theoretical. How was he supposed to do this—be a *daet* to an Englisher child? There was a time he thought he could be an Englisher himself, but that was when he was young and foolish, and he'd forgotten that it wasn't possible to change what a man was born to.

Tanya brought Rue indoors, and introductions were made. Amos. Noah. Mammi. Mammi's name was Mary Lapp, but she was never called Mary in this house. Rue stared silently around the room, looking stricken. Thomas sank down to his haunches in front of her.

"Hello, Rue," he said quietly.

"Hello..." she whispered.

"This is all very new, isn't it?" he said.

"Yes. I want my mommy..." Tears welled in her eyes, and Thomas reached out and patted her shoulder.

"Have you had a...daddy...before?" He hesitated over the English word. Had Tina moved on with another Englisher man? That was what he was asking.

"No, never," she whispered. His heart clenched. How much wrong had he done in that woman's life? He'd known better, and he wouldn't ever completely forgive himself for the way he'd conducted himself in that relationship.

"You'll call me Daet," he said softly. "And I'll take care of you. You'll be safe and happy here, *yah*?"

Rue wiped her eyes on her teddy bear and looked hesitantly around the kitchen again. Her bright pants and T-shirt were in stark contrast to their plain clothing.

"Where's the TV?" Rue whispered.

"We don't have a TV," he said.

"How come?" She frowned, peering past him as if he were hiding it somewhere, and Thomas couldn't help but smile.

"Because we're Amish, Rue. You'll get used to our ways."

It didn't seem to be the right thing to say because Rue's eyes filled with tears again, and he looked helplessly toward Amos and Noah. He wasn't quite so comforting for the little girl as he'd hoped, and he didn't know how to cross that divide.

"Thomas, pick her up," Mammi said, waving a hand at him. "She's just a tired little thing, and she needs to be held."

Thomas looked hesitantly around, and when Tanya nodded her approval of the idea, he gently picked Rue up and rose to his feet. She was light and small in his arms, and when he gathered her close, she leaned her little head against his shoulder and exhaled a shaky sigh. It was then that he felt it—that wave of protective love.

"All right, then," he murmured. "All right, then."

"Are you all set up for Rue to stay?" Tanya asked.

"Yes, she'll sleep in a little bed in Mammi's bedroom," Amos said, speaking up. "Mammi—" He hesitated. "That is, Grandma to us. So the child won't be alone."

"I'll take care of her with the washing and dressing and such," Mammi said. "She'll be well cared for."

"And we have another young woman coming to help," Amos added. "She'll arrive in a few minutes to meet Rue."

"It sounds like you're prepared, then," Tanya said. "I'll go get Rue's suitcase from the trunk."

The older woman disappeared out the door, the screen clattering back with a bang.

"So, the new schoolteacher said she'd help?" Thomas asked, shooting Uncle Amos a questioning look.

"She did," Amos replied. "I'm sorry, I meant to tell you. She's a nice young woman, too. You should take note—with a child, it's high time you get a wife."

As if Thomas could even think about courting right

now. He looked down into Rue's pale little face. The delicate skin under her eyes looked almost bruised from lack of sleep, and he reached up and brushed her hair away from her forehead. He was still taking her in, looking her over, trying to see himself in that little face. He could see her mother there—the hair, the eyes. Was he there, too? He must be, but it was hard to tell.

There was a tap on the door and Amos went to push open the screen. Thomas looked up, expecting to see the social services woman again, but this time a young Amish woman stepped inside. She wore a purple dress, and her apron was gleaming white. Her hair was golden—the part he could see before it disappeared under her *kapp*—and she smiled hesitantly, looking around the kitchen.

"This is Patience Flaud," Amos said. "She'll be teaching school here starting in September, and she's staying with the Kauffmans."

Hannah and Samuel Kauffman lived on the next acreage over, and Hannah and Mammi were good friends—they had coffee together at least twice a week and they'd been known to help each other out with canning and washing days.

Patience, however, was distinctly younger than old Hannah Kauffman…and prettier. Thomas swallowed.

"You asked me to help out?" Patience said.

"Yah," Thomas said, stepping forward with his daughter in his arms. "We haven't met yet. I'm Thomas Wiebe, and this is my daughter, Rue."

Patience smiled at the girl, cocking her head to one side. "Ruth, is it?" she asked in German.

"No, Rue. She's Englisher." As if her clothing wasn't

glaring enough. Thomas felt heat flood his face. "It's…
a long story. She doesn't know German. But she's mine,
and I'll need a woman's help."

"Besides me, of course," Mammi said. "I'm not as
young as I used to be, and I'm not sure I could chase
down *kinner* if the need arose. Safety, you know."

"Rue, then," Patience said, switching to English, and
her gaze flickered up to Thomas, sharpening slightly.
She'd have questions, no doubt. Everyone would, and his
reputation as a good, Amish man looking for a wife was
officially tarnished. He'd now be the Amish man with
an Englisher child looking for a wife—very different.

"Hello, Rue. I'm Patience," she said softly and she
glanced over to the table where the older woman had
set down a pan of cinnamon buns. "Are you hungry?
Mammi has some sticky buns."

Rue lifted her head from Thomas's shoulder and
looked toward the table.

"Have you ever had a grandmother before?" Patience
asked.

Rue shook her head.

"Well, you have one now. This is Mammi. *Mammies*
are kind and sweet and they cook the best food…" Patience bent down conspiratorially. "I'm glad to meet
your new *mammi*, too!"

Mammi smiled. "Come now, Rue," she said gently.
"I think you'll like my sticky buns."

Thomas put Rue back down and she went toward
the table, sidling up next to Mammi like a hurt animal
looking for protection. Mammi bent down to talk to
her, and Thomas heaved a sigh.

"She looks very sweet," Patience said, and Thomas

glanced over. Patience met his gaze with her clear blue eyes, and for a moment, he felt all the words clam up inside him. Why did the schoolteacher have to be so distractingly pretty?

"Yah," he said after a moment. "I've just met her, myself."

"How did that—" Patience stopped and blushed. "I mean, this is the first you've met her?"

"I had a rebellious Rumspringa," he said quietly. "One I learned from. I'm not proud of that."

In fact, he'd meant to keep the secret for the rest of his days, if he could. What use was it to the community to advertise his weakness? But that secret was no longer possible, and his mistakes were about to be very public.

"I'm not judging," she murmured.

But she was. Everyone would. Thomas would, too, if he were in their place. What did she think of him *now*?

The door opened again, and the social services woman came inside with a suitcase, and things turned official once more. There was discussion of dental visits, doctor's appointments and counseling for the family to help with the transition if they should feel the need.

"No," Thomas said, shaking his head. "We have our ways, and if there is one thing our people do, it's raise *kinner*. She'll be loved…dearly."

Emotion choked off his voice, and he forced a smile as he shook Tanya's hand in farewell.

"Congratulations, Mr. Wiebe," Tanya said. "You have a beautiful daughter."

"Thank you," he said.

That was the first anyone had congratulated him yet. Noah, Amos and Mammi had reassured him, but that was a different sentiment. In this community, Rue was a shock. Not only did Thomas have to confess to a rather large mistake in her conception, but he was bringing an Englisher child into their midst. The Amish understood the trouble he'd brought to everyone, and one did not congratulate a mess.

"I'm going to give you my phone number, and some information to help you in this transition," Tanya went on, and for the next few minutes, he attempted to grasp all that she was saying. The Englishers had their ways, but the Amish would pull together and deal with this the way they always had—with community. He accepted the pamphlets and brochures that she handed to him before walking out the door.

There were always consequences—to his own household and to the community. The Amish protected their boundaries for a reason—there were other young people who could be influenced. Their way of life was not only an act of worship, it was a wall between themselves and the world. He'd just brought a piece of the outside world into their midst in the form of his tiny daughter. There would be strong opinions, he had no doubt, and he couldn't blame his neighbors if they voiced them.

This was precisely why a man needed to behave himself before marriage, and now he must shoulder those consequences. Thomas stood there by the door for a moment as he listened to the social services agent start her car.

Gott, guide me, he prayed silently. *I know I went wrong out there in the world, but she's just a little mite, and… She's mine.*

He was Rue's *daet*. Nothing would ever be the same again.

* * *

Patience went into the kitchen and opened a cupboard, looking for the plates. Mammi stood at the table, slicing the cinnamon buns apart with a paring knife, but she'd need plates to serve them on. This was Patience's role in any Amish home—to help out in the kitchen. She didn't need to be asked, and she didn't need permission. She found the plates in the second cupboard that she checked, and she glanced over at the table to do a quick head count.

Thomas stood beside the table, and his gaze was trained on her. He was a good-looking man—tall with broad shoulders and dark eyes that could lock her down... But he didn't seem to see her, exactly. He seemed more to be deep in thought. And could she blame him? His life had just turned upside down.

Patience brought the plates to the table, and Mammi used the tip of the knife to pry up a cinnamon bun and plop it onto a plate. When she gave the first plate to Amos, he slid the cinnamon bun in front of Rue instead, and a smile lit up the girl's face.

The men were served first, so she accepted a cinnamon bun from Mammi and angled her steps around the table and over to where Thomas stood.

"For you," she said, holding out the plate.

"No, no..." Thomas shook his head. "You eat it."

Patience held the plate but didn't take a bite. "Are you all right, Thomas?"

He roused himself then. "*Yah.* I'm fine."

She followed his gaze to the little girl. Rue looked so out of place in her Englisher clothes. Pink and purple. And pants on a girl, too—it wasn't right. But all the same, Rue was such a slender little thing—her head looking almost too big for her body.

"She needs some dresses," Patience said.

"Yah." Thomas brightened. "The social services woman left all these Englisher clothes, but when we get her some proper Amish dresses, it will be better, won't it?"

"Yes," Patience said with confidence she didn't exactly feel. "I think so, at least."

Thomas relaxed a little. "Amos said you'd agreed to help us."

"It's no problem," she said. "For a week or two, at least."

Thomas nodded. "I'm grateful. This was a pretty big shock for me, so I'm not ready for...any of it."

"Understandable," she said.

"Would you be willing to do some sewing?" he asked, lowering his voice. "Because Mammi doesn't see as well as she used to—"

"I can sort out some girls' dresses," she replied with a small smile. "They're quick enough to sew."

"Rue doesn't know our ways, at all," Thomas said. "Rue's life, up until now, has been entirely English. I'm not even sure that her *mamm* told her who I was. Tina—Rue's *mamm*—didn't want me in her life, and I didn't have a whole lot of choice. I was coming home to rededicate my life to our faith, and Tina hated me."

So he *had* known of his daughter...

"Why did she hate you?" Patience asked, then she felt the heat hit her cheeks. This wasn't even remotely her business.

"Because I wanted to go home, and I didn't want

the life she did." Thomas looked away, pressing his lips together. He'd probably already told her more than he wanted to.

She had so many questions, but none of them were appropriate to pose. She'd been asked to come help, not to put her nose into another family's affairs.

"How can I help?" Patience asked quietly.

"I need my daughter to learn to be plain," he said. "And the sooner the better. I'll show her what I can, but she needs a woman to show her how an Amish woman acts. Mammi is getting old, and she can't chase down a four-year-old if she decides to bolt. I need Rue to know how to be one of us."

"That's a lot to ask," Patience said softly.

"I know. You're not here for this. You're here to teach school—" he began.

"No, I mean, it's a lot to ask of *her*," Patience said with a shake of her head. "She's very young, and only just lost her mother. We're all strangers to her, and she doesn't even speak our language. Teaching her to be Amish might be too much to ask of her. Right away, at least."

"What are you suggesting, then?" Thomas asked.

"That we just teach her that she's loved," Patience said. "The rest will come with time."

Thomas met her gaze, and his shoulders relaxed.

"Is that enough, do you think?" he asked.

"For now, yes." For as much as her opinion counted in this.

"And you would know *kinner*, wouldn't you?" he said. "How long have you been teaching?"

Patience dropped her gaze, suddenly uncomfortable.

"This will be my first position. I might not be much of an expert."

"Oh…" Thomas eyed her a little closer.

"I love *kinner*, though, and I really needed a fresh start."

"Why?"

It was a loaded question, because everyone knew that a girl didn't grow up longing to teach school. She grew up planning for her own husband and houseful of children. A girl didn't plan her life around a job—she planned her days around a home. And at twenty-three, Patience was very nearly an old maid. But she'd asked a few probing questions of her own, so she supposed she owed him an answer.

"There was a proposal," she admitted. "That I could not accept, and… It was better to come away, I thought."

"Oh…" He nodded. "I'm sorry."

Mammi approached with another plate, and Patience stepped back to allow the older woman to press the plate into Thomas's hands.

"Eat now," Mammi said, patting his arm gently. "It is what it is, Thomas. You still need to eat."

It was the same thing that Patience's mother had said when Patience had turned down Ruben Miller's proposal. Ruben's proposal had seemed quite ideal—he was widowed with five children of his own, all under the age of thirteen. And if Patience could be his wife, she could help him raise his *kinner*—a ready-made family. But when Ruben proposed, he'd spoken rather eloquently about the future babies they'd have together.

"Does it matter so much?" Patience had asked. "If

you have five children already, do more babies mean so very much to you?"

"Babies are blessings!" he'd said. "Patience, what is a marriage without *kinner* to bind you? You'll see—you'll want to have *kinner* of your own. And the *kinner* will want babies to play with, too. You're young. We could have another seven or eight before we're done."

Ruben had said it all with such a smile on his face that any other girl would have been swept off her feet in anticipation of all those babies, the children to raise, the family to grow. Patience's secret had been on the tip of her tongue, ready to reveal why the babies were a worry for her...

And she didn't tell him. She *should* have told him, perhaps. But she didn't.

"Eat," Mammi said, turning her attention to Patience, and the old woman tapped her plate meaningfully.

Patience peeled a piece of cinnamon bun and popped it into her mouth. Mammi was right, as was Patience's own mother. No matter what came a person's way, they were obligated to eat and keep up their strength. Because there was still work to be done—always more work.

"It will be better, Thomas," Mammi said, lowering her voice, even though she was speaking in German and Rue wouldn't understand. "When you marry and have more children, she'll be one of many. More children will nail her down properly. You'll see."

More children—yes, that was very likely the solution for Thomas Wiebe. If he got a good Amish wife and had more children, then Rue would grow up in a proper Amish household. She'd be an older sister. Responsibilities helped a child to feel like they belonged.

Hadn't that been Ruben's solution to any marital difficulties? And he wasn't alone. Amish people wanted children. Their lives and their faith revolved around the home. Even the rules of the Ordnung were set in place to keep families close together. Parents and children were the center of their lives.

Patience turned away from Thomas and Mammi, who continued to talk together, their voices low. She took another bite of the buttery, sweet cinnamon bun. She should have told Ruben the truth when he proposed—told him that she could not have any children of her own—because marrying a man who needed a *mamm* for his children was the perfect solution, if that man could be happy with no more babies. If she'd told Ruben the truth about the surgery to remove the tumors and how it left her infertile, would he have still married her? Patience hadn't been sure, and when faced with the older man's hopeful gaze, the words had died on her tongue.

Patience would never be a *mamm* to her own children. She'd never be pregnant or have babies. And she'd wanted nothing besides a family of her own since she was a girl. So she was grieving all that she was losing, too, and she hadn't had the strength to walk Ruben through it all. That surgery to remove the tumors might have saved her life, but it had ended any chance she had at living the life she longed for.

But work helped her not to think too much about the things she could not change, and teaching was supposed to provide that distraction for her. Until the teaching started, she could distract herself with this little Englisher child—there would be work enough to go around.

"Tomorrow, if you could find me some fabric, I could start making a dress or two for Rue," Patience said, turning back.

"Our carpentry shop is right next door to the fabric store," Thomas said. "I'll bring you with us to work in the morning, and you can choose whatever you need. Then I'll drive you both back."

"Thank you. That would work well." She glanced back at the men at the table, the old woman seated next to Rue, already coaxing a few smiles out of her. "Unless you need me for anything more, I could let you and your family have some privacy."

Sewing some little dresses would not be difficult, and it would be good for the girl to wear some looser, more comfortable clothing. And it would also be good for Patience to keep her fingers busy. Work made the hours pass by and brought meaning to the daylight hours.

It was the evening that she dreaded, when the work was done and she crawled alone into her bed at night. It was then that she faced all the things she longed for but would never have.

Like children of her own.

Chapter Two

Thomas stepped outside, holding the screen door open as Patience passed through. He pulled it shut behind him, giving a thin screen between him and the others— it was something. Closing the door outright wouldn't have been appropriate. They were both single, after all.

Thomas rubbed his hands down the sides of his pants, still feeling a little uncomfortable around this woman. The sun was sinking below the horizon, washing her complexion in a rosy pink, and Thomas did his best not to act like it mattered to him. He wasn't some young man looking to take a girl home from singing— he was a *daet* now. And a mildly confused *daet*, at that.

Thomas glanced over his shoulder toward the back yard; a white chicken coop sat next to the fence. The chickens had all gone back into it for the night, the cock standing outside, surveying the bare dirt surrounding the structure like a guard. The rooster crowed hoarsely.

"If you could come back in the morning, that would be really helpful," he said.

"I'll see you in the morning, then," Patience said, and

as she looked up at him, he realized that her blue eyes were fringed with dark lashes. An odd detail to notice, but one that he liked.

"*Yah.* I'll see you then," he said with a quick nod. "Thank you. I appreciate you helping us."

She shrugged. "We help where we can."

"I'd like to pay you back somehow—"

"That isn't necessary," she said. "I was here, and I was able. That's enough."

And maybe she was right. The Amish helped each other in times of need—it was what bound them together. But she was new here, and she already had a classroom waiting for her. To take this preparatory time and use it with his daughter was a sacrifice that he appreciated.

"I'm a carpenter," he said hesitantly. "I could help you, too. You should come by my shop. Maybe there is a piece of furniture, or—"

"I'd have nowhere to put it," she said. "I'm a single woman teaching school. I have no home of my own."

"Not yet," he said with a wry smile. Did she have no idea how lovely she was? There would be men lining up in Redemption for a chance with her. And perhaps that was why she came to a new community—for new marriage options. "When you marry, you can count on me to make you a cabinet."

"You're very kind." Her expression saddened and she dropped her gaze. Of course—he'd already forgotten about that man who had proposed... Maybe she'd loved him, and her reasons for turning him down had gone deeper.

"I'm sorry," he said awkwardly. "I'd forgotten about…the proposal."

"Life moves on," she said.

"Why did you say no?" he asked. "If I can ask that."

"Because I wouldn't have made him happy," she said, shrugging.

"He must have disagreed with that," Thomas said. She wasn't seeing herself through a man's eyes, obviously.

"He didn't know everything," she said. "And I know myself better. I wouldn't have been the wife he wanted."

Patience knew her mind, and she'd been willing to not only turn down an offer, but move to a different community. Thomas could only respect that she knew what she was talking about. Not every woman had such high character. Uncle Amos's wife ran away after less than a year of marriage, dooming Amos to a life of solitude, and Thomas had seen firsthand how lonely that had been for the older man. At nearly forty, Amos should have a houseful of *kinner*. There could be no remarriage for an Amish man. Those vows were for life. So if Patience had chosen the harder path, it was likely the right path to take.

"He might thank you later, then," Thomas said.

"I hope so," she replied. "He's a good man, and another woman will be happy to snap him up."

Yes, there would be women less beautiful than Patience waiting for a chance. And he looked at her quizzically. She wasn't what he expected.

"I'm grateful you're here to help me with my daughter," he said. "All the same."

Patience took a step down the stairs, then looked

back at him over her shoulder. "It will all work out for good, Thomas."

Was she talking about her situation, or his? Yes, that was what their faith told them, that all things worked together for good for those who loved Gott. But sometimes the working out took some time to get to. Hearts broke… And while Gott brought comfort, it wasn't immediate. It was more like spring growth.

"Good night, Patience," he said.

Patience smiled, and then turned and continued walking up the drive. His gaze lingered on her retreating figure for a couple of beats, and then he turned and pulled open the screen door once more. He went inside, past the washing-up sink in the mudroom and into the kitchen.

Noah stood with his hands in his pockets and he met Thomas's gaze with a helpless look of his own.

"She'll be back in the morning," Thomas said. It would be a big help.

"*Yah*, that's good." Noah looked toward the kitchen sink. "I'll do the dishes."

The older Mammi got, the more like bachelors they all lived—cleaning up after themselves. Mammi was elderly, and she couldn't do it alone.

"No, no," Mammi said, as she always did. "That's women's work."

"That child needs a woman tonight, Mammi," Noah replied. "I can wash up the dishes."

Rue sat at the table next to Amos, a half-finished cinnamon bun in front of her. Her eyes were drooping, and her little shoulders sagged as if under a heavy burden.

"I've got a nightgown for her," Mammi said. "It's a

bit big. Looking at her, I could probably wrap her in it twice."

"We might need to let her wear her own clothes," Thomas said, looking toward the suitcase in the corner. "Until we can sort out something more appropriate."

"Yah..." Mammi said with a sigh. "We might need to."

He could hear the regret in her voice—those Englisher clothes were jarringly different from their Amish garb, and for him they were a reminder of those years he'd spent away from their community.

"I'll carry the suitcase upstairs for you, Mammi," Amos said, rising to his feet.

Rue looked up as Amos stood, then she turned tear-filled eyes onto Thomas. "I want my mommy."

Thomas sank down on his haunches next to her. "I know, Rue."

"But she's dead," she whispered.

"Yes…" Thomas felt his throat thicken with emotion. "Did your mommy tell you about Heaven?"

"Yes…" Rue's chin trembled.

"Then you know that God is taking care of you," Thomas said quietly. "And He's taking care of her, too."

The girl looked at him in silence. Did it mean anything to her right now? He wasn't even sure. She was very young, and he didn't know how much faith Tina had raised her with. Tina hadn't been a strong believer when he'd known her… And he hadn't been much of an example of a Christian man's behavior, either. That was something he wouldn't forgive himself for, and a mistake he'd never make again. He'd keep himself under control, and he'd find an appropriately Amish wife.

"It is time for bed now," Thomas said.

"No."

Thomas looked down at her, uncertain if he'd heard the girl right. "Come, Rue. Mammi will help you get your pajamas and she'll show you your bed."

"No." Rue hadn't raised her voice, but she did tip her chin up just a little bit.

Amish children didn't say no at bedtime. At least he didn't think so. He didn't have any other children to compare this with, and he looked over at Mammi uncertainly.

"Come, Rue," Mammi said, smiling. "We'll get you dressed for bed."

"No!" Rue shook her head and leaned back into the chair. "I don't want to!"

Mammi's eyes widened, and Noah laughed softly from where he stood at the kitchen sink, filling it with sudsy water.

"You don't want to go to bed," Thomas said.

"I don't want to."

"What if…" Thomas rose to his feet and rubbed a hand over his rough chin. "What if you got your pajamas on, then you came back downstairs and I told you a story?"

Rue eyed him uncertainly. "I want TV."

"But without a TV, a story might be nice," he said, raising an eyebrow. "Don't you think? I know all sorts of good ones."

Mammi made a disapproving sound in the back of her throat, and Thomas realized he was likely digging himself into a hole with this little girl, but she couldn't be blamed for not knowing their ways, or even for resenting them just a little bit. She'd lost her mother, after all. What was the harm in a story or two to put her to sleep on this first night in a strange home with no TV?

"She must learn to obey," Mammi said in German.

"But first she must learn to like it here," Thomas replied, then a smile tickled at his lips. "And we have no TV. That is a serious problem for an Englisher child."

Mammi wasn't amused, but Thomas was the *daet*, so she held out her hand to Rue.

"Come, Rue," she said in English. "You'll get your pajamas on, and then come back down to your *daet*. Okay?"

Rue slid off her chair, casting a tiny little smile in Thomas's direction before she took Mammi's hand and followed her up the staircase.

Noah stood at the sink washing the dishes, the water turning on for a moment as he rinsed a plate and put it in the dish rack.

"Am I wrong?" Thomas asked.

"What do I know?" Noah said with a shrug. "I'm not a *daet*."

And up until yesterday when he'd heard that his daughter was coming home to him, he hadn't felt like one, either. But he'd have to catch up, and he'd have to teach Rue their ways. He was just grateful for the family surrounding him that would help him in this new role of father.

"I should tell you, Noah. I talked to our *mamm* yesterday," Thomas said, and his brother turned to look at him, his gaze suddenly guarded.

"When?" Noah asked.

"At the government office. She was the one who helped them find me."

Their mother, Rachel Wiebe, had looked so different dressed in a sleeveless Englisher dress and wearing a few pieces of jewelry. Her hair was dyed—the gray that had started to creep into it was now gone. She didn't look like a *mamm*. She looked… English.

"How is she?" Noah asked.

"She's healthy and happy." He'd wanted to see her miserable—realizing her mistake. But that hadn't been the case. "She wants to get to know Rue."

Noah sighed and turned back to the sink. Their *mamm* had left the community and gone English after their father's death.

"Rue is an Englisher child," Thomas added. "And our *mamm* is her real Mammi, you know."

"Rue is *your* child," Noah said curtly. "And if you want to raise her right, you'll raise her Amish."

Raising Rue Amish meant keeping her from Englisher influences. Did that include her grandmother?

"Obviously, I'll raise her Amish," Thomas said. "But Mamm also said she wanted to see you—"

"No."

Thomas eyed his brother. This was an old argument. Mamm came back to visit once every so often, and she sent letters, but Noah remained obstinately reserved. And yet, she was their *mamm*. She'd been the one to tuck them in, give them hugs and teach them right from wrong. She was their first love—the beautiful *mamm* who sang the strange Englisher hymns when there was no one else around to hear. When it rained, Thomas could still hear his *mamm*'s soft singing. *Rock of Ages, cleft for me... Let me hide myself in Thee...*

In English.

"She made her choice," Noah said, his voice thick. "She could have stayed for *us*!"

Thomas didn't answer that. He understood his brother's anger, because he felt it, too. When he was fourteen and Noah was fifteen, she'd given them the choice to leave with her, or stay without her. What kind of choice was that? She'd been their *mamm*, and one day she'd told them that that she couldn't continue this way, and their entire world had been thrown upside down. So Thomas could understand the anger in his daughter, because he carried around a fair amount of anger, too. He'd been trying to sort through it during his wild Rumspringa.

There was movement at the top of the stairs, and Mammi and Rue came back down.

Rue was dressed in a nightgown that showed a cartoon princess on the front, and it had little frilly ruffles around the arms. He glanced at his brother—their conversation would have to wait.

"Tell our schoolteacher that she will need a proper nightgown, too," Mammi said.

"Very good," Thomas said, smiling at Rue. "Now, I will sit in the rocking chair, and you will sit on my lap. I will tell you stories, and when your eyes get heavy, you must promise to let them close. Is that a deal?"

"You want to trick me into sleeping," Rue said.

"Yes." He met her young gaze. "That is exactly what I intend to do. With stories."

Rue regarded him for a moment, and she seemed to be deciding what she thought of him. Then she sighed.

"Okay," she whispered. "But I want stories."

Thomas smiled and scooped her up in his arms, then strode into the sitting room. Behind him, he could hear Mammi chiding Noah for having done most of the dishes.

Thomas was a *daet* now. And he had story after story saved up inside him, all meant for his own children one day. These were the stories that formed Amish children—Bible stories, family tales, stories of warning about people they used to know who took a wrong turn and lived to regret it. And tonight, Rue would have her first story.

Thomas settled himself into the rocking chair and Rue curled up her legs and leaned her head against his chest. She smelled of the soap Mammi had used to wash her face and hands, and he gingerly smoothed a hand over her flaxen hair.

"Are we ready, then?" he asked.

Rue nodded mutely.

"Tonight, I will tell you a story about the very first man and woman to live in this world. It was a very, very long time ago, in the days of *In the beginning*. So long ago, that no one remembers just what this first man and woman looked like…"

He would tell her the story of a snake in a garden, and a very tempting piece of fruit that had been forbidden to the inhabitants. That piece of fruit still hung before all the Amish community, just out of reach, just over the fence… And Thomas's own *mamm* had chosen the fruit.

The next morning, Patience dried the last plate from the breakfast dishes and put it into the cupboard. Cheerful sunlight splashed through the kitchen window and over the freshly wiped counters. Outside, she could hear the robins' songs, and she felt a certain excitement inside her that she hadn't experienced in quite some time. It was more than having a job to look forward to, though. And teaching school was definitely something new... But there had been something about Thomas and little Rue that had piqued her interest.

"A child needs a woman's touch," Hannah Kauffman said as she wiped the table. "You're kind to help him."

"The poor thing," Patience said. "This will be a hard adjustment for her."

"Hmm." Hannah straightened. "And for him. Mary and Amos raised him after his *daet* died and his *mamm* left, so I heard all the stories of his struggles as he grew up. I mean, Rachel did come visit, and she sent him letters in between, but it's not the same, is it? No one thought Thomas would come back after he went to live with his *mamm*. And when he did, we all knew there would be baggage. It wasn't just a Rumspringa—it was a boy's chance to spend time with the *mamm* who left him behind. Both of those boys were so heartbroken..."

Patience folded the wet towel and hung it up. "He's been through a lot."

"More than any of us know, I'm sure," Hannah replied, then she batted her hand through the air. "But you go on, now. I can handle the rest. Thomas will be waiting on you."

"Thank you, Hannah," Patience replied. "I'll make it up to you this evening."

It was a cool morning, and as Patience walked down the drive, she could feel fall coming in the air. A couple of leaves had started to turn—only one or two—but it was a hint at things to come.

Trees lined the gravel drive, and their branches stretched overhead, leaves trembling in the morning breeze. Some magpies chattered from the top of one tree, and they were answered by a group of crows—some sort of bird standoff happening above her head. She waved at Samuel Kauffman as she walked past. He was bent over a shovel, harvesting the last of the potatoes from their garden just past the horse stable. There were three draft horses grazing in the pasture beyond, and the animals looked up at her in mild curiosity.

Ruben had owned a property similar to this one, and there had been a time when she'd imagined what it would be like to be his wife, to be mistress of that home, to be the *mamm* calling those *kinner* down to breakfast. She still felt a pang of regret at all she'd given up in a life with Ruben, but she knew it had been the right choice. She wouldn't be able to give him what he truly wanted, and even if he left his offer of marriage on the table after he knew that she couldn't give him babies, she knew he'd be settling. It wasn't the kind of marriage a woman dreamed of, where a man had to lower his hopes in order to be with her.

In some ways, coming to a new community was a fresh start. She didn't know these people, their histories or their families. But the farther one went from home, the more it all looked the same. Amish lives all revolved around the same ideals—marriage, children, farming… A plain life was not an easy life, nor was it excitingly different in another community. Her problems would not change, but at least here in Redemption, she'd have a meaningful job.

When Patience approached the Lapp house, she could hear Rue's crying a good way up the drive. And when she arrived at the door, she knocked twice before it was flung open by a frazzled-looking Thomas. His hair was tousled and from inside she could hear the renewed wails of his young daughter.

"Patience!" he said, stepping back. "You're here."

"I am." She met his gaze questioningly.

"Go!" He gestured inside. "Help me with this!"

Patience swept past him, and she heard the door thunk shut behind her as she headed into the kitchen. The other men seemed to be out doing their chores, because it was only Mammi in the kitchen with Rue, and she was standing at the sink, completely ignoring the meltdown going on in the center of the kitchen floor. She looked up with a mild smile on her face.

"Good morning, Patience," she called, her voice hardly to be heard over the tantrum.

Rue lay there, drumming her heels against the floor, howling her heart out. Patience looked down at her for a moment, then pulled up a chair and sat down on it right next to Rue.

"What happened?" Patience asked.

"We told her that she was getting new clothes," Thomas replied, shrugging helplessly. "And then... this!"

The child continued to wail and pushed herself away from the chair another couple of feet, but when she got no more attention than Patience's watchful eye, her crying lowered in volume until she lay curled up in a ball, sobbing softly. It was then that Patience sat down on the floor next to her and held out her arms.

"Come for a hug, Rue," Patience said softly, and Rue crawled into her lap and leaned her tear-streaked face against Patience's shoulder, then let out a long, shuddering sigh.

"Now," Patience said. "What is the problem, little one?"

"I don't want a new dress," Rue said, her voice trembling. "I don't want it."

"Why not?" she asked.

"I don't want it…"

At this age, Rue wouldn't even know why not, and it likely wouldn't matter. What Rue didn't want was this—a new home, a father she'd never known, a way of life utterly foreign to all the things that used to comfort her.

"We aren't getting a new dress today," Patience said simply.

Rue looked up, startled.

"But Daddy said—"

"We're looking at fabric today. This is fabric—" She fingered Rue's nightgown between her fingers. "It comes in huge rolls. You'll see them."

"But no dress?" Rue asked.

"No. We're only getting fabric. I have to sew the dress myself. You can watch me. I'll use a needle and thread. Have you ever seen that?"

"No." Rue shook her head.

"It takes some time. But it's fun. And you can see how it works. And you'll be wearing your own clothes while I do it."

"Oh…" Rue wiped her nose across her hand. "I like my clothes."

"They are very nice," Patience said. "Did your *mamm* buy them for you?"

Would mentioning her *mamm* only make this worse?

"Mommy got me this nightgown," Rue said softly, holding it out to look at the picture on the front. "It's a princess nightgown."

"Very pretty…"

"And Mommy got me my unicorn shirt." Rue was looking up earnestly into Patience's face now, and she sensed that Rue desperately wanted someone to understand. "And Mommy got me my pink ruffle socks. And my purple shorts…"

All the clothing that would be taken from her—every item that was most inappropriate for an Amish girl to wear. But it had meaning to Rue because it was connected to the mother she lost, and Patience could suddenly imagine the disapproving looks of every single Amish adult who had looked into her precious suitcase of memories.

"I think I understand," Patience said quietly. "Should I explain it to your *daet*?"

Rue nodded quickly.

"Rue wants to keep her clothes," Patience said, looking up at Thomas.

Thomas stood there for a moment, looming over them, and then he pulled up that kitchen chair next to where Patience sat on the floor with Rue on her lap, and he sat down in it.

"*Yah*, I heard that," he said somberly.

"Her mother bought them, Thomas," Patience said quietly, switching to German. "This is her last connection to the mother she's lost, and I'm sure she knows that we're planning on getting rid of every last stitch of her Englisher clothes."

"Yah," he replied in German. "Of course!"

"It will break her heart," Patience said. "She isn't ready for that."

"No, she's not..." He sighed and rubbed his hands over his face. "I'm so eager to make her Amish that I forget she's not." Thomas looked up, his dark gaze meeting hers. "I will pray on it."

"And in the meantime, can I tell her she keeps the clothes?" Patience asked hopefully.

"In the meantime, yes."

"Your *daet* understands," Patience said, turning to Rue and switching back to English. "And you can keep your clothes. He just wants to give you *more* clothes."

"More?" she asked, and she looked up at her father with such hope in her eyes.

"More," he said solemnly. "Proper Amish dresses for my little Amish girl."

"Am I Amish, Daddy?" she asked.

"Yah," he said. "And I would like it if you called me Daet."

Rue frowned.

"It means *daddy* in German," Patience said.

"I don't like that..." Rue shook her head. "You talk funny."

"Okay," Thomas answered almost too quickly, and Patience had to smother a smile. He was afraid of another meltdown, and right now, she couldn't blame him.

"You're Daddy," Rue said seriously, fixing Thomas with a no-nonsense look of her own. Thomas looked at his daughter for a moment, then sighed.

"For now," he agreed. "I'll be… Daddy."

It was a painful concession, and Patience knew it. Daddies were of the Englisher world, but an Amish father was a *daet*. Tiny children learned to form the word, and it was a tender name, one attached to deep love and emotion. Thomas didn't want to be Daddy, and Patience understood all too well why he wouldn't.

Patience disentangled herself from the girl and boosted her to her feet. "Rue, have you had your breakfast?"

"Yes."

"Have you washed your face and your hands? Did you brush your teeth?"

Mary Lapp dried her hands on a towel at the sink and cast Patience a grateful smile, then held out her hand.

"Come, Rue," Mary said. "Let's get clean so you can see the big rolls of fabric."

It seemed to work, because Rue agreed to trot upstairs with the older woman. Thomas stood up, then held his hand out to Patience to help her to her feet. Patience took his hand, and his grip was warm and solid, calloused from the hard work he did every day. He was strong, and he pulled her easily to her feet.

"You're good with her," Thomas said, releasing her hand.

"I don't know why," Patience said, stepping back. "I don't know anything about Englisher children."

Thomas smiled sadly. "Me neither."

"We'll figure it out," Patience said.

"Gott teaches patience with children. Isn't that what they say?"

"It is." She smiled. "And I'm about to have a whole

schoolhouse full of them, so maybe you should feel grateful for just one."

Thomas cracked a smile then, and he laughed softly. "Maybe I should." He jutted his chin toward the door. "I'm going to go hitch up the buggy."

Patience watched as he headed out the side door, and she put a hand over her pattering heart. She wasn't blind to his broad shoulders and warm smile—it would be easier if she were, because it wasn't that she didn't want to marry... She did. But she was going to be a disappointment to whoever tried to court her.

Patience was a teacher and a helpful neighbor. Nothing else. She'd best remember it. Strong hands and broad shoulders didn't change that she wasn't the wife for Thomas.

Chapter Three

The horses trotted along the paved road, the scenery slowly easing past the buggy. Thomas flicked the reins and looked out past the ditch full of weeds and wild-flowers, to the fields beyond. Cattle chewed their cud, lying in the long summer grass, and overhead a string of geese beat their wings heading south. These were the last weeks of warmth, and soon there would be frost in the mornings.

"It's a carriage ride!" Rue said, seated between Thomas and Patience on the bench seat.

"A what?" Thomas asked, turning back toward his daughter.

"A princess rides in a carriage!" Rue said. "Like this."

Thomas looked over Rue's head and caught Patience's eye. She shrugged subtly. Rue wasn't raised with dreams of a gleaming kitchen or a neat new dress she'd stitched herself. She'd been raised with grander hopes, it would seem, the kind that elevated one person high above the rest. The Amish saw the danger in that.

Must this child be so foreign from everything he held dear?

Gott, I don't know how to raise her, he prayed in his heart. *She's so...different.*

And she was also his doing. He'd been the one to roam outside the community's boundaries. He'd been the young man who needed to see if his *mamm*'s world might be better, after all. And back then, he'd deeply hoped that it would be, because he missed his *mamm* so much in between her visits, and her letters said very little that meant anything to him. Those who said that a teenager was old enough, that he no longer needed his *mamm*, were dead wrong, because at the age of fourteen, he'd lain in his bed night after night sobbing his heart out, wishing his mother would come back for good.

"Would you like to see our shop, Rue?" he asked.

"What's that?" Rue asked.

"I'm a carpenter. I build things with wood, and I work at Uncle Amos's carpentry shop. We build everything from beds to cabinets to little carved boxes for Englisher women to put their jewelry in."

"A jewel box?" Rue breathed.

"*Yah*, but we Amish don't use them," he said. "We don't have jewelry."

"A princess does," Rue said.

Right. He sighed. This would be a long journey in the making of an Amish girl.

"You could still come see our shop," Thomas said. "Then you'll know where your *daet* works."

Rue looked up at him, silent. It didn't seem to mean much to her.

"Can I hold that?" she asked, pointing to the reins.

Thomas smiled. He couldn't exactly hand the reins over to a four-year-old, but it was a good sign that she wanted to try it herself. This was how children learned—they got curious and wanted to hold the reins.

"Come sit on my knee, and we'll hold the reins together."

The buggy ride into town wasn't a long one. Patience sat quietly the rest of the ride, and he stole a few looks at her over his daughter's head—noticing some details like the faint freckles across her nose and the wisp of golden hair that came loose from under her *kapp.* She was beautiful in that fresh, wholesome way that he'd missed so much when he'd left the community. But he was also feeling attracted to her, and that made him nervous. He needed to focus on his daughter right now, not the new teacher. Besides, Patience was comforting, and that was exactly what drew him to Tina in the city—a search for comfort. His comfort needed to come from his Father in Heaven, not a woman's arms. He'd learned that the hard way.

A couple of farmers, both of whom Thomas knew, looked at him in open curiosity as their buggies passed, going in the opposite direction. Thomas nodded to them, and they nodded back. Word would spread quickly when they started telling their neighbors what they'd seen. Patience could be easily explained, but Rue wearing a striped Englisher sundress would require more. Thomas had a child—a distinctly Englisher child. People would have opinions about that, to be sure.

The town of Redemption was an Amish-friendly town, which meant that the shops all had buggy parking out front, and there were parking lots with hitching posts. Many of the restaurants and stores were Amish owned and operated, including Redemption Carpentry. Englishers traveled from miles around to visit Redemption and buy up the authentic Amish crafts and food. They ordered Amish cabinetry for their homes and stared at the Amish folk with the open curiosity that only Englishers could pull off.

Redemption Carpentry was on Main Street, with a convenient buggy parking area behind the shop. They also had a stable for their horses, and every few days, they'd bring out a new bale of hay and cart out the soiled hay to be used as fertilizer. Even housing horses during business hours took extra work. That was the life of the Amish—putting their backs into the labor and their hearts into Gott.

Next door to their carpentry shop was Quilts and Such, the fabric shop, and after unhitching the horses and settling them with their oats in the stable, Thomas took Rue's hand and they all walked together to the front door. He felt the curious eyes of Amish and English alike sweeping over him. Benjamin Yoder stared in unveiled shock from his seat on his buggy, and his wife, Waneta, leaned forward to get a better look past her husband's chest. *Yah*, he'd have explaining to do.

Thomas pulled open the door to Redemption Carpentry first. He let Patience and Rue go in ahead of him, out of sight from the passersby on the street. He heaved a sigh of relief as the door shut behind him, the soft tinkle of a bell pealing overhead.

"It's you," Amos said, poking his head out of the workshop. They had a small display room for a few finished products, giving customers an idea of the types of furniture they could order. There were some chests of drawers, sections of headboards, wood and stain samples, and a display shelf of ornately carved jewelry boxes.

"Oh…" Rue sighed, immediately drawn to the boxes. "They're so pretty…"

"*Yah*, but why don't you come see where the real work happens?" Thomas said, and he led the way into the back where Noah was working on a bedpost on a gas-powered lathe.

Thomas let them look around. Rue seemed most interested in the curls of wood shavings on the floor, and she collected a few in her hands.

"You have a good business here," Patience said.

"*Yah*. It's doing quite well," Thomas said, and while he wouldn't brag, they were doing more than well. The Englishers loved their work, and with the three of them meeting orders on time every time, they had a reputation for being reliable, as well.

"This is where your *daet* works," Patience said, bending down next to Rue. "He makes all these beautiful things."

"Could I have a jewelry box?" Rue asked, standing up and fixing Thomas with a hopeful look.

"Those are for the Englisher ladies," he said.

"But I'm an Englisher lady!" Rue insisted.

"No, you're an Amish girl," he said. "And I will get you something that you'll love. You'll see."

He glanced at Patience, and she shrugged faintly. There would be plenty of this in the coming weeks and months, he was sure. His daughter wanted an English life—it was what she was born to. He was the one asking her to change everything she'd been raised to be—and for what? For *him*, a father she hardly knew.

Thomas waved to Noah and Amos, then held the door for Patience and Rue to leave the workshop, heading out into the summer warmth once more. As they left the shop, Rue's gaze lingered on their carved boxes. Maybe bringing her here hadn't been the best idea just yet, but he felt like there were pitfalls anywhere they went.

Next door was the fabric shop, and they ducked inside.

"Good morning!"

It was Lovina Glick, the owner of this shop. Thomas often helped her with mucking out the temporary stalls for her draft horses when she was forced to drive her own buggy into town for the day. Normally, her teenaged son drove her and picked her up again in the evening.

Lovina's gaze landed on Rue, and she looked up at Thomas and Patience in surprise.

"Who is this?" she asked in German.

"This is…" Thomas swallowed. "My daughter."

"Your—" Lovina's gaze whipped over to Patience, and Thomas could see that he'd have to explain right quick.

"My daughter is from my Rumspringa," he said in German, his voice low. "And this here is Patience Flaud—our new schoolteacher. She's completely unrelated."

"Ah…" Lovina came out from behind the counter and nodded slowly. Her gaze flickered up to Thomas's face, and he could see the disappointment there. She'd been a good friend of his *mamm*'s back in the day, and

Lovina had stepped up to be a sort of mother figure to them in their own mother's absence. "I don't think I have a right to ask more than that, Thomas. Not now that you're grown." She paused, and again he saw a flood of disappointment in her eyes. "So what do you need, then?"

Her sudden distance stung.

"We need to buy fabric enough to dress her," Thomas said.

"And you'll burn that, I suppose." Lovina's mouth turned down as she gestured to Rue's sundress. "But yes, I understand. She needs to be dressed properly."

Thomas cleared his throat. "We need enough fabric to make—how many dresses?" He turned to Patience.

"Three to start," Patience said. "She'll need more later, of course. But those will need to be warmer for winter."

"Do you want three different colors?" Lovina asked. "Or all the same for now? It might be good for character to keep them the same—take away the temptation to glory in oneself. It's best to quash that early. I've raised four daughters of my own, mind."

That was aimed at Patience.

"All good girls, I'm sure," Patience said with a smile. "I'm glad you can help me to sort this out, then."

Lovina's gaze moved down to Rue once more, and she cocked her head to one side, chewing the side of her cheek. Thomas knew that look from Lovina—that was her look when she was planning on fixing something, and Rue was the problem to be fixed.

Rue squirmed under that penetrating gaze and squeezed Thomas's hand a little bit tighter.

"You'll need a pattern, I take it?" Lovina turned to Patience, Thomas officially out of the conversation as they moved into more technical requirements.

"Yes, a pattern, thread…" Patience moved away with Lovina. "I brought my own needles, and I have some extra hook clasps, but we might need an extra package of those anyway…"

"You're our new teacher, then?" Lovina's voice this time, and Thomas sighed. He was glad Patience was here to take over this womanly task. He wouldn't have known where to start, and Lovina wouldn't have made it easy on him, either. In fact, if they were alone, she might have demanded a few explanations. She'd been more like an aunt in his teens, and she'd take his moral failing personally.

"I like that one…" Rue moved over to a bolt of fabric with a floral pattern, and she smiled up at him shyly.

"No, Rue," Thomas said. "That's fancy."

She didn't know what that meant yet, and he didn't have the energy to try to explain it to her in a way she'd understand. So he walked with her over to the fabric in solid colors—blue, green, pink, purple. All sober and muted. Rue's gaze kept moving back to the brighter patterns.

"Patience will choose for us," Thomas said.

"Will it be a princess dress?" Rue asked, her eyes brightening.

"No. It is an Amish dress."

"I can be an Amish princess." She beamed up at him, and he simply stared at her, because he had no answers. The Amish didn't have princesses, and he couldn't give her something she'd like better. That was the hard part.

He was offering her a life of humble work, of prudence and piety. How could that compare to her fantasies?

The bell tinkled again over the front door, and Thomas looked up to see two more Amish women come inside with two little girls. He knew the women by sight—one was a school friend's older sister. The other was a distant relative of the bishop who had moved to their community when she got married. One of the little girls looked about the same age as Rue, and the girls moved in the direction of the Amish-approved fabrics. The women nodded a friendly hello to him.

The little girls wandered ahead of the women, fingers lingering on the fabrics as they passed them. The smallest girl reached them first, and she startled when she saw Rue, concealed behind some tall bolts of fabric.

"Hi," Rue whispered.

The little girl frowned, and then started to smile when her older sister plucked at her sleeve.

"Stop," her sister remonstrated in German, and tugged her in the other direction. Both girls then turned their backs and headed back toward the women.

"I want to play with her," Rue said, loudly enough to be heard, and it was then that the women took notice. They looked at Rue, up at Thomas, and then steered their girls away from her.

"Englisher child…" he heard one whisper.

"With Thomas Wiebe, though? Who is she?" Their whispers carried, and Thomas felt his stomach clench in anger.

"You know about his mother…" the other woman replied.

And then he couldn't hear anymore, but they cast a

couple of sidelong looks in his direction. They wouldn't ask him directly—they didn't know him well enough for that. They'd simply ask anyone else who might know him better if they knew who that Englisher child was.

The Englishers were perfectly acceptable as tourists or as customers, but not as playmates for their children. Thomas knew that full well—part of the reason why Rue desperately needed plain clothing. When he was a boy, he'd learned the same lesson—don't chat with them, don't do anything more than give a quick answer to a question if forced, and never form friendships with other Englisher children. They wouldn't understand the Amish way, and they'd do what Englishers always did—try to find some common ground with which to lure you away from the narrow path.

Englishers were necessary for an income, but dangerous to their way of life. It was a delicate line to walk, and Amish children learned it early.

"Daddy?" Rue asked, her voice carrying. "Daddy?"

Thomas looked down at her, trying not to let his own tension show, but he wasn't sure he managed it. He would not let his daughter think that he was embarrassed of her.

"Yes, Rue?" he murmured.

"I like the one with flowers."

"We don't have dresses with flowers, Rue," he reminded her. "We're Amish."

And when Thomas looked up, he saw the direct stares of both women—aghast and suddenly understanding perfectly. They quietly herded the girls out of the store in front of them, and the bell tinkled as they left.

Judgment felt heaviest when it was deserved.

* * *

Thomas came up beside Patience, and she could feel the anger radiating off him. He placed a protective hand on Rue's head, but when she met his gaze, his eyes glittered, and his jaw was clenched. She caught her breath. Had she done something? She'd been focused on choosing cloth—

"It's not you," he murmured, as if reading her mind. "We need to get back. Have you finished choosing things?"

"Yah," she said. "This will do."

She'd chosen a blue color of fabric that would bring out Rue's beautiful eyes, and a soft pink, because she thought that Rue would like it.

"Good." He turned to Lovina and briskly pulled a wallet from his pocket. "How much?"

Patience waited as Thomas paid the bill, pocketed his wallet once more and picked up the bag.

"We'll see you," Lovina said with a smile.

"Yah." Thomas scooped up his daughter's hand. "Let's go now."

"Wait." Lovina picked up a basket of hard candies and lowered it down to Rue's level. "Because you were so good, Rue. You can have two."

Rue's eyes lit up and she took a moment to choose her two candies. Patience looked over at Thomas, searching for a hint of what the trouble was, and the bell over the door tinkled again, another group of Amish shoppers coming inside.

"Thank you, Lovina," Thomas said tightly as Rue picked up her second candy. "Let's go."

Thomas didn't look up as they made their way to the

door, but Patience nodded at the women. This would be her community, too, after all, and soon she'd get to know many of these women in kitchens and at hymn sings.

Thomas headed out the door, and Patience had to quicken her pace to catch up. The door swung shut behind them and the warm August air enveloped them once more.

"I was wrong to take Rue to town like this. She looks—" He sighed and changed to German. "She draws attention."

"People will look later, too," Patience pointed out, following his lead in speaking in the language the child wouldn't understand. "They'll get used to seeing her, though."

"It's not just the staring." Thomas led the way around the building toward the buggy parking in the rear. "They pulled their girls away from her."

As they would… But Patience's heart gave a squeeze. Yes, that would sting. Had Rue noticed? She looked down to see Rue watching them in mild confusion. She gave Rue a reassuring smile.

"It was my fault," Thomas said. "I shouldn't have put her in the middle of that kind of scrutiny. We'll go back home and…and…"

"And not be seen," Patience finished for him.

Thomas didn't answer, but he cast her one forlorn look. She'd been right—that was his hope. He just wanted to get her out of the public eye. They approached the buggy, still hitched, and Thomas took the feed bags off the horses.

"For how long?" Patience asked pointedly.

"What?" He ran a hand over the horses' muscular necks, then looked back at her.

"How long will you keep her hidden away at the house with Mary?" Patience asked.

"A woman's place—" he began.

"A girl needs friends," she countered, interrupting. It wasn't right for a woman to cut a man off when he was speaking, but her heart was beating fast. "A girl needs to know people—see people. Yes, her place is in her home, and one day she'll marry and make a home of her own, but if she's treated like a dirty secret—"

"She is *not* a dirty secret!" Thomas snapped back. "She's a vulnerable little girl and her *daet* has done wrong. I'm trying to protect her."

She knew he was only trying to protect his daughter, and he was right that some proper Amish clothes would make her more presentable...

"Thomas, I'm not saying we shouldn't go home right now. I'm only pointing out that there will be explaining anyway," Patience said. "She will be a surprise, regardless, and as uncomfortable as it is, you will have to tell the story again and again. As soon as she speaks, or can't answer a German question, it'll be clear she's Englisher. There's no hiding that."

"Yah." Thomas sighed. "But once she looks proper with a *kapp* and a dress, will they pull their children away still?"

Patience couldn't answer that. They may very well.

"Daddy?" Rue said, and instead of answering, Thomas picked her up and deposited her on the buggy seat.

"Wait there," he said with a forced smile, and then he

turned to Patience again. "I've been the subject of gossip before. My mother left the community when my father died. She couldn't do it alone—walk the narrow path. She said she had friends and family with the Englishers, and she missed them. I had no idea my parents had been converts, but there you have it. She didn't want to marry another Amish widower to provide for us. She said it was…" He swallowed. "She said it was too hard. But she'd raised us Amish, all the same, and she taught us to choose the hard choice, to take the narrow path. She just wasn't willing to do it without Daet."

Patience stared at him, shocked.

"Where did she go?" Patience whispered.

"To a nearby city. My *mamm* had gone to an Englisher college. She has a sister there in the city, and they hadn't seen each other since she and Daet converted—" His voice caught. "My parents had had this whole life we never knew about. I should have guessed with our last name. It's German, but not typically Amish, but I never thought to question it. So my mother went Mennonite on us… Or went back to being Mennonite might be more accurate. Sure she would come visit and she tried to keep up with our lives, but everyone knew she'd left the Amish life. And I had to endure the gossip and the sidelong looks for years afterward. I know what that feels like."

"I'm sorry," she murmured. So he had his own painful history, too…one that linked him to the Englisher world more than she'd ever suspected.

"We need to help Rue fit in as quickly as possible," Thomas said, his voice low. "She needs Amish clothes. She needs to learn a few German words."

"Yah," she agreed. "I'll do my best."

"That's all I can ask."

"Do you see your mother still?" Patience asked.

"Sometimes," Thomas replied. "She still comes to visit from time to time. She's my *mamm*. I suppose I'm still hoping she'll come back for good."

An Englisher mother, and an Englisher child. Thomas was indeed a very dangerous man, and she understood why a community would be cautious. Patience didn't say anything, but she felt the wariness in her own expression.

"I'm Amish!" he said fervently, reading her face. "I was born Amish, I was raised Amish and, given the choice, I was baptized into the church. Rue can be Amish, too. She's young enough to be formed—I was formed into an Amish man, wasn't I? She can learn our ways. We can teach her our language. And given a few years, the community will do for her what they did for me—"

"What's that?" she asked.

"They'll pretend that she's no different." Thomas held out his hand. "We'd best go now."

Patience put her hand in his warm, strong grip and hoisted herself up into the buggy. Rue was staring at her with wide, worried eyes. Understanding the language or not, the child understood the tension. Patience let out a slow breath. She couldn't let Rue shoulder these adult worries.

"Do you like pie?" Patience asked quietly, shooting Rue a conspiratorial smile.

"Yes," Rue said.

Patience settled herself on the opposite side of the girl so that Rue would be in the middle again.

"Good, because I make a wonderful lemon meringue pie. How are you at licking the whisk?"

Rue smiled again, this time more relaxed. Thomas settled himself onto the seat next to his daughter, and he gave Patience a small smile. Their conversation would have to wait…again.

"I'm a good licker!" Rue declared.

"I'm good at licking the whisk, too," he said in mock seriousness. "It might run in the family."

"No, Daddy, it's for me!" Rue complained, and Patience chuckled.

"Your *daet* will be working, Rue. So there isn't much worry that he'll get to the whisk first."

"You never know," Thomas replied with a teasing grin. "I might sneak back, just in time—"

"Daddy, no!" Rue was smiling this time, though.

"A *daet* deserves a treat, too," he joked, and then he flicked the reins and the horses started.

"A *daddy*…" Rue whispered so softly that Patience almost missed it.

This child would wear a plain dress, and she'd eat Amish food, but there was a stubborn spirit in Rue that would not accept an Amish *daet*.

Chapter Four

Patience helped Rue down from the buggy when they got back to the house. She was light—weighing about the same as a large cat. She was thin, and Patience could feel her ribs through that striped sundress. She was a naturally slight child, and Patience felt an urge to feed her—plump her up, if possible.

"Are those more horses?" Rue asked as Patience set her on the ground. Patience looked in the direction Rue was pointing.

"*Yah*, those are more horses," Thomas said, coming around to their side of the buggy. "But that big one—the black stallion, there—he's mean. Real mean. You stay away from the horse corral, okay?"

"Okay..." Rue frowned. "What's a stallion?"

"A boy horse," Patience said.

"How's it a boy?" Rue squinted up at Patience, and Patience chuckled. There were many lessons that a life on a farm gave to children, but this one could wait.

"If that horse were a human, it would wear a straw

hat and suspenders," Patience replied with a smile. "That's how you know."

"Huh." Rue seemed to accept this at face value. "I want suspenders, too."

"Little girls don't wear suspenders," Patience replied. "They wear pretty dresses, and when they get old enough, they get a *kapp*, like mine. You see this *kapp*?"

She tapped the white fabric that covered her bun.

"Can I have one now?" Rue asked. "Instead of suspenders, then?"

Patience looked over at Thomas and found him watching her, instead of Rue. His brows were knit, and when she caught his gaze, he straightened and dropped it.

"You have to get old enough," Thomas said to Rue. "Now, I'm going to unhitch these horses. You go inside with Patience, okay?"

Thomas waited as Patience caught the little girl's hand, then he took the lead horse's bridle and started toward the stable. Rue stared after him.

"You must be very careful around horses, Rue," Patience said, starting toward the house. "*Kinner* have been hurt very badly playing around horses."

There was so much Rue had to learn. She might not be very old yet, but Amish children her age knew all sorts of safety rules. Add to that, Rue would have to catch up on more than their culture, their clothing and their faith. The very foundation of an Amish child's life was obedience. Immediate obedience. From what Patience saw of the Englisher children in town, they weren't raised with the same expectation. Englisher children sassed back, said no when asked to do something, ignored their parents. It was unheard of in Amish communities—*kinner* who behaved like that were very quickly corrected. And they didn't do it again.

As Patience led Rue into the mudroom, she shut the door behind her. The house was silent, and Patience peeked into the kitchen. There were some dishes to be done, and Mary was nowhere to be seen. When Patience glanced into the sitting room, she saw the old woman in a rocking chair, her chin dropped down to her chest and her breath coming slow and deep.

"Mammi is sleeping," Rue said.

"*Yah*, it looks that way," Patience replied. "We have to be quiet to let her rest. In fact, I think it is your naptime, too."

"Naptime?" Rue eyed Patience uncertainly.

"*Yah. Kinner* like you take naps," Patience replied.

"I'm not a *kinner*!" Rue said.

"*Yah*, you are. *Kinner* means children. You're a child."

"Don't call me that," Rue said irritably.

Rue was tired. It had been a long morning, and Patience could only imagine how hard things had been for her recently.

"All right," Patience said softly. "I will call you sugar, then. Is that nicer?"

Rue considered this a moment, and Patience could see the fight seeping out of her.

"I'm not tired," Rue whispered.

"Then you lie on your bed and you think quiet thoughts," Patience replied.

"I don't want to." Rue's lips pressed together, and that defiant glitter came back to her eye. Patience had a choice in how she dealt with this, and she debated inwardly for a moment, then she squatted down to Rue's level.

"What if I lay down next to you?" Patience asked.

Tears welled in Rue's blue eyes and she nodded. "Okay."

Patience led Rue upstairs, and she found Mary's bedroom with a little cot all arranged next to her bed. Patience doubted that the old woman would mind her bed being used for a napping little girl, so Patience lifted Rue up onto the quilted bed top, and then lay down next to her. Rue let out a shuddering little sigh.

"I'm not tired," Rue repeated.

"I know, sugar," Patience replied, and she took Rue's hand in hers. "Me, neither. Let's just lie quietly for a little while. Maybe we'll even shut our eyes a bit."

It didn't take long for Rue to fall asleep, and Patience looked down at the girl with her long, pale lashes and the pink little lips. That striped sundress looked so strange against the blue-and-white Amish quilt, and Patience fingered the material. It was soft and stretchy, unlike the cotton of plain dresses and men's shirts. Rue needed new clothes—but would she wear them, or would she fight it? This girl was so small, and sleeping she looked even younger than her four years, but the spirit in her—she had fight. Downstairs, the side door banged shut, and Patience eased herself slowly off the bed. She could hear the steady beat of Thomas's footsteps on the stairs. She crossed the room on tiptoe, and when she got to the doorway, Thomas's face appeared around the doorjamb. Her breath caught, and for a moment they just looked at each other—his dark gaze meeting hers. He was so close that she had to tip her face up, and she could make out the faint stubble on his chin. He was handsome—dare she admit that? And there was something about the way his gaze moved across her face that made her hold her breath. She'd have to get over her way of reacting to him.

Patience put a finger to her lips. Thomas's dark gaze flicked over her shoulder to where Rue lay sleeping.

"Oh…" he breathed, a smile tickling the corners of his lips. "How did you manage that?"

"I'm not sure," she whispered, and they exchanged a smile.

Thomas angled his head toward the stairs and she let out a shaky breath as he turned away.

"Englisher *kinner* aren't raised the same way," Patience said, following him down the stairs.

"Don't I know it," Thomas replied. He headed for a cupboard and pulled down a sealed plastic container, then opened it. "Do you want a muffin?"

"*Yah.* Thanks."

Thomas passed a blueberry muffin to her, then took one for himself. Patience took a bite and swallowed before she continued.

"Englisher *kinner* don't obey like Amish *kinner*. The Englisher parents seem to do more pleading with their *kinner* to make them behave, and quite frankly, it's dangerous on our land."

"You think I'll be pleading?" he asked ruefully.

"I confess, I did a little pleading of my own up there," she replied.

Thomas laughed—a full, open laugh that she didn't

expect—and she blinked at him. His dark eyes met hers with a glitter of humor.

"So, I'm not the only one?" Thomas said, shaking his head. "If she were raised plain, she'd already know the rules. It'll take some time."

"And in the meantime, she's not going to know what's dangerous," Patience added. "From fire in the stove to the horses in the corral—this is all completely foreign to an Englisher child. She's an accident waiting to happen."

"That's why you're here, isn't it?" Thomas asked hopefully.

"Yah," she said. "But I don't think either of us knows what she'll get into once she feels more comfortable."

Thomas nodded. *"Yah.* Definitely. Maybe having her play with some *kinner* would help with that. Learning while she plays."

"It's a good idea," Patience agreed. "I don't even remember learning everything I gleaned while playing with my older sisters. Maybe there are some girls who would… I don't know…take her under wing a little."

Thomas looked at her, his expression sobering. "You saw the reaction of the women in the store today."

"Yah," she admitted. "Maybe that was rooted in surprise, though." Eventually, the community would learn who Rue was and why she was here.

"I'll see what I can sort out," he said.

Patience finished the muffin and then wiped the crumbs from her fingers. She went to the sink, put in the plug and looked around for the dish soap.

"Uh… I can do that," Thomas said.

Patience looked up at him, a little embarrassed. "This is women's work."

"I know it's not my place to tell you what needs to be done," Thomas said, his voice low. "But Rue needs dresses, and if you'd be willing to start on that, I can clean up."

"Oh…" She felt the heat hit her cheeks. Had she overstepped somehow?

"We're a houseful of bachelors," Thomas said. "We fend for ourselves a lot. We'll be right proper once we're married, I'm sure, but—" He shrugged.

"*Yah*, well, I can start sewing," Patience said.

As she stepped away from the sink, Thomas pulled a bottle of dish soap from the cabinet and squirted it into the running water. He rolled his sleeves up past his elbows and looked around himself for a moment, then started gathering the dirty dishes. He looked…practiced. He'd spent time with the Englishers… Was this his time away shining through?

For the next few minutes, Patience cut out the paper pattern for a little dress, then laid out the cloth and began pinning the pattern in place. Mammi's sewing basket was in the corner, so Patience made use of it. Girls' dresses were simple enough to sew, and they left lots of room for a child to grow, too. She'd helped her sisters make all sorts of clothes for her nieces and nephews over the years, so her hands knew the work.

But as she worked, she caught herself looking up at the quiet man who continued to wash, dry and put away the stack of morning dishes.

"I know that you spent time with the Englishers,"

she said after some silence. "I shouldn't be trying to inform you of how they raise their *kinner*."

"*Yah*. I went there to live with my *mamm* for my Rumspringa and stayed for three years. I'm twenty-four now, so I've been home for a while," he replied. "But they're different, the Englishers. They keep to themselves. You don't see as much as you think you will about how their families work. The young people spend time together, and the older people have their friends... The different generations don't come together very often."

That seemed sad—and lonely. All the same, a woman like her who wouldn't be raising children of her own might fit into an Englisher system a little easier than she would here with her own people. She wouldn't ask about that, though. It wouldn't be right to show curiosity about the Englishers. Still... He'd loved an Englisher girl, hadn't he? Obviously they weren't so strange and different to *him*.

Thomas seemed to feel her eyes on him, and he turned. She felt the heat hit her face and she dropped her attention to the pattern on the fabric. Was that jealousy she'd just felt?

"I had a choice," he said quietly. "I could stay with my *mamm* and live an Englisher life, or I could come back. It wasn't easy. Your home, your life... Your mother is supposed to be a part of that, isn't she?" He waited, as if he expected her to answer, and when she didn't, he went on, "But I'm Amish. And I came back. I'll be Amish until I die."

"I wasn't questioning your dedication," she said.

"I thought it should be said," he replied.

"Do you miss your *mamm*?" she asked quietly.

Thomas pressed his lips together, then nodded. "*Yah*. Of course."

But he was living away from her. An Amish family got together with all the grandparents, aunts and uncles and cousins regularly. Even coming out here to teach school, Patience knew she'd go back to visit her family at Christmas, and to help her *mamm* with all the Christmas baking. Would Thomas have his *mamm*'s cooking to look forward to come Christmas?

Thomas let the water out of the sink and wrung out the cloth. He hung it over the tap neatly.

"I'd best get some work done here at home," he said. "I'll be going back to the shop tomorrow, so…"

"*Yah*, of course," she replied.

Thomas nodded, then headed past the table, his fingers skimming over the tabletop next to the spread-out fabric as he passed her. She watched him disappear into the mudroom, and a moment later the door shut behind him.

There was a rustle at the doorway to the sitting room and Patience looked up to see Mary standing there. Her eyes looked bleary from sleep, and she patted at her hair, checking for any loose strands.

"I must have dozed off," Mary said. "I'd better get to the dishes."

"Thomas did them," Patience replied.

"Did he?" Mary's face pinked. "That boy… They're treating me like I'm old, you know. What is that you're doing, dear?"

"I'm starting on a dress for Rue," Patience replied.

"Well, let me help, then," Mary said. "I can cut out

the cloth still. I'm not as good with the stitching any-more, but—"

"That would be wonderful, Mary," Patience replied with a smile. "Before the day is out, I want her to have at least one proper dress."

Mary came to the table, and pulled out a chair. She reached for the shears, and Patience passed them over.

"She wasn't a bad woman," Mary said, setting to work. "Thomas's *mamm*, I mean. She wasn't a bad woman, just a sad one. She knew how to be Amish with her husband, but she hadn't been raised in our ways, and she didn't know how to do it without him. She couldn't change who she was."

Patience met the old woman's gaze. Did Mary guess at how much Patience was judging the woman who'd left her sons behind? She didn't answer, and Mary didn't say anything further.

There was a dress to be made—an Englisher child to be made over into a plain one. Like her grandmother, Rue had started out an Englisher. Was there any real hope that that this child would stay Amish in the long run?

Two hours later, Thomas came out of the stable with a wheelbarrow full of soiled hay. Sweat beaded on his forehead, and he paused to pull out a handkerchief and wipe his face. The sun shone warm on his shoulders and he pushed his hat up on his forehead as he looked toward the house. It was a bit of a relief to have a young woman around for Rue's sake, but also a little unnerv-ing. They were used to their ways in this house—bachelor men living with one old woman whom they all secretly went out of their way to take care of.

If only this schoolteacher were a little less attractive. He wouldn't be the only one to notice how beautiful she was. His older brother, Noah, certainly would, and Uncle Amos wasn't exactly dead yet, either. Except Amos was legally married still, so his days of courting were past.

And yet, it was silly to be feeling competitive over a woman who was clearly uncomfortable with all the untraditional parts to Thomas's heritage. Englisher convert parents, a *mamm* who didn't stay, an Englisher daughter of his own... Thomas wasn't going to have an easy time of finding a woman—some might see him as a threat to the very fiber of their community.

He dumped the load of soiled hay on the manure pile, and put the wheelbarrow back under the buggy cover where they kept it. The side door opened and Rue appeared on the porch. She stared at him somberly.

Amish *kinner* helped the adults and learned through chores. Work was how a family bonded, and while looking at her in those Englisher clothes was slightly jarring still, she could help with some little jobs.

"You're awake now, are you?" Thomas called.

"Patience tricked me into sleeping," Rue said, leaning against the rails.

"How did she do it?" he asked. Because he might need to use the same "trick" later.

"I don't remember, but it was a trick," Rue replied.

Thomas chuckled. "Well, if you're up now, you could help me with the chickens."

"I can help?" She perked up at that.

"*Yah*. Come on, then. We'll get the eggs. Go ask Mammi for the bucket and bring it out."

Rue disappeared back into the house and Thomas pulled off his work gloves, slapped them against his leg and tucked them into his back pocket. The screen door opened again, and Rue came out, dragging a blue plastic bucket half as big as she was. Patience held the door for her, letting her do the lugging on her own. He couldn't help but let his gaze linger on Patience as she smiled down at his daughter.

"Carry it on down to your *daet*," Patience said cheerily. "And when you're done with the chickens, your dress will be finished."

He dragged his gaze away from her—staring wasn't appropriate behavior.

"Patience is making a dress, Daddy!" Rue hollered as she thumped the bucket down the stairs. "And it's pink!"

By the time she got to him, she was breathing hard, and he bent down and picked up the bucket by the handle.

"Pink, you say…?" he said, and he started toward the chicken coop, Rue trotting along next to him.

"I don't want it," Rue said.

"I know," he replied. "But it's just an extra dress."

"I don't need more," she countered.

The chicken coop was quite large, since Amos wanted his chickens to have space to move about. There was an outside space where they could run and scratch that was portioned off with chicken wire, and then the whitewashed coop where the nesting boxes were.

"Now, you've got to watch for the rooster," Thomas said. "You just stick close to me, and I'll deal with him."

"Why?" Rue asked.

"He's protecting his hens. So he tries to show you that he's boss. You can't let him be boss."

Rue looked up at him, wide-eyed. "Is he naughty?"

"Yah," he replied. "He's very naughty."

"Do you punish him?" Rue asked.

Thomas laughed. "You can't punish a chicken, Rue. They aren't very smart. One of these days, we'll eat him, and then I'll get a new rooster."

"You can't just eat someone for being naughty!" Rue retorted.

"He's not a someone. He's a chicken!" Thomas said, stopping short and looking down at her. "That's where your chicken comes from on your plate, you know."

"What's his name?" Rue asked plaintively.

"He doesn't have a name. He's a chicken." Thomas shook his head. Not only was she an Englisher child, but she was an Englisher child raised in the city. "Rue, don't worry. I won't let him peck you. He'll be fine."

Thomas started toward the coop again, Rue in tow.

"He won't be fine if you eat him!" she said, tramping along behind him. "I'm going to name him Toby."

"You can't name him Toby," Thomas said, opening the coop door.

"Why not?"

"It's not an Amish name," Thomas said. "Besides, we don't name chickens. It's very awkward to eat a chicken you named."

"Daddy, you can't eat Toby."

She hadn't even met the silly bird yet, and she'd grown attached. This was not an argument he'd win, he could tell. "Come on inside, Rue."

The door shut behind them, and Rue wrinkled her nose at the smell.

"*Yah*, chickens smell, too," Thomas said with a low laugh. "Now come on, we're going to get the eggs and put them in the bucket—but very carefully. We don't want to break them, okay?"

"Okay..."

For the next few minutes, Thomas took her around to the nests, pushing his hand under the ruffled hens to retrieve eggs. He handed an egg to Rue, and she cautiously put it in the bucket.

"The eggs are warm," Rue said.

"*Yah*, they start out that way," he agreed.

The rooster eyed them with beady, mistrusting eyes. But he knew Thomas well enough that if he came at him with his spurs and beak, he'd get a boot. Later this evening, Thomas would come back and clean out all the wood shavings and put in some fresh ones to make the coop smell clean again, but it was always a challenge because Thomas couldn't turn his back on that bird. The rooster lowered his head and fluffed up his neck, and his wings came out.

"No, you don't," Thomas said, and he picked up a wooden switch and flicked it at the bird. The rooster backed off for the moment.

"Why is he mad?" Rue asked, accepting another egg to put in the bucket.

"Because he's a rooster," Thomas said. "And he wants to keep the hens to himself. He's a jealous, feathery little fiend."

"He needs a hug, maybe," Rue said.

Thomas looked down at her, bewildered. "Rue, never

hug a chicken, okay? That rooster will hurt you. He doesn't want a hug."

Rue didn't look convinced of that, and he sighed. When they gathered the last of the eggs, including three that had been laid on the top of a beam, Thomas nodded toward the door.

"All right, let's go out now," Thomas said.

"Goodbye, Toby…" Rue said softly, and Thomas pulled the door tight shut behind them. The bright sunlight shone off Rue's blond head and she hopped along next to him as he carried the bucket of eggs back toward the house.

When they got inside, Thomas lifted Rue up so that she could reach the sink, and with one hand he helped her soap up her hands, while he held her under his other arm, like a calf. When she was clean, he washed his own hands, then they dried them and headed into the kitchen.

Patience sat at the table, a mound of fabric in her lap that she was clipping some stray threads from. She lifted it and shook it out, and he saw a small pink cape dress. His heart gave a grateful squeeze.

"I see you brought us eggs," Mammi said with a smile.

"It's a lot of eggs," Rue said.

"We have a lot of baking to do," Mammi replied. "Cakes, and buns and bread and pies…"

"Can we share some with Toby?" Rue asked.

Mary and Patience both looked toward Thomas questioningly.

"She named the rooster," he said helplessly.

"That ratty, ugly, nasty rooster?" Mary asked with a shake of her head.

"His name is Toby, and I love him," Rue declared.

"Don't call him those things! Call him pretty and sweet... Call him Toby!"

"Come with me into the other room, Rue," Patience said. "I'm going to get you into your new dress and you can show your *daet*."

Patience took Rue's hand and they headed down the hallway together.

"I think Toby needs to be hugged..." Rue's little voice was saying as they disappeared into the laundry room.

Thomas rubbed his hands over his face, then shook his head. "She's so—"

"English?" Mary asked, but her tone was full of humor.

"Yah," he said. "She's English. To the bone, it would seem."

"I thought we were going to eat that rooster," Mary said.

"I'm not sure we can now," Thomas replied. "She decided she loved it sight unseen. I have no idea why."

Mary chuckled. "Welcome to being a *daet*, Thomas. Your whole world goes upside down. And *kinner* seldom make perfect sense. They are confusing little bundles of personality and willfulness. Gott grows us more through parenting than He does through anything else."

"Yah..." Thomas had heard the same thing repeated over and over again, but he was getting a firsthand view of exactly how true it was.

From the other room, he could hear Patience's soft tones... It was different having her here—but it was different having Rue here, too. Suddenly this house full of bachelors had more female presence to even them out. But he found himself straining to hear one particular voice—the soft, reassuring tones of their schoolteacher.

Rue emerged into the kitchen again first, clad in that small pink dress that fit her perfectly. Her feet were bare, and her hair was tangled, and she looked up at Thomas irritably.

"Very nice," Thomas said with a smile. "You look like an Amish girl now."

"I'm not an Amish girl," Rue replied.

Patience came up behind her, holding Rue's folded sundress. Patience looked as cool and neat as a spring morning, except for one tendril of honey-blond hair that had come loose from her *kapp* and fell down the side of her face. There was something soothing about their new schoolteacher. She calmed him, at least.

"Will it do?" Patience asked.

"It'll more than do," Thomas said. "It's perfect."

Patience smiled at that, her own blue gaze meeting his for just a moment, before she seemed to feel the hair against her face and she tucked it back up under her *kapp*. Then she turned toward the table with the scraps of cloth, bits of thread and the open sewing box and started to clean up. Thomas's gaze moved back to his little girl.

"Thank you for this, Patience," he said quietly.

"*Yah.* You're welcome. It's no trouble," she replied. "I'll make another one tomorrow."

But it wasn't about the trouble, it was about the transformation. If this little wildcat could be made to look Amish, then it was a step in the right direction. Because while he couldn't help the start she'd had in life, he could try to make up for it now.

Could he raise his daughter to become like this—an Amish woman who loved this life? Could he give his daughter a community, a place to belong and work that made her happy?

Maybe… But when he looked over at his daughter, she was looking down at her dress balefully.

"She looks very proper," Thomas said. Not happy, but at least she looked Amish.

"I think she looks like you, Thomas," Patience said, and then she moved past him toward the cloth scrap bag.

Hopefully that wasn't a comment on his expression, because Rue looked about as sweet as that rooster outside right now. Rue needed more than genetics to help her settle in. She needed a new mother, and some brothers and sisters to nail her down. Because her link to her *daet*, as well-intentioned as he was, wouldn't be nearly enough.

Chapter Five

The next day, Patience worked on a second dress for Rue with Mary's help in some of the hemming and the cutting. Between the two of them, the work went smoothly, and Rue played outside in the garden, picking the tender, tiny pea pods and crunching on them whole. She looked toward the chicken coop, standing, staring thoughtfully, and then gathered a few more pea pods and headed over there.

Patience watched her through the kitchen window.

"What's she up to?" Mary asked.

"Feeding peas to the chickens," Patience replied.

"Ah." Mammi smiled at that. "At heart, *kinner* are all the same. They like to eat and feed things."

Patience chuckled at that. She'd find out a lot more about *kinner* when she had a classroom filled with them from the first grade through to the eighth. She was used to caring for her nieces and nephews, and most young Amish women had plenty of practice in taking care of little ones. But this would be a whole new challenge.

Last night, sleeping in the upstairs bedroom of the

Kauffman house, Patience had lain awake wondering about the strange story surrounding Thomas. If she hadn't been told what had happened, he would seem like a regular Amish man to her. He loved his work, he seemed dedicated to the Amish way of life and there was nothing about him that stood out as different. And yet, everything about him was different.

But he wasn't the only one with a peculiar story, it would seem. These men were bachelors living together, or so she'd been told. And most had been married before.

Patience reached for an iron staying hot on the stove and smoothed it over a finished seam on the cape of the dress. The kitchen was overly warm because of the stove, and they had all the windows propped open, and the side door, too, trying to get some cooler air moving through.

Mary was making sure the stove did double duty, and she had some meat pies baking in the oven alongside some potatoes and some flatbread cooking on the stove top—all to feed the hungry men who'd be home soon for their dinner.

"What happened to Amos?" Patience asked. "He has a beard. Did his wife die?"

Mary looked up from her work, using her bare fingers to pluck up some flatbread and flip it on the pan.

"That's a sad story," Mary replied. "She didn't die. Her name is Miriam, and she left Amos after their first year of marriage. She went back home to her family in another community."

"Why?" Patience asked.

"They weren't happy," Mammi replied. "They were

both stubborn, and we all told him when he set his sights on her that it wouldn't end well. She was too well off, and Amos barely had two nickels to rub together." Mammi paused, thoughtful. "We aren't supposed to focus on money, but it does make a difference. He could afford a little cottage on the corner of someone else's land. And her *daet* owned two farms free and clear. They butted heads a lot, and Amos was more fiery-tempered back then."

"Oh…" Patience sighed. "That's sad."

"*Yah*, it is," Mammi replied. "And she broke his heart when she left him. But now they're both living their own separate lives, and… It is what it is."

"Isn't it worth patching it up?" Patience asked.

"He tried once. He went out to see her *daet*, but her *daet*'s a proud man, and he told Amos that if he wanted his support in bringing Miriam back home, then he'd better prove himself a better provider. That insulted him deeply, and he just couldn't forgive it."

"And she'd rather live without a husband?" Patience asked.

"Well… The way I heard it, she'd rather live without the fighting," Mary replied. "A marriage takes two, dear, and she wasn't used to Amos's ways any more than he was accustomed to hers. There is always another side to the story."

Patience brought the dress back to the table where she had better light and sat down to begin hemming the sleeves.

"Noah and Thomas came to stay with us because we had the room," Mary went on. "Besides, the boys were both working with Amos in the carpentry shop, so they all knew each other well. When their *mamm* jumped the fence, they had the choice to go with her, or to stay with us. They both chose to stay."

"Is he like a *daet* to them, then?" Patience asked.

"More like an older brother," Mammi replied. "He's protective. He gives advice. They're as close to *kinner* as he'll ever get, I suppose."

How many women had just walked away from the men in his household? Amos's wife abandoned him, and Noah and Thomas's mother did the same. From what she could see of these men, they were kind and decent—and lonesome. Men needed some nurturing as much as anyone—maybe even more so when they seemed the strongest.

Mary rapped on the kitchen window. "Rue, stay away from there!"

"What's she up to?" Patience went to the door and saw Rue stop short at Mary's call. Rue had been headed toward the horse corral. She looked just like any other Amish girl now in her little pink cape dress, except her hair was shorter, with bangs in the front, and she still wore her flip-flops.

"Come back inside, Rue!" Patience called.

Rue turned and came back toward the house, dragging her feet and glancing over her shoulder a couple of times.

"I wanted to see the horses," Rue said as she came up the steps.

"The horses aren't for playing," Patience replied. "They could squish you."

Rue sighed and came indoors, her little flip-flops making a slapping sound against the bottoms of her feet.

"You can take those off," Mary said. "Go barefoot."

Rue stepped out of the sandals and walked away from them.

"Put them in the mudroom, dear," Mary said. "We all have to pick up after ourselves, or else we'll have nothing but mess and confusion."

Rue looked up at Mary mutely, her eyes suddenly misting.

"It's okay," Patience said, and she scooped up the sandals herself, depositing them in the mudroom next to the men's big boots. "Are you hungry, sugar?"

Rue smiled faintly at the endearment. "Yeah…"

"Come have a taste of some flatbread," Mary said. "Come on, it's okay. Come try it. Supper is ready soon. We're just waiting on the men."

Outside, she heard the sound of a buggy's wheels crunching over gravel and the cheerful rumble of deep voices. The men were home. Rue came dancing across the room, a piece of flatbread in one hand, and she stood in front of the closed screen door, waiting.

Patience gathered up her work and put it into a sewing basket. The dress was nearly finished—two more hems and it was ready to be worn. When she'd cleared her work off the table, the door opened and Amos came inside.

"Something smells wonderful, Mammi," Amos boomed out, and then he looked down at Rue. "Hello, Rue."

Rue stared at him in wide-eyed silence.

"You can't be so noisy with little girls," Mary said, shaking her head. "Now, you wash up and sit down, Amos."

Amos cast Patience a rueful look, but did as Mary asked of him. Noah was next to come inside, and he squatted down to say hello to Rue.

"I like that dress," Noah said with a smile.

"It's okay," Rue said. "I can run in it."

"Well, I like it," Noah replied. "Did you know that I'm your uncle?"

Rue shook her head.

"Well, I am. I'm Uncle Noah. And when Uncle Amos gets too noisy, you just tell me, okay?"

Rue shot a look toward Mary, and Patience chuckled.

"Mammi can take care of that, too, I'm sure."

Noah grinned in Patience's direction and stood up to go wash his hands when Thomas came inside. His gaze moved over the kitchen, stopping at Patience for a moment, and he gave her a small smile. He had already washed, and he had a package in his hand—a white plastic bag.

"I brought something," Thomas said, turning to Rue.

"For me?" Rue whispered.

"*Yah*, for my little girl," Thomas said, and handed her the bag.

Rue opened it and pulled out a cloth doll wearing a purple Amish dress and a bonnet. She looked at it for a moment, then tears welled in her eyes.

"No," she whispered.

"What's wrong, Rue?" Patience asked, bending down next to her.

"No!" Rue said. "I don't like it! I don't want it!"

"It's a beautiful doll, sugar," Patience said. "I think it's lovely."

"I don't!" Rue shook her head. "I want a Barbie. I want a Barbie with long hair and pretty dresses."

A Barbie… Patience didn't even know what that was. When she looked up, she saw Thomas standing there awkwardly, his gift rejected. He took off his hat and ran a hand through his hair.

"What's a Barbie?" Patience asked.

"An Englisher toy. The *kinner* love them…" Thomas put his hat on a hook and heaved a sigh. "I'm sorry, Rue. We don't play with Barbies here."

Tears spilled down Rue's cheeks, her lower lip trembling, and Patience scooped her up in her arms, cuddling her close. Rue pushed her wet face into Patience's neck and let out a trembling sigh. The discarded doll lay on the floor next to the crumpled plastic bag.

Thomas looked at her with a helpless expression on his face. He bent down and picked up the doll and bag. He wadded the bag up in one hand, and placed the doll on the corner of the table.

"I thought I'd try," he said, his voice low.

"Give it time," Patience said. "She'll play with it eventually."

Maybe. Unless she decided to blame all things Amish for the depth of her loss.

"Yah." Thomas lifted his hand as if he wanted to pat his daughter's back, and then he let it drop. "Would you stay for dinner, Patience?"

"I don't mean to intrude on your family time," Patience said.

"No, it would be…helpful," Thomas replied. "If you wanted to, at least."

"Sure," she replied. "If it would help."

* * *

Thomas picked up the doll and carried it into the other room. He looked down at the fabric body, with the little purple cape dress that was a perfect imitation of the dresses worn by the women in their community. The doll had brown hair made of string that disappeared behind a crisp white *kapp*. Lovina Glick had sold it to him— one of several she had for sale. There had been one doll with blond hair like Rue's, but she'd been wearing a black dress, and Thomas thought she'd like a purple dress better.

He'd shown the doll to Noah and Amos, and they'd thought it was a great idea, too. He'd wanted to make his daughter happy, and her reaction cut him more deeply than he wanted the others to know.

When he came back into the kitchen, Rue was sitting next to Noah at the table, and Patience was in the kitchen with Mammi.

Noah gave Thomas a sympathetic shrug, silently offering some emotional support.

"Rue, why don't you come help me?" Mammi called. "We need someone to wash carrots. Do you think you could do that?"

Rue looked over hesitantly.

"The water is nice and cold," Patience added. "It would feel so nice on your hands."

Rue climbed down from her chair and headed over to where the women were working, and Thomas met his brother's gaze.

"I asked her about the doll," Noah said. "She says she likes the rooster better."

Thomas smiled at that and shook his head. "She's a stubborn one."

"A lot like her *daet*, might I add," Amos said, coming to the table with a stack of plates. "You were never one to settle into anything without a struggle. Look at what it took to get you home and Amish again."

Thomas had to admit that was true. He'd had to go out there and make his own mess of mistakes before he could see that the Amish life was the one for him. So maybe expecting a more submissive personality from his own daughter wasn't realistic. That possibility was also daunting. It was one thing for a man to accept his own mistakes in his journey home, but quite another to face the likelihood of his daughter doing the same.

"I'm going to pick three more carrots!" Rue said, running for the door. Thomas watched her slam outside, then looked over at Mary and Patience.

"Oh, she's fine," Mary said. "It's good to have young ones help. Besides, they have more energy."

Mary looked out the window, then rapped on the glass.

"No, Rue! Not those! Those are cucumbers!" Mammi called. "Over more…more…by the tree, Rue! Yes!"

Patience stood at the counter mashing potatoes, and he saw the smile tickle her lips. She glanced up and met his gaze, her eyes glittering with humor.

"She's gone to see the chickens…" Mary sighed, turning back to the stove. "The Englishers really don't teach their *kinner* how to fetch things, do they?"

Patience laughed. "She's new at this."

Mary muttered something Thomas couldn't make out, and he chuckled. "She'll come back with carrot tops, you know."

Four-year-old Englishers didn't know how to pull carrots, and he got up from his seat and headed to the side door to see how she was doing. But when he got there, all he could see was a single, dirt-covered carrot, several more carrot tops, as he'd predicted, but no Rue. She wasn't in the garden or at the chicken coop, either. His heart sped up, and as he scanned the property, he spotted her over by the corral.

"Rue!" he called.

Rue looked over her shoulder, but didn't stop moving closer to the horses. The unbroken stallion was closest to the fence, and Thomas's heart stuttered to a stop.

"Rue!" he barked, sounding a whole lot gruffer than he even intended. The girl stopped. She didn't turn, though, and she seemed undecided about what she was going to do. He didn't have time to find out.

Thomas headed out of the house and then strode across the yard in Rue's direction. She saw him coming, and instead of turning back, she climbed up on the fence and thrust her hand out toward the stallion.

The horse, whether in response to the unexpected hand, or to Thomas's thundercloud of a face, shied back just as Thomas arrived and slipped an arm around Rue's waist, plucking her neatly off the fence.

Rue set up a howl, and he stalked back toward the house, his daughter under his arm. His heart was hammering hard in his chest, and when he got to the side door, he was met with four mildly surprised adults staring at him.

"She went for the horses," he said, putting Rue down. She immediately collapsed into a pile, wailing her heart out.

"That's very dangerous," Amos said. "And she didn't listen."

"I'm telling you," Mary said, fire in her eyes. "It's those Englishers and their lazy way of bringing up their *kinner*. No discipline!"

But Thomas wasn't actually convinced of that. Rue couldn't be blamed for not knowing the dangers around her. She hadn't been raised with horses and chickens and carrots that came from the ground. She knew about cars, crosswalks and not to talk to strangers. Not much of that applied here—not on a daily basis, at least.

And yet, he was the *daet* here, and everyone was looking to him to decide on what should be done. It wasn't just a misunderstanding—she'd willfully disobeyed. She had to be disciplined, but the prospect of doing so clamped a vise around his chest.

"Come, Rue," he said firmly, picking her up and setting her on her feet. Then he led her out of the kitchen and up the stairs.

Rue continued to cry, but he could tell at this point that her crying was mostly put on for effect, and she watched him with teary curiosity as he led her up to the bedroom she shared with Mary.

He set her on the side of Mary's bed, and she sniffled and wiped her eyes.

"Why didn't you obey?" he asked, sitting down on the edge of the bed next to her.

Rue didn't answer.

"There are rules in this home, Rue," Thomas said slowly. "And they are going to be different rules than what you had with your *mamm*. You won't have to worry about the same things. There will be no day care, or holding a rope, or electrical sockets. But there are dangers here, too. And those horses are dangerous. They could crush you."

"I wanted to hug him," Rue said.

Thomas felt that rise of frustration. Why did she have to be so different? Why couldn't she see reason? Obviously, small *kinner* weren't going to be as rational as when they got older, but even the little Amish *kinner* knew better than to try to hug horses in a corral. They learned quickly from the adults around them.

"He could have bitten you," Thomas added. "That horse has very big teeth."

Rue pulled her fingers back into a small fist and licked her lips.

"You must never disobey like that again," Thomas said firmly. "What did your *mamm* do when you got in trouble at home?"

Rue blinked up at him.

"Did you get sent to your room? Did you get put in a corner?"

Rue didn't answer. Had she been corrected at all?

He looked around the room. He had to make a point, or else she might get herself badly injured next, all because of uncurbed defiance.

His gaze landed on her suitcase, and he rose to his feet and went over to it. Rue's gaze followed him, and as he opened the case, her entire body lurched forward.

"No!" Rue shouted.

Thomas pulled her pajamas out of the case and laid them on the edge of the bed.

"I am going to leave you your pajamas, but I am taking the rest of your old clothes until you can listen better. When you are able to do as you're told and obey the first time, you can have your suitcase back."

Rue's eyes stayed fixed on the case, filling with tears. The color had gone out of her cheeks and her hands trembled. "No…"

He could already feel how deeply this was cutting the girl, but he'd made a decision and he had to stand by it. *Kinner* didn't benefit from parents who swayed with the wind, and she had to learn to listen, if only for her own safety.

"*Yah*, Rue," he said firmly, picking up the case. "Now, you will come downstairs for your dinner."

Rue turned her back on him and laid her head down on Mary's pillow with a shuddering sigh. She didn't cry again, but she didn't turn to look at him, either, and he stared at that tiny form, filled with his own misgiving. Was this going too far?

But he'd made his decision, and he couldn't go back on it now, so taking the suitcase with him, he left the room and deposited it inside his closet. When he came back down the hall, he looked in Mary's room again and Rue hadn't changed her position. She lay on the bed, so small that she barely took up a corner, her entire body curved around her knees, and her tangled blond hair spread across the white cotton of Mary's pillow.

"You can come down for dinner, Rue," he repeated.

"No," Rue said.

So he carried on down the stairs. The meal was on the table, and Amos and Noah were both seated already. Patience was just putting a bowl of gravy on the table when she spotted him.

"Is she coming to eat?" Mary asked.

"No, she doesn't want to," Thomas replied.

"What did you do?" Noah asked. "A lecture?"

"A lecture, and—" He swallowed. "I took her suitcase."

"Just as well," Mary said, coming to the table. "Those clothes are inappropriate for our girls anyway. If she's going to be one of us, those clothes had to go. The sooner the better."

Patience didn't speak, but there was a tightness around her mouth that betrayed an opinion, and she dropped her gaze.

"Let's pray," Amos said, bowing his head. "For this food we are about to eat, make us truly grateful. Amen."

"Amen," the rest of them murmured, and there was the rustle of food being passed and the clink of dishing up.

"Was I wrong?" Thomas asked, turning toward Patience.

"You're her *daet*," she said simply.

"But was I wrong?" he pressed. "I know what Mammi thinks. I want to know what you think."

Patience accepted the bowl of mashed potatoes from Noah and handed them to Thomas.

"Those clothes are more than something she likes," Patience said, her voice low so that only he could hear her. "They are her last link to her dead *mamm*."

He knew that, and he hated the way she'd caved in like that when he took them. He wasn't going to burn them—and he knew plenty of men who might in the same situation.

"If she'd liked the doll, I might have taken that away. But something had to be done."

"I agree..."

"Any ideas?" he asked.

Patience shrugged weakly. "She's lost too much. I don't know. Maybe other *kinner* to play with—to see how they're expected to behave—might help."

And that seemed to be the only answer that kept coming back—she needed other *kinner* in her life, and the sooner the better. If he was already married, there would be siblings, but as it was, he'd have to find her some playmates one way or another.

Thomas accepted a plate of chicken from Mary and took a leg, then passed it to Patience. She took some white meat and passed it along.

"Ben Smoker asked if one of us would help him with a broken gate tomorrow," Amos said.

"I could do it," Noah said. "When does he want us to come?"

"In the morning," Amos replied.

But the timing was just too perfect. Thomas needed to show Rue other *kinner* so that she could see that their way wasn't some random, cruel list of rules to follow. She had to see that others were like them, too. And the Smokers had five girls, twelve and under.

"What if I went?" Thomas said. "I could bring Patience and Rue with me, and Rue could play with some *kinner*. It would be good for her. She might see how another family runs."

Amos shrugged, and looked over at Noah.

"*Yah*, I don't mind that," Noah replied. "I didn't want to get behind on that bedroom set that's due to be finished next week, anyway."

"Would you be willing to come along?" Thomas asked Patience.

Patience nodded, and from the stairs, there was a small, shaky voice. "I'm hungry."

They'd all been speaking German up until now, and Thomas looked up to see Rue standing there, her eyes red from tears, and looking so small that his heart nearly broke.

"Come have your dinner, then," Thomas said, patting the stool next to him. "It's chicken."

Rue froze, and he could almost see the cruel possibilities running through her little, tousled head.

"It's not Toby," he clarified.

"Oh, good..." Rue sighed, and she came up to the stool and stared at it.

"Here—" Thomas lifted her onto her seat. When she was settled, Thomas and Patience both set to filling her plate.

"Now, eat up," Thomas said.

And in those words, he meant so much more—he wanted to say that he loved her already, and that he wanted to keep her safe. He wanted to say that he was sorry that he had to punish her, and that he was only trying to teach her the right way.

But he couldn't say all that, so instead, he gave her a little extra gravy.

Chapter Six

The next morning, Thomas flicked the reins as the horses got into their pace, trotting down the paved road, their hooves clopping cheerfully. Patience sat across from him, with Rue between them, scooted forward so her legs could hang normally. This would help—he was sure of it.

He'd been praying last night about his predicament, and community was the answer to all of an Amish man's troubles. He'd been reading Galatians, and he came across the verse that said, "Bear ye one another's burdens, and so fulfil the law of Christ." This was what the Amish strove to live—but going to a neighbor with a vulnerability wasn't always easy. It took humility—a painful amount, he realized now. But Rue needed to belong to more than just him—she needed to belong *here*.

The day was sunny, with some fluffy mounds of cloud sailing overhead. The bees seemed extra busy this morning, circling the wildflowers that grew in the ditches lining the road, and he got that old feeling of nostalgia. It had been a long time since Thomas had driven out this way. Two or three years, actually. He'd been avoiding it ever since he got back from his extended Rumspringa. It held memories that he no longer knew how to process.

Thomas glanced down a familiar side road that led to a creek he and Noah used to play in as boys. It wasn't deep enough to swim, but it had been wet enough to play in on a hot summer day after chores.

"I used to live down here," Thomas said.

"Really?" Patience shot him a curious look.

"You see that house up ahead—the one with the trees in front?" It had been whitewashed when they lived there, but it was the same house. "That was ours."

He and his brother helped their *daet* whitewash the house and the chicken coop every few years. The winter wind had a way of blasting the paint, and they liked to keep their home looking bright and fresh. Daet worked as a farmhand at a local dairy, and Mamm had kept house, like the other Amish women did.

"You really had no idea they weren't born Amish?" Patience asked, switching to German.

Thomas shrugged. "I had no idea. You tend to think your home is normal... Looking back on it, I suppose there were a few signs. My parents spoke English when they were alone. I used to think it was their way of hiding what they were saying from us kids. And maybe it was. Sort of like we're doing now to keep Rue from understanding us... But now, I realize, it was more than that, because the only time they could have talked freely in their first language would have been when they were alone together."

How unsettling was this for Patience to hear about?

He'd worked through a lot of his own anger about his parents' secrets over the last few years, but there were still times when his feelings about it took him by surprise. When his father died and his mother left the community, he'd lost both parents and his sense of place within his own community all at once. He'd been bereft and adrift. He'd needed every ounce of charity that had been offered to him—including the home that Amos and his grandmother opened up for them to live in.

As they came closer to the drive that led up to his childhood home, Thomas noticed some signs of a new family living there—a truck in the driveway, the growl of a tractor coming from farther back on the property. There was a tree closer to the road with low, spreading branches, and a swing still hung from the straightest of them. The rope was new, though. There must be kids living here.

Thomas reined in the horses.

"I used to swing on that swing when I was a little kid like you, Rue," Thomas said, pointing.

"Can I swing on it?" Rue asked.

"No, it isn't ours anymore," Thomas replied.

The door opened and a woman in shorts appeared on the step. She shaded her eyes to look at them, then waved. Rue waved exuberantly back.

"Hello!" Rue shouted.

"Rue, stop that," Patience said briskly, and she exchanged a look with Thomas.

"Hya." Thomas flicked the reins.

"We could ask if I can swing!" Rue said, leaning around Patience to get a better look at the Englisher woman. "She'd probably let me!"

There was no doubt that the woman would let Rue swing, but the price for that would be conversation, and Thomas knew better than to get chatty with the Englishers. Friendships were a two-way street, and for better or for worse, the Englishers in these parts were bent on developing friendships—sharing their experiences, asking too-personal questions.

"Rue, we are Amish," Thomas said. "We keep to ourselves."

"But I'm not," Rue said.

"You're my little girl, so yes, you are," he countered.

Rue frowned at this and leaned back against the seat.

"Her people *are* Englishers," Patience said in German.

"Not anymore," Thomas replied. "I'm raising her Amish. And that's that."

"Of course, but she can't deny her own *mamm*," Patience replied. "Everything she knows and remembers…"

"So I should let her play with Englisher *kinner*, then?" he asked, shaking his head. "I should let her chat with Englisher neighbors? What would you have me do?"

There was a beat of silence, and then Patience said, "I don't know. But her situation might be more complicated than a child born here. That's all I'm saying."

And maybe Patience was right, but what was he supposed to do? Tina had kept him away, and now that Rue was under his care, he had to do what he felt was right. And an Amish life was right. So maybe, in a way, he was doing the exact thing that Tina had done…

"What would you have me do?" Thomas asked, shaking his head. "Her *mamm* was Englisher. Well, so is mine. Am I less Amish because of my parents?"

"I didn't mean that," Patience replied.

"There has to be something said for the life you were raised to, whether or not your parents were raised in the same way," he said. "I'm going to raise her Amish— and there will be no chatting with Englisher neighbors. She'll be Amish through and through by the time she's old enough for her Rumspringa."

And if God blessed his efforts, then she'd stay Amish, too.

"You're her *daet*," Patience said simply.

"I know what it's like to have connections…out there," he said.

"Then you understand how she feels, I imagine," Patience said.

"I understand what she *needs*," he replied. "And she needs to find her place in our community. She needs the stability, the sense of who she is on the narrow path. She doesn't need distraction or reminders of the life she came from. She needs a solid future."

He was frustrated, and he attempted to relax his iron grip on the reins. This child was so determined to cling to her Englisher upbringing, and while he couldn't entirely blame her, he didn't know what to do. There was no halfway with the Amish life.

"Thomas…" Patience said.

He looked over and she reached past Rue and put a hand on his upper arm. Her touch was warm and gentle, melting away the irritation rising up inside him.

"Yah?" he said.

"You're a good *daet*." She smiled then, and he sucked in a slow breath.

Amish families were calm and collected. Already, he was feeling himself getting riled up at the thought of everything he could not control, but at a touch from her hand, he was reminded of everything he was supposed to be. It made him want to close his fingers around hers, tug her closer against him… But there was a child between them, and this new addition to his life had to have his focus.

A man could make a good many mistakes in his life and manage to forgive himself, but the errors in judgment he made with his own *kinner* were the ones that haunted him. He couldn't afford to mess this up with Rue.

They carried on for another couple of miles, then turned down a gravel road that led to the Smoker farm. Patience was silent, and Rue, who hadn't understood any of their German conversation, swung her legs and watched the scenery go by.

As they turned into the Smoker drive, Rue leaned forward when she saw two little girls in the garden. They were barefoot, and they each had plastic ice cream pails that they were filling with weeds. The girls stood up when they saw the buggy and wiped their dirty hands on their dresses.

"There are kids here!" Rue said with a smile.

"*Yah*, you'll have some girls to play with for a little while," Thomas said, and he was glad to see that his daughter was simply happy to see other children, instead of judging whether they were Englisher or Amish.

"This is better than a swing," Rue announced.

Thomas looked over and met Patience's eye. She shot

him a smile. Then the door opened and Susan Smoker came out with a wave and a smile. Thomas pulled up the horses.

"Good morning, Susan," Thomas called. "I've come to help Ben with the gate."

"Yah, yah," Susan said. "He'll be glad of that. I think he's in the main barn right now."

"I've brought the new schoolteacher," Thomas said. "Meet Patience Flaud. She'll be teaching some of your girls this year."

"Pleasure to meet you." Susan's smile spread. "Well, come on down and let's get some pie, then."

It was then that Susan's gaze fell on Rue, and Thomas could see the question forming on her face before she said anything.

"This is my daughter, Rue," Thomas said, and he cleared his throat. "It's a long story, but suffice it to say, she's from my Rumspringa. I know I did wrong, and Gott has forgiven me, but... Her *mamm* passed, and she's mine to raise now."

"Oh..." Susan nodded twice. "So she's Englisher, is she?"

"Yah," he admitted.

"She looks it," Susan replied.

Rue, not understanding the conversation, just stared, her blue eyes wide and uncertain. After Thomas hopped down from the buggy, he lifted his daughter down, and then held a hand out to help Patience to the ground, as well. It felt oddly comfortable to have a little girl and a woman in his care today.

But when he turned back to Susan, her easy smile was gone and she was staring at Rue solemnly. The girls arrived from the garden just then, and an older girl opened the screen, a toddler on her hip. The girls were all in matching dresses—some dirtier than others—and he couldn't help but feel a bit of relief. This was the kind of family that Rue needed to see—respectable, well behaved, pious. Except Susan looked a little less welcoming now.

"I hope it's a convenient time for us to get to know each other," Patience said, seeming to read Susan's altered expression at the same time.

"*Yah*, of course," Susan said. "Do you need clothes and shoes for her, Thomas? Because we have some dresses the girls have outgrown and a couple of pairs of shoes, too—"

"*Yah*, thank you," he replied. "That would be a great help. We're starting from scratch, and this was a bit of a shock."

Rue looked up at Thomas uncertainly, and a part of him wished he could stay with her, help her feel more comfortable. But he was here to help Ben, and Patience could help her navigate. Patience seemed to sympathize with Rue's plight, at the very least.

"Go on inside with the women, Rue," Thomas said. "You'll have friends to play with."

It would be all right. This was where his daughter belonged—with Amish playmates and a community that would help her get a proper start...just as soon as they forgave her father for the mistakes that had brought her into the world.

Patience took Rue's hand and followed Susan Smoker into the little farmhouse. Susan looked over her shoul-

der again at Thomas, who was leading the horses toward the stable, then she sighed. Patience looked in the
same direction, watching Thomas's form as he walked
away. He was a strong man, but right now, Patience
sensed he was at his most vulnerable. It was all coming
back on him—his mistakes, his family's problems…
To simply look at him, a woman would never know. If
Patience had met him under any other circumstances,
he'd be just a handsome Amish man, laughter twinkling
in his eyes and good looks that could sway just about
any single woman.

"It's good to meet you… Patience, is it?" Susan said,
drawing Patience's attention back.

"Yes," she said with a smile. "Likewise."

The kitchen was neat, and the table had some basic
school worksheets laid out—some printing, some counting… Someone was getting ready for school. The older
girl stood by the door with the baby on her hip, looking
at Patience shyly. Patience smiled at her, then turned
to Susan.

"How many of your girls will be in school this year?"
Patience asked.

Rue leaned against Patience's side, and she smoothed
a hand over the girl's head.

"Three," Susan replied. "This here is Bethany—
she's in seventh grade this year. She's got baby Leora.
And Rose is in the fourth grade. Dinah is just starting
grade one."

Dinah and Rose were the girls who had been weed-
ing, and Dinah, the smaller of the two, wiped a stray
tendril of auburn hair away from her face, leaving a
streak of dirt behind.

"And let me see…" Susan turned to spy her fifth daughter munching on a muffin by the counter. "That is our little Ellen. She's only five, so she starts school next year."

Patience smiled at the girls. "I'm glad to meet you. This is Rue. She's four."

"Bethany, let me take the baby," Susan said. "And you take Rue upstairs. Get those dresses from the back of the closet—the ones Dinah outgrew…"

Susan set about giving instructions to her girls, and Bethany took Rue's hand and led her upstairs. The other girls followed, chattering away to Rue in German. Rue wouldn't understand, but they'd figure that out eventually.

"Could you hold the baby for me?" Susan asked. "I'm going to get us some pie."

Patience took the chubby baby girl with a smile, and overhead was the sound of laughter and giggling.

"Now that the *kinner* are out of the way, who is this little girl—Rue, you call her?" Susan asked.

Patience pulled out a kitchen chair and sat down, settling the baby on her lap. "He's Thomas's daughter, as he said. You'd know Thomas's family better than I do—"

"His *mamm*—Rachel—she left us," Susan said. "We know that, but she always was a little different. I'd heard that they'd converted in another community, then moved here. But you could tell—there was just something about them… They spoke English too well, for one. And their German was terrible. After Rachel left, Thomas left, too, for a while, then came back and got baptized. We had no idea there was an Englisher child."

"Yes, well…" It wasn't Patience's place to talk about anything that personal. "She's a sweet little girl. Her *mamm* died in a car accident, and she's doing her best. But she's a fish out of water out here. She's still adjusting to our ways."

Susan nodded sympathetically. "I'm sure she is. But she doesn't speak German?"

"No," Patience replied. "Not a word. Yet, at least. I'm sure her *daet* will teach her."

"And she's…wild and willful?" Susan pressed.

Patience knew what Susan was getting at. It was how they all seemed to see the Englisher *kinner*. And while Rue was Patience's first Englisher child to get to know, she could already see that their assumptions weren't completely true, either.

"She's a little girl with a broken heart," Patience said simply.

"*Yah*, of course." Susan came to the table with two plates of shoofly pie. "I'm just…surprised by all of it. It's a lot to take in. So… What about you, then? Where do you come from?"

"Beaufort," Patience replied.

"And single, it seems?" Susan raised her eyebrows. Patience laughed at that. "*Yah*. Very single."

"We'll see what we can do about that…" She took her baby back into her lap, then pressed a kiss against her head.

It wouldn't be any use setting her up, though. It wasn't that men her age weren't interested in her upon first sight, but she couldn't offer the family an Amish man yearned for. She wouldn't explain this to Susan Smoker, though. The woman meant well, but Patience would have to find another way to live her life...focus on the ways she could contribute to her community. Teaching school was a valid option.

"Mamm!" Dinah appeared at the top of the stairs. "This girl only speaks English!"

"Yah," Susan replied. "I know. See what clothes fit her, all the same."

"And she wants to know where our TV is!" Dinah added.

Patience felt her own cheeks heat at that. "She's still adjusting to our ways. She needs some time."

"And some scripture, it would seem," Susan said. "Was she raised believing in Gott?"

"I'm not sure," Patience admitted.

"And she says—" Dinah started.

"Enough, Dinah!" Susan said. "Find her clothes, then come back down."

"Yes, Mamm." Dinah disappeared again.

Susan stared up at the staircase for a moment, then turned back to Patience with a tight smile.

"I hope this doesn't reflect badly on our community as a whole," Susan said. "We're actually a very respectable bunch."

Patience didn't know how to answer that, except, this situation wasn't quite so cut-and-dried. Thomas was going through a lot more struggle than they were giving him credit for—all of which he'd confided in her, and she couldn't break his trust. Thomas had quickly become more than just a neighbor, she realized in a rush. He was truly a friend.

"Thomas thought you'd be a good influence," Patience said, lowering her voice. "He needs support—

he needs a way to raise her, and that involves a whole community. He sees your *kinner*, and he wants to do the same for his little girl."

"Either we'll be a good influence, or that child will be a bad one," Susan said bluntly. "One or the other."

Patience fell silent, and the girls came back down the stairs, bare feet slapping against wooden floorboards. Their hair was all wild, all except Bethany's, who carried herself like a small adult already, with three dresses in her arms and a pair of girls' running shoes. Susan brightened at the sight of them.

"That's wonderful. That should get you started, Rue," Susan said in English.

"Daddy will give me my clothes back after I'm good," Rue said.

Susan looked over at Patience questioningly, and Patience felt her heart tug toward the little girl. After she was good… Did that mean she thought she was currently bad?

"Thomas took her Englisher clothes," Patience explained. Thomas had meant well, but he'd been wrong there.

"Not forever!" Rue insisted. "He said he's going to give them back, after I'm good for a bit. So I have to be good."

"I don't think they're coming back," Susan said in German.

Rue's eyes narrowed—seeming to dislike the switch in language.

"You needed shoes," Patience said, turning to Rue. "That's so nice of the girls to share theirs with you."

"I don't fit them anymore," Dinah announced. "They're too small for me."

Rue looked at the shoes doubtfully. "I like pink."

"We wear black shoes in our community," Susan said.

"I like pink," Rue repeated. There it was—her stubborn streak that was so problematic.

"There are pink running shoes?" Dinah asked, switching to English, too.

"No," Bethany replied. "Not for us. That's what the Englishers wear."

"I'm not Amish," Rue said simply. "So I can wear pink shoes."

The girls exchanged looks, but Dinah's gaze was fixed on Rue with a look of open curiosity. Ellen was staring, too. Patience could all but see those little gears running for both girls. They were being exposed to a brand-new idea today—that Englishers had things that sounded downright wonderful to a small girl, like pink shoes.

"Rue, say thank you," Patience said, forcing a smile.

"Thank you," Rue said quietly.

Yes, she could see the problem here, but if that stubborn spirit could be turned to use her strength of resolve in favor of the Amish life, all would be well.

"Come play outside, Rue," Dinah said, holding her hand out to the smaller girl. "I'll show you the chickens."

Rue smiled at that. "We've got a rooster named Toby, and my daddy wants to eat him!"

"Toby will probably be tasty," Ellen said in a matter-of-fact tone, following the other girls as they clattered outside, leaving Bethany in the kitchen with them. She reached for her baby sister, and Susan handed her over with a smile.

"Dinah's very interested in Rue's Englisher stories," Bethany said, her voice low.

"What kinds of stories?" Susan asked sharply.

"Oh, TVs, their toys, princesses..."

"The Englishers don't really have princesses," Patience said. "It's only a game, and a foolish one, at that. Gott made each of us equal, and we ought not to raise ourselves above each other. It's wrong and only leads to unhappiness. An honest wife with a kind husband and houseful of *kinner* is far happier than a princess in a tower somewhere."

"You're telling the wrong person," Bethany said, casting a too-grown-up gaze onto Patience. "It's Dinah who needs to hear it. And maybe Ellen."

Patience swallowed. Bad ideas could spread just as quickly as that. It was why the Amish *kinner* were kept away from the Englishers—*kinner* were impressionable. Rue was just a little girl, but she was also a child who didn't want to be Amish, even now. And somehow, Patience felt protective of little Rue...

"Bethany, could you go out and keep an eye on them?" Susan asked.

"*Yah*, sure, Mamm," Bethany said, and she headed out the side door, the baby on her hip.

When the door shut behind her, Susan cast Patience a tired smile. "I know she's just a little girl, and I know you have nothing to do with this... In fact, I feel terrible for you that this is your introduction to our community. But we need to be careful with our girls. I'll suss up some more clothes for her for winter—I've got some warm clothes put away in storage that she can have, and some boots, too. But I can't have her back here to play with my girls."

Patience met the woman's gaze. "She's very young…"

"So are mine."

Patience nodded.

"Look, I'm sorry to put you in the middle of this," Susan said with a shake of her head. "My husband can tell Thomas himself. I just thought I should mention it, all the same."

Patience looked toward the window where she could see the girls out by a white-painted chicken coop beside which the chickens ran free. Rue had squatted down to be closer to the hens that were pecking at the ground, and Ellen and Dinah stood close by. There was a peal of laughter and Rue looked up, her eyes glittering with delight.

"You haven't started your pie," Susan said. "And Patience, you make sure you come back to see me, yourself. It'll be so fun to have another woman around to chat with…"

But Patience wasn't listening. Rue would never be Amish enough, Patience realized, her heart sinking. She'd always be the girl with the Englisher *mamm*, and there'd be no changing people's knee-jerk reaction to that fact. They had families of their own to protect, *kinner* they longed to shelter, and Rue was a walking, breathing threat to their careful plans. This was going to break Thomas's heart.

Chapter Seven

They all left after Thomas was finished helping Ben Smoker with his gate. As the horses made their way back home without much guidance from Thomas, Rue chattered excitedly about her new friends, which only made Patience feel worse for the poor thing. Even Thomas seemed cheerier after the visit—apparently, Ben hadn't had the chance to fill him in on his wife's request that Rue stay away from the Smoker girls. When they got back to the house, Mary needed help with the laundry, and Thomas went to work at the carpentry shop, leaving the women to their own work. There was no chance to talk to Thomas alone, not without drawing undue attention to herself, so she needed to wait until the men returned that evening and it was time for her to head back to the Kauffmans' house.

By dinnertime, a clothesline of laundry fluttered outside—and this time, there were men's shirts and pants, two of Mammi's dresses and two tiny dresses lined up next to all the adult clothing.

The men came inside smelling of wood shavings and

hard work. Amos was telling a story that made Noah laugh, but Thomas remained silent, his gaze immediately seeking out Patience in the kitchen. There was something about the spontaneity of his attention that warmed her cheeks. Rue spotted her father and gave him a shy smile.

"I have something different for you today," Thomas said, squatting down. He had something wrapped in a handkerchief, and Patience paused to watch.

"What is it?" Rue asked, coming closer. She pulled aside the cloth and her eyes lit up.

"It's a rooster!" Rue exclaimed, holding it up. "It's a Toby, Daddy!"

Patience got a glimpse of the gift—a little carved rooster about the size of a tin of tuna. Rue hugged it to her chest, then she sidled up closer to her father and tipped her head onto his shoulder. Thomas patted her head tenderly, then rose to his feet again.

"Did you want to stay for dinner?" Thomas asked Patience.

"Thank you, but I won't stay tonight," she said.

Amos and Noah had turned their attention to nabbing a bun each from the dish Mary had been guarding.

"Would you like to…walk with me back?" Patience asked hesitantly. It was forward of her—far too forward, actually. They were both single, and this would look an awful lot like courting. But she needed to speak to him alone, and she wasn't sure how else to do it.

"Uh—" Thomas's gaze looked uncertain for a moment, and then a smile tickled his lips. "*Yah*, I'd like that."

After saying goodbye, Patience hurried to the door.

How this must look! When she got outside, her face felt like it was blazing, and when she glanced over at Thomas, she found him looking mildly amused.

"This looks terrible," she burst out. "I'm not really this forward."

"I didn't think you were," he said.

"I'm not trying to start something, Thomas," she added.

"That's too bad," he replied, his warm gaze catching hers. He was teasing—she could see it in the glint in his eye.

They started their walk down the drive, but Thomas didn't seem in a big hurry. He sauntered along slowly enough.

"I just had to talk to you alone, and I didn't want to draw any attention to it because Rue has been through enough lately, and—" Patience looked back over her shoulder and Thomas did the same. Mary was looking out the door after them, and when she was spotted, she whisked back inside.

"I don't think it worked," Thomas chuckled. "What's going on?"

"It's Susan Smoker," Patience replied. "Did Ben say anything to you?"

"No." He sobered now. "What's the problem?"

Patience licked her lips. "Oh... Well, it seems that Susan—" She didn't want to have to say this out loud. It was cruel, and when she turned to look at Thomas again, he reached out and caught her hand. It wasn't a casual touch, either—it was purposeful, steadying.

"Patience, what is it?" He kept her fingers clasped in his, and there was something about his warm, strong grip—she couldn't let herself appreciate it. So she tugged her hand free. Thomas seemed to realize what he'd done then, too, and he pulled his hand back to his side.

"She says that Rue can't come back," Patience said. "I'm sorry. I tried to point out that her daughters could be a good influence for Rue, but…"

Thomas was silent for a moment, and Patience could see the emotions clashing over his face—anger, frustration, hurt. These were people Thomas thought he could trust to help him in his most vulnerable time as a brand-new *daet*. He'd been wrong.

"Did Rue do something bad?" Thomas asked.

"No! She was fine. She…just talked. As *kinner* do."

"About Englisher things," Thomas surmised.

"*Yah*, about Englisher things."

Thomas sighed, and he started walking again, and she fell in at his side.

"I'm sorry," Patience added. "I don't think Susan is being fair to her."

"I don't think Susan is thinking about Rue at all," he replied quietly. "She's thinking about her own girls."

"That's true…" Patience rubbed her hands over her arms. "Do you want my advice, for whatever it's worth?"

"*Yah*, I do." Thomas looked down at her. "What do you think?"

"Maybe it's better to start out with time alone with you," Patience replied. "It's her relationship to her *daet* that will be most meaningful. Maybe until people relax a little more, you could do some special things with Rue alone."

Thomas chewed the side of his cheek, and they reached the top of the drive. He walked over a few paces until he was shrouded from view at the house by some lilac bushes, the blooms wafting fragrance. He smiled faintly.

Patience went over to where he stood and looked past his shoulder. Anyone in the house could no longer watch them—was that on purpose? They had some privacy—for a moment or two, at least.

"You know how this looks, Thomas," she said.

"They can't see us," he said.

"You know what I mean!" she laughed. "And I know it's my own fault, but I'd really rather not start rumors right away. You should go back."

"I don't want to go back," he replied, and he caught her gaze with a challenge in his eye. "Do you?"

She didn't, actually. It felt nice to stand here in the cool shade of the lilac bushes, this handsome, kind man inches away from her... This was the very thing she couldn't be getting used to, or playing with.

"I'm your first friend here," he said. "And I will make sure to set everyone straight as soon as I get back to the house."

"Do you promise?" she asked quietly.

"*Yah.* I promise. Besides, we haven't figured out what I'll do with Rue all by myself."

Patience was silent for a moment, her mind going back to her own childhood. "My *daet* used to take me and my sisters to the river. We had one that ran through our property, and we'd pack up a picnic lunch, and he'd take us out to the river to eat it together. Once, when my *mamm* and sisters had gone to a quilting circle, my *daet* took me to the river alone, and we sat and threw stones into the water…"

She smiled at the memory. Her *daet* had been a loving man, and he had a way of making every single one of them feel like the favorite.

"There's a creek I used to play in as a boy," Thomas said. "My brother and I used to go there together after chores were done, and we'd dam it up with stones, and then let the water through again in a rush… I pointed it out on the way to the Smokers' place."

"That's right. I remember. A creek is part of a complete childhood," she said.

"I don't know if Rue would even want that much time alone with me," Thomas said. "I'm the gruff one—the one who punishes."

"Rue loves the rooster," Patience countered.

"Yah." He smiled. "I got that one right." He paused, the sound of birds twittering filling the silence as his gaze moved slowly over her face. "Would you…come with us?"

Did she dare? It wasn't that she didn't want to, it was that she might want this time with Thomas and Rue a little too much. She didn't belong here—not like that.

"I'm not sure I should," she admitted.

Thomas nodded. "Okay. I understand. I'm sorry if I'm crossing lines I shouldn't. I know you'll find some nice man sooner or later and he'll marry you, but—"

"It isn't that," Patience said, shaking her head. There wouldn't be other men. She knew that already. "I don't want to intrude. You don't have to entertain me or anything. And this is about you and Rue. I'm…an outsider."

"No more than I am," he said with a sigh.

A bug fluttered next to her face and Thomas reached out and brushed it away. The movement was impulsive, but once his hand was next to her face, he didn't pull back, and neither did she. He touched her cheek with the back of one finger, and that warm gaze met hers. She felt goose bumps rise on her arms, but she didn't drop her gaze. His eyes moved down to her lips, and he stepped closer.

"She's comfortable with you," he murmured.

Patience meant to answer him somehow, but there were no words in her head, and all she seemed able to feel was the warmth of his chest emanating against her and the tickle of his breath against her face. The moment seemed to deepen around them—even the sound of the birds seeming to drift away. She swayed toward him, and he caught her hand in his, stepping closer, too. But the growl of a car engine was too much to ignore, and they both took a step back as a car swept past them, a whoosh of air ruffling her dress around her legs.

She let out a shaky sigh, suddenly feeling very alone on that street with the gulf between them. What had just happened there? If it weren't for the car, would he have kissed her? She dropped her gaze.

"Thomas—"

"Patience, I—"

They both started talking at once, then they both halted. Patience looked up at him again, some heat in her cheeks.

"I'd like it if you came along for our picnic to the creek. That's all," Thomas said, clearing his throat.

That was all… And maybe whatever had just happened in that moment was just in her imagination.

How could Patience say no to going with Thomas and Rue to the creek? Because she wanted to go along, too, and somehow some time with this man, even if it was nothing more than friendship, felt like a chance at some fleeting happiness. She smiled hesitantly.

"Okay," she said.

"Yah?" A smile turned up his lips. "The shop is closed tomorrow, so... It's a day off anyway. Come over after breakfast, and we'll head out to that creek I used to know."

"Are you sure you wouldn't rather bring your brother?" she asked. He shared the memories with Thomas, after all.

"Nah." A playful grin came back to his face. "I think I prefer you."

Was that flirting? She rolled her eyes. "You could bring the whole family."

"I could." Was that confirmation that he would? He didn't say anything else, but he smiled again teasingly. "Will I see you?"

"Yah." Patience nodded. "I'll see you then."

Patience paused, then turned and took a few steps toward the Kauffman property.

"Are you flirting with me, Thomas?" she asked, turning.

Thomas turned back and hooked his thumbs into the front of his pants. "What if I were?"

"I'm not a good one to flirt with, you know," she said.

"Then don't worry about it," he replied, but that teasing glint hadn't left his eye, either.

Patience didn't have an answer for that, so she hid her smile by turning around and continuing down the road. When she glanced over her shoulder, Thomas was heading back to his drive.

And what if a man flirted a little? It was nice to be noticed and appreciated. It didn't have to go any further than that. She'd just have to be careful not to let things go too far. And she could do that—she knew where things stood. She was helping a man bond with his little girl, and that was a good thing.

Rue needed all the bonding she could get.

As Thomas walked back down the drive toward the house, his mind was spinning. He hadn't intended to flirt—he knew better than that. Amish courted—they thoughtfully and purposefully moved toward a marital union. They didn't flirt and fool around. But there was something about Patience that sparked the competitive male inside him, and the ability to make her blush or smile just like that… But he wasn't looking for romance right now. He was trying to find his balance being a *daet*, so trying to make her smile—it was inappropriate.

But there was something about her—something that tugged at him in spite of all the reasons he should be keeping his distance. And he'd almost kissed her. That realization in itself was a surprise, because he hadn't been thinking of that when he asked her to step behind the lilacs on the street. He'd only been thinking of Mammi, who was likely standing at the front window, watching hopefully for some sign of blooming romance. And knowing Amos, he wouldn't have been far behind.

But that instinct to flirt, to draw her eye—that came from a different source. And the last time he'd listened to it, he'd found himself in a relationship with Tina. His instincts led him wrong, and he needed Gott's guidance if he was going to be the kind of man his daughter could be proud of.

When he got back to the house, the food was on the table—roast beef and mashed potatoes. It smelled wonderful and his stomach rumbled in response to it. Everyone had started eating. They looked up as Thomas came back inside, and he caught Noah's knowing glance.

"Sorry about that," Thomas said, and he slid into his place next to his daughter. She had the carved rooster sitting next to her plate. He smiled down at Rue as she plunged her fork into a fluffy pile of mashed potatoes, topped with a pool of gravy.

"So you saw her off, did you?" Amos said in German. He passed a platter of beef down the table toward Thomas.

"Yah," Thomas said, accepted the platter and served himself two slices.

"She's very pretty," Mary added. She didn't look up from her plate, though. She took a bite of meat and chewed deliberately slowly.

Thomas chuckled. "I know what you're doing."

"Us?" Mary said innocently. "She's a lovely woman. We're just...pointing it out."

"And single," Amos added with a grin. "We've all confirmed that."

"She also seems to like you—which is a point in her favor, because look at you," Noah joked.

Thomas laughed, and shook his head. "It isn't what you think."

"What are they talking about?" Rue asked, leaning closer.

"They're teasing me," Thomas replied. "They think Patience is pretty, and that I should take more notice of it."

Rue frowned slightly. "Oh."

Thomas shook his head. "Someone pass me the potatoes, please."

But despite his protest to the contrary, he was noticing her. She was beautiful, but even so, in their friendship, he sensed that she was holding back in that regard. Was it the man she'd left behind who still filled her heart? And was that all this was—some petty jealousy over a man he'd never even met? Some male competition? Because that would be disappointing.

"Can I go back to see the girls again?" Rue asked.

"No," Thomas said softly.

Noah looked up when he said that. "Why not?"

"It's nothing," Thomas said quickly. "I have something else for Rue and me to do tomorrow. We're going on a picnic."

Mary smiled at that. "Good! That sounds fun."

"Just the two of you?" Amos asked.

"Patience is going to come along," Thomas replied, and he knew how this looked, so he added, "If you all want to come, that would be…very nice."

Amos shook his head, his mouth full, and Noah chuckled.

"Nah," Noah said. "I've got some things to work on here at home."

"And I have some sewing of my own to do, dear," Mary said. "I couldn't possibly."

They were making it so that he'd get time alone with

Patience, and he knew it. But at least he'd invited them, even if he was relieved they'd turned him down flat.

"It will be fun, Rue," Thomas said. "I'll take you to a creek I used to play at when I was a boy. You can play in the water and look for tadpoles. We'll pack a lunch to take along."

Rue smiled up at him, and he felt a well of love for his little girl. Some time together—Patience was probably right. What Rue needed was her *daet*, not a bunch of strangers. She needed family, and if there were to be *kinner* in her life, maybe they ought to be siblings.

Chapter Eight

Saturday morning, Thomas, Noah and Amos went out to do their morning chores—mucking out the stable, bringing hay for the horses, cleaning the chicken coop and gathering eggs. Rue came with them wearing her new-to-her running shoes instead of her pink flip-flops, and she stood to the side obediently when they told her to. There was no wiggling or laughter. She was utterly serious, watching everything they did.

"Are you trying to learn how to do the chores, little one?" Amos asked her with a smile.

"I'm being good," she replied seriously. "And I'm not getting in the way."

"Come carry the egg bucket," Noah said.

She looked askance at Thomas first.

"Sure," he chuckled. "Why not? But don't hug Toby."

"I won't hug him," Rue replied. "Not even once."

The men chuckled to themselves and carried on with their chores. Thomas was rather impressed with Rue's improved behavior. Was that because she'd seen some Amish girls who knew what was expected of them?

While there wouldn't be more visits with the Smokers, maybe that one visit had been enough. Maybe his fatherly instinct had been right, and he felt a wave of gratefulness for one small step that had seemed to work in his favor, after all. Gott surely did work in mysterious ways, and maybe this was one of them.

When they got back to the house, Amos and Noah sat down with some hot coffee and Mary went off into the sitting room with her Bible. Thomas set about packing their picnic lunch and Rue waited until Thomas was nearly finished before she tugged at his pants.

"Yes, Rue?" he said.

"Was I good?" she asked.

"*Yah*, very good," he said. "Get me three napkins out of that drawer there." He pointed with his socked toe.

Rue opened the drawer and pulled out three cloth napkins, and he tossed them on top of the food and then closed the basket up. It would be a tasty lunch—roast beef sandwiches, pie, apples, some slices of cheese and a bottle of apple juice.

"Have I been very good?" she asked, and she fixed him with a direct stare.

"*Yah...*" For such a small girl, she was filled with a strange intensity.

"Can I have my clothes back, then?" Rue asked, her voice shaking just a little.

"Your clothes." Her connection to the Englisher world—the clothes all the adults knew had to go. He'd been hoping she'd forget, quite honestly, that after she settled in she wouldn't even think of her Englisher clothes again and he could quietly dispose of them.

"Yes. I need them. They're mine." Her eyes welled

with tears, but she didn't cry, and she didn't look down. She stared up at him hopefully. He looked at Amos and Noah. They'd overheard Rue's request and they stared back at him in silence, offering no hint into what they were thinking.

"Well…" He swallowed. "You can't wear them, Rue. You know that, right?"

She didn't answer, but her lip trembled. Her face was so pale, but those eyes were filled with a determined fire.

"They aren't Amish," he added gently.

"They're *mine*," she whispered hoarsely, and the intensity of her gaze nearly choked him.

Thomas had a choice here—keep the clothes, and possibly destroy them, or give them back. She was only a child and didn't know what was best for her life yet. And he was her father—it was his job to guide her, whether it made her happy in the moment or not. But that little suitcase of Englisher clothes… He knew what they meant to her, and even if he wanted to erase her Englisher side, it wouldn't be possible anyway. Nor did he have the right to do it. She'd come into this world because of his relationship with her Englisher mother. And now he was trying to undo it?

"Rue, I'm going to promise you something," Thomas said quietly.

"Okay?" Rue said hopefully.

"I am not going to do anything to your clothes. They're safe in my closet right now, and I won't hurt them or get rid of them. They're still yours, okay?"

Maybe that would be enough and given time she'd finally forget about them. Maybe she'd see that the Amish life he offered her was worth more than a suitcase of purple and pink summer wear.

"Can I have them back *now*?" Rue pressed earnestly. Her hands were balled up into fists at her side. "I was *good*. I'm a good girl. Can I have them?"

The "no" was on the tip of his tongue, and he almost said it, but he couldn't bring himself to. She wanted those clothes so desperately, her whole body trembling with her desire to have them back, and he couldn't be the one to keep them from her.

"Of course you're a good girl," he said tenderly.

She stared at him, mute, and her eyes filled with hopeful agony. He was beaten. He knew it, and when he looked over, Amos and Noah had both dropped their gazes into their coffee cups. They knew it, too, apparently.

"Yes," he said, at last. "You can have them back. But you can't wear them."

"Okay..." Rue visibly deflated with relief, and the tears that had welled up in her eyes finally rolled down her cheeks. "Thank you, Daddy."

"Oh, Rue," he said softly, and he squatted down next to her and gathered her into his arms. She leaned her face into his shirt and her tears soaked into it, wetting his chest beneath. She cried softly with big, shuddering sobs. Had she been carrying that around inside her all this time? Had he been too harsh on her? He rose to his feet, picking up Rue in his arms as he stood. "I'll give them to you now."

He went up the stairs, his daughter in his arms, and he carried her into his bedroom. His bed was neatly made, the floor swept, and his window open just enough to let a breeze inside. He set Rue on the edge of his bed and went to his closet and pulled out the little suitcase.

Rue jumped down and gathered it up in her small arms.

"Oh, thank you!" she breathed. "I love my clothes, Daddy. I do! I really love them."

And he knew it wasn't about her clothes so much as her mother. She loved her mother most desperately, and this was her last link to the mother she'd likely forget over the years. She wouldn't retain many of her memories of Tina, and he was sorry for that.

"All right, then," he said, a lump in his throat. "Go put those in your room, and then we'll go down, okay?"

Thomas waited for her at the top of the stairs, and when Rue rejoined him, they headed back down, Rue scampering happily on ahead. There was a knock at the door when he got back into the kitchen, and Amos rose to open it.

As expected, Patience stood on the step, and Thomas felt a wave of relief as she came inside.

"I think we're ready to go now," Thomas said. "Come on, Rue."

"I got my clothes back, Patience!" Rue said as they all headed outside. "Because I was good. I was extra good. I didn't hug anything. Nothing at all!"

Patience laughed and held out her hand for Rue, and Thomas headed over to the stables to hitch up horses. He felt deflated, exhausted and not entirely sure he'd done the right thing, either with taking her clothes away to begin with, or with giving them back. He'd certainly made an impression on her, but what would she take away from that? That her *daet* was capable of strange cruelty? That she was required to behave perfectly in order to keep what was rightfully hers?

Gott, I don't know how, but I've already gone wrong here. I need Your help.

Within a few minutes, they were in the buggy and headed up the drive to the road.

"So you gave her back the clothes?" Patience asked in German.

"Yah," he replied. "I did. I… It might have been a mistake. I realize that. The elders would tell me so, I'm sure."

"But you're her *daet*. It's your call," Patience replied.

"It is," he said grimly.

"For what it's worth," Patience said, "and this coming from a schoolteacher who's never once taught school, so you can take that into account… I think you did the right thing."

"Yah?" He looked over at her, surprised. "I thought I caved in, actually."

Patience shrugged. "But you didn't break her heart."

Thomas smiled to himself. *Yah*, that was true. How fondly would she think of the Amish life if her Amish *daet* was the one to keep breaking her heart?

"I do have an idea of what you could do with her Englisher clothes," Patience said.

"What's that?" he asked.

"You could make a quilt from them," Patience said. "That way, her clothes would be preserved in an Amish way, and she'd still have those memories of her *mamm* close by."

Thomas nodded. *"Yah.* That's a good idea, actually."

It was a solution that hadn't occurred to him. Maybe

it took a woman's touch to get there. He glanced over at Patience and smiled. Did she know how much she did for him, just by being here at his side while he waded through the biggest challenge of his life?

"What's a good idea?" Rue asked.

Had he said that in English? He hadn't meant to, but there was no harm done.

"What if we made a very special quilt—that's a blanket for your bed—out of your old clothes?" Thomas asked. "You see, you're growing fast, and soon you won't be able to even squeeze into those clothes. And in the winter, they'll be too cold. But if you had a quilt, when it's cold, you could wrap yourself up in it."

"Ooh…" Rue smiled. "*Yah*, I like that."

Yah. Had he heard that right? She'd answered like an Amish girl. He looked over Rue's head to find Patience smiling, too, with a twinkle in her eye.

"Good, then," he said, not wanting to draw attention to it. "We'll see what we can do."

The creek was set back from the road a little way, shaded by spreading trees. Patience could feel all tension seeping out of her at the tranquil scene—grass rippling in a warm breeze, lush trees, the babble of water that she couldn't yet see, although she knew the land well enough to know that the line of trees would be along its banks. A swarm of sparrows flapped up like a sheet in the wind farther on down the stream, billowed, then settled again in the trees. Thomas tied up the horses with a long enough line to let them graze, and he carried the basket as well as a worn blanket down toward the water with Rue dancing along ahead of them.

Patience had been thinking about that tender moment between them at the lilac bushes all evening, and she'd prayed earnestly that God would simply take away whatever it was that seemed to be brewing between them. She prayed for God to provide for Thomas and Rue—to give them the *mamm* in their family that they needed. She knew that wouldn't be her, and while the prayer did stick in her throat just a little, she prayed that Thomas's wife would capture his heart and they'd love each other well.

It was the kind of prayer that a good woman prayed— at least, that's what she thought. A good woman should be able to pray a thankful prayer for other people's blessings, but she still found that it hurt to pray it. Maybe it was some selfish, sinful corner of her heart that wished he could stay single, too, and they'd remain close friends, and she wouldn't have to watch him move on with another woman.

But out here by a babbling creek, the wind ruffling her dress and Rue laughing at the sheer freedom of the morning, she had to silently pray for strength. It would be too easy to fall for this man, and there would be no benefit in it. She wasn't the wife for him.

"So you used to play here?" Patience said in English.

"*Yah.* My *mamm* would pack me and Noah a lunch and send us off on her floor-washing days. She always said we got in the way more than we helped, so we'd carry our lunch down here and we'd play for hours until our food was gone and we were good and hungry again. I used to use a rope and put it over a branch and we'd swing over the water."

Patience could almost see them—two sun-browned boys whooping and playing.

"Were there only two of you in the family?" Patience asked. It was a noticeably small family for the Amish.

"Yah." Thomas frowned. "I asked my *mamm* if she'd have more babies, and she always said that Gott was the one who gave *kinner*, and that I should take it up with Him. I never got more explanation than that."

Patience could understand that kind of answer. She had a similar one, herself, except she wouldn't have the pleasure of having even one child of her own. She often wondered why Gott had taken away this ability for her. There didn't seem to be any benefit to anyone else by denying her the simple ability to be a *mamm*. She was born Amish, with one duty to a husband, and unable to provide it.

"So you wanted more siblings?" she asked.

"Yah, of course," he said. "My friends all had big families and lots of little brothers and sisters to pester them, and I felt like I missed out a bit. I had Noah, but our home was a quiet one. I liked the mayhem."

"I suppose you could make up for that with a houseful of *kinner* of your own," she said, hoping her voice didn't sound strained.

He shot her a grin. "I suppose I could."

Was he imagining those *kinner* belonging to them? Because she was…even though she knew it wasn't a possibility.

"Come on," he said, putting down the basket. "Let's find a spot for the blanket."

Thomas unfolded the worn quilt and handed her one

side of it. They shook it open, and then spread it down on the lush grass that lined the water.

"Can I go in?" Rue pleaded. "Can I go into the river?"

It wasn't much of a river, and there hadn't been much rain that spring, either, so it was only a few inches deep and rippled over the rocks in a merry babble.

"*Yah*, go ahead," Thomas said, and he crossed his arms over his chest, watching Rue pull off her shoes and dip her toes into the water.

"It's warm!" Rue said, and she lifted her dress up above her knees and stepped farther in. "Are there fish, Daddy?"

"There might be," he said. "If you look really closely."

Patience couldn't help but smile, and she put the picnic basket on one corner of the blanket, then lowered herself down to sit on it, adjusting her skirt to cover her legs. Thomas settled himself next to her, leaning back on his hands, and she couldn't help but notice the ripple of muscle that was visible in his forearms. She purposefully looked away, and her gaze fell on the initials sewn onto the edge of the quilt—RW.

"Who made this quilt?" she asked.

"My *mamm*. Years ago."

It was a simple block quilt, and she could see a few blocks that hadn't lined up perfectly. It was the kind of quilt a girl started on, learning as she went. Although, Rachel would have been a wife already when she started learning, she realized.

"I made a few quilts like this," Patience said, running her fingers over the stitching. "In fact, a basic block quilt would be best for Rue's quilt, I think."

"Would you be willing to make it for her?" Thomas asked. He looked over at her, and there was something about his warm gaze that made her look down again.

"Sure, *yah*. I could."

"I'd pay you for your time," he said. "I'm not trying to take advantage of your good nature, or anything."

"You don't have to pay me," she said with a faint smile. "It will give me something to work on in the evenings."

It would give her something to do besides grading papers, quite frankly. And it would help her to feel like she was useful, because that was the thing that had been hanging on her these last few years—a feeling of general uselessness. Yes, she could cook and clean, but so could her *mamm*. She was the barren, single daughter left at home—loved, of course, but not really needed for the running of things. Teaching school was supposed to help with that, but now that she was here in Redemption, she wasn't so certain that it would fill all the gaps. There were a few left over. What Patience wanted most was a home of her own, but that didn't seem likely.

"I messed up by taking Rue's Englisher clothes away," Thomas said.

Patience looked over at him, surprised by the abrupt change in subject. His expression was less guarded now, and he watched his daughter play in the water as he talked.

"I shouldn't have done that," he went on. "If you'd seen her doing her very best to be good—so solemn and careful—and then begging me with tears in her eyes to give them back…"

Patience's heart gave a squeeze. "She's learning, but so are you."

"*Yah*, but I'm the parent, and it's in my power to ruin her. She can't ruin me." Thomas sighed. "If you ever notice I'm doing something that I probably shouldn't, tell me, okay?"

"Are you sure you want me to?" Patience asked. "It would be intruding, interfering."

"It would be insight from a friend," he replied, and he turned his dark gaze toward her.

"Am I a friend?" she asked.

"*Yah*. I thought so. You don't?"

Patience smiled, then shrugged. "I don't know. I'm a neighbor lending a hand. I wasn't sure if you'd want more from me after this."

She knew that her words were loaded—wanting more from her... And she didn't really mean the implied intimacy, because even if he did want more from their relationship, he'd change his mind once he knew that she'd never have *kinner*. She caught Thomas's gaze locked on her, and she looked up, smiling self-consciously.

"What?" she said.

"You're very beautiful," he said quietly.

His words slipped beneath her defenses, and she felt her cheeks heat. Why did he say things like that?

"I'm the plain sister in my family," she said with a low laugh, trying to push away his compliment. "I was never the pretty one. Trust me on that."

"You're the pretty one for me," he replied.

Did he really think so, or was he flirting? It was hard to think of herself in that way.

"You shouldn't talk like that," she said. "I'm the schoolteacher, and you'll be embarrassed later when

Rue is in my classroom and you'll remember sweet-talking me by the creek."

"I won't be embarrassed," he said, and his expression was completely honest. "I'm only telling you the truth."

He'd be married to someone else, no doubt, and that would change things. But she didn't want to say that out loud. There was something about this quiet morning that she wanted to protect. Even if he never thought of it again, she would.

"Tell me about you," he said after a moment of silence. "You have sisters, you said."

"There are six of us—and I'm the youngest," Patience replied. "They're all married now with *kinner* of their own. So I'm the favorite aunt of seventeen youngsters."

Thomas chuckled. "I like that."

"One of my nephews has a learning disability, and I was the one who taught him to read and write," she said. "His name is Mark, and when he was born, he had the cord wrapped around his neck so he didn't get oxygen fast enough. It affected him."

"That's awful," Thomas said.

"Gott brought him through. And now, he's the funniest kid—he tells jokes and has the other kids in stitches. The teacher couldn't take the time with him, though, and I think he distracted the class a lot because he'd rather joke than admit the work was too hard for him. He kept getting notes sent home, and his *daet* was just beside himself trying to get him to behave. But I sat him down and took the time he needed to really understand. And after that, I thought I'd like to teach. It's very satisfying watching *kinner* catch on, especially when they've really struggled with it."

"They must miss you," Thomas said.

"Oh… I suppose. Somewhat. But they all have their own families."

"You're a part of their families," he countered.

"I know. And they do miss me, I'm sure. I'm just feeling the—" She stopped. She was talking too much.

"Feeling what?" he asked.

"I needed this change," she said, and she forced a smile.

"There's a fish!" Rue called from the creek. She stood there, water just past her ankles, looking down at something. "Patience, come look! There's a fish!"

The distraction was well-timed, and Patience pushed herself to her feet. She kicked off her shoes and went barefoot to the bank of the creek, and then stepped into the rippling water. Rue was right—it was warm, and she made her way slowly over the smooth rocks to where Rue stood.

"See?" Rue said, pointing down at a little stick.

"That's not a fish, Rue," Patience chuckled. "That's a piece of stick."

"Oh." Rue straightened and looked around, but just then Patience saw a flash of silver, and then another one.

"Rue, look—" Patience pointed. "There. Do you see that flash? And there. Those are fish."

Rue bent down to look, her dress drifting in the water, but then she shrieked with delight.

"It's fishes, Daddy!" she hollered. "All sorts of them!"

Patience looked up to find Thomas sitting in the same position she'd left him, leaning back on his hands, his legs crossed at the ankles in front of him and his gaze locked on them. It wasn't just Rue he was watching…

She'd better not get used to this. It wouldn't last—it couldn't! And if anyone spotted them, they'd assume they were courting, when they weren't. Once a rumor like that started, it could be very uncomfortable.

"Are you hungry, Rue?" Patience asked.

Maybe it was better to keep things focused on the little girl who had tugged them together in the first place. Because whatever had started to develop between them could only end in someone getting hurt…and she suspected that someone would be her.

Chapter Nine

Thomas opened the picnic basket, and Rue sat on her knees on the blanket, bouncing while she waited for her food. She ate ravenously, much more than he thought a girl that size could consume. But then, when she'd finally eaten her second piece of pie, she seemed to fill up, and she laid herself down on the blanket with a deep sigh.

"Daddy," Rue said quietly. "Do you know any more stories?"

"Yah," he chuckled. "All sorts."

"Tell me a story about when you were little," she said. "Little like me."

"Like you?" he said.

Patience looked over at him with a smile tickling the corners of her lips, and he suddenly felt shy. What kind of story could he tell that would both please his daughter and impress the teacher? That wasn't going to be easy.

"I'm not sure Patience wants to hear stories," he hedged.

"Oh, I do, though," Patience said, breaking into a full smile. "Tell us a story, Daet. We want to hear one."

Daet. The term warmed his heart, and there was something about how Patience said it—with warmth and familiarity. It almost felt like she could be the *mamm* here.

"Okay, you want a story," Thomas said. He frowned to himself, sifting through his memories of childhood antics, punishments he'd received, his brother's tricks and games... "All right, I have one."

"Is it from when you were little like me?" Rue asked.

"I was a little bit bigger than you," he replied. "But I was still a little boy."

Rue fixed him with a direct stare, and then she yawned. "You can start."

Patience seemed to sense Rue growing tired, too, because she reached out and started to stroke the girl's blond hair in a slow, methodical way.

"One spring, when I was a little boy," Thomas began, "my *mamm* got sick with a terrible flu. The flu turned into pneumonia, which meant that she was sick for a few weeks and had to stay inside. So she gave me a very special job to do—I had to plant the garden."

His mind went back to those days, when his *mamm* and *daet* were the center of his world, and he'd never once suspected that they'd ever been anything other than exactly what they were—Amish. Life had been simple back then, and sweet.

"My *mamm* gave me very specific instructions," Thomas said. "I was to plant three rows of carrots, three rows of peas, three rows of cabbage... But it all seemed very tiring. Mamm said I had to put three seeds in a little hole, and then move down a foot, and put three more seeds in a hole, move down another foot... We had a very, very big garden."

Rue's eyes started to drift shut, but she said, "You were helpful."

"*Yah*, I was helpful," Thomas agreed. "At least I intended to be. At first. But when I started planting, it was a very warm day, and I was tired and cranky, and all by myself out there. It was just me and the dirt. I started to get lazy. I started putting more than three seeds in each hole, and I started putting more space between the holes, just trying to finish up faster. And every time I got to a new row, it just seemed like it would take forever to finish up."

Rue's eyes were shut now, and her breath was coming slowly.

"Rue?" he said softly.

There was no reply. She'd fallen asleep. Just as well. He didn't come out well in this story. Maybe he should have chosen a different one.

"So what happened?" Patience asked.

He looked up, then chuckled. "Oh... I did a terrible job of planting, and my parents found that out when it all came up a couple of weeks later. They got some advice from a neighbor about putting some more seeds in between the ones I'd planted too far apart, and I think they were also advised to give me extra chores for a while."

"Did they?" she asked with a small smile.

"*Yah*. They did." He still remembered that punishment, not because it was so painful, but because he'd known that he deeply deserved it. He'd been so ashamed of himself, not helping properly when his *mamm* had been so sick. "But the most important lesson I learned that day was that what you plant will eventually come up, in life as well as in gardens."

"A good lesson," she said softly.

"*Yah*, a good one." He looked down at his daughter asleep on the blanket. "I made mistakes in my life, Patience, and I am certainly reaping from the mistakes I made, but I can't regret my little girl."

"Sometimes Gott gives us some grace in the middle of our consequences," Patience replied.

And that was what Rue had turned out to be—the most generous gift Gott could have given him, in the form of one little girl whom he hardly deserved.

Rue stirred a little in her sleep, and Thomas pushed himself to his feet, then held out a hand to Patience.

"Let's let her rest," he suggested.

Patience accepted his hand and he tugged her to her feet as well, and as they walked the few yards to the creek bank, he kept her hand in his. Her fingers were soft, and the contact with her felt natural in the moment. He turned to look back at Rue, and Patience leaned into his arm. It was an innocent enough movement, but it reminded him of just how close she was, and he dropped her hand then, and slid his instead around her waist.

She felt good there next to him, his arm around her, her face leaned against his shoulder, and looking down at her, he didn't know why he'd been holding himself back all this time. She was beautiful, insightful, kind…

"Patience," he murmured.

She lifted her cheek from his shoulder and looked up at him, and when her gaze met his, he felt like the rest of the field and trees, the creek and the twitter of birds all seemed to evaporate around him. It was just the two of them—this beautiful woman who had tumbled into his life, and himself. His stomach seemed to hover in the center of him, and he swallowed. She was beautiful, but it was more than that... Looking down at her, he was feeling a tumble of emotion that he couldn't even name. But it felt good, and scary and—he just wanted to be close to her. She met his gaze easily enough, and without thinking better of it, he leaned in, wondering if she'd pull back, but she didn't. Instead, her eyes fluttered shut, and as his lips covered hers, he let out a sigh of relief.

That kiss felt like the culmination of everything he'd been longing for, and when they pulled back and he opened his eyes, he saw Patience staring up at him in surprise.

"Oh..." she breathed.

He couldn't help but grin. "I've been thinking about doing that for a little while now."

"We shouldn't do that," she whispered.

"You didn't want that kiss?" he asked. Because it had felt like she did. If he'd gotten that wrong, he'd feel terrible.

"No, I wanted it," she said, and pink infused her cheeks. She pulled out of his arms. "But we can't."

But why not? They were both single and Amish. They both seemed to be feeling something here—unless she was still uncertain about him because of his family... Or was it her own history?

"Is it the man you left behind?" he asked.

"No..." She shook her head. "Thomas, I'm not the wife for you."

"How do you know?" he asked. Was it his history? His parents? His daughter? Was he not Amish enough for her, after all? All the possibilities tumbled through his head.

"You want marriage and *kinner* and a houseful of life," she said.

"*Yah*. Of course," he said, and he smiled faintly. "Don't you?"

"Thomas, I can't have *kinner*."

Her words hit him in the stomach, and he frowned slightly, trying to make sense of it. "What?"

"I had surgery that left me...unable to have children. I'll never get pregnant. I'll never have babies of my own."

Thomas licked his lips, this new information clattering through his mind. "Never?"

"Never." Her voice shook. "I don't tend to announce these things, but I should have said something earlier... before this."

"It isn't your fault," he said. "I kissed you. Not the other way around."

"Still, we can't do that again," she said. "You don't just want a family, you *need* one. Rue needs one! And you'll need a woman who can give you that family and fill your house with babies and laughter."

She was right—he did need that family, but it didn't change how he felt when he looked at Patience, or when he thought of her. She'd seeped in through the cracks somehow.

"I can't help how I feel about you," he said at last.

"We should try, though," she replied, and she met his gaze earnestly. "We really need to try."

And somehow, the serious glint in her eye, the pink in her cheeks and her complete intention to shut down whatever this was sparking between them made her even more beautiful to him. Because she wasn't just an attractive woman, she was a good woman…and that appealed to him most of all. Her beauty sank right down to her core.

"Yah," Thomas said nodding. "I'm sorry. I won't kiss you like that again."

She shrugged sadly. "It's no use breaking our hearts over something that will never work, is it?"

"Not really," he agreed.

"You're a good *daet*," she said, and her voice caught in her throat. "You deserve to be a *daet* many times over."

That had been his dream for a long time—a wife and *kinner* of his own. He'd wanted to be ready to be a good *daet*—to mature into it. But the woman he'd have those *kinner* with had stayed a misty blur in his imagination. Suddenly, she seemed to be taking shape—but Patience couldn't be that *mamm* to his *kinner*.

"Have I ruined things between us?" he asked. "By kissing you, I mean. Can we still be friends after that?"

Patience shrugged, but a smile tugged at her lips. "I could forgive it."

Thomas was relieved to hear that, because he didn't want to send her out of his life, either. He wanted her insights, her presence, her advice. And maybe she was right about a romance not working between them, but she was still an exceptional woman.

"Then I'll curb whatever this is I'm feeling," he said.

"Me, too."

Those words made his heart skip a beat, because it meant that she was feeling this, too. It wasn't just him attracted to the wrong woman...

"You, too?" he breathed.

"Yah." She gave him a nod. "But stopping this now is the right thing to do. We both know that."

The right thing was often the hard thing—as an Amish man, he knew that.

"Should we head back, then?" he asked, his voice low.

"Yah. That would probably be smart."

Because staying out here with her by the creek with all this privacy, he wasn't going to be able to back his feelings off quite so easily. She wouldn't know exactly how she made him feel, but he did.

So he headed over to where his daughter was still sleeping on the quilt, and he crouched down, scooping her up in his arms. Her head lolled against his arm, and he felt a rush of paternal love looking into her pale face. He'd never been able to see her as a baby—but he'd wondered about the child Tina had kept from him. He'd missed so much, but he wasn't going to miss anything more.

Rue was his... And she had to be his priority.

"Could you hold her on the ride back?" he asked, rising to his feet.

"Yah, of course," Patience said.

He'd have to be careful, because his feelings for Patience were growing, and if he messed up this fragile friendship with her, he wouldn't be the only one to suffer. Rue did better with Patience in her life, too, and she didn't have many friends who could look past her beginnings and see the bright little girl she was. She needed Patience more than he did—and if friendship was the way to keep her in his daughter's life, then he'd have to protect that friendship with all his might.

His growing feelings would have to be curbed. There was no way around it.

The ride back to the house was a slow one, and the bright sunlight, the tumble of scattered clouds, the buzz of the bees around the wildflowers and the soft, floral-scented breeze weren't enough to soothe Thomas's heart. The ride out to the creek, with his boyhood memories, was so much sweeter than this ride back.

He couldn't help but feel the weight of what he'd done. He should never have kissed Patience. It was wrong, overstepping... And on this side of it, he felt incredibly stupid. Would Patience ever be comfortable with him again? Amish courting was a slow process that involved much conversation before any kisses were exchanged. A man and woman needed to be certain of each other, to truly understand each other. Then there would be no regrets later on if the relationship didn't work out—no lines crossed that would cause any undue embarrassment.

He'd moved too quickly with Tina in the city, too. But that had been pure rebellion—as was his entire time spent with his *mamm* away from Redemption. And it had been loneliness, too, because he'd missed his brother, his friends, the community that had become a part of him. He'd thought that being with his *mamm* would give him the comfort he'd been missing while he was in Redemption, but as it turned out, a *mamm* wasn't enough. He'd needed more than her presence in his life, and he'd reached for a different kind of comfort. He'd known his relationship with Tina was wrong, and he'd done it anyway.

Was he making a similar mistake now—reaching out for comfort where he shouldn't be? Because Patience was a comfort, a definite help, and having her around made an already difficult situation that much sweeter. Was he leaning on her because of his own longing for some compassion and support? Was that even fair?

And maybe on his Rumspringa, his loneliness was just part of growing up when a man realized that "home" was no longer at his *mamm*'s apron. Home started to take on a new meaning, to come with a new sense of urgency to create his own home with his own wife. But Patience had already made it clear that she couldn't be the wife he needed.

Thomas flicked the reins, urging the horses to speed up again. One horse shook its head, making the tack jingle. He was letting his heart lead when he should be praying a whole lot harder. Hearts could go wrong so very easily, and there was no getting around the fact that his heart was definitely entangled with the woman at his side.

Gott, I'm sorry, he silently prayed. *I don't want to go back to old ways. I want to live a pure life that will please You. I don't want to play with this. I want to marry the right woman. Obviously, I was wrong in kissing her, but...*

He looked over at Patience with his daughter cradled in her arms, her cheek resting tenderly against Rue's blond head. Her gaze was on the road ahead, and she seemed to be equally deep in thought.

I'm feeling things for her that will only lead to heart-break if I let it continue. She's beautiful, and kind, and sweet, and...never to have kinner. *And I know what Rue needs—a family to give her a sense of who she is here in our community.*

Whatever they were feeling for each other didn't matter, because even Patience saw that Rue needed siblings if she was to have a hope of settling into the Amish life on a heart level. He couldn't just raise his daughter for the inevitable heartbreaking day when she left them. If Gott had brought his daughter to him, there had to be a way to raise her so that she'd feel that an Amish life was home. There *had* to be. And Rue's future had to be his top responsibility, not his own comfort.

Take it away, Gott. These confusing feelings that just keep growing—douse them for me. Because I can't seem to get them under control on my own.

The horses knew their way home, and as soon as they got to the drive, they turned in and carried them at an easy pace down the gravel way toward the stables where oats and hay were waiting. Rue woke up and rubbed her eyes. Patience loosened her grip on the girl as she sat upright and looked around herself for a moment in bleary confusion. Then Rue's face fell.

"We left?" Rue asked plaintively.

"We did," Thomas replied, reaching over and giving her leg a pat. "We had to get back."

"Why?"

"Because—" Thomas glanced over at Patience. Because if he'd stayed longer with Patience, it would have made everything harder. He'd have kept feeling this draw toward her, and she'd likely have felt it, too. Leaving had been the right choice—getting back to the bustling distraction of other people.

"Because grown-ups get tired, too," Patience said.

It was a good answer, and he cast her a grateful smile. Thomas reined in the horses, and the side door to the house opened and Amos came outside. He looked almost gray, and he strode up to the buggy, his expression grim. Had something happened? Thomas's first thought was of Mammi.

"Thomas, I'll unhitch the horses," Amos said in German. "You're needed inside."

"What's going on?" Thomas asked.

"Your *mamm* is in there."

Thomas's heart hammered to a stop, and he tightened his grip on the reins, looking toward the house. His *mamm*? She wasn't due for another visit—and when she came, she didn't usually come to the house.

"Did you talk to her?" Thomas asked.

Amos shrugged. "Not much. I mean…pleasantries."

Thomas looked over at Patience, unsure of what to say. Here it was—their family embarrassment.

"You need privacy," Patience said.

He did. He couldn't ask Patience to come help him deal with his mother—this was on him. Rue seemed to sense the tension, even if she didn't understand the language, because her eyes were wide and her little lips were pressed together in a tight line.

"It's okay, Rue," Thomas said. "Come with me. There is someone you'll want to meet."

"Who?" she whispered. "Are they taking me away?"

"No, no," Thomas replied. "No one's taking you anywhere. It's your grandmother."

"Mammi?" Rue sounded confused.

"You have another grandmother." A biological grandmother. A *real* one.

Rue brightened at that, and Thomas got out of the buggy and lifted Rue down beside him. Then he held a hand up to help Patience from the buggy. When she hopped down next to him, he didn't release her fingers right away.

"What do I do?" he whispered.

"You pray," she whispered back.

Thomas licked his lips. He was already praying—a wordless sort of uplifting toward Gott, asking for… He wasn't even sure what. Just wanting to feel Gott there with him—even more of a comfort than this woman beside him. He realized then that he was still holding her hand, and he released her.

"I'll go on back to the Kauffmans', and you'll know where to find me if you need me more today," she said. She made it all sound so rational and simple.

"Yah," he said, his voice thick. "I suppose I'd better go see what she wants."

Patience headed back up the drive, walking briskly, and Thomas looked toward the house. There was no cheery clatter of dishes or the din of laughter. It was ominously silent.

"Come on, Rue," Thomas said, forcing himself to sound cheerier than he felt. "Let's go in."

When Thomas opened the door, Rue went inside ahead of him. She stood in the doorway of the mudroom staring.

"Is that my granddaughter?" Mamm's voice said in perfect, accent-free English. "Hi there, Rue. I'm your grandma."

Thomas followed his daughter into the kitchen, and his *mamm* sat at the kitchen table with a glass of water in front of her, nothing else. She wore her Amish clothes—they looked worn and a little snug. She needed new Amish clothing for her visits, it seemed, but she was still the mother he loved so well—the same laugh lines around her eyes, and her dyed hair had started to grow out a little bit. The last he'd seen his *mamm*, she'd been wearing Englisher jeans and a T-shirt. The memory was strikingly different from the Amish-clad woman before him. Mammi was nowhere to be seen, and Noah sat at the table across from their mother glowering at an empty space on the table.

"Hi, Mamm…" Thomas said.

"Son—" Rachel stood up and circled the table to give him a hug.

"We normally get a coffee in town," he said. "And I thought we were getting together at the end of the month."

"I know," she said. "I just—" She smiled hesitantly. "I want to come back."

Noah's gaze jerked up as she said the words, and Thomas could only assume that his brother was just as surprised as he was.

"What?" Thomas breathed.

"I want to confess and come back to the community," she said, tears welling in her eyes. "I want to come home."

After a decade away, after leaving her sons behind

and forging ahead, building a new Englisher life with her sister in the city. After all the things she'd told him—how the Amish life was too controlling, too restrictive, too hard to live… After she'd shown him how the Mennonites could live a life to honor Gott while using all the modern conveniences, too… She'd been so certain. She'd said that their *daet* was the one who wanted to live an Amish life, and she'd been willing to do it with him, but when he died she just couldn't face another canning season.

Thomas shook his head. "I don't understand. Why?"

"And why now?" Noah interjected. "You left us when we needed you most, Mamm. And now that we're grown men, you want to come back?"

Noah's eyes misted, and he looked away again, his jaw set. Rachel sucked in a wavering breath and she looked pleadingly toward Thomas.

"You have Rue now," she said. "You might need my help with her. I can understand where she came from, and the kind of life you want for her. I understand little girls. I could help you in ways that you aren't even considering yet!"

"I want my daughter to stay Amish," Thomas said, shaking his head. "I don't want her to have more connections with the Englisher world."

Mary came to the top of the staircase, and Thomas stared up at her mutely. She met his gaze for one agonizing moment.

"Rue," Mary called. "Come upstairs with me."

Rue looked at Thomas.

"Go on," Thomas said. "You go with Mammi. This is grown-up business."

"Mammi?" Rachel said softly. She looked like the endearment stung a little—technically, she was Rue's *mammi*, too. Rue walked slowly past Mamm, looking at her in open curiosity as she went by, then headed for the stairs where Mary stood impatiently. The old woman snapped her fingers.

"Rue. Now," Mary said curtly, and Rue picked up her pace as she went up the stairs. When Rue disappeared onto the second floor, Thomas rubbed his hands over his face.

"Did you talk to the bishop yet?" he asked.

"I wanted to talk to you first," she replied. "I'll talk with him afterward."

"You know that's the wrong way to do it," Thomas said. "If you want to come back, you've got to go to him first! You have to talk to the church leadership, confess your wrongdoing, ask to be rebaptized and to be admitted into the community again. This—this is just more flouting of the rules, Mamm!"

"And who taught you those rules?" she snapped. "I did! I raised you to be good Amish men, and I did a good job of it, might I add!"

"So you really want to be Amish again?" Thomas demanded. "After all of it…after you halfway convinced me that this life isn't even what Gott wants of us… Now you think you were wrong?"

"I…" She paused, and then shook her head. "I see things differently now."

They all fell silent and Thomas looked over at his brother. Noah's hands were balled up into fists on the tabletop.

"Are you coming back, then?" Noah asked curtly.

"Do you *want* me to come back, son?" Rachel asked, turning toward her oldest boy.

Noah was silent. He'd never admit it—he was too angry—but Thomas couldn't let this spiral down into anger and emotional punishment.

"*Yah*, we want you to come back," Thomas interjected. "Of course we do."

"Will you…give me a place to live when I do?" Rachel licked her lips, and Thomas could see that was a hard question for her to ask.

"This is Amos's house," Noah said curtly. "And Mary's."

"Mamm, even if I have to find a house of my own, you'll have a place to live," Thomas said.

Tears welled in her eyes. "I miss you both so much… You don't know how much I've missed you. I didn't think I could face an Amish life without your *daet*. He was the one who was most convinced about the theology and all that… But I've had my own Rumspringa, I suppose you could call it. I craved some freedom, to just be my own woman again. I was raised to have a career and an education. I missed theater—operas and plays, especially. I missed that life I used to have… As you know, the Amish life doesn't really allow for all the things that had made me who I was before I got married."

"But do you believe in the church's teachings?" Noah asked dubiously.

"I do. I've gone back to the Bible and looked at the teachings all over again," she said earnestly. "It was having Rue come back to the family that gave me a good mental shake. Tina died so unexpectedly, and I realized that we don't always have the time we think we do."

She wanted to help with Rue, and while he could never turn his own *mamm* away, he couldn't be sure that a *mammi* who'd jumped the fence was the answer for his daughter, either. What he needed most desperately was a deeply devoted Amish wife, and to begin growing the family that would give Rue her roots.

Coming back... Would his mother really do it? Would she come back to the life she found so stifling? Because ten years ago, she'd left this life for the rest of her Englisher family that she'd missed just as desperately. She missed being a "modern woman" with cultured interests and other opportunities. Even if Mamm did come back in earnest, Thomas didn't know how she'd ever find a balance.

Would Rue have any more success than her grandmother?

Chapter Ten

The next day was service Sunday. It was a more lei-
surely morning than usual. Samuel went out to tend to
the horses and chickens, but the regular work would
wait until Monday and the family would get a sem-
blance of a break.

Patience helped Hannah clean up the kitchen after
breakfast, and they put some salad fixings aside to bring
along for their contribution to the light meal served
after worship was done. Last night, Patience and Hannah had baked cinnamon buns, some tarts and oatmeal
cookies, and this morning they packed them into tubs
to carry with them.

Patience couldn't help but think about Thomas,
though. She'd waited to see if he'd ask for her to come
back and help with Rue, but he hadn't, and she didn't
dare go back. It wasn't her place to insert herself into
their family problems, but she was concerned all the
same. Thomas had been through more than most men
had, and she suspected that his mother's visit was an
emotional confusion.

News of Rachel Wiebe's visit had already spread. Samuel saw her waiting for a cab at the end of Thomas's drive, and while he hadn't spoken to her, they had exchanged a silent look.

"Will the Wiebe boys tell the bishop that their mother was here, I wonder?" Hannah said, closing a plastic container. She'd been talking about it all morning.

"I don't know," Patience replied. "Do they need to?"

"She didn't do anything bad enough to get excommunicated from the church, but she's not exactly Amish anymore, either, is she? All after she was baptized."

"*Yah*, there is that..." Patience sighed. "But we're talking about a *mamm* and her *kinner*."

"A *mamm* who certainly knew better." Hannah didn't look inclined to feel much pity. "There are consequences to everything we do in life, and we need to face them. As does she. I think the bishop should have shunned her—for leaving like she did. Mary Lapp took over with those boys when their *mamm* left—and I know that Mary did her best by them. But Rachel was the one who left them in a difficult position. She was their *mamm*—she owed them better than that!"

"*Yah*..." Patience wasn't adding much to the conversation. She didn't know any more than Hannah did— that Rachel had arrived, Thomas had most certainly seen her, and then...silence.

"Rachel was a good woman," Hannah went on, her voice softening. "I didn't see the tendency to jump the fence in her. She seemed so...proper. But there is no saying how grief will affect some people, I suppose."

"She had a more complicated situation, though," Patience added.

"*Yah*. We found that out too late, didn't we?" Hannah shook her head. "And if we all just abandoned our faith and our *kinner* when we faced loss, what would be the point of even having our community? What is your faith if it crumbles at the point of testing? There are vows we take in marriage, and they are similar to the vows we take at baptism—we vow to be faithful. She broke hers."

"Not in her marriage," Patience qualified. She felt the need to defend Thomas's mother, if she could. She was his *mamm*, after all.

Samuel pulled the buggy up to the side door, and Patience heard the nicker of horses. She'd be attending service this morning with her landlords, but she wasn't sure if she'd even see Thomas today. Would he skip service Sunday? Samuel came inside, and Hannah looked up at her husband with a smile.

"Carry that, would you, Daet?" Hannah said, gesturing to a cloth bag filled with vegetables for salad.

Samuel took the bag, and a stack of treat-filled plastic containers, too. He tramped back out to the buggy, and Patience and Hannah grabbed the last of the food and followed him out.

Service Sunday—the time when everyone gathered together, worshipped Gott as a community and got to see everyone after two weeks. Patience had always looked forward to it, but this Sunday seemed to be a reminder that she needed to keep an emotional distance from Thomas and Rue. There was no future there for her with the handsome carpenter—and he *needed* a wife.

The services were being held at the bishop's farm, and when they arrived, the buggy field was already nearly filled. A large tent had been erected for the service, and the young men were busy arranging the benches beneath it from the Sunday service wagon. Every Amish community did things in a similar way, but each gathering of a community felt a little different. These were new families with new challenges, and her *mamm* had asked her rather pointedly to keep her eyes open for any single men with *kinner*. Mamm was absolutely convinced that a happy marriage was possible for Patience, and she dearly wished that she shared her mother's optimism there.

After helping Hannah to carry the food to the refrigerated wagon—a community investment that came in handy when keeping food from spoiling during weddings and church services—Patience scanned the unfamiliar faces for a familiar one. She spotted Thomas over by the horse corral in a pair of black pants, a white shirt rolled up to his elbows and his black suspenders and hat. Rue clung to the side of a fence, and Thomas leaned against the top rail, both of them looking out at the horses.

"*Yah*, he's over there," Hannah said with a knowing look.

"It isn't like that," Patience said.

"No?" Hannah's eyebrows went up, but she didn't look convinced.

"I should go say hello," Patience said.

"*Yah*... But don't be locking yourself to one man in the public eye just yet, my dear," Hannah said meaningfully. "You're young and attractive. We have a few single men who will want to meet you."

Patience forced a smile. "I'm more concerned about

how Rue is doing after seeing her Englisher grandmother."

"Ah." Hannah sobered. "That's understandable."

Patience nodded to a few different families as she
made her way across the farmyard and toward the
horses. Thomas seemed to be deep in thought; neither
he nor Rue heard her approach until she was right behind them, and then Thomas startled and turned.

"Hi," she said with a hesitant smile.

"Hi." Thomas relaxed at the sight of her. "How are
you?"

Rue grinned up at Patience. "Patience, there's horses.
But you can't hug them. That's very dangerous."

Patience chuckled. "It is very dangerous. I see you've
been listening to your *daet*."

"I want a horse," Rue said seriously.

"You have horses. Your *daet* has horses that pull the
buggy," Patience replied.

"No, I want a horse of my own," she said.

Patience looked over at Thomas and he gave a tired
shrug. "Another battle for another day."

"Is everything okay?" Patience asked. "With your
mamm, I mean. Samuel saw her waiting on a cab, so
we know she left, but…"

Thomas licked his lips. "She…says she wants to return to the community."

Patience started to smile. "That's good news!" But
when he didn't match her smile, she let it fall. "Isn't it?"

"Rue, do you see those girls at the pump?" Thomas
said, pointing. "Why don't you go get some water to
drink? I'm sure they'd help you."

Rue ambled off in the direction her father had indicated, and Thomas stood there, his eyes glued to the back of his daughter. She got to the pump and the older girls looked down at her in stunned curiosity—they'd likely just realized this little girl was speaking English, not German. There would be many, many introductions just like that one for little Rue. She'd get used to the initial shock she caused.

"What happened?" Patience asked. "And I won't tell anyone what you tell me, if that's what you're thinking."

"No, I trust you," he said, his gaze flickering down toward her. "The problem is, I don't know what's a good outcome anymore. Two weeks ago, I would have been thanking Gott for my mother's return, and now? I'm worried. She'll be a major influence in my daughter's life—an Englisher *mammi*. Am I raising my daughter just to have her jump the fence the minute she's old enough? Will she stay? If she has a grandmother who did the same…"

"But who came back," she countered.

"But she's still English, and only now do we realize how English she really is…" Thomas stepped a little closer, lowering his voice further. "She's coming back because she misses us, and because she has a grand-daughter now."

"Not only for Rue, though," Patience said hopefully.

"No, but Rue factors in rather heavily," Thomas replied seriously. "She wants to help."

They exchanged a meaningful look. She understood his worries very well.

"Oh…" Patience leaned back against the sun-warmed fence, and Thomas did the same, leaving a proper six inches between them. He looked over at her, his dark gaze filled with misery.

"My *mamm* missed the English life so much," he said.

Patience frowned. "People come back when they see the error in their way, and she came back. So she must have seen that the English life was empty and…" Her voice trailed off.

"I don't think it was empty, actually. She's coming back because she realized life is short, and you don't always have the time to repent that you think you do." Thomas sighed. "When she left the first time, it was because she didn't like the restrictions in an Amish life. She said she didn't think Gott requires that, that it only cuts us off from the rest of the believers."

Patience didn't know how to answer that. She rolled the words around in her mind. "But she came back…"

"And if my daughter says something to her about the Amish way not being Gott's will—one day when she's old enough to think she knows it all—what will my *mamm* say to her?" Thomas eyed her for a moment, then shrugged. "I know she's repented and she wants to come back to the narrow path, but will my mother harbor some of those dangerous views still? I might not have cared before I had Rue in my life, but now—"

"Will you turn her away?" Patience asked softly.

"Oh, Patience…" he sighed. "She's my *mamm*! I love her too much to turn her away. But we'll be the ones to pay for it."

"Gott is still working," she said.

"Yah…"

"You have to trust that."

"But the right thing to do is often the hard thing, isn't it?" he said.

Was he thinking that the right thing would be to turn away his *mamm*? He didn't elaborate. Right now, the easy thing would be to reach out and take his hand. It would be to lean into his strong shoulder, to comfort him… The easy thing was not the right thing to do.

"But you're good for Rue," he added. "She's doing as well as she is because of you. You're…really good for her."

"I'm not good for you, though," she said.

Thomas dropped his gaze, then shrugged. "You're comforting for me."

Tears misted Patience's eyes. She longed to be his comfort right now, but she knew where that would go. It wasn't only him who was feeling this strong attraction; she was, too, and last night she'd lain awake thinking not of his *mamm* and the drama that had unfolded before him, but of his kiss. His arms around her had felt so warm and safe, and she'd never been kissed quite like that before. She'd never had the experience of feeling heady and grounded all at the same time…

Over at the pump, Amos and Noah stopped for some water, then took Rue's hand. People were moving toward the tent now. It would be time for service to start soon.

"Where will Rue sit?" Patience asked.

Thomas looked toward the tent, then shrugged.

"With me," Thomas replied. "Mary can't chase her down, and she's *mine*. She'll sit with me."

There was no *mamm* to take her to the women's side of the tent, so one little girl would sit on her *daet*'s knee on the men's side—a fair-haired little ray of sunshine amid a sea of males clad in black Sunday clothes. Patience felt a well of compassion for this man and his little girl. They were doing their best together, and she couldn't overstep. She must be available for other men, just in case there was a widower who wanted a wife but no more *kinner*. And Thomas must be available to find a good Amish *mamm* for his daughter.

It was time for service.

Thomas wasn't sure what he expected from his daughter during her very first Amish service. From what he'd gathered already, Rue had never gone to church in her life. Tina had told her a little bit about Gott, a confusing tangle of information that included Heaven for those who had died, but that was the extent of Rue's spiritual education thus far.

Every night, Thomas had been telling her Bible stories, tricking her into listening with rapt attention by beginning each one with "Once upon a time..." It worked. And whenever she asked for another story, he never said no, because she was finally getting the foundation that she so desperately needed.

There was a Bible verse that guided much of Amish parenting: *Train up a child in the way he should go: and when he is old, he will not depart from it.* At least he could give her a reason for her faith—the stories from scripture that could be a bedrock for every choice she made in the future. And if his prayers were answered, those stories would keep her rooted in their faith—*here*.

The raising of a child was such a deep commitment,

and he was only now appreciating how much lay on his shoulders as Rue's *daet*.

Thomas sat next to his brother and Amos on the very edge of the bench. If he had to get away from the service for whatever reason, he'd need an exit that didn't cause disruption. Other *daets* sat with their young sons next to them, and he caught their eyes on him. Word would have traveled by now, and he'd already fielded a few questions when they first arrived, but people seemed to know enough from the spread of gossip that they weren't coming forward with more curiosity.

Across the tent, the women's side of the service faced the men's. A couple of single women were looking at him with undisguised interest. He was in need of a wife, and that little detail would have made it into many a kitchen in their community before anyone ever spotted him at service. But he couldn't summon up any interest in other women. The only one he was looking for as he scanned the familiar faces was Patience, and he finally spotted her sitting next to Hannah Kauffman near the front.

Patience caught him looking at her and smiled slightly. What was it about her that made him feel better just by a tiny smile like that one?

"Daddy," Rue said, her voice rising loudly above the murmuring of settling people.

"Shh." Thomas winced and bent his lips down to her ears. "You have to whisper and be very quiet. And please... Call me *daet*."

"That boy has a feather," Rue whispered loudly.

"Rue." He tapped her leg. "Shh."

Rue settled in quietly, but the boy in question turned

around, looking at her in open curiosity. His own *daet* tapped his shoulder and he turned back. The feather was confiscated.

The singing started, and Rue was amply drowned out by several hymns, but by the time an elder stood up to pray, Rue was drumming her feet against Thomas's shins and wriggling to get a more comfortable position. She wasn't used to this, and he couldn't blame her, but compared with all the other *kinner* sitting quietly next to their parents on either side of the service, her unruliness stood out.

Would it be appropriate to bring her over to Patience? Would Patience be any better at calming this child than he was? But Rue wasn't Patience's obligation. She was just the teacher next door… And *he* was Rue's *daet*. She was his to raise and guide, and to figure out.

Noah tapped Rue's leg and then passed her a hard candy. Noah had thought of pocketing a few candies? Even Thomas hadn't thought of that. He shot his brother a grateful smile as Rue noisily unwrapped the candy and popped it into her mouth.

By the time the first preacher stood up to speak in German, Thomas knew he was beat. She couldn't understand anything that was being said, and even if she could, it would all be far too complicated for a four-year-old to grasp.

He caught Patience's gaze on him, and he shook his head slightly, letting her know all was well. He couldn't keep leaning on her—it wasn't fair to either of them.

"Come, Rue," he whispered, and he eased off the bench and carried her out of the tent. When he looked back, Noah and Amos were watching him, but they both looked as helpless as he felt.

He was a single *daet* to an Englisher... How was he going to do this?

A few women had some small children playing on a blanket outside the tent.

"Would she like to come play here?" one of the women asked in German.

But Rue didn't speak German, and she didn't obey terribly swiftly, either. Suddenly, leaving her to play with other Amish children felt like it was setting her up for failure. The women would talk about her afterward—the little girl who spoke only English and didn't obey. He didn't want that. Things had already gone wrong with the Smoker family.

"Thank you, but we'll be fine," he said.

Another time, when Rue was more settled maybe. When she'd picked up some German and saw what kind of behavior was expected of the *kinner* here. He'd wait until the people wouldn't judge her harshly, because while there would be kind people who wouldn't, there would be others with less patience of an Englisher child, and he wasn't sure which would be which just yet.

Thomas had been looking forward to seeing Patience today, to spending a little time with her... But maybe it was better to go early. People would start jumping to conclusions, and it would only complicate things. Besides, he wasn't going to be able to hide his feelings for her—he was too tired to manage it. Patience deserved a chance to settle into the Redemption community, free from the taint of the Wiebe men.

"Where are we going, Daddy?" Rue asked as he carried her toward the buggies.

"We're going home," he said.

"How come?"

"Because—" He looked over at her, wondering how to explain the tumble of emotion, his fears, his caution, his exhaustion... "Because I want to."

"Okay." It seemed to be a good enough answer for her, but it wasn't a good answer. Amish looked to their communities to help them through difficult times, and he was pulling back, much like his *mamm* had done when her husband passed away and she'd needed support the most. Was he more like his *mamm* than he liked to admit, too?

The problem was, he didn't want the community's support—he was longing for one woman, and he knew better than to allow his ever-so-observant neighbors to witness that.

Gott, make me a better father. I feel like I'm failing already.

Chapter Eleven

Patience saw Thomas leave the service, and she followed him with her gaze until he disappeared outside the tent. She shouldn't feel so drawn after Thomas and Rue—they weren't hers to worry over—but she couldn't help it. Did he need help with Rue? Should she go out and see?

But there were several women on the bench between her and freedom, and she'd only draw more attention if she had to get past them. So she tried to focus on the service and waited to see if Thomas would come back.

He never did. One sermon turned into singing, and then there was a second sermon. And she did her best to listen to the preachers expound upon scripture, but her heart wasn't in it… It was following after Thomas and his little girl.

Gott, this isn't a good sign if I can't even worship because I'm thinking about him. He isn't for me! I know that. Help me to stop feeling this…

With that kiss, things had changed between them. For her, she felt even more drawn to the man, and his

mother's arrival had made that attraction more dangerous. Thomas was a man without the same deep roots
that she had—his *mamm* had jumped the fence, and now
Rachel was back in time to help with an Englisher child.
Nothing here was easy or straightforward, and maybe
that was Gott's way of showing her that Thomas wasn't
for her. She might know it logically, but sometimes Gott
had to "*bapp* her over the head with it," as her *mamm*
would say. So Patience had to admit that Thomas was
right in keeping his distance.

Sitting on the bench, her back straight and her
thoughts refusing to settle, Patience felt tears welling up
inside her. Sunday service wasn't supposed to be about
Thomas Wiebe, and she wouldn't let it become that, either. She fixed her mind onto the preacher's words, and
tried to find the peace that normally came with worship.

The next day, Patience had Samuel Kauffman give
her a ride to the schoolhouse. She hadn't heard from
Thomas after service, and all she could assume was
that he had things under control. He was Rue's father,
after all. He was the one raising the little girl, and it
wasn't like there weren't three men in that house to
pick up the slack when Mary wasn't able to keep up.
Among Thomas, Noah and Amos, they'd figure things
out, she was sure.

That was what she told herself, at least. His absence
stung, even if she didn't have a right to feel the rejection. They'd talked this over—more than friendship
wasn't going to work, so she had no right to expect him
to come by just to see her.

The schoolhouse was located on the corner of two

rural roads. A field of young wheat rippled across the road from the school, and it was flanked by farmers' fields on either side. Outside, there was some play equipment and some hitching posts in the parking lot. The schoolhouse itself was a squat, white building with a small bell tower on top.

Patience let herself inside with the key she'd been given when she first arrived, and Samuel helped her to unload the school supplies that the community had provided for her.

"Would you like me to stay and help at all?" Samuel asked. "It looks like a lot of work."

"Oh, you're too kind, Samuel," Patience said. "But I'll be fine. Thank you for the offer. I'd rather just putter about on my own and figure out how I want my classroom. It might take me some time to figure out."

Samuel gave her a nod. "No problem. If you need anything, just ring the bell. We can hear it from our place."

The schoolhouse was walking distance—a long walk, mind, but it was doable. When Samuel left, Patience set to work with some cloths and cleaning supplies, scrubbing the room from top to bottom.

Back in Beaufort, she and her *mamm* had shopped for some classroom decorations—paper birthday balloons for each student's birthday, some hangable signs with multiplication tables, some math equations, some sight words for new readers that they had picked up at the dollar store… She would be teaching everything from the first grade through to the eighth, and while she had books to show her what information needed to be covered for each grade, it was daunting, to say the least.

Patience wiped down the last windowsill, cleansing away dust and a few dead flies, leaving the entire room smelling of Pine-Sol and possibilities. Just as she wiped off the last windowsill, there was a knock at the front door, and she startled. She wasn't expecting anyone.

Patience went to the door and pulled it open, and she couldn't help but smile when she saw Thomas standing there with Rue at his side. Rue had her hands folded in front of her and an excited smile on her face.

"Hello, Rue!" Patience said, then she looked up at Thomas. "Hi, Thomas…"

A smile tickled the corners of his lips. "We wanted to see if you needed help."

So he'd come to see her after all, and she felt a sudden rush of relief that whatever they'd shared wasn't completely changed and forgotten. But then another possibility occurred to her—this was Monday, after all. Was he here for a favor?

"Do you need me to watch her while you work?" she asked.

"No, I took the day off," Thomas replied. "With Rue settling in still, Amos and Noah said they could handle things on their own for today."

"I would have offered to watch her," Patience said. "I did agree to help you out. It's just… I thought you… were finished with me."

"Finished—" Thomas swallowed. "No, not at all. I just—"

They stared at each other, without the words to capture it all, then Rue broke the moment by brushing past Patience and heading toward one of the boxes of supplies that sat on a desk. She stood up onto her tiptoes to look inside.

"Rue, do you want to play with some of that modeling dough?" Patience asked. "You can take it to one of the desks, if you want to."

Rue liked this idea, and she grabbed a pot of red dough and went to a desk on the far side of the room next to the teacher's desk.

"Daddy, I'm in school!" Rue announced.

Thomas smiled in his daughter's direction, then turned his gaze back to Patience. "I didn't mean to seem like I was pushing you off. It's just been complicated lately, and I'm trying not to take advantage of our friendship here. I'm sure there are other men you'd like to meet."

"Not really," she admitted.

"Fine, then other friends you'd like to make. I'm sorry, I didn't mean to come off as...a jerk."

Patience shrugged. "Of course not."

Obviously, they both had been afraid of overstepping, and knowing that helped.

"So, you wanted to help?" she asked.

"*Yah.* That was the plan."

Patience pulled out a box of supplies. "I need to get these organized in the bins up there at the front. I'm thinking I can have all the markers, glue and scissors in those bins, and when the *kinner* need them, I can pass them out."

"Sure." Thomas easily lifted the heavy box.

"I could have helped you during the service, you know," Patience said as they headed toward the front of the classroom.

"I felt like I should do it myself," Thomas said. "After I kissed you, I mean. I know I ruined things there, and I didn't want you to think I was taking advantage or…"

"I don't think that," she said.

"Are we becoming more to each other?" Thomas asked, turning toward her. He put the box down on a desktop.

"Maybe we are," she admitted.

"The thing is," he said quietly, "I'm the one at fault here. I'm feeling things I shouldn't. You're beautiful, and I'm attracted to you. I'm just trying to pretend that I'm not. I think it's the smart thing to do. It just gets a bit awkward sometimes."

Patience felt warmth hit her cheeks. He'd called her beautiful again… No other man had told her that before. Even Ruben had called her "good-looking" and "strong." Not beautiful. Beautiful was different… It came from a different place.

"I'll never have my own *kinner*, Thomas," she reminded him. "I'd be happy to help out with Rue. She needs someone who can love her for who she is, and one of these days soon, if I stay in Redemption as a teacher, I'll have her in my classroom. So, don't be afraid of taking advantage. Really, you're just giving me a chance to be more than a teacher to one little girl. I won't have that offer very often."

"Yah?" His gaze softened. "You sure about that?"

"Positive. I can be your friend, Thomas. I'm going to be the old maid schoolteacher, so I'll need friends."

"Don't say that," he chuckled.

"I've very nearly made my peace with it," she said with a shrug. "I'll get there."

"There might be a widower—" he started, but Patience shook her head, and he fell silent.

"I tried that once," she said. "It didn't work for me, and I'm not in a rush to embarrass myself or a good man in that way again."

"Just tell me if I'm overstepping, or asking for too much when it comes to Rue," he said. "Because I don't want to ruin the friendship we have. You mean a lot to me."

"Okay."

She'd try to keep her feelings in line with her rational expectations. She'd stop hoping to hear from him when he didn't need her help with something. She could be reasonable when she needed to be.

Patience filled the first bin with markers, and the second with rulers and protractors for the higher grades' math. And when she turned for the box again, she nearly collided with Thomas. He was pulling out a bundle of rulers, and they both froze.

Thomas was so close that she could feel the fabric of his shirt touch her dress—that soft scrape of cotton against cotton. She sucked in a breath, and he smelled musky with a hint of shaved wood. That smell had seeped into her over the last while—a scent she associated with this carpenter *daet*—and it made her heart ache.

She felt his work-roughened hand brush against hers, and he moved one finger up her skin in a slow line. Her breath caught, every fiber of her being focused on that one place on her body. She knew she should move back, move her hand at the very least… But she couldn't quite bring herself to do it. She lifted her fingers toward him, and he twined his through hers. They didn't move—not toward each other, and not away, just standing there breathing the same air, their hands clasped.

What was it about this man that made her do this? Why did something as simple as standing this close to him, or touching his hand, feel like it could stop the entire earth from spinning?

But then Thomas did what she wasn't strong enough to do on her own, and he let go of her hand and took a deliberate step back. She released a shaky sigh.

"We have to be more careful," she whispered.

"Yah..." He cleared his throat.

She missed him—even standing right here next to him, she missed his fingers twined through hers—and all she could think about was the feeling of his lips, his arms around her, the tickle of his stubble against her face... But she had to stop this. Whatever they were feeling had no future. Why was she punishing herself like this?

"Why don't I get those chairs from the corner? That's across the room."

She smiled at his dry humor. "Maybe a better idea."

He caught her gaze with an impish grin.

"I made a family," Rue announced from her seat at the desk. There were four blobs of modeling dough lined up. "They're Amish. You can tell because they have a rooster named Toby."

"Yah?" Thomas said. "And who else is there?"

"That's a *mammi*," Rue said. "And that's a *daet*."

Patience looked over at Thomas, her heart suspended in her throat. Rue had used the Amish words

for a grandmother and father... And it was her represen-
tation of a family. She saw that Thomas's eyes misted.

"And who is the other one?" he asked, his voice
catching.

"That's just me. I'm next to Toby."

"*Yah*, I can see that," he said. "Right next to Toby."

"He's part of the family, Daddy," Rue said seriously.
"I just want you to remember that we don't eat family."

Thomas burst out laughing. "No, we don't." He
turned to Patience with a rueful smile. "I'm stuck with
that rooster until it dies of old age, you know."

And he was, Patience had to agree, all because a
little girl loved a scruffy, bad-tempered rooster. It was
amazing what the love of a little girl could do.

That evening, after Rue was already asleep in her
little bed with the curtains pulled shut to block out the
last of the summer sunlight, Thomas sat on the steps of
the house, a piece of wood in his hands, and he whit-
tled away at it. Rue had given him an idea, and he was
now working on some little wooden Amish people—a
mammi, a *daet* and even two uncles. But right now, he
was working on the *mammi*. Wood curled as his knife
pared away another slice of wood, and he blew on it,
scattering the shavings into the summer wind.

The funny thing was, as he worked on what was supposed to be the *mammi*, the figure was turning more slender, more lithe and much more like a *mamm* in a family...
He didn't carve a face, but the figure was one he recognized—this looked very much like Patience. Would anyone else notice that? What was it about this woman that
had crept into his head, coming out in his work?

Because he couldn't stop thinking about her… And that was wrong, because he had to put his daughter first. She hadn't asked to be born, and yet here she was, thrust into a world that must seem incredibly foreign to her. She was trying to adjust—he could see that—but the burden couldn't rest on those tiny shoulders. He was her *daet*, and he had to smooth the way for her.

A buggy turned into the drive, and he looked up in the lowering light. He recognized Bishop Glick with the reins in his hands, and he was alone. The sun was near setting, and the shadows were long and soft. Thomas put down his carving, then rose to his feet and headed toward the bishop's buggy.

"Good evening, Bishop!" Thomas said, as he ambled over. "How are you doing tonight?"

"Well, I'm enjoying this dry weather," the bishop replied. "After all that rain last month, it feels good to have dry feet."

"*Yah*, it does," Thomas said with a nod. "What can I do for you?"

"Well… This affects both you and your brother, so maybe I should discuss it with the both of you."

"Mamm?" he asked.

"*Yah.*" The bishop tied off his reins and hopped down from his buggy. "Your *mamm* came to speak with me, and… I thought it best to come see you about it."

Thomas led the way inside, and Amos and Mammi both greeted the bishop with smiles, but when his intention to talk with Thomas and Noah was made clear, they excused themselves and left the three in privacy.

The sitting room was lit by a kerosene lamp hanging on a hook overhead. There was another reading lamp between the couch and a chair, and the bishop took the chair, his expression solemn.

"Our *mamm* came to talk to us," Noah admitted.

"*Yah*, I understand that," the bishop agreed. "And she did come see me. She wants to return."

"A little late," Noah muttered.

"Are you angry still, then?" Bishop Glick asked.

"You could say that," Noah admitted.

"And now that she's wanting to come back," the bishop said, "will you give her a home when she returns?"

"*Yah*," Thomas interjected. "I will, at least. Of course."

"Can you forgive her, though?" the older man asked. "Both of you. Can you offer her your sincere forgiveness for her past mistakes?"

Thomas looked over at his brother and they exchanged a silent, miserable stare. Forgiveness wasn't quite so easy to deliver.

"We'll try," Thomas replied after a beat of silence.

"You left the service early on Sunday," the bishop said. "I wanted to ask you why. The sermon was about forgiving others, and—"

"It wasn't because of the sermon topic," Thomas replied. "Rue isn't used to worship, yet. Bishop, I'm doing my best. She hasn't been raised in our community from babyhood. There is a lot for her to learn—for both of us. We'll need a little grace."

"Your *mamm* said something quite similar," the bishop said, his voice low. "She said she's made mistakes, and all she could hope for at this point was a little grace and forgiveness."

Tears misted in Thomas's eyes and he swallowed,

blinking hard. His *mamm*... Facing life as a single parent was not easy, but she'd left them! She'd given them an impossible choice, and she'd gone alone to the city, to her sister and to that life that they'd been taught was fraught with evil.

"This is the part that is difficult for me," the bishop went on. "If we vote to let her come back, then we're opening our community to her influence. We all influence each other, whether we like it or not. But if I turn her away, then perhaps I'm going against Gott's will. He asks us to forgive, not to judge, and Gott works in mysterious ways. He's brought his wayward daughter to our door. She's asked to be permitted to live a plain life again. What do we do with that?"

Thomas licked his lips, but he remained silent.

"What would you like us to do under these circumstances?" the bishop pressed. "This is your *mamm*. You must have missed her desperately."

"*Yah*, we've missed her," Noah confirmed.

"As her *kinner*, your lives will be directly affected by this decision," the bishop said. "This will be voted on by the elders, but I'd like you both to give us an idea of how it would impact you if she returned, or if she stayed away. To have your *mamm* back in your life would be wonderful, I'm sure. But it would also impact your daughter, Thomas. I wanted to hear from you what you would like the outcome to be."

"You want us to be part of the decision?" Noah asked.

"Indirectly, yes. I want you to let us know how you feel about your *mamm*'s return. And then we will pray for Gott's guidance, and vote. But your feelings in this matter to us."

"I don't know what to say just now," Thomas admitted. He loved his *mamm*, but he also loved his daughter. There was a grave risk in his *mamm*'s return, and yet… It was another impossible choice. How could a man be asked to choose between his child and his *mamm*?

"You'll need to talk as brothers," the older man said. "So you can tell me in a few days, then."

The bishop took his leave, shaking both of their hands before he went back out to his waiting buggy. Thomas and Noah went back onto the porch and Thomas picked up his whittling again. Together he and his brother stared out at the dusky sky. Bugs circled the kerosene lamp that gave Thomas enough light by which to work, and for a few minutes they were both silent.

"I am angry," Noah said quietly. "And I'm insulted that she doesn't believe what she taught us anymore. But all the same, I want her back. Maybe even to argue with her about all we went through—maybe just for that."

Thomas sucked in a wavery breath. His experience of their *mamm*'s life with the Englishers was different, because he'd joined her there for a few years. He knew what she'd experienced out there—it was a whole different way of seeing things, and when you were out there in the midst of the Englishers, their ways didn't seem so wrong. It was a strange experience.

"I miss Mamm," Thomas said quietly. "But will she make an Englisher life look that much more appealing to my daughter?"

"If Mamm stays English, it might give Rue somewhere to go to," Noah replied.

"I hadn't thought of that…" Thomas worked at the details of the *kapp* and hair on his little figurine, the work calming the clamor in his head. There was no clear path here—no easy decision that protected his daughter's innocence. His own mistakes were shadowing him here, as were his *mamm*'s.

"Is this cruel of the bishop to ask our input?" Noah asked.

"Maybe," Thomas said. "But we're the ones who will live with the impact of her return most closely. Maybe it's just wise of them to listen to what we have to say."

"So what *do* we say?" Noah looked up at his brother.

Thomas turned back to his whittling, his heart heavy. He didn't want to sit here—he wanted to get away from the house and get alone with his thoughts. He needed to walk.

"Maybe we just say that we love our *mamm*," Thomas said. "It's the only thing we can be sure is true."

Noah swatted at a mosquito on his arm, and Thomas tucked his whittling aside, snapped his knife shut and put it back into his pocket.

"I need to clear my head," Thomas said. "I'm going to take a walk."

"*Yah*, okay," Noah replied, and he sucked in a deep breath.

And Thomas headed off across the lawn and toward the gravel drive. The sun was bleeding red along the horizon, and his heart was bleeding within him.

Gott, I can't choose between my daughter and my mamm. *And I can't read the future, either. What do I do? What do I say? Can You redeem this mess that we've made?*

Chapter Twelve

Patience sat on the edge of her bed up in the guest room of the Kauffmans' home. The older folks were downstairs in the sitting room. She could hear the murmur of their voices through the floorboards, but her attention wasn't on their muffled conversation. She was looking outside the window at the slowly setting sun. It flooded the sky with crimson, matching her mood tonight.

She'd thought that talking things through with Thomas would be enough to banish whatever they were feeling for each other, but it hadn't worked—not in the schoolhouse, at least. Her hand tingled where he'd touched it, and she balled her fingers into a fist.

She had to stop this! Whatever was sparking between them couldn't last. She didn't think he meant to toy with her, any more than she meant to toy with him. But she was no longer a young thing with giddy hopes of romance. She didn't have what a man like Thomas needed, and adults with responsibilities were obligated to be practical.

She couldn't relax, and while she'd get used to living with the Kauffmans this year, it wasn't like being at home with her *mamm* and *daet*. If she were home right now, they'd all be sitting around the kitchen table talking about the latest gossip in the community, or playing a game of Dutch Blitz. Being with family was easier, even if she was the last one left at home.

She'd wanted this move to a new community—desperately. And now that she was here, she felt nothing but homesick.

Patience sucked in a breath. Maybe a walk would do her good, clear her head, give her some fresh air and a bit of perspective again.

She headed down the stairs, and when she got to the bottom of the staircase, she poked her head into the sitting room.

"Oh, hello, dear," Hannah said with a smile. "Are you hungry?"

"No," Patience said and smiled in return. Hannah seemed to feed people on instinct—whenever she saw them, she offered a snack. "But thank you. I thought I'd go for a walk."

"Oh, of course. Enjoy yourself."

Samuel smiled, too, then passed the folded newspaper over to his wife. "Look who's gotten married— that's old Ben's grandson, isn't it? Ben Yoder—the one who built that silo, and the storm crushed it, remember? His son, with the one leg a bit shorter than the other..."

Patience went back through the kitchen and out the side door, the sound of the older couple's discussion whether this was the right young man in question or someone with a similar name following her until she got out onto the step. This old couple knew the family stories of everyone, it seemed. That's how a close community worked, and it was that very intimate community knowledge that she'd been trying to escape in Beaufort.

She sucked in a deep breath, the aroma of lilacs and freshly cut grass soothing her nerves, and she angled her steps across the lawn and toward the field. She wanted to walk and pray and feel like there might be a purpose in her life again. Because after Ruben, whom she hadn't really loved, but whom she respected a great deal…and now after Thomas, whom she'd started to feel things for that she had no right to feel, she just wanted the solace that only Gott could give her.

But Gott wasn't soothing her heart! He wasn't taking these feelings away! Why not? She was trying to do the right thing—not to toy with something so powerful as this kind of attraction between a man and a woman— and Gott wasn't doing what everyone assured her He would do if she just took a step in the right direction. Gott was not making this easier.

The grass was long and lush. There was only about two acres between the Kauffman house and the fence at the end of their property, but Patience liked this walk— wildflowers mingling with grass, the birds twittering their good-nights in the copses of trees, and the warm wind reminding her that there was still life on the other side of loss.

As she came within sight of the wooden fence that separated the two properties, she saw a figure standing there, head down, shoulders stooped, leaning against the top rail. It was Thomas—she'd know him anywhere. She slowed her stride, wondering if she should turn back. He lifted his head, looking out toward the sunset—away from her and to her left. What was he doing out here—the same as her? No one walked out this direction unless they wanted privacy, and it wouldn't be right to interrupt his, and yet—

Thomas turned then as if on instinct—and he seemed to have spotted her, because he straightened.

"Patience?" he said, his voice surfing the breeze toward her.

She couldn't turn back now, and if she had to be utterly truthful, she didn't want to.

"I just came for a walk," she said, closing the distance between them. They stood on either side of the wooden fence, the grass rippling around her as she looked into Thomas's pain-filled face.

"Are you okay?" she asked.

"I'm...just thinking, I guess," he said. "Are you?"

Did her own misery show on her face, too? "I'm praying," she said.

"What are you praying for?" he asked.

"Comfort," she said. She didn't want to tell him that she was praying for Gott to empty her heart of whatever it was she was feeling for him.

Thomas leaned against the fence. It came up only to just below his chest, and he reached for her hand. She came closer and reached out, and he caught her fingers in his strong grip. It was a relief to have this contact with him, and she shut her eyes for a moment, wishing she didn't feel it.

"I missed you," Thomas said, his voice low and gruff.

"Thomas..."

"I know, I know," he said. "I'm supposed to turn this off, aren't I? I'm supposed to recognize that it won't work and do the honorable thing."

"Yes!" she said. "We both are! What are we, if we aren't honorable?"

Patience took a step closer. The fence loomed between them, the grass tickling her legs, and she looked down at his work-worn fingers moving over hers.

"Have you managed to stop feeling this?" he asked.

"No," she whispered. "But I'm praying for it… Oh, how I'm praying…"

Tears misted her eyes and she swallowed hard. Thomas released her fingers and she pulled her hand against her apron. She didn't know what to say. She had no words of wisdom here, no answers that would fix this problem for them.

"You're all I seem to think about," Thomas said. "And when I see you, I—I don't know even know how to explain it. It's like I can't be content until I've held your hand, or…kissed you."

"But Thomas, you know what you need… And I've already turned down one man because I can't live my life being the second best he settled for. I can't be that for you, either."

"Should we avoid each other, then?" he murmured.

"Maybe…" But the very thought was a painful one. It would hurt for a long time, but eventually, she'd find her balance again.

"The bishop came to visit tonight," Thomas said.

"The bishop? Why?" she breathed. Had gossip already spread? Had someone seen them together? Possibilities tumbled through her head, and she couldn't help but feel that welling sense of guilt. A couple couldn't play with these things. Especially not the schoolteacher!

"It was about my *mamm*," he said.

"Oh…"

He gave her a brief overview of the bishop's visit and his request for their input, and then he heaved a sigh. "I can't ask the bishop to turn my *mamm* away, and yet, I'm scared for Rue."

"You'll raise Rue right," Patience said, but even as the words came out of her mouth, she knew it wasn't enough.

"I'll need to get married," he said, and his voice caught.

Patience stared up at him. She could hear in his voice that it wasn't her that he'd wed, either. He'd have to find someone who could give him *kinner* to fill in those gaps in his home.

"*Yah*, you will," she said, trying to sound braver than she felt. "It will be okay."

"Will it?" he asked. "Really?"

"I think you need to—" she started.

"No, tell me how you *feel* about it," he interrupted her. "Because I've been thinking myself in circles. What really matters here is how we feel."

"No!" she snapped. "No! I'm not doing that, because it isn't fair! I hate it, okay? I hate it! And I won't go to your wedding, either!"

"Good. At least you hate it as much as I do."

Thomas reached for her hand again and pulled her up against the fence. He dipped his head down and caught her lips with his. His kiss was sad, and filled with longing. She let her eyes flutter shut, leaning against that rough wood that held them apart as he kissed her tenderly. When he pulled back, she opened her eyes again and found him looking down at her miserably.

The sun had set now, the last smudge of red along the horizon, and they stood there in the growing darkness, a fence between them, and her heart aching in her chest.

"How am I supposed to just walk away from the woman I love?" he whispered.

The breath whisked out of her lungs as the words hit her.

"You love me?" she whispered.

Thomas looked at the fence between them irritably. "*Yah*, I do."

Thomas climbed the fence, and then vaulted himself over the other side. He tugged her into his arms and pulled her close. She could feel his face against her hair, the stubble on his cheek scraping against the stiff cotton of her *kapp*. It felt good to have his arms around her, his heart beating strong against her.

"The question is," he said, his voice low and gravelly, "do you love me?"

Patience felt the tears rise up inside her. She'd been fighting this for longer than she'd realized. This man had managed to slip beneath her cautious defenses, and she'd fallen for him. She'd been praying and praying for Gott to take this away, but... It was too late.

"*Yah*," she whispered. "I do."

The inevitable heartbreak she was trying to protect herself from had arrived. She'd fallen in love with him in spite of all her best efforts. And now all she could do was pray that Gott would take her through.

The dusky darkness was growing ever deeper, and Thomas looked around them. In the distance, the Kauffman house's downstairs windows glowed with light from the gas lamps, but it felt far away, and the chill of oncoming autumn whispered through the grass. He'd been standing out here praying for some sort of insight, some wisdom that could come only from Gott, and instead he'd come face-to-face with the woman he couldn't seem to get out of his system.

Was she his answer? Dare he hope it? Thomas cupped her cheek with one hand, and she leaned into his touch. Her skin was so soft, and her eyes glittered in the lowering light. She loved him... Somehow, he hadn't expected her to admit it. But he wasn't alone in this ocean of emotion—she loved him, too! His heart welled up inside his chest. If she loved him, there was hope, wasn't there? He wasn't just some foolish man pining for a woman who didn't see him the same way. This was different...

"You love me," he repeated. "Then let's find a way."

"What way?" she asked.

"So I'm supposed to find someone else?" he whispered.

"Yah." Her voice sounded strangled.

"And if I want you?"

"I want you, too... But it isn't about that, is it? Do you think I want to be the one who holds you back from the full life of a growing family?" Patience demanded, her voice strengthening. "You seem to think this is about your sacrifice only, but I'm not the kind of woman who can give a man *half* the life he wants and figure I've done well for myself. Getting a husband is a fine accomplishment, but marriage is about a whole lot more than a wedding, because after the excitement and when things calm down again, you'd still want *kinner.* You'll still *need* them! That isn't going away. And when women in our community got pregnant, women I've made quilts with, I'd constantly wonder what you were thinking, because I would know that you settled for me. I wouldn't be sure if I was enough, after all."

Enough! Could she even wonder that?

"You would be," he insisted.

"No!" She took a step back. "No, Thomas! I have older sisters. I've seen the rhythm of marriage. It starts out passionately where nothing else matters but the two of them, but a family matters. And your needs won't go away. Neither will Rue's."

Rue... She was the one he needed to worry about, and Patience had made a painfully accurate point. He was afraid that he wouldn't be able to give his daughter enough reason to stay Amish, to stay with *him*... But there was an Amish proverb that said, *Don't bother telling your child what to do, she'll only copy your actions anyway.*

And what would Rue do as an only child in an Amish community? She'd be different in two ways then—born English, and having no siblings at home. She needed stability, and it was very difficult to achieve that when Thomas couldn't give her what all the other Amish *kinner* would have. When she got to be a teen, she'd do what her own *daet* had done—she'd launch herself out into the unknown, away from the community, away from her *daet*. He'd lose her, and he couldn't take that chance.

"It won't work," he breathed.

"No, it won't." Patience's chin quivered.

How much heartbreak had this woman gone through already? He hated being the cause of more pain for her, but sometimes love wasn't about a feeling. Sometimes love had to be broader and deeper. It had to persevere and sacrifice, and it had to do the right thing, even when it didn't want to. He had to be a *daet* first. He'd brought Rue into this world, and Gott had brought her home to him. He could no longer follow his own heart when it came to the woman he longed to be with, not when being with her would jeopardize his daughter.

A child was a gift from Gott, and she was lent to him for only a little while. He'd never forgive himself if he let his daughter go in order to satisfy his own romantic longings. Whatever his daughter chose when she grew up, he had to know that he'd done his very best by her and have no regrets to haunt him in his old age.

"I'm still going to love you, even if we can't make this work," he said huskily.

"*Yah*, me, too…" Her voice was thick was tears.

"So what do we do?" he asked.

"We carry on," she said hollowly. "We put one foot in front of the other, and we put our backs into our work. That's what we do. We can't be the first couple to realize they loved each other but there was no hope. And we won't be the last."

Maybe not, but it felt like the universe began and ended in their feelings for each other, as foolish as that might be.

Thomas looked toward the Kauffmans' house with the lights shining from the windows in the distance. A car swept down the rural road, headlights cutting through the darkness, and then a pickup truck came thundering afterward, Englisher teenagers whooping out the windows.

That was the foolish life he was trying to keep his daughter away from, but more immediately, whooping, half-drunk Englishers were also the kind of danger he needed to protect Patience from this evening. The sky was almost fully dark now, and he couldn't let Patience walk to the Kauffman house alone—for safety's sake.

"Let me get you home," he said, and he caught her hand in his.

She squeezed his hand in return.

"We shouldn't—" she started.

"Let me get you home," he repeated, his voice low. "And then I won't touch you again, or ask you to love me. I'll let you focus on your work. I won't make this harder on you. But just for now... Let me hold your hand."

"Okay," she whispered.

And they walked through that long, lush grass together as the moon started to rise and the first pricks of stars materialized overhead. Her hand was warm and soft in his grasp, and he wished that this walk, and these stars and that crescent of a moon could last forever. Because while his heart was breaking, at least he had her at his side and his goodbye could be postponed.

When they got to the gate, he stopped, and she opened it, hovering for a breathless moment as if she might come back into his arms.

"Good night," she said, her voice broken.

"Good night," he replied.

The front door opened and Samuel appeared, light from indoors spilling out onto the porch. Patience picked up her pace, and Thomas waved at Samuel, trying to act like this was nothing more than a friendly walk—like no hearts had been shattered this evening.

Patience got to the door, and he held his breath.

Look back... Look at me...

But she didn't. She disappeared inside, and the door shut behind them, leaving Thomas alone in the darkness.

He couldn't ask her to continue loving him. If he cared for her at all, he'd pray for Gott to rinse him out of her heart completely. But he couldn't pray for that for himself. He wanted to remember... Because in all his life, he'd never loved a woman like this.

Chapter Thirteen

Patience stood at the window in the laundry room and watched as Thomas disappeared into the darkness. The older folks wouldn't look for her here—not at this time of night—and all she wanted right now was a moment or two to try to collect herself. She'd cry upstairs alone, but she'd have to pass the Kauffmans to get up there. She wrapped her arms around her waist, tears welling up inside her. She loved him… And it wouldn't work. She'd never felt this way before. She'd had a few crushes, and had even accepted a proposal based on profound respect, but what she felt for Thomas was deeper and broader and cut much more sharply at the realization that it could never happen.

She realized now that falling in love with Thomas hadn't been a choice—hadn't even been avoidable. Whatever they felt for each other was something outside their ability to wisely sidestep. How was this fair? Gott asked them to walk the narrow path—to do right when the rest of the world took the easy way. And she was doing her best to do right—to put Rue and Rachel ahead of her own deepest desire. There should be some comfort in knowing she'd done the right thing, and yet all she could feel right now were the cracks in her heart.

"Patience, dear?"

Patience wiped her eyes and turned to see Hannah in the doorway. Hannah held a kerosene lamp, lighting up the laundry room in a cheery glow. Her plump figure was illuminated—an impeccably white apron against a gray dress. She squinted through her glasses.

"I'm sorry, Hannah, I'm just a little emotional," Patience said. She turned away again, blinking back her tears.

"I'm sure that some pie would help," Hannah said.

"Not this time," Patience said, and she wiped at her cheeks again. "I'll be fine."

"Is that the Wiebe boy?" Hannah asked.

"Uh… He walked me home. It got dark faster than I thought, and—" She couldn't lie, so she stopped. There was so much more to the story, but it was private.

"And you've had some sort of lover's spat?" Hannah pressed.

How obvious had their relationship been? They'd done their best to hide it—especially at Sunday service.

"I was helping with Rue," she said.

"And falling in love, I dare say," Hannah replied.

"It's not that—" It was so much more than that. "We're not engaged. There's no agreement between us…"

"Ah, but so much happens before those understandings, doesn't it?" Hannah asked. "A heart gets entangled before any proposals come along. Come now. I know you want to go upstairs and have a cry, but I'm going to suggest something else that works much better. Come to my table and have a cry there. I'll bring you some pie and we'll talk it all out. It might not fix what's gone wrong with your young man, but it will start the healing that much faster, I can tell you that."

Patience paused to consider. Hannah seemed to understand a whole lot more than Patience even realized, and if she were at home with her own *mamm* right now, she'd likely do the same. Except, she and her *mamm* liked to take walks together—walking and talking, and sorting out all the things that seemed so impossible on her own.

Tears spilled down Patience's cheeks, and Hannah reached out, took her hand and led her down the hallway and into the kitchen. Hannah left the lamp on the table, then passed a handkerchief to Patience.

"Let it out, dear," Hannah said softly. "I'm going to whip you some cream to go on top of your pie. I think you could use a little treat…"

Patience felt the tears rise again, and this time she didn't stop them. She lowered her head onto her arms and cried.

Tuesday morning, school was set to open and Samuel waited patiently by the door, the buggy hitched and ready. When Patience brought her last bag of school supplies to the door, Samuel took it from her and put it up on his shoulder.

"All ready, Mamm!" Samuel called. "I'll be back in a short while."

"Drive safe, Daet. And you have a good day with those *kinner*, Patience," Hannah said.

Samuel carried her bag out to the buggy and Patience got settled in her seat while Samuel put the bag in the back and came around to hoist himself up.

"It's a beautiful morning," Samuel said, flicking the reins.

And it was—warm, bright and a cloudless sky. But it was hard to feel cheery this morning. A good cry last night, and another one upstairs in her bed, had drained her of tears, but her heart still felt heavy in her chest.

"How many *kinner* do you have, Samuel?" Patience asked, more by way of making conversation than by any real interest.

"Oh…" Samuel's cheeks pinked. "None, I'm afraid."

Patience looked over at him, surprised. "But you called her Mamm."

"And she called me Daet. I know…" He sighed. "You see, we wanted *kinner*—a whole house filled with them—but Gott never gave us any. We were heartbroken about it for years, and then we remembered that Gott doesn't make mistakes. He brought us together, gave us a love like no other and didn't choose to give us *kinner* to love. So we decided to look at it differently."

A love like no other, and an inability to bring children into the marriage. She could identify with that a little too keenly.

"How?" Patience asked.

"We decided to be the *mamm* and *daet* that young people needed when their own parents were far from them," Samuel replied. "We've had traveling students stay with us. A few Englisher college students came to see how we Amish live and we gave them room and board. We also opened our home to the teachers."

Samuel cast her a shy smile. "In hopes that we could be a little piece of home when you are far from yours."

"That's...beautiful," she said.

A life of meaning, even without *kinner* of their own. She'd been wanting to create something like that for her own life—a loving teacher to help guide these *kinner* toward Gott, even if she never did have any babies of her own.

"Can I ask you something, Samuel?" she asked hesitantly.

"*Yah*, you can ask," Samuel replied.

"Did you ever...lose your faith in Gott's leading? Gott led you to Hannah—and I believe that—but did you ever, in a moment of weakness, regret your marriage? Did you ever think that if you'd married someone else, you might have had that houseful of *kinner* after all?"

Samuel looked over at her, his eyebrows raised, and she felt a flood of shame at even asking him such a thing.

"I know it's a terrible question," she said quickly. "I don't mean to disrespect your marriage, or your wife."

"Not once," he said quietly. "And that is not just the answer of a loyal husband. That is the honest truth. My wife is a wonderful woman, as you probably already know. And being her husband—that was Gott moving. I have never questioned that. And what Gott has joined—"

"—let no man put asunder," she finished for him.

"*Yah*, that, too," he said. "But I was going to say, what Gott has joined, He joins for good reason. No one can love me just like my Hannah. And no one can love her just like me. And I'm grateful every day for the woman Gott gave me. *Yah*, I missed out on being a *daet* to my own little ones, but we remind each other that we're still able to love the ones Gott puts in our paths. When we were younger, we focused on the *kinner*. And as we aged, so did the ones we reached out to. It happened naturally, I suppose. So she calls me Daet and I call her Mamm. Because we still have a job to do—it's just a little harder."

The horses clopped along, early morning dew shining like diamonds on the tall grasses in the ditches on either side of the road. Samuel hummed a little song to himself, and Patience's heart pounded in her chest.

Here was a couple that had never had *kinner*, had never resented each other for the loss, and had made life so meaningful and rich that she'd never have guessed their childless state if he hadn't told her himself.

She'd been so certain that Thomas would regret giving up that houseful of *kinner* of his own... But was it possible that he might not? Could this love that had blossomed between them be something wonderful enough that he'd never regret the day he chose her?

But as soon as the hope started to rise up inside her, she remembered that this wasn't just about Thomas and a desire for children. This was about the daughter he already had—the little girl who needed her roots, her stability and a family that could anchor her to an Amish life.

Even if Patience could take the leap for a love like theirs, she knew what Rue needed, and she still couldn't provide it.

Samuel pulled the buggy to a stop in front of the

schoolhouse, and Patience took out the key. She was
here, ready to teach her very first day of school—and
she'd have to find a way to fill that aching hole in her
heart alone.

"Let me get that bag for you," Samuel said.

"Oh, I can get it," she said, forcing a smile.

"Now, now," Samuel said gently. "Let an old man
treat you right, my dear. It does me good."

And she realized that it did. By showing kindness to
a new teacher who was very near the age his own *kinner* would have been, she was letting him be the *daet*
he'd so longed to be. So she let Samuel pull the bag out
of the back of the buggy and carry it into the schoolhouse for her. Then he headed back out to his waiting
buggy and was on his way again.

Patience stood in the center of the schoolroom, the
air cool and quiet, and lifted her heart to Gott.

Give me purpose, she pleaded. *I have so much love
to give, and no one to take it. I might not ever have a
family of my own, if that is Your will, but give me purpose and people to love, anyway.*

This was her classroom—may Gott bless the *kinner*
who passed through these doors, and may Gott fill her
aching, lonely heart.

Thomas left Rue with Mary that day, with some solemn promises on Rue's part to obey the older woman
without question.

"All right?" he'd asked her. "You do as Mammi says.
If I come home and find out that you haven't…"

"Then what?" Rue whispered.

And he really didn't have an answer to that, so instead he shook his finger meaningfully, bent down to kiss the top of her head and headed out to work.

His mind wasn't on the bedroom set he was building, though. He knew the work well enough that he didn't need to think too much about it as his hands went through the motions. He was sanding and getting the wood ready for the first layer of stain.

Thomas rubbed the sandpaper over the headboard, back and forth, a fragrant powder of wood falling to the ground and clinging to his pants and the hairs on his forearms. He normally felt calmed and soothed in his work, but today his heart seemed to beat with the weight of all his grief.

He loved her... Oh, how he loved her...

But he needed a *mamm* for his daughter and a family of his own, and yet his heart couldn't let go of the woman he'd so recklessly fallen in love with.

The day crawled by, and Amos and Noah took care of customers and let him stay in the back workroom, avoiding people for the rest of the day.

But then in the afternoon, Noah came into the workshop.

"Thomas, Ben Smoker wanted to talk to you," he said.

Ben Smoker—the family that didn't want his daughter to play with their girls. Susan had made herself clear enough to Patience, and Ben had stood behind his wife. Rue was too much of a danger for their *kinner*, it seemed, and the last week had left Thomas with a tender spot in his heart when it came to the way his daughter had been treated.

Thomas stopped the sanding and shook the wood powder off his arms. "What does he want?"

"He just—" Noah started, but then fell silent when Ben appeared at his side.

"Thomas, how are you?" Ben asked with a friendly smile, but when he saw Thomas's face, the smile faltered. Thomas hadn't even bothered to try to look friendly. He didn't have the energy today.

"I'm fine. You?" Thomas asked, forcing the pleasantries out.

"Look," Ben said, coming closer and glancing over his shoulder as Noah left the shop once more. "I feel badly for how things went when you last came to help me out with that gate."

"It's fine," Thomas said with a sigh. He had no intention of fighting over it. They'd made themselves clear.

"Susan put together some winter clothes for your daughter," Ben said. "She dug them out early. She wanted to make sure Rue had what she needed."

"She needs friends, Ben," Thomas said curtly.

"Yah." Ben nodded a couple of times. "Maybe we can sort something out in that respect, too."

Rue didn't need friends who had been guilted into spending time with her, either. Rue needed real, honest love—like the kind she'd been getting from Mary and Patience.

"I dropped the bag of clothes by your place before I came to town," Ben said. "Rue was very polite and well mannered. I thought you might like to know that."

"Yah, that's good to hear," Thomas agreed.

"Your rooster attacked me, though," Ben said with a low laugh. "I thought you were going to eat that bird. He'll be tough as rubber by the time you get him in a pot."

"I can't cook him," Thomas replied. "Rue's attached to him."

"She named him, I think?" Ben asked.

"Toby. That's Toby the rooster." Thomas met the other man's gaze, and for the first time, he realized, he was having banter with another *daet*. It felt good—better than he imagined it would.

"I got overly attached to a turkey when I was a kid," Ben said. "I named it and begged my *daet* not to kill it for Christmas dinner."

"Did he save it?" Thomas asked. Was there an elderly turkey running around their farm because of a small boy's love?

"What? No…" Ben shrugged. "We'd raised that turkey specifically for Christmas dinner. So my *daet* butchered it. It took me a full year to forgive him, though. And by the next Christmas, I still carried a small grudge against him. But we had a family of ten *kinner* to feed, plus the guests who'd come by. That turkey was food, and there was no getting around it."

A family with ten children… That was the kind of family an Amish man dreamed of. That was the kind of family that would give Rue the siblings who would help her feel her place in this community. They'd belong to each other… Or that was what he'd thought, at least. Thomas looked at his friend thoughtfully for a moment.

"Do you wish he'd saved it?" Thomas asked, at last. "I mean, you know that they had to eat it, and all, but do you wish he'd done it for you?"

Ben's expression softened and he rubbed a hand through his scraggly beard. "It would have meant the world to me if he had."

A family with ten *kinner*, and a boy's heart had still turned to the Christmas turkey. But even with all that family around, a loving gesture for one little boy would have made all the difference for him.

"Look, if you want to sell me the bird, you can tell her that it went to a farm, and I'll cook that rooster myself," Ben said. "If that helps you in getting rid of it."

"No," Thomas said. "Rue has already decided that Toby is part of the family, and I've been informed that we don't eat family. I suppose we shouldn't let neighbors eat family, either. It's the spirit of the thing."

Ben chuckled. "Fair enough. Well, I just wanted to make sure that we were square between us, Thomas."

"*Yah*, we're fine," Thomas replied. "Thanks."

Ben nodded and turned toward the door. Thomas watched him go, then picked up the sandpaper once more. But this time he stared down at it, his mind spinning.

Was it possible to love his daughter so well that she found the roots she needed without brothers and sisters? Maybe he'd been defining family wrong… Sometimes families looked different because of how life had unfolded. He was a single *daet*, and his *mamm* was returning to the community… Maybe Rue needed to see his *mamm* loved well, in spite of the hard times, in spite of her changed views. Maybe Rue needed to see a wife loved deeply, whether or not she could have babies. Maybe the family Rue needed to see wasn't the traditional Amish family of a *mamm*, a *daet* and a large group of siblings. Perhaps his daughter needed to see their family just as it was, complete with imperfections, hurts, hopes and devotion. And maybe, just maybe, Patience could be a part of it...

She didn't want to be the one who held him back from the family she thought he wanted, but there might be a way to convince her that if she agreed to be his, he wasn't settling at all—he was reaching for the highest happiness he could hope for on this earth.

"Noah!" Thomas brushed off his clothes with a sweep of his hands, and headed for the door that led to the sales shop.

An older Amish couple were just leaving, and both Noah and Amos looked up.

"I know this is a lot to ask since I've been taking so much time off for my daughter, but would you mind if I left a couple of hours early today?" Thomas asked.

The clock on the wall showed it was nearly three o'clock, and school would be letting out in a matter of minutes.

"What's the rush?" Amos asked with a frown.

"I'm going to do something that might be incredibly stupid," Thomas admitted. "But then again, it might be wonderful."

Noah exchanged a look with Amos and both men grinned.

"So you're going to propose, are you?" Amos asked.

Thomas shot them an irritated look. "I'll make up the time. However, this goes, I'll need to be working—either to save for a wedding, or to drown my sorrow."

"Don't let us keep you," Noah said, gesturing toward the door. "And I'm praying for the wedding, Thomas. She's a good choice!"

Thomas headed for the door and refused to look

back. He knew that Noah and Amos meant well, but right now he didn't want their good-humored ribbing. What he wanted was to get to the schoolhouse and see Patience... Because that was where his heart already was. He needed to see her once more, hold her hand again, and if she'd accept him, pull her back into his arms for good. He didn't know if she would accept him, but he was adding his prayers to his brother's.

Gott, I believe You've shown me the wife for me...if only You'd bring us together.

Chapter Fourteen

"Bartholomew, you may ring the bell now," Patience said.

If she had to be honest, she'd been looking forward to the sound of that clanging bell overhead, too, and not just because she was tired. The *kinner* were wonderful—three first graders, and four eighth graders, with a spattering of *kinner* in the grades between. They were good kids—smart, eager and funny. She was looking forward to this year together, and it would be better still when she could finally put her heartbreak behind her.

But today, her pain was very, very fresh.

Bartholomew, an eighth-grade boy, opened the door that revealed the bell's cord and gave it a hard pull. The bell clanged above them, and the *kinner* jumped to their feet, chattering away excitedly.

There were a couple of buggies waiting for some smaller *kinner* who had too far to walk, but most of them would walk home, their lunch boxes swinging at their sides and backpacks holding their first homework.

"Goodbye, Teacher," said Naomi, a little girl not

much bigger than Rue was. She had similar straight blond hair pulled back into a ponytail and she smiled up at Patience adoringly.

"Goodbye, Naomi," Patience said with a smile. "I'll see you tomorrow."

Naomi dashed out, her older sister and brother already outside the schoolhouse, and Patience tried to soothe the sadness that welled in her heart when she thought of Rue. One day, she'd be Rue's teacher, but it wasn't quite enough. Not for the love she already carried for the girl. To be called Teacher would be an honor, but to be called Mamm…

She pushed back the thought—it wasn't wise to let herself think of such things. She knew better than to allow herself to long for things that couldn't be hers.

"Have a good day, Patience," one of the *mamms* called into the door.

"Thank you! You, too!" Patience called back.

She went down the rows of desks, picking up bits of garbage on the floor and straightening a chair or tucking a paper inside a desk. She stood and looked around. This was her classroom, and it would mean something different to every student she taught, but to her, it would be a refuge—somewhere she could be something more.

The front door opened again just as Patience bent down to pick up a little carved horse. It was Naomi's, and Patience had made her promise to take it home and not bring it back to school again. But she hadn't confiscated it. She wanted to give Naomi the chance to do the right thing.

"Patience?"

She froze at the sound of Thomas's voice, and then

looked up, breathless. Thomas stood in the doorway, then the door swung shut behind him, leaving them alone. She held the little horse in the palm of her hand, and she put it down on the top of Naomi's desk.

"Hi…" she said. "I wasn't expecting you."

"I know," Thomas said. He wound his way through the desks toward her, and when he got to her, she felt the tears well up inside her. She'd pushed her heartbreak back all day for the sake of the *kinner*, and now facing him…

"This isn't fair, Thomas," she said. "I'm trying to be strong—"

"Patience, let me tell you about something, and then I promise that I'll leave you be. But hear me out."

Patience nodded, sucking in a stabilizing breath.

"I want to marry you," he said.

She shook her head. "But we've been over this—"

"I had a bit of an epiphany today," he said quietly. "It had to do with Toby the rooster and Ben Smoker's turkey, and…"

"This doesn't make any sense," she said, a smile toying at her lips.

"Long story short, my daughter needs love," he said. "She needs real, honest love. She doesn't need a perfect Amish setup, she needs to see her grandmother loved in spite of a difficult history, and she needs to have a ratty rooster that is part of the family just because she loves it. I've been seeing this all wrong, Patience. A family's love isn't purer for the number of *kinner* born to it, and a child doesn't feel more loved because of a wealth of siblings. Love is…love! It's a mother finding a place with her family, even after years of heartbreak. It's two brothers who look up to a man like a father, even though he is no blood relative. It's a man and a woman who love each other so deeply—" he reached out and caught her hand "—that they choose to face whatever Gott brings them side by side, shoulder to shoulder."

"Is that me?" she whispered.

"Yah." He tugged her closer. "I want that to be you. I'm not going to regret anything, Patience. I believe Gott brought us together for a reason. How many women would be able to love my little Englisher girl the way you do? How many would be wary of her influencing the other *kinner*? But you've loved Rue for the little person she is right from the start. I want my daughter to grow up with you as her *mamm*. And I want you as my wife."

"Even with no other *kinner*?" she asked.

"That is in Gott's hands," he replied. "Maybe we'll adopt. Maybe we won't. But Gott started something in us, Patience, and I believe this is something…" he touched her cheek with the back of one finger, the scent of wood shavings close and comforting "…this is something wonderful."

She nodded slowly, and she thought of the Kauffmans with their devoted marriage and their life of loving the ones who needed a *mamm* and *daet*, even for a little while. A life together, finding a way to love those around them, raising one little girl with love and purpose and direction…

"Patience, I love you," he added pleadingly.

"I love you, too." She lifted her gaze to meet his.

"Enough to marry me?" he asked hopefully. "Enough

to trust me to never look back, never look to the side…
Enough to be ours?"

"*Yah.*"

Thomas slipped his arms around her and lowered his lips over hers. He pulled her in close, his stubble tickling her chin as he kissed her. His arms were strong and she let herself melt into his embrace.

The door opened just then, and Patience startled. She pulled back, instinctively putting her hand up to her *kapp* to make sure her hair was in place.

"Teacher?" Naomi said uncertainly.

"Naomi!" Patience laughed breathily, tugging herself out of Thomas's arms. She went to her desk and picked up the toy horse. "You forgot this, didn't you?"

"*Yah…*" Naomi looked over at Thomas uncertainly, and Patience brought her the toy.

"You run along home now," Patience said. "And no more bringing toys to school, okay?"

"Okay." Naomi headed back out, and Patience nearly wilted when the door closed once more.

"You said yes, right?" Thomas said. "You'd just agreed to be my wife?"

"I said yes," she confirmed, and a smile spread over her face.

Thomas crossed the distance between them and kissed her once more. "I'll talk to the bishop today, then, because I have a feeling the rumors are about to explode around here—starting at that little girl's house. He'd better be in the know."

Patience couldn't help but laugh. "I think you're right."

And this time when Patience looked around the schoolroom, she saw more than a chance at a life where she could contribute, she saw a future with a husband by her side and a little girl who'd call her Mamm. A family of her own—maybe not the most traditional in appearance, but purposefully pieced together by Gott's own hands.

And when Gott brought a family together, let no man put it asunder.

Epilogue

The wedding was held in late October after all the harvesting was done and the community was free to celebrate. Patience's family came for the wedding, and the community of Redemption pulled together to cook and prepare for the only wedding that fall.

Thomas rented a house on another Amish family's property. It was a little house originally meant for some farm employees to live in, but it was just perfect for their little family—three bedrooms, a large kitchen, a small sitting room and a bathroom. That was all—but what else did they need? Patience had already set up the kitchen the way she wanted it to be arranged, and Thomas had carefully built their new bedroom set—polishing it by hand. He'd made a special little bed for Rue, too—she'd need more than just the cot she'd been sleeping on so far.

But this wedding wasn't only about him and Patience, it was about Rue, too. This wedding was going to join Thomas and Patience as husband and wife, and Rue would get a *mamm* of her very own. And for this happy day, Thomas's handiwork wasn't what would matter most to his little girl.

So that morning, while the women put the last of the food into the refrigerated trailer, and while Patience got ready for the wedding in Mammi's bedroom with the help of her mother and two of her sisters, Thomas sat with his daughter in the bedroom that used to be his. He was already dressed in his Sunday best, and Rue was wearing a pink dress just like the other women who were standing as Patience's *newehockers* for the day.

"It's a wedding quilt," Thomas said as Rue unfolded the quilt that Patience had sewn late into the evenings, stitching together squares of Rue's clothing from the suitcase. "But it's a special one. Patience said it was more important that you have your quilt than we have a new one for our bed."

Besides, his mother and Mary had been staying up late into the evenings, too, sewing some quilts to be used on their beds during that winter. Each stitch was sewn with love.

"That's my unicorn shirt," Rue whispered, running her fingers over the familiar fabric. "And that's my striped dress—and my pink shorts!"

Thomas ran his hand over Rue's pale hair.

"Do you like it, Rue?" he asked.

"*Yah.* It's my favorite," she said, and she hugged the quilt against her chest. "And today is a happy day. It's the day you and Patience become a mister and missus."

"Well, we Amish don't use those titles, Rue," he said.

Rue put her small hand on his knee and gave him

a serious look. "It's an important day, the day you become a mister, Daddy."

Thomas laughed and scooped her off the bed and into his arms.

"I'll explain all of that to you later. But right now, I want you to go into the bedroom where Patience is getting ready, because she's going to need you."

"And what will you do?" Rue asked.

"I'm going out to the tent. I have to wait there until you and Patience come. It's what the men do when they're getting married."

Thomas carried Rue out into the hallway, and he put her down in front of Mary's bedroom door just as his *mamm* came up the stairs. There were female voices coming from inside and a peal of laughter.

"Oh, no, you don't!" Rachel said with a laugh. "The bride is to be left alone until the ceremony. You know that, son."

Thomas bent down and kissed his *mamm*'s cheek. "I'll leave Rue with you, then."

He shot his mother a grin as she paused with her hand on the doorknob to Mary's bedroom, refusing to open it even a crack until he headed down the stairs. And Rue stood there, standing tall and proud with a smile on her face.

"He's gonna be a mister," Rue told her grandmother seriously. "And I think then I'd better call him Daet."

Thomas pretended not to hear, but he smothered a laugh. Was that the line for Rue when she'd finally let him be her Amish *daet* instead of a daddy—the day he married Patience? To finally be called Daet by his little girl would be the finest wedding gift anyone could offer him, and he sent up a prayer of wordless thanks to Gott for all of these blessings.

Patience was up there getting dressed, hearing all the last-minute advice from her married sisters and from her *mamm*. And they'd need all of it—all the advice and love and support that their families and their community could offer them.

As for Thomas, Amos and Noah didn't have much advice for him between them except to say, "Remember how blessed you are in marrying that woman. And treat her like you're grateful. We think that should cover it."

It likely would. And he was grateful. Thomas paused in the kitchen and looked up the stairs. He couldn't wait to say his vows and to finally claim Patience as his own.

"Out, out, out!" Mary said, flapping a towel at him. "Everyone is ready for you in the tent—they sent one of the *kinner* to tell me. Let's get you wed, Thomas. It's high time."

Thomas headed out the door to where Amos and Noah waited for him under trees ablaze in golden splendor. The men rubbed their hands together in the chilly autumn air, their breath hanging in front of them as they hunched their shoulders up against the chill. It was colder than usual, and while there wasn't snow yet, there would be soon. Noah grinned at him and Amos just stood there with a goofy smile on his face.

"Let's go," Thomas said. "I'm getting married today."

Then the three of them headed for the tent, the golden leaves swirling free in a gust of wind. Today was his wedding day, and in the presence of his family and community, he'd vow to love Patience, to stand by her, to defend her and to honor her.

At last, Rue would have a *mamm*, and his heart would be filled right to the brim.

Gott was good.

* * * * *

On Wednesday after work, Hannah drove toward home, the twins in the back seat, and tried not to be nervous that Luke was in the front seat beside her.

"I really appreciate this," he said. His car hadn't started this morning, and he'd walked the three miles to Rescue Haven.

Of course, Hannah had insisted on driving him home. What else could she do? It was cold outside, spitting snow, and he was her next-door neighbor.

"I hate to ask another favor," he said, "but could you stop by Pasquale's Pizza on the way?"

"No problem." She took a left and drove the two blocks to the only nonchain pizza place in Bethlehem Springs.

He jumped out, and she turned back to check on the twins, trying not to watch Luke as he headed into the shop. He was good-looking, of course. Kind, appreciative and strong. And he had the slightest swagger in his walk that was masculine and appealing.

LIEXP0921

But he was also about to go visit his brother, Bobby, if he kept his promise to his ailing father. And when she'd heard about that visit, it had been a wake-up call: she shouldn't get too close with him. The fewer chances she had to spill the beans about Bobby being the twins' father, the better.

He came out of the pizza shop quickly—he must have called ahead—carrying a big flat box and a white bag. What would it be like if this was a family scenario, if they were Mom and Dad and kids, stopping for takeout on the way home from work?

She couldn't help it. Her chest filled with longing.

He climbed into her small car, juggling the large flat box to make it fit without encroaching on the gearshift.

She had to laugh at the size of his meal. "Hungry?"

"Are you?" He opened the box a little, and the rich, garlicky fragrance of Pasquale's special sauce filled the car.

Her stomach growled, loudly.

"Pee-zah!" Addie shouted from the back seat.

"Peez!" Emmy added, almost as loud.

"That's just cruel," she said as she pulled the car back onto the road and steered toward Luke's place. "You're tempting us. I may have to order some when I get these girls home."

"No, you won't," he said. "This is for all of us. The least I can do is feed you, after you drove me around."

Her stomach gave a little leap, and not just about the prospect of pizza. Why was he inviting her to have dinner with him? Was there an ulterior motive? And if there was, would she mind?

Don't miss
Finding a Christmas Home *by Lee Tobin McClain,*
available October 2021 wherever
Love Inspired books and ebooks are sold.

LoveInspired.com

LOVE INSPIRED

INSPIRATIONAL ROMANCE

UPLIFTING STORIES OF FAITH, FORGIVENESS AND HOPE.

Join our social communities to connect with other readers who share your love!

Sign up for the Love Inspired newsletter at **LoveInspired.com** to be the first to find out about upcoming titles, special promotions and exclusive content.

CONNECT WITH US AT:

Facebook.com/LoveInspiredBooks

Twitter.com/LoveInspiredBks

Facebook.com/groups/HarlequinConnection